# DANCE OF DESIRE

They were playing a polka, and Stuart whisked me off my feet, twirling me around and around until we had advanced to the other side of the room. The danger was behind me now . . . at least for the moment.

French doors opened out to a flagstone terrace that overlooked the garden. As the music slowed and drifted into a waltz, he danced me outside, onto our own private dance floor under the stars. Holding me close, and with his lips brushing my ear, Stuart whispered, his breath warm and fragrant. "You fit my arms just right." He smiled down at me, and I felt my foolish heart begin to melt.

I looked up and met his eyes.

"Your lips fit mine just perfectly too. Let me show you, Katherine."

Time stood still under the magic of his kiss. A new moon beamed down on us and stars flickered in a black velvet sky. A gentle breeze brought us a fragrance of lilacs.

Hypnotized by a force I could no longer control, I returned his fevered kisses, let his hands caress me, surrendered to the bliss, the ecstasy of his touch.

# ROMANTIC SUSPENSE WITH ZEBRA'S GOTHICS

THE SWIRLING MISTS OF CORNWALL        (2924, $3.95)
by Patricia Werner

Rhionna Fowley ignored her dying father's plea that she never return to his ancestral homeland of Cornwall. Yet as her ship faltered off the rugged Cornish coast, she wondered if her journey would indeed be cursed.

Shipwrecked and delirious, Rhionna found herself in a castle high above the roiling sea—and in thrall to the handsome and mysterious Lord Geoffrey Rhyweth. But fear and suspicion were all around: Geoffrey's midnight prowling, the hushed whispers of the townspeople, women disappearing from the village. She knew she had to flee, for soon it would be too late.

THE STOLEN BRIDE OF GLENGARRA CASTLE     (3125, $3.95)
by Anne Knoll

Returning home after being in care of her aunt, Elly Kincaid found herself a stranger in her own home. Her father was a ghost of himself after the death of Elly's mother, her brother was bitter and violent, her childhood sweetheart suddenly hostile.

Elly agreed to meet the man her brother Hugh wanted her to marry. While drawn to the brooding, intense Gavan Mitchell, Elly was determined to ignore his whispered threats of ghosts and banshees. But she could *not* ignore the wailing sounds from the tower. Someone was trying to terrify her, to sap her strength, to draw her into the strange nightmare.

THE LOST DUCHESS OF GREYDEN CASTLE      (3046, $3.95)
by Nina Coombs Pykare

Vanessa never thought she'd be a duchess; only in her dreams could she be the wife of Richard, Duke of Greyden, the man who married her headstrong sister, Caroline. But one year after Caroline's violent and mysterious death, Richard proposed and took her to his castle in Cornwall.

Her dreams had come true, but they quickly turned to *nightmares*. Why had Richard never told her he had a twin brother who hated him? Why did Richard's sister shun her? Why was she not allowed to go to the North Tower? Soon the truth became clear: everyone there had reason to kill Caroline, and now someone was after *her*. But which one?

*Available wherever paperbacks are sold, or order direct from the Publisher. Send cover price plus 50¢ per copy for mailing and handling to Zebra Books, Dept. 3634, 475 Park Avenue South, New York, N.Y. 10016. Residents of New York and Tennessee must include sales tax. DO NOT SEND CASH. For a free Zebra/ Pinnacle catalog please write to the above address.*

# THE LOST LADY OF HATHAWAY MANOR

## ANNE KNOLL

**ZEBRA BOOKS**
**KENSINGTON PUBLISHING CORP.**

*Juggy—This one's for you!*

*My thanks to Renee for enthusiastic support
and many helpful suggestions
and to the members of my Critique Group
for their expertise.*

ZEBRA BOOKS

are published by

Kensington Publishing Corp.
475 Park Avenue South
New York, NY 10016

First printing: January, 1992

Printed in the United States of America

*Oh, what a tangled web we weave,*
*When first we practice to deceive!*
*Sir Walter Scott,*
*"The Marmion,"*
*"Lochinvar"*

# Chapter 1

*New York—1895*

We left a fictitious forwarding address and departed the Barclay Hotel at dawn.

The yawning desk clerk showed little interest in Beau's elaborate attempt at laying a false trail. "Please see that all of my mail is forwarded to this theater. I'll be opening in a new play there next month. That's Carsville, Indiana."

"I can read."

"I'm amazed," Beau replied, causing the man's sleep-drugged eyes to pop open, and guaranteeing that the name Beauregard Chantelle would be remembered.

The clerk gave a short laugh. "You two-bit actors kill me. Carsville, Indiana," he sneered. "You gonna play in a barn?"

He was still laughing as we went out the door, pushing the two trunks that contained all our earthly possessions.

"By the time they locate Carsville, Indiana, we'll be in merry old England," Beau said, smiling with satisfaction.

I gave him no answer. In fact, I had spoken very little to my father since hearing about this, the latest of Beau's many indiscretions, all of which necessitated our leaving town in a hurry.

My father is fifty years old, going on fifteen. He is an actor, onstage and off, and this combination has gotten him into more scrapes than I care to mention, but a few of the worse come readily to mind.

There was the time when I was twelve and Beau had posed as a French Count to impress a beautiful southern belle. Unfortunately, the lady had a father with a violent temper, and when he found out about Beau, he almost succeeded in having him tarred and feathered and run out of Mississippi on a rail. We had to sneak through swamps in the middle of the night to escape.

Then there was the time when I was fourteen and. . . . What's the use of thinking about them, I decided. I've been taking care of Beau ever since Mama died and my two older sisters defected to Grandma's. I could have gone with them, they begged me to go, all of them, even my father, but I just couldn't leave him all alone.

"You're making a mistake, India," my sister Persia had told me, and maybe she was right.

There were three of us, all girls, all two years apart, and all named by Beau: Persia, Alexandria, and India. How we hated those odd names, and what we wouldn't have given for normal ones like Mary, or Elizabeth, or Jane.

Beau hailed a hack and handed me in with as much aplomb as if we were off on a vacation and not running for our lives.

I glanced back to see if we were being followed. Now that he had calmed down, my father was treating this like an adventure, but he hadn't been so nonchalant last night.

"Pier Six," he called out to the driver and leaned back in the seat. "I wonder if they'll let us board now," he mused, taking the tickets out of his pocket and looking at them.

I hadn't even asked him what ship we were sailing on, and I glanced idly at our boarding passes. *"The Servia,* first class Accommodations," I read. "Oh, Beau. How much did those tickets cost?"

"Now, don't be spoiling things, Indy. It's a magnificent steel ship, and it'll be a wonderful crossing."

"Of course, but what are we going to do for money after we land?"

"Things will work out. Don't you worry your pretty head about it."

"Oh, Beau," I said. "We should be saving our money. We

don't know when we'll find jobs."

"Nonsense, my dear. Your father's a famous actor. London will receive us with open arms." His eyes shone with visions of glory, and it was no use trying to persuade him to be practical. Beau prefers his daydreams to reality.

Of course, they wouldn't let us board for several hours, and we wound up drinking tea in a run-down cafe and glancing nervously up at everyone who entered.

The men who were after my father *this time* were killers. I shuddered, remembering the bullet hole in his black velvet cape and the terrified look on Beau's face when he'd shown it to me.

I didn't have to ask why. Beau was a gambler, and he'd been in scrapes before, but this was no penny ante game, not if they meant to kill him!

At long last we were able to board, and I think we both held our breath until we felt the ship pushing away from the shores of New York and heading out to the safety of the Atlantic.

Beau turned to me and smiled. "Care to take a stroll around the deck, my dear?"

"No thank you," I answered coldly. "I'm going to my cabin and take a nap."

I was still irritated with him, and his nonchalant attitude was not helping matters. Typical of Beau, now that the danger was past, he was ready to enjoy a frolic on this luxury liner that we could ill afford, giving little thought to how we would manage once we landed in England.

I love my father, despite his faults, and I would go to the ends of the earth for him, but his easy acceptance of that fact rankles me.

Nevertheless, I gave him a weak smile. "I'll feel better after I've had a nap, Beau."

"You go ahead, my dear. Of course you're tired. It's been a long day." Taking out his pocket watch, he checked the time. "And morning has not yet dampened a rose with dew."

A line from *The Impoverished Aristocrat,* one of Beau's earlier triumphs. It was uniquely suited to his talents and present circumstances, I might have added, but didn't.

7

I shook my head, and an earnest look appeared on his still handsome face. "I'm going to make this all up to you, Indy. You'll see. Beauregard Chantelle will take London by storm!"

I retired to my cabin, which was small, but infinitely more modern than my room at the Barclay Hotel. It was done in the Renaissance style, with heavy curtains, and a bed rail which I gathered might be necessary should the ship roll or pitch during the night.

The extent of my travels by water had been confined to occasional ferryboat crossings, and one trip down the Mississippi when I was a child. So whether or not I was a good sailor remained to be seen.

I unpacked my trunk, surveying my wardrobe with a critical eye. A succession of wardrobe mistresses had taught me early on to sew, and I had altered several dresses that a fashionable leading lady had discarded. These were evening gowns, and until now, I had had no occasion to wear them.

My favorite was a peach silk brocade. I had removed the outdated bustle and attached a train to the back, copying the design from a gown pictured in *Vanity Fair*. Lace, which I removed from an old costume found in the wardrobe room, provided the flounce that encircled the low neck and stood out over the sleeves. The transformed gown was now in the height of fashion, and I wondered if I had nerve enough to wear it.

I have always been rather shy, preferring the shadows to the foreground. My older sisters, Persia and Alexandria are similarly inclined. Obviously, we all take after our mother, rather than Beau. But I am not as compliant as my mother, having a stubborn nature and often a quick temper.

Mama was just eighteen, two years younger than myself, when she eloped with Beau. Her father never forgave her for running off with an actor, but Grandma relented after he died. We visited her once when I was quite small. I vaguely remember the white clapboard house in Columbus, Ohio and the small, pinched-faced woman who looked at my

8

father with disapproving eyes.

When Mama died, our grandmother offered us a home, and Persia and Alexandria accepted. I didn't blame them. They were fourteen and sixteen and they wanted to stay in one place and make friends, but I could not leave Beau any more than our mother could.

My sisters are both married now, and have families of their own. I haven't seen them for several years, but they are still my sisters and I feel bad that I can't even let them know where we are.

I stretched out on the narrow bed, which proved to be very comfortable and I didn't wake up until Beau tapped on the door to announce it was time to dress for dinner.

The nap had improved my disposition and the prospect of spending five days on this floating mansion suddenly overwhelmed me. I felt different, almost daring, and I dressed carefully, taking great pains with my toilette.

I arranged my heavy dark hair into an elaborate twist, back combing the sides and top for added fullness; a trick I had learned from one of the actresses. It gave me a sophisticated look, and as I stared at my reflection in the mirror, I hardly recognized myself.

Should I take it all down, part my hair in the middle and fasten it into a plain knot as usual? And this gown, I wondered, is it too theatrical? Maybe my own purple taffeta with the leg-of-mutton sleeves would be more appropriate.

Beau's voice from outside the door intruded on my thoughts. "Come on, Indy. We'll be late for dinner. I've never known you to take . . ." He stopped abruptly when he looked up and saw me, framed in the doorway. "My God, Indy. What have you done to yourself?"

I blushed in embarrassment. "It's only a joke. I'll change and be ready in ten minutes."

"You'll do no such thing. Turn around. Let me see you."

Feeling like a fool, I slowly turned, and when I again faced him, he had tears in his eyes.

"My little India, all grown-up. I guess your old father just hasn't kept track of time, my dear." He kissed the top of my head. "You're a beautiful young woman, and I'm very proud of you," he added, offering me his arm.

I was still nervous as we entered the ornate Dining Salon which was softly lit by electric bulbs built into the ceiling.

We were escorted to a long table with swivel chairs that had been bolted to the floor, and as we were the last to arrive, we were introduced to all our dinner companions at one time. They were middle-aged to elderly people, except for one other young woman like myself.

"I'm so glad you're sitting next to me," she whispered. "There's not many young people on board."

Her name was Katherine Hathaway, and she was traveling to her uncle's estate in Cornwall.

She was vibrantly pretty, with dark hair and a friendly manner. Younger than myself, I decided, for she had the eager charm and innocence of a schoolgirl.

"How exciting to meet someone from the theater," she exclaimed. For in his introduction, Beau had added, "Shakespearean Actor," like a title after his name.

I nodded. I was a little defensive on Beau's behalf. He was proud of his profession, but some people, I knew, looked down on it.

"And are you an actress, too?" she asked.

"Heavens, no. I lack the talent." I didn't think it necessary to add that I worked as a Wardrobe Assistant.

She turned admiring eyes on Beau. "Mr. Chantelle, will you be appearing in a London production?"

"Oh, yes indeed," he answered. "But the arrangements have not been completed as yet."

The elderly gentleman on my right claimed my attention then and the conversation turned to other matters.

Katherine Hathaway seemed to favor my company and I, too, was grateful for the companionship of someone my own age. I invited her to stroll the deck with us after dinner, and she accepted eagerly. She seemed to be traveling alone, and I thought that rather strange for someone so young, but I found out that there was a tragic reason for it.

"My parents are both dead," she explained. "Mother died when I was quite small, and I lost my father this past spring in the flu epidemic." Sighing, she added, "I'm being sent to

10

England to live with my aunt and uncle, Lord and Lady Hathaway of Cornwall."

"How sad for you!" I said. "I mean about your parents, not Cornwall," I added hastily.

"Oh, it's sad about Cornwall, too," she replied with childish frankness. "I don't want to go. New York is my home. I've lived there since I was ten years old." A determined look crossed her face. "But I shan't stay in England. In six months, I'll be eighteen." Smiling suddenly, she added, "I'll come into a rather generous portion of my inheritance then, and I shall lose no time in returning to America."

I wondered a little wistfully how soon we should return to America. "Six months isn't long," I said cheerfully.

She gave me an enthusiastic hug. "Oh, you make me feel better already. Now, I want to dance. Could we go to the ballroom?"

"My pleasure," Beau said gallantly, taking us both by the arm. "Won't I be the envy of all the young ship's officers tonight!"


It was after two o'clock when a very handsome ship's officer walked me back to my cabin. He gallantly kissed my hand, and bade me good night.

I was more amused than flattered, for I was sensible enough to know that the ship's officers were expected to dance with unattached young ladies on board.

It had been a delightful evening though, and one I would not soon forget, for despite my theatrical background, I have led a very sheltered life.

I had hardly closed my stateroom door when I heard Katherine's voice on the other side. "May I come in for a minute, India?"

I unlocked the door, and she rushed in, bubbling over with girlish giggles. "You've made a conquest, India. Why, he never took his eyes off you, and he's so handsome. Aren't you thrilled?"

I smiled indulgently. "And tomorrow night, he'll dance

with another girl and kiss her hand. It doesn't mean a thing, Katherine."

"How can you be so calm about it?" She looked at me and sighed. "I suppose you're used to men falling in love with you."

"On the contrary," I said.

"I don't believe that. You're so beautiful, India. You must have had dozens of proposals by now."

I laughed. She was an engaging childlike girl, but I couldn't let her credit me with her fantasies. "Not even one," I said. "You've probably had more than that yourself."

"Oh, no. I haven't come-out yet."

"I see." I didn't really, and not being one for pretense, I added, "I don't know much about these things, Katherine. What does that mean exactly?"

She looked suprised. "You didn't . . ." Then she giggled. "It's rather silly, but fun. You see when a debutante is eighteen, she's presented to society. There's a Coming-Out Ball, and everybody who is anybody attends. A girl is then on the market, as it were, and there are teas and dances and all sorts of lavish parties for a whole year." She paused, and then added knowingly, "That's when the proposals come." A wistful look crossed her face. "Now, I'll be presented in England, and it won't be nearly as much fun."

"Oh, I don't know," I said. "I'm sure the British do these things very well. Why, you'll probably be presented to the Queen!"

She made a face. "La-di-da! That doesn't sound like fun."

"It sounds exciting to me."

A strange expression crossed her face. "But, nothing could be more exciting than the theater."

I smiled. "The smell of greasepaint, the roar of the crowd. . . . Some people feel that way; I know Beau does. I don't think he could live without the theater. It's in his blood." I shook my head. "For some reason, it never got into mine."

She gave me an incredulous look. "I'd trade places with you any day, India."

If you only knew, I thought, and my composure

suddenly snapped. I'd kept my emotions pent up inside me, but now they exploded, and tears that I could no longer control rolled down my cheeks.

Mortified beyond words, I covered my face with my hands. "I'm sorry," I sobbed.

"Oh, India, what is it? Have I said something to upset you?"

I shook my head. "It has nothing to do with you, Katherine. It's just that . . ." I don't usually confide my troubles, but at that moment, I needed a friend. "You wouldn't want to change places with me," I said. "You can go home again, but I can't."

She was full of concern. "But, why not India? Why can't you go home?"

"It's Beau. Someone is trying to kill him. That's why we're running away."

"But, can't you go to the police?"

I shook my head, and wiped the tears away. "You don't understand. These people are gamblers, and Beau owes them a great deal of money."

Katherine's eyes glittered with excitement. "It sounds like a play!"

"Well, it isn't," I said impatiently. Oh, how could I expect this spoiled child to understand! "Our life is not what you think, Katherine. Beau's a dear and wonderful man, but he lives in a dream world. We don't belong in first class. If we had any sense, we'd be in steerage!" I felt the tears coming on again, and I bit my lip. "I'm sorry. I have no right to burden you with all this."

"I'm glad you did, India," she answered, patting my shoulder in an absentminded way. She seemed lost in her own thoughts, and added softly, "Perhaps we can help each other."

I had no idea what she meant, and I attached no significance then to such a casual remark. "I know you've helped me, just by listening," I said, giving her a sheepish smile. "I don't know what came over me, but I feel much better now, and I do thank you."

She seemed anxious at that point to leave, and I was just as anxious to extricate myself from an embarrassing situation. I am not one to court sympathy, and I hoped that in her childish way, Katherine would forget all about this in the morning.

She returned to her own cabin, and I quickly undressed and got into bed. I felt like a baby, being rocked in a cradle, as the ship's gentle motion lulled me into a pleasant, euphoric state.

Sunshine was streaming through the stateroom's tiny porthole when I awoke. Disoriented at first, I expected to see the Barclay Hotel or some similar establishment's faded wallpaper instead of cream colored walls offset by dados of rich oak paneling.

My mind quickly caught up with my surroundings, and I jumped out of bed. I was anxious to get up on deck and view such an endless expanse of ocean in daylight.

I was fully dressed before I checked my watch. It was 7:00 A.M., too early to awaken anyone else, so I passed by both Beau's and Katherine's doors without knocking. I preferred the solitude anyway.

Alone, I could look out over the horizon and give my imagination free rein. I would not have to make idle conversation, and instead I could visualize this same ocean, hundreds of years before when buccaneers in sailing ships plied its waters. I could look down into its depths and wonder about all the mysteries that are buried at the bottom of the sea.

"India's a romantic," my mother used to say, and I suppose I am, although life has forced me to compromise my daydreams and assume a practical nature.

I swung back the heavy door that led to the Promenade Deck, and a strong wind billowed my skirts about me, as I walked toward the rail. I breathed deeply, drinking in the smell of the sea. Shielding my eyes with my hands, I looked out on a majestic sight, an endless expanse of ocean sparkling in the sun.

For the moment, I had the deck all to myself, and I

mentally cast my troubles on the waters along with the kerchief that a playful breeze whipped from my hair. It fluttered down past the lower decks and was scooped up by a passing wave. I watched it drift away toward England, and I smiled. My kerchief and my troubles may meet me on the other side, I mused, but for now, I was free of them both. Or so I thought.

I was joined at the rail then by other passengers who had wandered up on deck after an early breakfast, and feeling slightly hungry myself, I left the Promenade Deck and headed for the dining room.

Katherine and Beau greeted me with smug smiles, and Beau took out his pocket watch. "Eight bells, and our sleepy head has just come down to breakfast," he teased.

I took my place and smiled back. "I hate to disappoint you both, but I've been on deck for an hour communing with nature."

"Foiled again," Beau proclaimed in exaggerated anguish and Katherine giggled. "Now, she'll tell us she's been up since 5:00 A.M., and . . ."

"6:00 A.M.," I interrupted, taking a sip of my orange juice.

"6:00 A.M., then," he conceded. "India's an early bird, and a nature lover," he explained to Katherine.

"She would probably like to live in the country," Katherine said, looking at Beau and smiling like a conspirator.

"That I would," I answered, and without realizing it, played right into their hands. "Preferably in an isolated spot where I could do my communing in peace!"

They exchanged hurried glances and laughed at my little joke. The waiter appeared then, and I ordered a hearty breakfast.

Katherine and Beau were finished eating, so I said, "Please don't feel you have to wait for me."

Beau pushed back his chair, "Well, if you don't mind, my dear. I would like to stretch my legs."

Katherine chimed in, "Me, too. Activities for the Day are posted in the Winter Garden on A Deck. We'll meet you up there, India."

"Fine," I said, and they both rose.

As they left the table, Katherine looked at Beau and then quickly back to me. "We have something really exciting to discuss with you, India. It's my idea, but Beau thinks it's wonderful, too."

The waiter arrived with my breakfast then, and I waved them off. In between bites of plump sausages and poached eggs, I thought about what Katherine had said.

Whatever are they up to? I wondered. I had heard there was to be a masquerade on the last night out. That's it, I decided. Between the two of them, they've come up with something outlandish, and they need my help.

They didn't have to be so mysterious, I mused, smiling to myself. I'll make their costumes as long as they leave me out of it. Masquerades don't appeal to me all that much.

Later those thoughts would come back to haunt me, for I was soon to play a leading role in a much more sinister masquerade; a masquerade that would have far reaching consequences for us all.

Feeling deliciously stuffed, I left the dining area to look for the Winter Garden.

I passed through the music room, which doubled as a reading room when not in use for recitals. The beamed, wooden ceiling contained overhead Edison bulbs, and the floor was carpeted in deep wine with a diagonal pattern.

Round tables and chairs in dark mahogany were grouped cabaret style about the room, and the piano which dominated one corner was covered in a fringed silken drape, also in a deep wine color. Tied back, floral curtains in shades of wine, green and white allowed daylight to enter the room, but accustomed as I was to economizing, I found the still lighted overhead bulbs a shocking extravagance.

A portrait of Queen Victoria hung over the piano, and her sober countenance matched the stiff formality of the room.

I opened a glass door with a small sign in gold letters that read Winter Garden, and was pleasantly surprised at the contrast I found.

The Winter Garden had a lush and tropical flavor, with its palm trees and lattice work entwined with ivy and clematis. An overhead skylight gave the room brightness and no artificial light was used.

Stark white rattan furniture, and inside walls painted in a pale lime green, added to the gardenlike atmosphere. The outside wall was lined with windows looking out to sea, and I thought it quite the loveliest room I had ever seen.

Katherine and Beau were seated at a table at the far end and they waved me over.

"Isn't this charming?" Katherine exclaimed, as I joined them.

"It would make a wonderful setting for a play," Beau mused. "That one we did in Chicago last year. What was it called, Indy?"

"'Gardens of Delight,'" I answered.

"Ah, yes. My love is a vine that wraps itself around thy heart, fair Roseamunde," he recited.

I sat down. "Well, what is this exciting idea you two have? Something to do with a masquerade, I imagine."

They turned startled faces in my direction. "You know?" Beau asked.

"No, she doesn't. She must have guessed," Katherine added.

Beau looked amazed. "The decision is yours, Indy. I'm pleased you're ready to consider it, though. I was afraid you'd . . ." He let the sentence hang.

Katherine seemed ready to burst with pleasure. "Oh, India. This is just about the most wonderful thing anybody has ever done for me. Oh, you won't be sorry. I promise you."

I leaned back in my chair and let her ramble on. Such a fuss over making a few costumes, I thought.

"You love the country and I hate it. And, the theater . . ." She rolled her eyes in a dramatic gesture. "Oh, I've always been in love with the theater!"

Beau joined in. "It'll be an experience you'll never forget, Indy. I want you to have the opportunity, and when it's all over, we can go home again."

"Whatever are you talking about?" I asked, looking from one to the other of them in confusion.

"What did you think we were talking about?" Beau said in a weak voice.

"Making your costumes for Masquerade Night."

Beau cleared his throat. "It's not exactly that sort of masquerade we had in mind, Indy."

# Chapter 2

One week later, I was sitting in a train, bound for Cornwall. For the next six months I would be living my life as Katherine Hathaway, seventeen and a half year old daughter of the late Roland and Emily Hathaway; heiress in her own right to an American fortune; and the ward of Lord Fenton Hathaway of Hathaway Manor, a remote mansion on the wild Cornish coast.

I hadn't immediately agreed to Katherine's proposition as we sat that day in the tropical splendor of the ship's Winter Garden. I was too cautious, and I might add, too sensible for that, but I wondered now if the make-believe setting had not influenced my decision just a little.

My initial reaction had been one of shock. The idea was preposterous, and I told them so.

"Not preposterous, ingenious," Katherine had replied. "You want to spend time in an isolated spot where you can commune with nature?" Her hazel eyes gleamed with triumph. "Well, I am offering you a chance to spend six months at the most remote, and the most beautiful, spot in England. Oh, India, you'd simply adore it." She took a quick breath and hurried on. "The house is built on a high cliff, and you can hear the roar of the sea, crashing against the rocks below. It's a little frightening, but then you love the sea," she added as an afterthought.

"There's a cave, too . . ." Suddenly she hesitated. And a look of bewilderment, or was it fear, crossed her face?

Shrugging her shoulders, she continued. "There's something about it, but I can't remember what. As a child, I was probably afraid of it. There's so much folklore down there. Pirate tales, hidden treasure, smugglers—that sort of thing," she added and laughed. "There's even a buccaneer among our illustrious ancestors, but the Hathaways won't admit to it."

She followed this argument by declaring that it would only be for six months. "You said yourself that wasn't a long time," she reminded me.

"Then we'll all go back to America, and resume our former lives. With one big difference," she added dramatically. "I'll be the richer for my experience in the theater, and you and Beau will be richer by ten thousand dollars!"

I think I gasped, for it was then that Beau entered the conversation. "Katherine has more to lose by this than we do, Indy. I've er-um confided our circumstances to her."

Assuming a little more of his usual bluster, he continued. "I've explained that the London theaters may not be familiar with my work, so for the present at least, I might have to accept supporting, rather than leading, roles."

Poor dear Beau, always the optimist, I smiled in remembrance. I had left him with Katherine at Paddington Station. Full of good spirits, they had smiled, and waved me off. Both of them, I'm sure, were anxious to assume their own roles in this bizarre little masquerade.

Now that I was alone, I felt my courage deserting me. I was insane to have agreed to this! Desperately, I tried to arm myself with the arguments Katherine and Beau had used to convince me.

"No one will suspect anything, India. We look enough alike to be sisters. We both have fair complexions; same color hair; my eyes are hazel, your's are green, but nobody remembers a child's eyes. All you have to do is remember everything I've told you about the family."

"You'll carry it off, Indy. You're a Chantelle. We never forget our lines."

"They haven't seen me since I was ten years old, and they paid scant attention to me then!"

"Think of it as an adventure, Indy. You'll be living in a mansion, waited on hand and foot, like a great lady."

"Beau will be able to settle his debt."

"And I'll never gamble another penny, I swear it! The rest of the money will be yours, Indy, to put in the bank."

Enough, I thought. It's done. You've given your word, and you'll just have to make the best of it. Better to spend your time memorizing instead of sermonizing . . .

I went over my list: Lord Fenton Hathaway, third Earl of Melton—eldest son of Lord Duncan Hathaway, deceased. He was Katherine's. . . . No, I thought, correcting myself. He was *my* father's oldest brother.

"Immerse yourself in the role," Beau had advised me. "Shed your own persona, and *be* Katherine Hathaway."

Beatrice Hathaway—Uncle Fenton's wife, a Hathaway in her own right. She was Fenton's cousin.

Jordan Hathaway—Fenton and Beatrice's son—he was sixteen when I left. Would be twenty-three now. Very quiet and serious. Interested in chemistry.

Willa Hathaway—Fenton and Beatrice's daughter. Nineteen now. We didn't like each other much, but then, we were only children.

Stuart Hathaway—another cousin. Son of Gilbert Hathaway, the family's rake. Stuart's mother was a London actress and the marriage caused a rift between Gilbert and his father, Lord Duncan Hathaway. The couple divorced and Gilbert brought his young son home to Hathaway Manor to live. Stuart would be twenty-five now. I probably won't get to see him. His father and Uncle Fenton did not get along, and after our Grandfather's death, they moved to London. Uncle Gilbert died several years ago and Stuart is probably still living in London.

So much for the residents of Hathaway Manor. As for myself: I was born in London. My parents moved to Hathaway Manor when I was nine. We stayed until I was ten. Then we suddenly packed up and moved to America. I was never told why.

My father, Roland Hathaway invested heavily and made a killing in the American stock market, but he was a conser-

21

vative man. Although we lived on 87th Street, and my family were members of New York society, we lived a quiet life, especially after my mother's death in 1892. Then, my father became a virtual recluse, shutting himself up in the house and spending all of his time pouring over his stamp collection.

A decided contrast to India Chantelle's hectic life, I mused. Perhaps that accounts for the fascination with each other's lifestyles. We always find the pastures so much greener on the other side.

I looked out the window then, and the beautiful English countryside passed before my eyes. The rolling hills were dotted with quaint little white cottages, and I began to relax and enjoy the view. We wouldn't reach Cornwall for several hours. Time enough then to worry, I told myself.

The compartment door opened, and to my surprise a man entered. "This isn't taken, is it?" he inquired, glancing at the seat across from mine.

"No," I answered, looking uneasily toward the door to see if someone else was joining him.

It appeared that he was alone, and I thought it rather bold that he would choose my compartment. Surely there were others in first class that were not occupied by a lone woman.

I kept my head turned toward the window, refusing to look at him, though he made a great show of removing his heavy cape and bowler hat before slamming his luggage up on the rack overhead.

At last he seated himself, and I was annoyed to feel his eyes on me.

"Going far?"

"To Cornwall," I answered stiffly.

"What a coincidence! So am I."

He was smartly dressed in a grey frock coat, and quite handsome, with insolent grey eyes that made me blush when they met mine. His dark hair was slightly disheveled, and he exuded a rakish sort of charm. He wore a neatly trimmed moustache, and it gave him a look of sophistication though I doubted he was much over twenty-five. India Chantelle

22

would have squelched him on the spot, but Katherine Hathaway would have struck up a conversation with him.

"Do you live in Cornwall?" I asked.

He laughed. "Not on your life! Just visiting. I live in London."

The thought suddenly struck me that I could learn some valuable information from this passing stranger. "You don't recommend Cornwall then," I said.

"A little too quiet for my taste. I prefer London." He studied me a moment. "You're an American, aren't you?"

"Yes."

"Do you have relatives in Cornwall?"

Now, I can practice my role, I thought. "My uncle is Lord Fenton Hathaway," I said, "and I am his ward, Katherine Hathaway."

He gave me a slow smile. "Your servant, Miss Hathaway. I am . . . Stuart Cousin," he added. "I hope you have a pleasant stay at Hathaway Manor."

"You're familiar with it?"

"Most people are," he answered, and then quickly changed the subject. "Tell me about America. I've never been there."

"I haven't seen that much of it to tell. We lived in New York City, and I suppose most big cities are somewhat alike. America is a huge country, Mr. Cousin," I added.

"You've lived there all your life?" he asked.

"Oh, no. I was born in England. We left when I was ten."

"Then you must remember it very well; your family, too, I would imagine."

"Not really," I said. "Young children forget, and are forgotten quite easily."

He shook his head. "I shouldn't imagine anyone forgetting you, Miss Hathaway."

I blushed, and turned to look out the window again. He was a disturbing man, and for some strange reason, he gave me the impression that he was laughing at me.

The train was slowing down, and he said, "We'll be coming into Plymouth in a few minutes. Do you like

23

chicken, Miss Hathaway?"

I thought he must surely be mad. "Chicken?" I repeated.

"Yes. Those little feathered things that cluck about the barnyard. Don't you have them in America?"

"Of course," I answered primly.

"Good. Then you're familiar with them. I'll just hop off at the Plymouth station and get us one."

I suppose I gave him what Beau calls a "royal sneer," for he smiled and shook his head. "My dear, Miss Hathaway, I'm talking about a cut, dressed and cooked to perfection chicken for us to eat. They sell them at the station in Plymouth. They're called, 'box lunches.'"

He was gone before I could decline his offer. It was true, I was hungry, but to accept lunch from a gentleman I had so casually met did not seem quite proper.

Perhaps I was being provincial, though. The man is obviously a gentleman and I have identified myself as Lord Hathaway's ward. This is not New York or London, I told myself. English villages, like small towns in America, are probably just friendly places.

I smiled with satisfaction. Let India Chantelle quibble over the proprieties. Katherine Hathaway was going to enjoy her chicken!

I looked out the window, but I saw no sign of Mr. Cousin. I would swear it was all a joke if I didn't see his hat and cape on the seat, and his suitcase still on the rack.

The train began to move, and it quickly picked up speed. So much for Mr. Cousin and my chicken, I thought, making a mental note to have the porter take charge of his belongings.

The compartment seemed very quiet now, and I closed my eyes and almost immediately dozed off.

"Miss Hathaway." The voice was low and seductive, and the unfamiliar name did nothing to alert my subconscious. My head rolled to the side, finding a very comfortable position, and I settled into a deep sleep.

My eyes opened, I don't know how much later, to a close range view of a highly polished black shoe. I raised my head

24

and the shoe disappeared, as he uncrossed his leg, and I suddenly realized my head had been resting on a man's broad shoulder.

Shocked, I jumped up, and in doing so, startled Mr. Cousin out of his own nap. "Oh, good, you're awake. Now, we can have our chicken."

"Mr. Cousin!" I said, overcome with embarrassment. "I, I . . ." My face aflame, I stuttered over my words. "Really, sir, this is most unacceptable behavior!"

He grinned up at me. "No need to apologize, Miss Hathaway. I didn't mind a bit." He thrust a white box into my hands. "Better eat now. We'll be coming into Penzance soon."

I gave him a disdainful look, and shoved the box back. "No, thank you, sir. Please take your own seat, or I shall be forced to call the porter."

Unruffled by my outburst, he got up and moved to his own side of the car. Really, I thought. The man is insufferable. However, I should have followed my own instincts and not gotten into a conversation with him in the first place.

I returned to the window, and was startled to see a large expanse of water.

"We're crossing the Tamar," he said in a conversational tone, but I ignored him.

"Before the bridge was built, Cornwall was a godforsaken spot." He paused. "Parts of it still are, like where you're going to Hathaway Manor, but of course you already know that," he added, giving me a long look.

"I remember little about it," I said stiffly. I might as well reinforce this point to everyone I meet, I thought.

"How strange," he said. "I should think that whole area would be fascinating to a child."

He was watching me closely, and in the gathering twilight, his face took on a sinister rather than a teasing look. "Hidden coves, and pirate caves. Didn't you ever go exploring when you were there?"

"I don't remember," I said, impatient with myself for getting involved in another conversation with the man.

"Why did you leave England?" he asked abruptly.

"I have no idea," I said, suddenly angry. "And Mr. Cousin, since we have only a short time left to spend together, could we spend it in silence?"

He put his hand on his chest and bowed his head. "Miss Hathaway, your every wish is my command."

I turned my head and looked out the window.

"Just one last thing, Miss Hathaway."

"What is it?" I asked without looking at him.

"If you aren't hungry, could I eat your chicken?"


The sun was just setting when we arrived in Penzance. Mr. Cousin, acting the fool again, put on an elaborate pantomime about bidding me farewell and left in a hurry.

He must have jumped off the train before it had actually stopped, for I saw him from the window, risking his elegant apparel, as he ran down a slight embankment toward a dirt road behind the station.

"You'll have to take the fly out to Hathaway Manor," Katherine had said. "It's about an hour's drive from the station. There's no telephone at the manor, so they can't be expected to meet you."

I was glad that my ordeal could be postponed for yet another hour. On an impulse, I thought, Why not even longer? They have no way of knowing that I've arrived in Penzance. I'll get a bite to eat and look around the village.

The small station was almost empty, but I spied the Station Master and called to him. "What is it?" he asked, furrowing his brow with impatience.

He was a dour-faced man with muttonchop whiskers. "Cornish people are not exactly hospitable," Katherine had warned me. "Anybody from the other side of the Tamar is a foreigner to them."

"Another one, down from London. And I suppose ye be needin' directions," he grumbled. "Shouldn't have built the bloody bridge."

I was almost afraid to speak. If Londoners were foreigners, what would he think of me?

26

"Please, could you tell me where I might get something to eat?" I asked.

He pointed. "Walk up that road a block. There's a tea shop." And scowling, he turned his back on me.

The shop was small and looked like a place where ladies would stop after shopping. Two middle-aged women sat at one of the tables and they glanced up and smiled as I entered.

The waitress was young and friendlier than the station master. She took my cape and looked approvingly at my green wool traveling suit with its fashionable leg-of-mutton sleeves. "Just down from London?" she asked with a smile.

"Yes," I answered. "But, I'm not from London. I've only just arrived from America."

The two ladies at the corner table looked up, forks suspended in the air, and the waitress exclaimed, "What d'ye know bout that. All the way from America!"

I ordered the shepherd's pie, which the waitress had recommended, and drank the tea she brought me.

I'm accustomed to coffee. It's a mainstay in the theatrical world, but the English tea was delicious and it soothed my nerves.

My thoughts turned to Mr. Cousin, and I wondered what such an obvious rake would be doing in a place like Cornwall. He had all the charm of an actor, and I didn't wonder that Beau had been somewhat like him when he had captured my country-girl mother's heart. But I am no country girl, I thought. No, neither am I a schoolgirl like Katherine Hathaway, and with my background, I should have known better.

"I beg your pardon." One of the ladies from the other table spoke. "We couldn't help but overhear that you are an American."

"That's right," I answered.

They were spinsterish looking women in their fifties. Thin, angular faces peered out at me under their sensible, short-brimmed hats. They might have been retired school teachers, but I didn't visualize them in a classroom. No, I rather saw them as gym teachers, whistles resting on their flat chests, as they lined up bloomer-clad girls for exercise class.

"How interesting! We've never met an American before."

Her companion chimed in. "My sister and I come down from Devonshire every spring. We're a little early this year. We usually come in April."

"Then you must be very familiar with the area," I said.

"Oh, dear me, yes."

"I'll be taking the fly up to my uncle's home," I commented. "It's toward Newquay."

"The fly? Oh, you've missed it. You'll have to stay over and go up in the morning."

"How stupid of me," I said. "I should have inquired about it with the station master."

"It shouldn't be a problem. We're staying right here at the Inn. Oh, let us introduce ourselves," she added. "I'm Violet Shaw, and this is my sister, Clara."

"How do you do? I'm Katherine Hathaway."

The waitress brought my dinner then, and Violet, who had a take-charge manner about her, said to the girl, "This young lady missed the fly, Grace. Can your mother put her up for the night?"

Grace smiled. "Mum's got plenty of room, that's for sure. I'll tell her to make up something for you, Miss."

"Thank you all so much," I said, ready to do justice to my meat pie. Again, I had managed to postpone my inevitable meeting with the Hathaways.


I awoke to the mournful sound of a foghorn in the distance, and looking out the inn's window I saw that the whole coastline was shrouded in a thick mist.

Perhaps I should have left Penzance yesterday, I mused. The weather had been clear then. In fact, it had been a beautiful, mild evening for March. The Shaw sisters had walked down to the station with me after dinner and we had all remarked about it.

Violet had spoken to the station master on my behalf, instructing him to check my trunks and to have the fly wait for me around ten in the morning.

"These old Cornishmen are a surly lot," she had confided,

as we walked back up the hill to the inn. "They resent the rest of us coming down here to enjoy the coast. You'd think it belonged exclusively to them and not to the whole British Empire," she added with a pompous shake of her head.

"There are some fascinating old caves up near Newquay," her sister remarked. "Pirates are said to have hidden treasures there, but I never heard of anything being found."

"More than likely it was smugglers' loot that was hidden," Violet said. "In the last century the Cornish coast was notorious for that sort of thing."

"Aye," Clara added. "There were wreckers, too. They used to lie in wait for ships, murder the crew and then steal the cargo." She seemed fascinated with the subject. "They say that's how some of the wealthy old families in Cornwall came into their fortunes."

Recalling our conversation, I thought now of the station master. His descedents would have been wreckers, I decided, and perhaps the Hathaways had been mixed up in the shady business, too. Hadn't Katherine said one of their ancestors had been a pirate?

I could see where my imagination could run wild down here. I was a Chantelle, and if I had not inherited a talent for projecting myself on stage, my ability to fantasize was no less creative. Perhaps I was destined to write plays instead of appearing in them!

I left the neat little room and hurried downstairs for a quick breakfast in the tearoom before returning to the station.

The Shaw sisters were not about, and I supposed they were sleeping in, since the day did not promise to be a fair one.

The fly was waiting when I got to the station, and the driver could have passed for the station master's brother, another crusty, disagreeable old Cornishman.

He slung my trunks on top of the fly, looking like he wished he could do the same with me. "T'ain't a fit day to be drivin' out to Hathaway Manor," he grumbled. "I'll have charge you'm more. We won't make no time in this fog."

I climbed inside and closed the door. I only hoped we

29

could make it in this rickety looking old carriage.

I wished I could have stayed in the inn at Penzance with sunny Grace and practical Violet and Clara. Their business-like approach had a charming effect on me, but instead, I was off on a journey to God knew where with a descendent of shipwreckers and murderers.

The fog was so thick, I could see nothing at all, and I wondered how the horse would ever find his way.

"How long will it take us?" I called up to the driver.

"How should I know? Several hours, if we don't land in a ditch!"

Wonderful, I thought. Katherine and Beau are probably having a late breakfast in Browns Hotel. Katherine was paying for their reservations in the exclusive establishment, as naturally, she was not about to stay in a boarding house.

Later they will take a plush, velvet lined hack to one of the casting agencies, where between Beau's silver tongue and Katherine's brass, they will probably immediately secure roles in some London production.

And here I sit in a hack that has to be a relic from the seventeenth century, with a driver who looks capable of slitting my throat just to get rid of me, and if I do arrive unscathed at my destination, who knows what lies in store for me there?

Several hours later, after being jostled over what must surely be the rockiest roads outside the civilized world, we climbed the narrowest and steepest path I have ever seen. And to say I saw it is an overstatement, for the fog was so thick, it seemed like we were ascending into the emptiness of space.

I could feel gravity pulling at the carriage as the poor horse struggled to rise against it. I thought, Dear God, if we get to the top, it will be a miracle.

I closed my eyes and prayed until I heard, "This is it, Hathaway Manor." The carriage door was opened, and I was practically pulled out of it.

I stood in what I supposed to be a driveway and I could hear the sea crashing against rocks somewhere below us. Straining my eyes, I searched for the house, and then faintly, through the swirling mists, I saw it, looking like some medieval castle, dark and forbidding.

A sudden premonition, as strong as it was terrifying, took hold of me, and my blood ran cold. *I should not have come. I should not have come.* The words resounded against the crash of the waves and filled me with dread.

# Chapter 3

I shrank back as a figure materialized out of the fog. Tall and wearing a long, black cloak, I thought him a figment of my imagination until he drew closer, and I could see that he was flesh and blood.

"Katherine? Is that you?"

I wanted to deny it. I could laugh and say, *We became lost in the fog. Can you direct us to Penzance?*

One of my trunks landed on the ground with a thud. "I'm owed me fare," the driver bellowed.

"I'm Katherine Hathaway," I heard myself say in a weak voice.

"I would never have known you, my dear. Welcome to Hathaway Manor." He brushed my brow with cold lips, and spoke in a stern voice to the driver. "I am Lord Hathaway. Get the other trunk down and mind how you handle it. My man will pay you."

Taking me by the arm, he guided me down a walkway towards the house. Two servants hurried past us, and he gave them brisk instructions. "Bring Miss Katherine's trunks inside and pay the driver."

A third servant was waiting at the open door. He took our wraps, and Lord Hathaway said, "Tarleton, this is Miss Katherine, my niece." The butler bowed and mumbled some pleasantry. Evidently I was not expected to remember him, and I was grateful for that.

We stood in a large mosaic tiled entrance hall, resplendent

with wall hangings. Tapestries, I believe they are called, and I stole a glance at the magnificent rococo ceiling that Katherine had mentioned. The plasterwork was picked out in gilt, and I tried not to gape like the newcomer I was to elegant surroundings.

"Your Aunt Beatrice is in the morning room," he said, "Come, let us join her."

I followed him down the hall and into a charming room that made me feel I had stepped into an English garden. The sofa and chairs were upholstered in a beautiful print, spilling over with large cabbage roses, and the floor was covered with a Persian carpet in shades of wine and teal blue.

A woman, her back to us, was seated at a desk, and she rose when Lord—I must remember to call him Uncle Fenton—opened the door. "My dear, our guest has arrived," he said in that same even tempered voice.

She turned then and came towards us, and I thought that they could have easily passed for brother and sister. Both of them tall and slender with rather pinched, long-nosed faces and colorless, ash blond hair.

"How nice to have you, Katherine," she said. There was no warmth in her greeting; neither had there been in her husband's. She, too, gave me a perfunctory, cold-lipped kiss on the cheek. "You must be tired. Such appalling weather to travel in. It's almost time for lunch. Would you like to freshen up first?"

"That would be nice," I said, anxious to be alone, if only for a few minutes. I don't know what I had envisioned Hathaway Manor to be, but this palatial mansion was beyond anything my limited background had prepared me for.

Their pale blue eyes looked into mine, assessing me. I felt if I have to stand here another moment, I shall break down and confess that I am an imposter.

Lady Hathaway—Would I ever be able to think of her as Aunt Beatrice?—rang for a servant and a young maid appeared. "This is Maureen. She'll show you to your room. You shan't be long, shall you, Katherine? Luncheon is served at one o'clock."

"Certainly, thank you, Aunt Beatrice," I managed, and retreated behind the maid.

We passed through the hall and ascended a handsome curved stairway to the second floor. Circling around the balcony, we continued on down a long corridor and around several corners. I shall never find my way back, I thought, when the maid suddenly stopped.

"Here we are, Miss Katherine. And a lovely room it is, if I might say so."

She opened the door, and I caught my breath. It was quite the loveliest room I have ever seen, light and airy with none of the heaviness and clutter so much a part of our Victorian inheritance.

The room was done in pale green and cream, with splashes of pink; a chaise lounge in pale pink slipper satin and bed hangings with those wonderful cabbage roses predominant in the print. The walls were painted in the palest of green and uncovered, casement windows looked out on what I thought must be a spectacular view of the sea.

I felt like I had been transported to paradise. Why would anybody turn their back on all of this? I wondered.

The maid stood waiting for me to make a comment, and I said, "It is indeed a beautiful room."

She smiled. "Course, I'm sure it's nothin' like what you've been used to."

I panicked. My throat went dry and I thought, She knows. I've given myself away somehow.

"Why whatever do you mean?" I asked, giving her a nervous smile.

"I've heard all about America, Miss Katherine. Everything fast and modern over there." She rolled her eyes. "I guess you had electric lights and a horseless carriage?"

I laughed with relief. "We're not all that modern yet, Maureen. Some people have electric lights, but plenty more use gas and oil lamps the same as over here, and as for horseless carriages, I haven't seen but one."

She looked a little disappointed, and I supposed I had shattered her illusions. Picking up the pitcher, she said, "I'll bring some hot water, so's you can freshen up."

When the door closed, I removed my hat and unlaced my boots. In my stocking feet, I walked back and forth over the plush carpet, feeling my toes sink into the deep pile. Then I sat on the edge of the bed and sank down into the thick feather mattress. Stretching out, I let myself luxuriate in it, feeling like a child in wonderland.

I could hear the roar of the sea, and I got up and looked out the casement windows, but the fog was still thick and I could see nothing of the view.

When I heard Maureen's footsteps in the hall, I quickly slipped into my shoes and stood before the mirror, patting my hair back into place. "Come in," I said in what I supposed to be the slightly bored voice of a rich young woman.

Maureen filled the bowl with water, and I washed my face and hands and dried them on the towel she handed me. I would have preferred pouring my own water and fetching my own towel, but for the next six months I would be waited on hand and foot, as Beau had predicted. I supposed I would just have to get used to it.

Once again, I followed Maureen through a maze of corridors to the balcony overlooking the entry hall. We went downstairs, and entered what the maid referred to as, "the small dining room."

Uncle Fenton, Aunt Beatrice, and a young woman were already seated at the table. I assumed the young lady to be Willa, Uncle Fenton's daughter, but I dared not speak first. Now comes the acid test, I thought. If anybody can trip me up, it will be Cousin Willa.

Uncle Fenton rose. "We've been waiting for you, Katherine. Your cousin, has been anxious to see you again."

The young woman looked more angry than anxious, and Katherine's words came back to me. *We didn't like each other much, but then we were only children.*

Looking down her long, Hathaway nose, Willa measured me from head to toe. She was tall and thin like her parents, long of face, and with the same pale blue eyes and ash blond hair. "Nice to see you, Katherine," she said, embracing me stiffly.

I mumbled something equally false and we took our places

at the table. I wondered why the son was not present, and almost jumped when Uncle Fenton seemingly read my mind. "Jordan will not be joining us for lunch. Something about an experiment he's working on."

"Those horrible experiments," Willa said. "I hope he's not going to . . ."

Her father interrupted her quickly. "Jordan is a chemist, Katherine. Perhaps you recall what a keen interest he had in the subject."

I shook my head. "Not really."

Better show from the beginning that I have a poor memory, I thought.

"He read chemistry at Oxford," Aunt Beatrice added pompously. "Jordan has a brilliant mind."

While the soup was being served, I stole a glance at Willa. She wore the same, sullen expression, and it was perfectly obvious that none of the Hathaways were overjoyed by my presence. I wondered why. Did they suspect something?

In my nervousness, I spilled a little soup on the cloth, and like a child fearing a scolding, I covered it with my napkin.

When the maid came to remove the plates, Aunt Beatrice said in her strange monotone, "Bring Miss Katherine another napkin."

I blushed, but made no comment. Why make an even bigger fool of myself, I decided.

I could feel Willa's eyes on me, and my panic increased when she said, "You've changed, Katherine."

"So have you," I replied, trying to sound matter-of-fact. "I wouldn't have known you, Willa."

Lady Beatrice eyed me critically. "It's true. Seeing you now, Katherine, it's hard to believe you are the same child. You were a caution," she said, forcing her thin lips to smile. "A chatterbox and a little mischief maker, you were, and now here you are, a poised and lovely young woman."

She had described Katherine Hathaway to a tee, but I was not about to attempt an imitation. I was not that good an actress, so I would just have to pass myself off as a more subdued, grown-up version of Katherine.

The second course arrived and I was spared further discussion on the subject, as the maid claimed our attention with the serving dishes.

I was not accustomed to such rigid formality in dining. Although it was the maid who served, the butler, too, was in attendance, observing the poor girl's performance like a director in the wings of a theater. I reminded myself that this was only a luncheon, and shuddered to think of the formal dinners I would be subjected to every evening.

However, Beau had not been remiss in teaching me proper table manners. So despite my nervousness, I presumed I should manage to conduct myself adequately on that score.

The long, drawn-out luncheon finally came to an end and mercifully I heard Aunt Beatrice say, "I'm sure you're exhausted, Katherine. I, myself, nap from two o'clock until four o'clock. Doctor's orders," she added, placing a hand over her heart. "Why don't you rest, too, dear? Maureen will wake you for tea."

I gratefully accepted her suggestion. I was tired, that was true, but the strain of playing the imposter was wearing me down. And this was only the first day!

I was sound asleep and dreaming I was back in the theater when I heard someone knock on the door. I fully expected to hear a shout, "Five minutes to curtain time," followed by the shuffle of feet as actors and actresses scurried from dressing rooms into the wings.

"It's four o'clock, Miss Katherine. Time for tea." Maureen's soft Irish accent brought me suddenly back to Hathaway Manor and I lit the lamp on the bedside table.

"Thank you, Maureen. I'm up," I called back.

I didn't bother to change. All too soon it would be time to dress for dinner. I combed my hair and patted a little cologne on my wrists. Glancing out the window, I saw that the fog had lifted, and looking down I could see waves crashing against the rocks.

It was a spectacular view, for the house was built on a high cliff. Directly under my room was a garden and in the gathering dusk, I thought I saw a figure move among the hedgerows. A big, lumbering figure. Rubbing my eyes, I looked again, and it was gone. There had been something unnatural about its movements, and I concluded it had merely been a figment of my imagination.

I closed the door and hurried down the corridor. It wouldn't do to be late for tea. The British are very punctual people, or so I had heard. Katherine, of course, was an exception, but then, I reminded myself she was more American than English.

I stopped as I came to the end of the corridor. Where is the balcony and the staircase? I thought. Annoyed with myself, I concluded I must have taken a wrong turn. Now, I would surely be late!

I gathered up my skirt and walked briskly back through the maze of corridors, becoming more confused than ever until I spied a small, back staircase. Better to take this, I thought, than to continue wandering around on the second floor.

The staircase was narrow and extremely steep, with short little treads which made descending it dangerous. There was no handrail, and I prayed I would not trip and land in a heap at the bottom. I had little doubt that such a fall would result in serious injury.

It ended, to my dismay, before a blank walk, and I was frustrated enough to cry. What use was a blind stairway?

I was about to start back up again when I heard voices on the other side. They were as clear to me as if I had been in the same room, and I suddenly realized that I was. This back stairway opened into a concealed wall, allowing the occupants to escape upstairs, unnoticed by visitors who might be detained in the entry hall.

I had seen a similar set designed for one of Beau's plays, "The Disappearance of Lady Agatha," Chicago, 1885. As a child, it had fascinated me, but the play closed after a month's run.

The voices in the room rose, and I recognized Lady Beatrice's. "Believe me, Willa. I shan't let her spoil your chances."

"How can you stop her? Have you looked at her, Mother? She's turned into a beauty. Oh, why did she have to come?"

"Your father felt it his duty, dear."

They're discussing me, I thought and shrank back, terrified lest I touch something that would release the wall and expose me as an eavesdropper.

Uncle Fenton spoke then. "It will only be for a little while."

"That's right," Aunt Beatrice said. "And in the meantime, we'll go right along with our plans. We'll have a lovely time in London and Sir Alex will be captivated by you."

Willa answered her in a sullen voice. "Not with Katherine around, he won't."

Oh, dear, I thought. She's afraid I'll steal her beau.

"I'll think of something," Lady Beatrice said, "Now, go to the hall mirror and fluff out your hair, dear. Margaret has it pulled too tightly back."

"Adopting Katherine's hairstyle won't help, Mother," Willa retorted.

She must have left the room though, for Aunt Beatrice spoke in a different tone of voice to Uncle Fenton. "I told you not to bring her here."

"Don't worry me with foolishness, Beatrice."

"I'm not talking about Willa. You know what I mean, Fenton. Katherine may remember more than we think she does." Suddenly her tone of voice changed back, becoming light and lilting again. "That looks lovely, dear. Have Margaret do it that way from now on."

Uncle Fenton spoke again. "It's quarter past. Where is that girl?"

"She never did have any regard for time," Aunt Beatrice replied.

I practically crawled up the stairs. Suddenly this masquerade had taken on a different tone. There was no question now that I was an unwelcome guest. And what had Aunt Beatrice meant about Katherine's memory? I wondered.

I reached the top, and I followed another long corridor that miraculously brought me by sheer luck out to the balcony and the familiar grand staircase.

I was spared another search when a young maid rescued me in the hallway. "I been waitin' to lead you to the Small Salon, Miss Katherine. The family'll be having their tea in there now."

I entered a very ornate room, typical of our Victorian era of clutter. Red and gold dominated the color scheme and the effect was one of ostentation, and overindulgence.

I scanned the walls for the location of the hidden stairway, but even my practiced, theatrical eye could detect no telltale sign that would give it away.

Uncle Fenton and a younger man, whom I presumed to be his son Jordan, both stood as I entered.

"I apologize for being late," I said. "I overslept."

"Think nothing of it. I'm sure you were tired, my dear." Uncle Fenton radiated good humor, and I would have been quite taken in if I hadn't overheard their conversation. "You remember your cousin, Jordan," he said.

The younger man was heavier than the other Hathaways, but the same pale blue eyes stared into mine. "Of course," I said. "Good to see you, Jordan."

There was something trancelike in the look he gave me, as if he didn't see me at all. He kissed my hand, and automatically murmured a greeting.

His father's eyes regarded him a little anxiously, and then Uncle Fenton said, "Jordan was late, too. He was working in his laboratory and lost track of time."

I thought it only polite to ask, so I said, "I understand you're conducting experiments, Jordan."

"Yes. I'm working with Dr. Langston Cummings in London, a very brilliant and innovative man. He has a theory that diseases of the mind are caused by a chemical imbalance in the brain."

Uncle Fenton looked anxiously at his wife and spoke in an undertone to Jordan. "Please don't distress your mother, Jordan. This is hardly a subject for teatime."

"Sorry, Father," Jordan replied, and turned back to me. "You must visit my laboratory sometime, Katherine. It's located up on the moors, not too far. You do ride, don't you?"

"No," I answered. Both he and Uncle Fenton looked surprised.

I was well aware that genteel ladies even in New York were taught to ride, and while I was wracking my brain for a plausible excuse, Uncle Fenton said, "But, Katherine, I do recall you rode as a child."

"Yes," I said quickly, "but I had a bad fall, and lost my nerve."

Uncle Fenton shook his head. "I can't imagine Katherine losing her nerve, can you, Jordan? But we'll remedy that," he said in a jovial way. "Our groom will find you a good mount. He's an excellent instructor, and it'll all come back to you. Living in the country, one needs to ride."

"I'm sure," I answered. I had always wanted to ride and here was a golden opportunity. The moors, I thought. Even the word sounded mysterious. Yes, I would love exploring the moors, innocent fool that I was.

Aunt Beatrice suddenly joined the conversation. "An excellent idea. It will give Katherine something to do next week while Willa and I are in London." I thought she gave her husband a sly look before she turned to me and added, "I feel terrible about this, Katherine, but Willa had already accepted this invitation before we knew you were coming. Naturally she cannot go alone, so . . ."

"Think nothing of it, Aunt Beatrice," I replied, trying to keep the eagerness out of my voice.

This was more than I had dared hope for. A whole week without having to worry about them! I was beginning to feel wonderful.

We were interrupted then by the arrival of Tarleton and a young footman who covered the tea table with a damask cloth, and set down the silver service and a tray of small cakes and crumpets before Lady Hathaway.

Aunt Beatrice poured and Willa sat on her right, passing the steaming cups to the rest of us.

I relaxed for the first time since I had arrived. I shall have all next week to myself, I thought. Uncle Fenton and Jordan will pose no problem. They will be busy with their own activities, and I can take long nature walks, perhaps even learn to ride and explore the moors.

Willa, too, seemed happier after her mother's announcement, and I felt a little sorry for this sullen, unattractive girl who was so concerned about my outshining her.

I supposed she would see the sought after Sir Alex in London. Perhaps she could wangle a proposal out of the gentleman next week, and then I would pose no problem for her at all. I sincerely hoped so. In fact, I would be elated should she elope while in London.

My thoughts were interrupted by the return of the butler. He spoke softly to Lord Hathaway, and a look of annoyance crossed Uncle Fenton's face. Turning to the rest of us, he said in his dry monotone. "We have another guest for tea."

Lady Beatrice looked up in surprise. But before she could ask a question, the door was opened and I almost jumped out of my skin when Mr. Cousin entered the room.

"Sorry to arrive at teatime," he said in his breezy way. "None for me though. I had something more bracing on the way up here." He reached into his pocket and produced a silver flask which he waved with a wink before Aunt Beatrice's horrified eyes.

I sank back in the large wing chair, hoping to be shielded from his view. What is he doing here, and what connection could he possibly have with the Hathaways? I wondered.

An annoying neighbor, I decided, one of those pesky kind of people that abound in even the best of circles. Hopefully he won't stay but a minute.

"Stuart, let me introduce you to our other guest," Uncle Fenton was saying, and I thought, now there's no escape for me.

I sat forward, and raised my eyes to meet Mr. Cousin's. He glowed with unsuppressed mirth, a condition brought on no doubt by the contents of his flask as well as my embarrassment.

"Mr. Cousin and I have already met," I said quietly.

Uncle Fenton looked confused. "Of course you've met

your Cousin Stuart, Katherine, but it's been seven years. He hasn't changed that much, but you certainly have." He turned to the man beside him. "Isn't that right, Stuart?"

My head was whirling. Cousin Stuart, Stuart Cousin! Good heavens! I thought. He is Katherine's cousin, Stuart Hathaway, and he has been making a fool of me all along.

# Chapter 4

Waves of panic washed over me. What had I said to this man on the train? Had I given myself away? The two masculine figures of Uncle Fenton and Stuart Hathaway took on giant proportions as they loomed over me, and I felt myself shrinking under their gaze like a tiny Alice in Wonderland.

All the blood drained from my face as two penetrating sets of eyes, the one so pale as to appear almost colorless, the other dark as slate stared into mine.

It seemed an eternity before Stuart Hathaway spoke. "Katherine certainly has changed," he said, giving me an appraising look. "Our little duckling has turned into a swan!"

I smiled with relief, and secretly indulged myself in some choice ruminations about this newest addition to Katherine's unsavory lineage.

A rake and a blackguard, if ever I saw one. This cousin could prove to be more trouble than the rest of them put together, I decided.

He leaned down then and whispered in my ear. "Don't be nervous. They're a little strange, but you'll get used to them again."

"I am not nervous," I said, and then followed his gaze to the teacup that rattled in my hand.

He smiled with satisfaction and took it from me. "Shall I get you a refill?"

"No, thank you."

"You aren't upset with me because of my little joke, are you Katherine? It was unfair, I must admit, but I simply couldn't resist it." He gave me a disarming smile. "Friends again? Or should I say, cousins again?"

I smiled back. What else could I do? "How long will you be staying at Hathaway Manor?" I asked, hoping he would be leaving in the morning.

He shrugged. "I usually stay until I become bored." His eyes traveled about the room. "Which, as you can see, would be early on." Returning his gaze to me, he grinned. "But now that you're here, Katherine, I just might stay indefinitely."

A pained expression crossed Aunt Beatrice's face and I knew that she had overheard him.

"Do you get down from London often?" I asked.

Pulling up a small footstool, he sat by my chair and lowered his voice intimately. "Often enough to annoy our dear relatives." He raised an eyebrow. "Didn't your parents clue you in on the family? My father was the black sheep, and I in turn have inherited his title."

I took the opportunity to establish that my knowledge was sketchy. "I was only told they didn't approve of your father's marriage."

He laughed. "That's putting it mildly. My father was disinherited. The entire estate including holdings in Sussex and Kent which were unentailed, and promised to my father. were turned over to Fenton. Your father, as you probably know, received a cash settlement." His face changed, and a sarcastic smirk replaced his smile. "It seems it is permissible to intermarry with first cousins, but someone from the stage would taint the pale blue blood of the Hathaways." He gave me a strange look. "No offense meant, Katherine. I get carried away sometimes."

My head went into another whirl. Why was he apologizing to me? Surely, he didn't connect me with the stage, or could it merely be that Katherine's parents were also cousins? I settled on the latter, as his face held no trace of guile.

It was obvious that he was referring specifically to Fenton and Beatrice, and I understood now the tension that had invaded the room with his presence. He was a thorn in all their sides, and in his perverse way, he reveled in making them uncomfortable.

Beneath their cool exteriors, the Hathaway family was seething with jealousy and hatred, and I was convinced now that Katherine was more aware of the situation than she had led me to believe.

Dinner that evening was an ordeal. Despite a delicious and beautifully served meal, rigidly formal as I had anticipated, with all of us impeccably turned out in evening clothes, undercurrents of malice crisscrossed the table.

"How charming you look, Katherine," Uncle Fenton remarked in his detached manner.

"I say gorgeous is a better word," Stuart added. "Don't you agree, Jordan?"

"Indeed."

"Is your wardrobe from New York or Paris?" Aunt Beatrice asked, giving my made-over peach gown a critical eye.

"Both," I answered, smiling sweetly at her.

"It hardly matters," Stuart insisted. "American women always manage somehow to look smashing."

Aunt Beatrice raised an eyebrow. "Oh, and do you consider yourself an American, Katherine?"

I floundered a little before coming up with what I thought was a diplomatic response. "Yes, but like all Americans, I have a great fondness for the land of my birth."

Willa sniffed. "I shouldn't be too quick to shed your English heritage, if I were you, Katherine. We see some frightful American women in London these days."

Aunt Beatrice nodded her head. "The *nouveau riche*. They come over here hoping to marry a title."

Stuart's eyes twinkled with a suppressed smile. "Coming in droves they are for the season. Why, I do believe I saw one of them with Sir Alex Lighthizer the other night at the opera."

Aunt Beatrice turned white and Willa turned red. With

undisguised fury, she stabbed at a piece of meat and impaled it on her fork.

Poor, Sir Alex, I thought. I don't know you at all, but you certainly have my sympathy!

Uncle Fenton's eyes, cold and colorless as ice, glared down the table at Stuart. "Still enjoying London's night life, I see." He took a sip of wine and dabbed his lips with a corner of the napkin. "Such a lifestyle can soon deplete a young man's capital, I should think."

Stuart's eyes danced with mischief. "Oh, absolutely, Uncle, but not for a while, I hope. I'm not ready to retire to the country just yet." Glancing quickly at his aunt, he gave her a devilish smile and added, "Keep my room ready though, just in case."

She ignored him, and turned quickly to me. "Speaking of rooms, Katherine, dear. Are you comfortable in yours?"

"Oh, yes," I answered. "I love looking out on the sea."

Stuart looked startled. "Katherine has Grandfather Duncan's room?"

"We opened up the wing and redecorated when we heard dear Katherine was coming," Aunt Beatrice said.

"It's quite lovely," I commented. "But I didn't expect you to redecorate on my account."

"It was our pleasure," Aunt Beatrice cooed and Willa nodded her head in agreement.

Jordan, who had been silent for the entire meal, suddenly turned those startling pale eyes in my direction and said, "I should like to show you my laboratory, Katherine. Perhaps next week while Willa and Mother are away—"

Stuart interrupted him. "Katherine's committed to riding lessons next week, old man. I plan to keep her in the saddle every spare minute."

To my surprise, Uncle Fenton concurred. "Plenty of time to show Katherine the laboratory, Jordan. Stuart can make himself useful as a riding master while he's here."

I was relieved. There was something strange about Jordan and I wasn't sure I wanted to be alone with him.

The long, tense meal finally came to an end and it wasn't too much later that Aunt Beatrice and Willa, pleading an early start for London in the morning, said their good nights.

I took advantage of the opportunity to retire early myself, effectively avoiding any further interrogation by the remaining family members, especially the annoying Mr. Cousin.

I'll have to stop calling him that, I told myself. But the stupid name had somehow stuck in my mind, and I feared Cousin Stuart would remain Stuart Cousin at least in my thoughts.

I hurried to my room, anxious to shed the flamboyant Katherine Hathaway and revert back to India Chantelle, but my performance was not over yet, for when I opened the door, I found Maureen waiting for me.

She had come to help me undress, a task that I, with my theatrical experience, could have performed blindfolded and with one hand tied behind me. Nevertheless, mask in place, I submitted to her efforts with all the helplessness the role required.

She offered to brush my hair, but I declined, pleading a headache. She reluctantly left, feeling I'm sure, that she had not been allowed to perform her duties properly.

After she had gone, I picked up the brush and languidly drew it through my long, black hair. The woman who stared back at me from the mirror looked different. The mauve satin dressing gown that had belonged to Katherine caressed my body with sensuous decadence. It shimmered in the candlelight, opening and closing to reveal the fullness of my breasts with each rhythmic stroke of the brush. What would Cousin Stuart say if he could see me now, I wondered. Would he smile and say "Smashing!"?

Shocked that I should even entertain such a thought, I got up and paced the floor. I am not even slightly interested in Stuart Hathaway, I told myself. The man's a rake and a mischief maker, and besides that, he's your first cousin.

*No, he's not. He's Katherine's first cousin,* my other self answered.

I blew out the candles and got into bed. Sinking down into incredible softness, I listened to the waves crashing on the rocks below. "What do you have to lose?" Beau had asked me after Katherine had presented her proposition.

The satin sheets suddenly felt cold, and I shivered, as a small voice inside me answered, *Perhaps myself!*


Aunt Beatrice and Willa were already gone when I awakened.

"Left before six o'clock, they did," Maureen informed me. "And never did I see so many trunks and hatboxes piled on a carriage." She placed a tray on the bedside table and opened the drapes. "Brought you a cup of coffee, Miss Katherine." Plumping my pillows, she smiled down at me. "I made it myself. Over here, they just drink tea. But the Irish are like the Americans," she added confidentially. "We like something a little stronger now and again."

I was glad Maureen was Irish. The other servants intimidated me with their strange Cornish accents and pompous airs, but her countrymen had immigrated to America in droves and Maureen's lilting speech and levelheaded personality made me feel at home.

"How nice! Thank you, Maureen."

She beamed, and I reached for the cup and took a sip. It was the strongest coffee I'd ever tasted. I think my hair actually stood on end, but under her beaming gaze, I managed to drink it down. All the same, I hoped this was not to become a daily ritual.

She meant well, I reminded myself, and so far Maureen was the only person at Hathaway Manor I could trust. Perhaps she could fill me in on some of the facts that Katherine had so conveniently omitted.

"Have you been at Hathaway Manor long, Maureen?" I asked.

"Four years, Miss."

That was longer than I had expected, and I wondered why a young woman would stay in such a remote place.

She seemed to read my mind. "The pay's good and I'm saving my money to go home. Besides," she said, "I ain't no Lily. All the same, I stay away from the moors."

I found the expression odd, but before I could ask a

question, we were interrupted by a knock on the door.

Maureen opened it, and then leaving the door ajar, she turned back to me. "Mr. Stuart would like a word with you, Miss Katherine."

Before I could gather my wits about me, he was in the room. His insolent eyes took me in from head to toe, making me suddenly aware that I was still in my dressing gown, with my hair hanging down my back. "What! Not dressed yet? Have you forgotten our riding lesson, cousin?"

He looked ruggedly handsome and disturbingly masculine in his riding attire, and I was acutely conscious that I had fantasized his seeing me like this. Mortified by the feelings this annoying man aroused in me, I spoke sharply. "I can't get dressed until you leave my bedroom, *cousin.*"

"I'll give you fifteen minutes, no longer," he said genially. Then with a wink, he added in an undertone, "You look smashing in your dressing gown."

He murmured something to Maureen as he left the room and she giggled. "Mr. Stuart's a caution, he is. Why he could pass for an Irishman with all his blarney." She gave me a knowing look. "He ain't nothing like the rest of them and that's the Lord's truth."

I wondered if "by the rest of them," she meant the other Hathaways, or just the British in general. In any case, I smiled to let her know she hadn't overstepped her bounds as far as I was concerned. Let her feel free to speak here in the confines of this room, I thought. It's the only way I'll find out what I need to know.


He insisted I eat breakfast. "You can't ride on an empty stomach, and I shouldn't want you to get sick."

"I don't have a weak stomach," I replied.

He looked at me curiously. "So I recall."

It irritated me that he had wormed his way into taking over for the groom. I would have been much more comfortable with someone who didn't know Katherine Hathaway had ridden as a child.

Fortune smiled on me though, as his first words in the

stable were, "I want you to forget everything you did before, unless you still plan on riding astride."

I sighed with relief. "I hardly think that would be appropriate now."

He was a good teacher, and I surprised myself by catching on quickly. I almost laughed when he said, "The basics are still there. All you need is practice."

"Naturally," I answered smugly.

His smokey grey eyes took me in boldly, and raising an eyebrow, he said, "You have a good seat, Cousin."

I knew he meant to be insolent, but I could only answer primly. "Thank you."

The first lesson was a short one for which I was grateful. My "good seat" was becoming a little sensitive.

"Soak in a hot tub," he instructed me. "Then you won't be sore tomorrow. A massage would help, too," he added and then smiled wickedly.

"Never mind," I answered. "I can do without it."

He laughed. "Shame on you, Katherine. Surely, you didn't think I was suggesting . . ."

My face scarlet, I turned on him angrily. "Oh, you are the most exasperating man!"

Gathering up my riding skirt, I flounced off, feeling like an *ingénue* in a silly play.

He caught up to me and grabbed my arm. "Don't be angry, Katherine. I apologize." All the mockery had left his face and an emotion I could not read flickered momentarily in his grey eyes. "We're both outsiders here. Trust me, Katherine. You may need my help."

His sudden departure from the role of outrageous rake startled me and made me question if I was the only one at Hathaway Manor to be wearing a mask. But I accepted his apology and we departed on friendly terms; he to the moors, or so he informed me, to exercise his restless stallion, and I to my room to soak my tired muscles and wonder about this strange warning I had just been given.

I was sleepy and completely relaxed after my soak in the hot tub and I wanted to nap and avoid a repetition of the heavy, formal luncheon that I had endured the day before.

"I suppose Lord Fenton would be very upset if I didn't appear for lunch," I remarked in an offhand manner to Maureen.

To my surprise, she informed me that neither Lord Fenton nor Mr. Jordan took the noonday meal at home. "Yesterday was a special occasion, you just arriving," she said. "But ordinarily, only Lady Hathaway and Miss Willa have luncheon in the dining room."

I pictured the two of them, alone at the massive table, servants stationed behind their chairs, accepting the whole ostentatious display as nothing more than their due.

"In that case," I told Maureen, "ask cook if I might have a tray in my room; nothing fancy, just some biscuits and a cup of hot tea."

"I'll fix it meself, and be right back," she promised.

She returned in a few minutes with a platter of cold meat to go with the biscuits and a pot of freshly brewed tea. Would that I could have all of my meals in my room, I thought, preferring both the company and the informal service to that of the dining room.

I sat by the window at a small table eating my lunch while Maureen busied herself brushing my riding habit, all the while chatting incessantly about the weather and other inconsequential subjects.

Hopefully, I steered the conversation back to the family. "I suppose Lord Hathaway is too busy with estate matters to return home for lunch."

"Aye. He's gone from early morning til dinner time, he is. Lord Hathaway's a mighty busy man."

"And Mr. Jordan," I asked. "Does he work at his laboratory all day?"

"Aye."

"Is it a very large laboratory?"

"I don't know, Miss Katherine. It's on the edge of the moors, and I don't go there."

I recalled her quaint expression, "I ain't no Lily." "Why are you afraid of the moors?" I asked.

She gave me a startled look. "On account of Lily."

"Lily," I repeated.

"You know about Lily, don't you, Miss Katherine? Lily Beacham. Cook says she disappeared right before you and your family left for America."

What else had Katherine omitted? I wondered.

"I was very young, Maureen," I said, falling back on my standard excuse. "Perhaps if you refresh my memory."

She spoke more to herself than to me. "Maybe you don't know. You were long gone when they found her, and probably your parents wouldn't have wanted you to know." Satisfied, that such was the case, she nodded her head and continued.

"Lily Beacham was upstairs maid here seven years ago. She was a comely lass, only she liked anything in trousers. Cook says she was a little too free with her favors, if you know what I mean." She stopped suddenly and blushed. "Begging your pardon, Miss Katherine."

"That's perfectly all right," I said. "Speak freely, Maureen."

She lowered her voice, and it was evident she relished the telling of it. "Anyway, she just disappeared in thin air. Everybody thought she'd run off with one of her gentleman friends, but Cook says she knew Lily would never leave all her clothes behind." She took a deep breath and continued in an awed whisper. "Three years later, right after I'd come to the Manor, they found her body buried out on the moors." Her eyes grew wide and she shuddered. "She'd been murdered!"

A classic tale, not so terrifying as Jack the Ripper, I mused, but it gave Maureen a thrill to imagine herself on the edge of danger, as it were.

She took my tray and feeling drowsy, I climbed into bed for my nap. I hadn't done a very good job of pumping Maureen, I thought. And in my innocence, I rejected the lurid tale of Lily Beacham, finding it of no consequence in my quest to discover family secrets.

I woke up an hour later, feeling refreshed and full of energy. An afternoon, all to myself, stretched before me, and I certainly wasn't going to spend it in bed.

The morning mist had lifted and looking out the casement windows, I could see the coastline clearly. The huge rocks that jutted out into the water directly below my window gave way to a sandy stretch of beach a little farther down.

It looked inviting, and my spirit of adventure was suddenly awakened. A wonderful day for exploring, I decided.

There was no one about as I strode through the maze of corridors to the grand staircase, and peering over the balcony, I saw the downstairs hall was also deserted.

I don't know why that pleased me. Surely I was not a prisoner here, neither was I a child who needed permission to walk the beach, I told myself.

The garden that I could see from my bedroom window stretched out almost to the cliff's edge, and when in full bloom, I thought that it must present a startling contrast to the ruggedness of the rock strewn coast beneath it.

Perhaps it mirrors the Hathaways themselves. Were they also orderly and civilized on the surface, but dangerous and violent underneath? I thought.

It was obvious that there was bad blood between Stuart and the other Hathaways. Stuart's father had been disinherited and Fenton had profited from it; sufficient grounds to sow the seeds of jealousy. But, if Stuart suspected that Fenton had perhaps influenced old Duncan Hathaway against his father, then that could really provide him with an obsessive hatred.

And what had Stuart meant this morning when he had said we were both outsiders? Katherine's father had not been disinherited, but it was also obvious that the Hathaways did not welcome their niece's return.

Willa, of course, had some foolish notion that I might outshine her and spoil her chances with Sir Alex, but it had to be more than that.

I thought back to the conversation I had overheard in the passageway. Beatrice had sounded frightened, and she had said, "She might remember more than we think she does."

Oh, Katherine, I thought. What have you gotten me into, and why?

I walked to the edge of the cliff, and stood, looking down.

Fascinated, I watched the giant waves crash against the jagged boulders and burst into sprays that rose high in the air. There was something savage and yet so beautiful about it that I could not tear myself away.

Over and over, the spectacle was repeated, as wave after wave rolled relentlessly to shore. I felt myself being hypnotized by the sight, and then suddenly I froze.

Someone was standing behind me. I sensed their presence with an uncanny certainty, and yet I could not bring myself to turn around. Instinctively, I knew that I would see something so shocking that it would cause me to plunge backwards through space and land on the rocks below.

The sensation passed, and my paralyzed limbs came to life again. Quickly stepping back, away from the edge, I whirled around to confront. . . . Nothing! No one was there!

My knees buckled under me, and I slid to the ground. Tears blurred my eyes, but I thought I saw a dark, lumbering figure move through the brush.

Like a flash, it disappeared, and I wondered even then if I'd seen it at all. Like last night, I thought. There was something similar in the garden, or had I only imagined it?

# Chapter 5

Picking myself up, I hurried like a frightened rabbit back to the safety of the house.

I would have welcomed anybody's company, even Stuart's, but no one was about. If I returned to my room, I knew I would be drawn like a magnet to the window, and I didn't want to look down on the scene of my near accident.

Had it just been a figment of my imagination? I speculated.

I supposed it had, but I found it hard to accept. I was not given to histrionics, despite my theatrical exposure to imaginative and high-strung people.

Even as a child I had not been fearful or timid. How many nights had I stayed alone in a strange hotel room waiting for Beau? My imagination had not played tricks on me then. Why now? I wondered.

There was no doubt in my mind that this pretense, this immersing myself in another person's character, was having an adverse effect on me. Also, there was something about this house and the people in it that bore watching.

Right now, I was badly frightened, but there was a mystery here and though my common sense told me to leave it alone, I knew my curiosity would eventually get the better of me.

My badly shaken nerves gradually returned to normal, and heading for the drawing room, I decided to do a little exploring on the inside of the house.

The stage set in "The Disappearance of Lady Agatha" had been designed with a revolving panel, and I was sure the hidden stairway I had stumbled upon was concealed in just such a manner.

I ran my hands over all the walls, pushing first this way, and then that way, but nothing moved. I had to conclude that the opening had been sealed and was no longer in use.

I left the drawing room with its clutter and formality, and wandered into the cheerful morning room where an older and more tasteful decor predominated.

Tarleton suddenly appeared, and with a pained expression announced that it was teatime, and asked where he should serve it.

"Will any of the other family members be present?" I asked him.

"No, Miss Katherine. Lord Hathaway and Master Jordan will not be home until dinner time, and Master Stuart has not returned from his ride."

"In that case," I said. "I'll have mine in here. Informally," I added. "This little side table will do fine."

Looking disgusted, he nodded his head, and left the room. I was given the impression he did not approve of this at all. The complicated ritual was probably performed whether or no, and I had just upset the daily routine. Too bad, I thought. Your act was boring, Tarleton, and I've just eliminated it from this performance.

Alone again, I let my eyes travel about the room. Someday, I thought, I might be fortunate enough to have a home of my own and if I do, I should want a room like this.

I noticed an unusual carved secretary in the corner, and wanting a closer look, I walked across the room to examine it. The carvings were exquisite with the figures depicted having a medieval look about them, and I wondered how old the piece might be.

Opening it, I was surprised to see that all the little cubbyholes were lined in leather. Either it was not as old as I had imagined, or the leather had been added at a later date. I was about to close it again when my eye centered on an open journal.

I must confess that before I could stop myself, I had read the brief entry dated yesterday, April 1, 1895.

"Jordan had a dazed look about him tonight and I fear for him. Katherine's presence here is another worry. I don't care what Fenton says, associations with the past could bring it all back to her, and then, to whom, or to what would that lead?"

I closed the desk quickly as Tarelton's soft footstep announced his return with the tea.

"Thank you, Tarleton," I said authoritatively. "You may leave it on the tray, and I'll help myself."

He left the room and I felt compelled to open the desk again and reread the entry to assure myself I hadn't imagined it.

Afterwards, I was consumed with remorse. Had I left my honor behind with my name?

Overcome with guilt, I poured myself a cup of tea and drank it slowly. Exploring the house is one thing, I chided myself, but reading another person's diary is despicable! When I had finished my tea, I left the morning room, effectively removing myself from further temptation.

Later, I was to mull over the entry in Aunt Beatrice's diary—I was certain it was hers—but for the present I put it aside. Perhaps I wanted to forget it, along with my own reprehensible behavior.


I was glad to have Maureen chattering in the room with me while I dressed for dinner. The roar of the sea had taken on a menacing quality after my experience this afternoon, and I had no desire to look out the window, lest I see again that dark and lumbering figment of my imagination.

"How grand you look, Miss Katherine," Maureen commented as she hooked me up the back. The dress was one of Katherine's, a simple, but elegant, gown in green watered silk with long sleeves and a daring neckline.

The only jewelry I owned was a single strand of pearls and matching drop earrings. Beau had given them to me on my eighteenth birthday, and I thought of him a little sadly as I put them on.

"You deserve better," he had said. "Diamonds, or better yet, emeralds to match your eyes." Then he had patted my hand, and added, "But you shall have them, Indy. This new play will make Beauregard Chantelle the toast of New York."

The pearls had been in and out of pawn shops, but I hadn't minded. Beau had given me more than jewels, he had given me love, and I missed him more than I had thought possible.

Maureen clapped her hands with approval. "Just the right touch, Miss Katherine. American ladies certainly know how to dress." She pursed her lips and added, "Lady Hathaway and Miss Willa load themselves down with too much jewelry. Less is best, I always say."

I joined the gentlemen in the dining room, and I must admit I was flattered by the attention I received. I was complimented lavishly by all three men, and it was a relief not to have to worry about Aunt Beatrice and Willa taking offense.

"Well, how did the riding lesson go?" Uncle Fenton asked.

"Very well," Stuart replied. "Of course, one can always tell when a person has ridden before. Don't you agree, Uncle Fenton?"

My blood ran cold. Was he mocking me? I stole a glance at his profile, but it gave nothing away.

"Absolutely," Fenton answered. Then he turned to me. "There, Katherine, didn't I tell you it would all come back? Why, as I remember, you were a regular little . . ."

"Hellion," Stuart said.

Fenton looked embarrassed. "I was about to say, a regular little horsewoman."

Undaunted, Stuart insisted. "A regular little hellion is what she was. Used to ride astride with her skirts all hitched up, showing everybody her underdrawers."

My face turned scarlet, and Jordan said, "Stop teasing Katherine, Stuart. You were quite a hellion, yourself, as I remember."

Stuart sipped his wine, and I detected a vague insinuation in his comment. "I don't pretend otherwise."

Was he referring to Jordan, or to me, I wondered.

Fenton must have sensed an undercurrent in the conversation, too, for he forced a smile and closed the subject with an offhand remark. "Katherine's always been courageous. No question about that."

They've had their jests with me, I thought, let's see how they react to my insinuations.

"Not so courageous as you may think, Uncle Fenton," I said. "As a matter of fact, I had quite a scare this afternoon."

All three of them gave me their full attention, but it was Fenton who looked at me through hooded eyes. "How was that, my dear?"

"I saw something strange in the garden today. A big, slow moving figure, a man, I suppose. He disappeared into the hedgerows before I could see him clearly." Hesitating, I added. "I think I felt his presence almost before I saw him."

Fenton and Jordan exchanged hasty glances and then Fenton, his eyes hooded again, spoke. "The mists come up from the sea and play tricks on the eye sometimes. What did it look like?"

I suddenly remembered the first time I had ever seen a possum. It was after one of Beau's escapades when we were hiding in the swamps of Mississippi. This big, lumbering animal had come out of the woods and for a split second, the light from our lantern had picked it up. "Actually," I said, "it looked like a giant, brown possum."

All of them laughed—deep, hearty, male guffaws—and I could have bitten my tongue off for reducing this to a joke.

I detected a note of relief in Fenton's voice. "Forgive us, Katherine. We're being rude." Smothering a chuckle, he added, "I don't think there are any giant possums hereabout. Like I said, my dear, the mists are known to play tricks."

I could have slapped them all for their accursed attitudes of male superiority, and I could have slapped myself, too, for falling so stupidly into their trap.

I might have imagined the phantom figure, but I did not imagine the look that passed between Fenton and Jordan when I first mentioned it.

Never one for peace, Stuart instigated friction on another

front. "I say, Uncle. Why didn't Katherine join Aunt Beatrice and Willa in London?"

"I believe the invitation had been accepted before we knew of Katherine's arrival," Fenton answered coldly.

Stuart shrugged. "I'm sure Lighthizer would have welcomed another lovely lady to his little *soirée.*"

I broke in. "I wouldn't have considered it. Besides, I wanted to spend time at Hathaway Manor."

"And we're so glad you did," Jordan commented. "We have to get to know our cousin all over again. Don't we, Stuart?"

Stuart focused on my low neckline and raised an eyebrow. "Ah, yes. And it's certainly a revelation. Our little cousin has turned into a very sedate young lady." He gave me a capricious look, "Sometimes it's hard to believe she's the fiery little thing we all knew and loved so well."

My eyes flashed in anger. "Don't test me," I said, gritting my teeth.

Jordan laughed. "That's our Katherine. What do you say to that, Stuart?"

Stuart's eyes narrowed. "I just might do that, test her, I mean."

Fenton looked puzzled, and I knew I had to bury this dangerous subject. "How are your experiments coming along, Jordan?"

"Research is slow," he said seriously. "But I think we've made some progress."

In the candlelight, his pale eyes seemed to have no pupils. It gave him an eerie, strange appearance, yet his voice was perfectly normal. He was more animated than he had been on the previous evening.

I recalled Lady Beatrice's reference to Jordan in her journal, and despite my remorse, I pondered what she had meant by it.

"When you have time, I should like to show you the laboratory," Jordan was saying, and I rallied from my deliberations and gave him my attention.

"I would be very interested in seeing it," I said.

Fenton cut in. "Plenty of time. Katherine must concentrate on her riding this week."

Tarleton and the unobtrusive serving maid had been tip-toeing about the table, giving us impeccable service while we chatted. Now, they removed the dessert plates, and Fenton said, "You may bring the port into the drawing room, Tarleton. Miss Katherine will join us in an after-dinner drink."

I appreciated his thoughtfulness, for I should have felt foolish being sent from the room while the gentlemen remained; a custom I found particularly degrading, anyhow. Did they think women too stupid to engage in serious conversation with them?

I suppose my theatrical way of life was more disposed to equality among the sexes, for women certainly had as much say in the theater as men, and not a few actresses could outmatch the actors in smoking and drinking.

We retired to the drawing room where Stuart and Jordan tried to outdo each other in vying for my favor. Fenton ignored us, and lost in his own thoughts, he quietly drank his port in the far corner of the room. When he had finished, he joined us and leaning against the wall, he impatiently drummed his fingers on the mantle.

At a break in the conversation, he interrupted and said, "Might I have a word with you in my study, Katherine?"

I'll admit the request made me feel a little uneasy, but I immediately replied, "Of course, Uncle Fenton."

I followed him into a small study off the library. A massive desk dominated one end of the room and heavy, leather chairs in dark nondescript colors made up the other furnishings.

The coldness of the leather and the somber colors gave the room an uninviting, judicious atmosphere, and I felt my muscles tense with apprehension.

He seated himself behind the large, mahogany desk like a judge about to hear a case, and I took the chair he indicated directly opposite him.

Regarding me with eyes that were unusual, but not quite so startling as his son's, he said, "I have received a letter from your New York solicitor, Katherine."

I felt my courage desert me like lines on opening night. Of course there would be legalities to deal with, and of course the three of us would not have anticipated such a contingency.

We had blithely assumed, like the fools we were, that this masquerade could be perpetrated on men accustomed to dealing with the law.

I was ready at that moment to confess the whole thing, admit my mistake, and beg Lord Hathaway for leniency.

I was jolted out of my reverie when Fenton chuckled, and I suddenly realized that he had been speaking for a long time. What had he said?

"And so, my dear," he purred, "As you can see, you have been well provided for. Your father has shown wisdom in setting your inheritance up into a trust fund to terminate on your fortieth birthday."

He gave me an ingratiating smile. "In the meantime, you will receive a monthly allowance from New York, and until you have reached your majority in September, I, as your guardian, will act on your behalf."

He picked up a sheaf of papers and handed them to me. "It's all there in black and white just as I've explained it to you." Then he rose and came around the desk to stand beside me. "Just sign the last page at the bottom, to let the solicitor know you understand the terms."

What could I do?

I took the pen he offered with a shaking hand, and as I laboriously copied Katherine's signature, my eye rested on a line at the top of the page.

*Should Katherine Hathaway die before reaching her majority, the aforementioned trust will be rendered null, and the entire estate will revert to the next of kin.*

"Thank you, my dear." He gathered the papers together, and walking back to the front of the desk, stuffed them into a drawer. "Come now, let us join the young men. I'm sure they're impatient for your company."

"Did he warn you about me?" Stuart whispered after we

had returned to the drawing room.

"Should he have?" I asked.

The meeting in the study had unnerved me. I was getting in too deep. Now, I was even guilty of forgery!

My heart was beating fast, and I was almost afraid it would be noticeable in a gown cut as low as mine. Stuart was observing me with his sharp eyes, and I had an insane wish to put my hands against his chest and push him out of the room. Nothing ever escaped is eagle eye, and I found it exasperating that he could read my emotions with such unfaltering accuracy.

Fenton, however, came to my rescue with a sudden, loud clap of his hands. Rubbing them together, he skewered Stuart with a penetrating look. "Well, nephew, are you ready for another match?"

An expression of annoyance flashed briefly across Stuart's face, but he recovered himself quickly. "You'd have me desert Katherine for chess!"

"Jordan will keep Katherine company. Come along, you can't deny me a chance to recoup my losses." Fenton turned to me. "You shan't mind, shall you Katherine?"

"Not at all. I want to hear about Jordan's research," I said.

Fenton looked smug. "We'll be in the card room." Leaning down, he landed a cold kiss on my feverish brow. "I'll say good night then, my dear."

Stuart gave me a masterful look. "Good night, Katherine. Don't stay up too late. I want you in the saddle by seven."

Jordan laughed. "And what will you do if she's not?"

Stuart's steely grey eyes met mine briefly. "I don't know. Punish her, I guess. My riding master used to use the crop on me."

"No doubt, you deserved it," Jordan commented as Fenton and Stuart left the room.

I wrestled with my temper. What an arrogant, swellheaded, infuriating man Stuart Hathaway was! I don't know why I let him annoy me so, particularly when I have so many real worries to contend with, I groused.

I composed my face in what I hoped was a more friendly

expression, and said, "Do tell me about your research, Jordan."

He reiterated the theory that a chemical imbalance in the brain can lead to severe mental disturbances. "Up to now," he said, "Not much has been done to reverse the process of deterioration." The lamp flickered, and again his eyes appeared to crystallize, pupils disappearing into the colorless mass. "As you probably know, laudanum has been widely used for years."

I smothered a yawn and he continued.

"Laudanum is derived from opium, and has a calming effect on the brain. Opium, of course is a plant derivative, as are most of the drugs we know." He leaned closer toward me, and spoke in an excited whisper. "But chemical combinations can produce far more powerful drugs—drugs that can make even a normal person hallucinate!"

I must have had a blank expression on my face, for the truth of the matter was, I didn't know what hallucinate meant.

"Don't you see," he insisted. "If we can induce a normal brain to mimic an abnormal one by injecting a particular combination of chemicals; another combination may allow an abnormal brain to mimic the norm."

I thought his zeal bordered on the fanatical, but I told myself he was a scientist and totally absorbed in his work. Nevertheless, I found the subject morbid and after the many shocks I had been exposed to this afternoon, I did not feel up to hearing anymore. "That's a fascinating theory, Jordan," I said. "I would love to hear more about it, but I must be up early, as you already know, so I think I'll say, good night."

"Of course. I'll explain more when you come to my laboratory," he said, taking my hand and forcing it to his lips.

I felt a shiver of revulsion at his touch, and I chided myself for it. Cousin Jordan was a perfect gentleman and a serious scholar, which was more than I could say for Cousin Stuart. Still and all, there was something about Jordan Hathaway that made me recoil from him.

I lost no time getting ready for bed. Not bothering to ring

for Maureen, I undressed quickly and threw the green silk gown over a chair. The careless act was so typical of Katherine, and so unlike herself, that I felt a compulsion to go back and hang up the dress.

That done, I rummaged through the bureau until I found one of my own old nightgowns, and putting it on, I turned down the lamp and got into bed.

Lying in the darkness, the events of the day flashed before my mind like scenes in a tableau. I think it had to be the longest day of my life, and certainly the most unsettling. Although life with Beau had been hectic, I had coped, and now I found that hard to do. Why? Was it because I was wearing Katherine's name, and Katherine's clothes—living Katherine's life?

Or could it be that in my other life, I had an advantage that was not afforded me here; the advantage of knowing who my enemies were, and why.

That was a theory that made sense to me, for everyone at Hathaway Manor was shrouded in mystery.

Lord and Lady Hathaway were cold, strange people, and they evidently thought Katherine was unconsciously privy to a secret. A secret they seemed determined to keep at all costs. What would they do should they suspect Katherine's memory had returned?

And then there was the matter of Katherine's inheritance. Her entire fortune would revert to Fenton should Katherine die before reaching her majority.

Jordan was another mystery. In the short time that I had known him, his personality had undergone dramatic switches ranging from the lethargic to the fanatical. A regular *Dr. Jekyl and Mr. Hyde,* I thought, recalling the novel that had been turned into a play several years ago. Too shocking for average taste, it had opened and closed in Baltimore after a week.

As for Willa, her jealousy could be troubling, but hardly dangerous, I decided.

My thoughts then turned to Stuart Hathaway. Why was he here? And what had he meant this morning when he had referred to us both as "outsiders?" Stranger still, why did he seem to bait me constantly about the past? Did he suspect I was an imposter? More and more I was beginning to believe that Stuart, too, wore a mask, and I wondered if underneath it, I would find a friend or an enemy!

And last, but not least, the lumbering figment of my imagination. Was I disturbed enough to. . . . I wracked my brain for the word Jordan had used.

It came to me slowly, ringing in my ear like an ominous warning, hallucinate, hallucinate, hallucinate!

# Chapter 6

Stuart looked up as I entered the stable.

"You're early, Cousin," he said, giving me a smug smile. "It's amazing what a little intimidation can do."

"Don't flatter yourself. You have not intimidated me. I'm anxious to finish these riding lessons and be rid of you, that's all."

He shook his head. "You have a sharp tongue, Katherine, but I probably deserve it." Holding out his hand, he gave me a disarming smile. "Truce?"

"If you promise to stop harping on my childhood," I said. "After all, I'm a different person now."

As soon as the words left my mouth, I wanted to bite them back, but his expression never changed, and he continued to stand there with his hand outstretched.

I tried to shake hands impersonally, but he held on to mine, and his touch sent a shiver of excitement up my arm. Then, grabbing me about the waist, he lifted me into the saddle.

My body's reaction to his touch both shocked and alarmed me. I may be inexperienced, but I am not innocent. I know what physical attraction means and where it can lead.

Stuart Hathaway is everything I don't want in a man, and I absolutely, positively will not be attracted to him, I told myself.

Since I was proving to be a natural horsewoman, Stuart said we could now venture away from the area immediately encompassing the stables. "Each day, we'll go a little farther," he said, "and by the end of the week, I shall show you the moors."

"Is that where Jordan has his laboratory?" I asked.

He nodded his head, and a guarded look entered his eyes. "Why? Are you interested in our cousin's experiments?"

I shrugged. "I don't know."

His arrogance returned and he said, "Perhaps you're more interested in our pale-eyed cousin. You certainly gave him your rapt attention last night. What was he telling you?"

"I don't remember," I said. "But I find Jordan interesting. At least he has a purpose in life," I added pointedly.

He laughed. "And I don't, is that it?"

"If the shoe fits," I said with a smile.

He shook his head. "You're an enigma, Katherine. By God . . ." He suddenly stopped, and raised his hand. "I promised not to bring up the past, and I won't. I shall try to remember that you are a different person, now." His eyes regarded me coolly. "Isn't that what you said, Katherine. You're a different person?"

My careless remark had not slipped past him, and I felt somebody walk over my grave. Did he suspect something? Or was I letting my imagination run away with me?

"Let's just say, I grew up. Perhaps you should try it."

Again he laughed. "Ouch! I deserved that. But come on, Katherine, let's not quarrel. It's a beautiful day and I want to show you Hathaway Manor."

"Fine," I said, and added indifferently, "But don't expect me to remember too much about it."

Recalling the fly's harrowing climb on the rocky road leading to the manor, I wondered how we should ever manage it.

Stuart must have read my mind, for he said, "Don't worry. We won't be using the road. The estate is much more accessible on horseback."

The sea was to the left of us. I could hear the roar of the waves, and the salty smell of it rose up from the cliffs. Taking a deep breath, I filled my nostrils with that peculiar scent that is like no other.

He must have been watching me, for he said, "We'll go to the beach one day. Do you remember the cove, and the time you almost got trapped there when the tide came in?"

"I tend to forget unpleasant things," I said warily.

"So I notice, but perhaps it will come back when you see it again. And the cave," he added. "Surely, you remember the cave?"

"I don't think so."

"Well, no matter. You'll find it interesting, I'm sure. It's quite a natural wonder."

I looked up in surprise, as suddenly the geography of the land dipped and flattened out, and the sea came into view again. Here the water lapped gently onto a little sandy beach; a peaceful contrast to the violent waves that crashed below my window.

"What a beautiful spot!" I commented.

"Would you like to stop a minute?"

"I want to walk over and look!"

He dismounted, and wanting to avoid his touch, I thought to jump down myself. Measuring the distance a little uncertainly, I hesitated, and he was instantly in front of me.

"That's a long way down," he said, reaching up and grasping my waist with strong hands. This time he lifted me down slowly, and needing support, I placed my hands on his shoulders.

My feet touched the ground, but I remained in his embrace. Anticipating a kiss, I closed my eyes, but nothing happened. Feeling like a fool, I opened them quickly and found that he was staring at me with a puzzled expression on his face.

Overcome with embarrassment, I slipped out of his arms and ran toward the beach. He remained behind, tethering the horses to a tree, and I stood on a little incline that overlooked the sea, watching the waves roll gently ashore.

I thought how dangerously close I had come to making a fool of myself over Stuart Hathaway. Glancing quickly back, I saw that he had left the horses and was walking toward me, hacking the tall grass indifferently with his crop.

I feigned an intense interest in the view, and he stood

silently behind me. My heart fluttered like a butterfly caught in a net. If I feel his arms go around me, will I be able to resist him? I wondered.

But he never laid a hand on me, and his voice when he spoke was casual. "There are several of these nice little coves scattered about. Years ago, the wreckers made use of them."

I tried to make my own voice just as casual. "So I heard. And wasn't there a buccaneer in the family closet?"

"Aye, indeed there was. That's where the money originally came from." He brushed sand from a huge rock and said, "Let me offer you a chair, Miss Hathaway."

I sat down, and he joined me on the rock. "Of course the family has always been very secretive about this," he said.

"Then, how did you hear of it?"

"My father told me. He was the black sheep, remember? So, he had no compunction about revealing family secrets."

"And did he tell you any other family secrets?" I asked.

He smiled. "Every last one of them."

I smiled back. "And you're not going to tell them to me?"

"Then they wouldn't be secrets anymore."

"Come on," I coaxed. "Tell me about our dark and devious ancestor?"

He laughed. "Devious, for sure, but certainly not dark." Pausing dramatically, he added, "Our great-great-great-grandfather Anthony Hathaway was an albino!"

"An albino pirate!"

Somehow the two didn't go together, and I reached back into my childhood to recall a little girl I'd met once in Chicago. Her hair had been snow white, her eyes pink!

"She's an albino," Beau had said, and I thought at the time that was her nationality.

Stuart continued. "They called him the white devil, and it's said his strange appearance terrorized his victims so much that they died of fright, sparing him the trouble of slashing their throats."

Thinking aloud, I blurted out, "The other Hathaways. That white skin and pale eyes!"

"They're probably throwbacks," he said. "And then, I suppose genes become more pronounced when there's so

71

much intermarriage within a family."

But you don't look like them, I thought, and neither does Katherine.

Again, he read my mind. "I look like my mother, and she was not a Hathaway." Studying my face, he added. "It certainly didn't show up in you either, Katherine. But then your parents were distant cousins, weren't they?"

I nodded mutely, still trying to reconcile my mental picture of a pirate with the portrait Stuart had just painted for me. Recalling Jordan's unnatural, crystal-like eyes staring back at me in the candlelight, I shuddered. No wonder the poor victims of this infamous ancester died of fright!

"Those that followed Anthony were not paragons of virtue either," he was saying. "The Hathaways were involved in smuggling right up to our grandfather's time." He gave a short laugh. "That's probably why they married within the family. They needed to preserve their secrets as well as their money." He looked at me sharply then. "Do you remember him?"

"Who?"

"Grandfather Hathaway."

"Oh, of course, but vaguely."

"You probably only saw him occasionally. The old devil stayed holed up in his room most of the time."

I nodded, relieved to have an excuse for not remembering Katherine's grandfather.

We spent a pleasant morning inspecting a small portion of the estate which was bounded by the sea to the south and the moors to the north, and stretched for a hundred miles in between.

True to his word, Stuart refrained from teasing me about Katherine's escapades, and I found myself enjoying his company.

Although he ridiculed country life and proclaimed London his home, I suspected that Stuart felt a kinship with Cornwall. This untamed, strikingly beautiful land of sudden and startling contrasts is so like him, I thought, stealing a glance at his handsome profile. There was a gentle

72

look about him now, but I was aware that like a chameleon, he could change from benign to bedeviled, and I felt I could never completely trust him.

"Look, there's an osprey," he shouted, as a large bird struck out from the cliff and swooped down into the water. "They dive feet first and catch fish in their talons," he explained.

"You know this country well, don't you?" I asked.

"I should. I came to Hathaway Manor with my father when I was five."

Hardly more than a baby, I thought, feeling a surge of sympathy for him. I wanted to hear about his childhood, and I said, "Let's take a rest. There's a nice shade tree over there."

We sat down under it, and he said, "I used to hide in this tree when I was a lad."

"Why?"

"So I could jump down on Jordan and Willa and scare the living daylights out of them."

"You must have been a little devil," I said.

"I don't deny it."

"Did you see much of your mother?" I asked.

"No. Grandfather Hathaway wouldn't allow it." His eyes smoldered with resentment. "That was the bargain, you see. He would provide for my father and me and she was to stay out of the picture."

"But why did your parents agree to it?" I asked.

He shrugged. "The old story, I guess. Love flies out the window when poverty walks in. My mother went back on the stage and my father came home with his tail between his legs."

"Then why was your father disowned?"

There was a long pause before he said, "I'm not sure, but I mean to find out!" His tone was menacing, and I was sorry I had brought the subject up. We had been getting along so well, but now he seemed angry with me. Jumping up, he took hold of my hand and none too gently pulled me to my feet. "Come on. It's time we were getting back."

When we were mounted, he turned to me and said,

"Brutus needs to race. Wait here, I'll be back for you."

Lowering his head, he leaned close to the stallion's sleek neck and took off in a cloud of dust, leaving me staring open-mouthed after him.

It's not Brutus who needs to race, I thought, it's you! Possessed by secret demons of your own, you think to lose them this way. But, if you think I'm going to sit here like a dummy and wait patiently, you're mistaken. I can find my way back without you!

Acting purely on instinct, I brought the crop down on the mare's flanks and was almost jerked out of the saddle, as she broke into a gallop. I held on for dear life, as we raced across the field. My heart was pounding as fast as the mare's hooves and I had no earthly idea how to stop what I had so foolishly begun.

I sucked in my breath, as the wind whipped off my hat, blowing my hair loose and into my eyes. Through the blur, I could see Stuart ahead of me. He was shouting something, but I was too terrified to understand him.

His words, however, had a startling effect on the mare, for she immediately altered her gait, slowing down to a canter. Stuart, beside us now, reached over and grabbed the reins.

"What the hell do you think you're doing!" he shouted, jumping down and pulling me out of the saddle.

I fell into his arms, gasping for breath, but I managed to meet his eyes and shout back, "So, I made a mistake, but I stayed on, didn't I?"

"I ought to lay the crop on you," he said. "You frightened that horse to death, you little fool!"

I burst into tears. I'd almost gotten killed and all he cared about was the stupid horse! I turned away from him, mortified to death that I should further disgrace myself by crying.

"Ah, now, Katherine, come on, you're all right," he said, putting his arms around me and holding me close. My heart ached to let him comfort me, but common sense warned me to beware.

I pulled away, but he put his hand under my chin, and forced me to look at him. "If you weren't my cousin, I'd kiss

74

you soundly," he said. Our eyes locked, and he added, "What the hell! We've not seen each other for a long time."

Our lips met, and sparks of fire raced through my body. His hands were on my back, pressing me tightly to him, and I could feel his heart pounding against mine.

"I don't understand this, Katherine," he murmured, brushing my ear with his hot breath. "I shouldn't feel this way. I can't . . ." Abruptly, he stopped and pushed me away, and I saw the mask slip over his face. "Sorry, cousin," he said flippantly. "I forgot for a minute who you were."

Blushing with embarrassment, I said nothing.

"Can you ride?" he asked.

The last thing I wanted was to get back on that animal, but the alternative would be to ride with him, and that I could not do. "Yes, I can ride," I answered, steeling myself to resist the thrill of his touch when I mounted.

We rode in silence for awhile, and then he returned to conversing casually, as if nothing at all had happened between us.

I followed his lead and concentrated on safe subjects. "What's on the moors?" I asked, for they still held a strange fascination for me.

"Granite, bracken and gorse, some sheep and wild ponies."

"No heather!"

He laughed. "What a romantic you are! Aye, there's some heather, also bogs that lay in wait for the unsuspecting." His voice took on an ominous tone and I shuddered as he said, "You can step into them and in a flash be stuck in the marsh. If you're alone, you can drown in that peat infested, black water and die with the smell of it in your nostrils."

"You make it sound like a dangerous place," I said.

"It can be. It also has a strange sort of beauty to it." He paused and looked directly at me. "I'll take you there, Katherine, but promise me you'll never go alone."

I wasn't about to make him any promises, so I merely said, "Thank you, Stuart. I'd like to see it."

No more was said, for by this time, we had reached the stable and my attention was drawn to an old woman who stood outside talking to one of the grooms. I caught my breath, for her appearance startled me.

Her long black cape and hair, dark as a raven's wing, contrasted sharply with the chalky whiteness of her skin. Standing tall and stately, she towered over the young groom, and it was obvious she was berating him, for the lad shrank back at her words.

My theatrical mind immediately thought of *Macbeth,* and I heard the witches' chant, "Double, double toil and trouble; Fire burn and cauldron bubble."

"Who is that?" I asked without even thinking.

"Surely you remember Mrs. Janney, the housekeeper." His eyes challenged me, and again I could have bitten my tongue. "She hasn't changed in twenty years," he added and then smiled, "But, as you say, you tend to forget unpleasant things." Then he laughed, a little unkindly, I thought. "Come, let old Janney see what a fine young lady you've turned out to be." And before I could protest, he was off his horse and walking over to the woman. "Mrs. Janney, look who's back!"

The young groom, anxious to escape, rushed over to help me dismount, and then walked both horses back to the stable. Reluctantly, I joined Stuart and the formidable looking housekeeper.

"What do you think, Janney?" Stuart said with a broad wink. "Would you have recognized our little Katherine?"

The woman stared at me with hostile eyes. "Welcome home, Miss Katherine. I heard 'ee were back."

"It's good to see you again, Mrs. Janney," I said politely.

"Turned into a beauty, didn't she, Janney?" Stuart insisted. "And a real lady, too," he added.

He was being annoying again, and I could have slapped him for it. I had no desire to be patronized by this woman who was even more overpowering up close.

Like an evil queen, she stared down her long nose at me without smiling. Her white face, as expressionless as a death mask, was long and narrow; the eyes small and dark. Her black hair was parted in the middle and pulled severely back, emphasizing a widow's peak so sharp it might have been

76

painted on her forehead.

The ghost of a smile flickered for a moment in the corners of her thin lips, as she said, "T'weren't nothing wrong with 'ee looks when 'ee were young. Tis actions what counts, me lady."

I met her gaze without flinching. "You're so right, Mrs. Janney. I judge people by that same standard myself. Good day," I added with a smile.

Beau would have been proud of me, I thought, as I walked regally away, leaving the two of them standing speechless behind me.

Stuart and I managed to avoid each other until dinner time. It was obvious though that we were both painfully aware of our earlier indiseretion, as we went to great lengths to avoid both physical touching and verbal sparring. The latter was such a sharp departure from our previous form of behavior that I'm sure both Fenton and Jordan noticed it.

I sensed an undercurrent of resentment in Stuart's attitude that evening. Even his most innocuous remarks seemed to be laced with bile. "How's the property in Sussex faring, Uncle?"

"Deteriorating, I'm afraid."

"Is that so? When my father managed it, it did quite well."

Fenton's lips curled in a half-smile. "Oh? I wasn't aware that your father managed anything, Stuart. When was that?"

"After Grandfather Hathaway promised it to him."

Fenton patted the napkin to his lips and continued to smile. "I wasn't aware of that, either, but I do recall your grandfather mentioning that quite a bit of money had been squandered on repairs to indulge the tenants." He took a sip of wine and added, "Was that due to Gilbert's astuteness or yours?"

Stuart's eyes narrowed dangerously. "I don't care for your choice of words, Uncle, but since you admit the properties are deteriorating, perhaps you need to try a little squandering yourself." Leaning forward, he fixed the older man with a superior smile. "Property kept in good repair attracts good tenants. Good tenants produce good crops, which in turn reap a profit for the landlord."

"A very nice theory," Fenton countered. "I'm sure the professor who expounded it in class made quite an impression on you, Stuart, but property management is better learned through experience."

Stuart's face turned red, and I quickly changed the subject. "How is your experiment coming along, Jordan?" I asked.

He'd been lost in his own thoughts, and I doubt if he'd even heard the exchange between Stuart and his father.

"What? Oh, yes, the experiments." Suddenly he was back at the table with us and he seemed grateful for my interest. "I'm working with morning glory seeds and ergot." My face must have gone blank, for he explained. "Ergot is a fungus that occurs in rye, and of course, you're familiar with the morning glory." His strange eyes glowed with a martyr's zeal, as he added, "I still hope to produce a drug that will reverse the distortions that occur in the minds of the insane."

I thought it a noble endeavor, but I still wondered how such a theory could be tested.

Immediately after dinner, I pleaded a headache and begged to be excused. It had been a disturbing day and I preferred my solitude to the alternatives for this evening.

Having had quite enough of thinly veiled insults and scientific jargon, I looked forward to losing myself in the sugar-coated novel I'd been reading on shipboard.

I had just reached the top of the stairs when I heard the front door open, and immediately a chorus of shrill voices assaulted my ears.

Peering down from the balcony, I saw that the chorus consisted of only two. Lady Beatrice and Cousin Willa had arrived home.

Like twin hurricanes, they swept in, disturbing the very air with their commands and countercommands. "Put that trunk down over here. No, over there. Good heavens, not on top of the hatboxes!"

Fenton appeared and was instantly subjected to a litany of

complaints from both his wife and daughter concerning the fly and the recklessness of its driver. "It's a miracle we're alive," Beatrice fumed.

Recalling my own trip in the fly, I could sympathize with them on that score.

"But why didn't you let me know? I'd have met you in Penzance," Fenton said, sounding irritated.

Willa giggled like a simpleton. "We didn't know until today, and then we just had to come back for more clothes." She stopped suddenly. "Where's Katherine?" she asked, and I shrank back into the shadows.

"She had a headache and retired early," Fenton answered.

"Good," Beatrice said. "We need to talk about Katherine." Then the three of them turned and walked toward the drawing room.

Hating myself, I hurried down the corridor to the hidden staircase. I know all about eavesdroppers and that they never hear anything good, but for my own protection, I felt I needed to know what was being said about Katherine.

The stairwell was dark, and I had to light a candle to find my way down. Holding my skirt in one hand and the candle in the other, my descent was not only slow, but hazardous. Dear God, don't let me fall, I prayed.

At last, I reached the bottom safely, and consumed by guilt, I nevertheless placed my ear against the wall.

Beatrice was speaking. "If I'd known this, we wouldn't have come back. I told you, Willa, to make do with what you had."

"And be seen wearing the same ballgown twice! Mother, you know, it's just not done!"

"That's enough!" Fenton said emphatically. "Either take Katherine with you, or stay home."

Beatrice's voice turned sickly sweet. "There, there, dear, don't fret. I'll find some distraction for Katherine. She'll hardly get to see Sir Alex."

Good Lord, I thought. Sir Alex again!

"Run along and eat some supper, now," Beatrice added. "I'll join you in a minute, dear." A pause followed and then Beatrice spoke again. "Fenton, I don't really see why . . ."

Fenton's voice betrayed his irritation. "Some disturbing things have happened since you left. I won't go into them now, but suffice it to say that getting Katherine out of Hathaway Manor will buy me some time."

She sounded frightened. "Is it Jordan?"

"I said, I'd handle it, Beatrice."

She started to cry, and at that point, the candle went out, and I was plunged into sudden darkness. I couldn't risk being discovered here, and so with superhuman strength, I dragged myself blindly back up those treacherous steps and fled down the corridor to my room.

Once inside, I threw off my clothes, turned down the lamp and got into bed. So, Fenton wants me out of the house, I thought. I was glad to be going to London, but I wondered what disturbing things had forced his hand. He had said he would handle them, but Beatrice had certainly been upset.

At any rate, I thought, I'll soon be in London, and no place on earth would I rather be!

My thoughts turned then to Beau and Katherine, and the other side of this bizarre masquerade. Were they, too, finding it hard to live a lie?

Somehow I didn't think so. It was a game to them and they probably enjoyed the challenge of it, while I was constantly on guard, fearful to have my secret discovered, and fearful, too, to discover the secrets of others.

Hathaway Manor has many secrets, I thought. And in my innocence I was completely unaware that I held the key which could unlock the deadliest one of all.

Hours later, something woke me, and I sat bolt upright in bed and stared into the nothingness of total darkness. An eerie feeling that I was not alone washed over me, and my blood ran cold.

My scalp began to tingle, and I swear my hair must have stood on end. I was afraid to get out of bed, and at the same time, I was afraid to lie down again. Suppose that phantom, lumbering figure was hiding, ready to pounce on me if I moved.

Gradually my eyes became accustomed to the darkness and I could make out objects in the room. I gasped as I thought I saw someone sitting in the rocker by the window. Straining my eyes, I saw that it was only my own gown that I had neglected to hang up, throwing it instead over the chair.

The huge hulk, lurking in the corner, turned out to be nothing more than a piece of furniture, the wardrobe that held my clothes.

I began to breathe easier as I identified each object: the washstand, the pitcher, and the mirror that glittered as a moonbeam touched it with light.

I listened for sounds and heard no movement but the crash of waves hitting the rocks. Taking a deep breath, I lay back down in the bed and turned on my side.

A scream died in my throat, as two dead eyes in a white face stared back at me!

# Chapter 7

I don't know how long I lay there, unable to move, unable to utter a sound, while all the while the lifeless eyes stared into mine. Could this be a dream? Oh, God, yes, I prayed, let this be a dream!

I closed my eyes, then opened them again, but it was still there, lying next to me in the bed. Cautiously, I inched my body away from it, sliding ever so slowly, little by little to the other side. Reaching the edge, I rolled off, and landed on the floor.

I sat there stunned for a minute, my breath coming in short gasps, my heart pounding in my ears, and then cautiously, lest someone be watching me, I stood up. Groping around on the bedside table, I searched for matches, and when I found them, lit the lamp.

Lying in the bed and staring blankly back at me was the painted face of a large porcelain doll!

I held the lamp high and let it illuminate every crevice and corner of the room, and when I was satisfied that I was completely alone, I sank down on the bed and cried.

Afterwards, my relief turned to anger. Who was responsible for this cruel trick, and why? And then fear, cold as death, began to creep slowly and insidiously back, filling me with dread. Someone in this house is my enemy, and whoever it is has a twisted mind!

In the morning, I decided to tell no one about the doll. It may be true that terror and darkness walk hand in hand;

nevertheless, prudence warned me not to trivialize my fears in the cold light of day.

There was something evil about Hathaway Manor, and I had felt from the very beginning that somehow that evil was directed my way. Or should I say Katherine's way?

Last night after discovering the face on my pillow belonged to a doll, I had gingerly picked the thing up and deposited it in the closet, away from my sight. But now, wanting to examine it, I brought it out again and laid it on the bed.

The porcelain head was covered with natural hair arranged in little girl, corkscrew curls; and yet there was something decadent looking about the painted face with its worldly, blue eyes and full, pouting lips.

The body was kid, marking it an expensive doll, for I had seen a similar one in an exclusive shop when I was a child. My sister, Persia, had pleaded with our mother to buy it for us, but Mama, being more practical than Beau, had refused. "That's a French doll," she had said simply, as if our not being French precluded us from purchasing it.

The blue striped dress and white pinafore were dirty, and both of the doll's shoes were missing, but I wrapped it carefully in an old petticoat and stuffed it under a pile of clothes in the drawer.

If I manage to survive Hathaway Manor without dying of fright, I told myself, I shall show it to Katherine for I was convinced it was her doll. But, what significance did it have? And why the mystery? Why sneak around under cloak of darkness and slip it into bed with me?

I rang for Maureen, and I found myself questioning her motives when she arrived. Was her friendly, outgoing personality genuine, or was it, too, a mask? Had Maureen been sent to help me, or could she perhaps have been sent to spy on me?

Suspicion feeds upon itself, and consequently, that morning, everything Maureen said or did became suspect in my eyes. "Good morning, Miss Katherine. Did you sleep well last night?" Her eyes traveled around the room, and it was obvious she was looking for something. Then suddenly, wearing a satisfied smile, she opened the closet door.

I watched her hang up the dress, and then she stopped, and began to rummage around on the floor. The gesture confirmed my suspicions, and made me angry. "What are you looking for?"

She jumped up, and regarded me with a hurt expression. "Why, only these riding boots, Miss Katherine. I figured to give 'em a lick and a polish before you went riding today."

"Take them downstairs and clean them," I said. "You can leave them outside the door when you've finished."

I was overreacting, and I knew it, but I just couldn't help myself. I felt betrayed, and I wasn't ready yet to give anybody at Hathaway Manor my trust.

Her, "Aye, Mum," was accompanied by a curtsy, but her customary smile was absent.


Stuart informed me before leaving the stable that Beatrice and Willa were home. "They're going back though," he said, chuckling to himself. "Old Alex Lighthizer might just as well hoist the white flag and surrender. Aunt Beatrice'll have him marching up the aisle with Willa before the poor fool knows what struck him."

"I take it, you don't approve of weddings," I said.

"On the contrary, I love them. All that champagne, and free, too."

The young groom brought out our mounts, and Stuart patted Brutus on the nose. "Aye, I'd say weddings were just about my favorite entertainment."

The lad helped us both mount, and as we rode out of the stable, my curiosity got the better of me. "Isn't it about time you were taking that step yourself?"

"You mean, get married?"

"Of course. Don't you have a fiancée?"

He smiled evasively. "Why, Katherine, I do believe you have designs on me."

Outraged, I glared at him. "I don't know how you manage to find hats!"

Wearing a humorless expression, he swept off his handsome derby and minutely inspected the headband. "It says right here, size fifty—for swollen heads."

We looked at each other and burst out laughing. He was outrageous and positively exasperating, and yet I couldn't stay mad with him for long.

We spent the morning practicing hurdle jumps, small ones to be sure, but my performance was faultless and Stuart seemed amazed.

"Well done!" he shouted after every jump.

But I was more disturbed than pleased. It had seemed so natural, like I had jumped hurdles higher than those many times before. Good God, I wondered. Who am I? India or Katherine?

Acting on a sudden impulse, I spurred the mare on and soared over a fence twice as high as the practice hurdles. Both the mare and I landed gracefully, like seasoned performers, and out of the corner of my eye, I saw Stuart take the jump, too.

He rode up to meet me, and I braced myself, expecting him to be furious. But the look he gave me was more an astonished one, and I thought I saw a flicker of disappointment burn briefly in his eyes before they turned cold and calculating.

"You see, nothing is ever really forgotten," he said, swinging his leg over the stallion's side. "Let's see if you remember the cave now, too." Leaving his own horse, he walked over to mine, and without another word, he reached up, grabbed me about the waist, and literally pulled me out of the saddle.

I was still trying to come to terms with my own identity, and his reaction reinforced my fears. Were we both trying to prove something?

Taking my arm, he propelled me down the beach to a sheltered cove that nestled in between the cliffs that jutted sharply out to sea.

"This was our pirate ancestor's cove," he explained with a leer. "Can't you just picture him standing on that precipice over there? Looking like a demon from hell, red eyes blazing, as he watches his cutthroats spread the spoils of battle out on the bloody sand."

I could see it vividly and my fertile imagination supplied the details. He would be wearing a tricornered, black hat that he had just snatched from the head of a dying victim. His long white hair would be tied back with a red scarf, and the sword hanging at his belt would be dripping with the blood of those he had murdered.

I felt a sudden urge to run away, away from this place, and away from Stuart, the chameleon who had changed into a hard-eyed stranger. Had he put a mask on? Or torn one off?

"Come on," he said, grabbing my hand and pulling me along.

It was difficult walking in the soft sand, wearing riding boots and with my long skirt trailing behind me, but Stuart was a man possessed. I felt like I was being dragged to my doom. What was so significant about this cave? I wondered.

When we reached it, I hung back. The opening was narrow, and looking inside the yawning black mouth, I knew a moment of sheer panic. Stuart, holding me tightly by the hand, drew me inside.

I thought it would be pitch dark, but light from the opening filtered through, and I could see that we were standing in a chamber, perhaps eight or nine feet wide.

The smell of the sea was stronger here than out-of-doors, a clammy, pungent odor that seeped through the walls in sweat-like drops. They glistened and made a pinging sound as they puddled on the rocky floor.

Never having been inside a cave before, I found it fascinating. I thought how centuries of waves, relentlessly pounding into the cliff, had produced this magnificent cavern. It had probably been used by cave dwellers in ancient times as a haven, and perhaps in Anthony Hathaway's time as a place to hide the spoils of plunder.

I was jolted back to the present by the sound of Stuart's voice. "Well, Katherine. Are you going to tell me you don't remember this cave?"

Cautiously I met his eyes. No trace remained of the affable, lighthearted rake who had joked with me in the stable. There was a hardness about him now, and I felt slightly apprehensive, being alone with him in this secluded cavern. "I don't know," I said, trying to control the tremor in my voice. "If you say, I've been here, I suppose I have, but I really don't remember much about it."

"Don't remember? Can't remember? Or won't remember! Which is it, Katherine?"

He covered the distance between us in two strides, and digging his fingers into my arms, he shook me. "Why are you so evasive?" His voice was husky with emotion, and a shiver ran down my spine, as he said, "Sometimes, I wonder who you really are!"

I tried to pull away from him and my own voice sounded shrill and hysterical. "I'm your cousin, or have you forgotten that?"

"I wish to God, I could!"

I felt his arms go around me, crushing me to him in an embrace so fierce, it took my breath away. His kiss scorched my lips and burned my body with spasms of passion.

Sinking slowly to the ground, he cradled me in his arms and kissed me again, this time parting my lips and exploring my mouth with his tongue.

I felt the hot touch of his hand on my breast, and I lay sprawled across his lap, compliant and too weak to protest. I let him unbutton my riding habit and a delicious warmth exploded in my loins as his hand touched my bare flesh.

I felt like I was entering a forbidden world where carnal pleasure was all that mattered and one discarded modesty along with one's clothes. The thought jolted me back to sanity. "Stuart, no," I said, but he smothered my protests with savage kisses that took my breath away. I struggled vainly against his superior strength, and then I instinctively uttered the only words that could cool his ardor. "I am your cousin!" I hissed, holding our supposed relationship like a club over his head.

The look he gave me was a tormented one. I wished, with all my heart, I could tell him the truth. But, I still did not completely trust him.

Later, I was to wonder about something else. Why was Stuart so afraid of falling in love with his cousin?

87

*　　*　　*

Hurrying to my room to change before lunch, I spotted Mrs. Janney at the end of the corridor. There was no way of avoiding her, save to turn around and retreat back downstairs, which I had no intention of doing.

A ghost of a smile played about her thin lips when we met. "Good morning, Miss Katherine."

Did I really see a smirk in that smile and triumph gleaming in those glittering black eyes? Or, did I want to believe that it was Mrs. Janney who had crept into my room last night?

"Trust 'ee slept well."

The words, spoken in that strange Cornish dialect, made me wary. "Too well," I said. "I might have missed my riding lesson had Maureen not awakened me."

Let her think her little prank had missed its mark, I thought.

She stared down at me, and this time there was no mistaking the hate I saw in her eyes. "I knowed t'would be trouble if 'ee came back. I have the sight, and I saw it afore 'ee came, saw it afore 'ee came the first time, too."

She had passed me, and was at the other end of the corridor before her words sank in. What trouble had she foreseen the first time? What trouble did she foresee now?

I shuddered and a chill ran down my spine at the thought of that black clad figure with the creepy smile bending over me while I slept.

Glancing up at the hall clock, I suddenly realized that I would be expected to present myself downstairs for lunch in exactly thirty minutes. I wasn't looking forward to seeing Beatrice and Willa again, but I was eagerly looking forward to their announcement that I should be accompanying them back to London.

I hurried to my room to get out of my riding habit and change for lunch. Not wanting to ring for Maureen, I struggled to pull off my boots by myself. Then, I took a quick sponge bath, using cold water from the pitcher. Taking no chances on outshining Willa, I dressed in one of my own outfits, a high-necked white shirtwaist and a simple black skirt.

88

Stuart would not be joining us for lunch. I already knew this and was grateful for it.

After his shocking behavior in the cave, he had silently accompanied me back to the stable and then roared off to lose himself in a punishing ride across the moors.

He had neither apologized, nor declared his dishonorable intentions. That, coupled with the doll incident and Mrs. Janney's warning, had me virtually in a state of distraction.

A sudden silence descended on the group, and all eyes focused on me as I entered the dining room.

"Katherine, my dear! We were just talking about you," Fenton said, coming forward and taking my arm.

I was sure that was true, for both Beatrice and Willa looked even more disagreeable than usual. They rattled off unpleasant pleasantries in identical monotones.

"Good to see you, Katherine."

"How nice to be together again."

I took my place opposite Willa and the footman pulled out my chair. As soon as I was seated, Fenton fixed his wife and daughter with penetrating eyes. "We must tell Katherine our news, mustn't we?"

Willa glared at her father, and Beatrice colored slightly. "Of course." Turning to me then, she gushed, "It's wonderful news and we hope you'll be as excited about it as we are."

Watching her performance, I was amused. Overacting is the hallmark of an amateur.

Beatrice forced herself to smile, as she said, "We want you to come to London with us, Katherine." Then her eyes lit up with sudden inspiration, and she added, "That's why we came back!"

Giving her husband a triumphant look, she continued. "We felt just awful, leaving you here while we went galli-vanting off to London. But, of course, we couldn't help it. We had already accepted the invitation!"

I nodded and smiled to show I understood. Let her take me for an idiot. I didn't care. I was going to London, and that was all that mattered to me. Once there, I would have to figure out how to see Beau and Katherine, but I'd cross that bridge when I came to it.

She was still talking, but I barely heard her words. What did it matter? They were all lies, anyway. I was going to London for one reason, and one reason only, because Fenton wanted me out of the house.

I thought back to the conversation I had overheard in the passageway. Some disturbing things had happened, he had confided to Beatrice, and getting me out of Hathaway Manor would buy him some time.

I didn't understand what it all meant, but I was perfectly willing to go along with it. I certainly had no desire to remain at Hathaway Manor and risk having even more disturbing things happen.

Besides, I was worried about Beau, and I needed to talk to Katherine. I wanted to know what was going on at Hathaway Manor.

Not that I intended to back out. It can't be really dangerous, I decided.

"Katherine!"

Willa's high-pitched voice made me jump, and I suddenly realized she must have been talking to me. "I'm sorry, Willa. I guess I was thinking about London," I said, hoping my face had not betrayed my somber thoughts.

"You're as bad as Jordan. He can go into a trance at the drop of a hat."

"I'm sorry," I repeated. "What did you say?"

"I said, since you haven't come out yet, you won't be able to attend all the functions in London."

I waved my hand, and it almost collided with Tarleton's nose. He had tiptoed behind my chair to offer me vegetables from a silver serving dish.

Murmuring an apology, I blushed and helped myself to a small portion of carrots and potatoes before assuring Willa that I would be perfectly content to forego such pleasures. "I understand perfectly," I said. "I just want to sightsee and shop. And I'm used to doing those things alone," I added hastily. "Papa had business engagements out of town and when I accompanied him, I was often on my own."

I hoped with all my heart it was not out of the realm of

reality for Katherine's father to have traveled out of town on business.

Aunt Beatrice looked shocked. "American girls are certainly daring!"

I would be willing to swear that Willa kicked her mother under the table.

"This is 1895, Mama. Young ladies go about London unchaperoned, too."

"Oh! Well, I suppose it's not all that shocking." Beatrice turned a false smile in my direction. "You have to excuse me, Katherine. We're a little provincial, here in Cornwall."

This was working out better than I had hoped, and I silently gave thanks for answered prayers.

As was her custom after lunch, Beatrice retired to her room to take a nap. I would have welcomed a chance to escape myself, but Willa, at her father's insistence, reluctantly agreed to show me the house.

"I suppose you don't remember much about it," she said, and I gratefully acknowledged that I didn't.

"Have you seen the gallery?" she asked.

"No."

"It's on the second floor of this wing. There's some valuable paintings there, besides the family portraits."

I said I should be interested in seeing it, and I followed her up the staircase, taking a right turn instead of my customary left one. The bedrooms in this wing were on the floor above, she explained, and this floor, which was called the mezzanine, housed both a large and small gallery, an auditorium, and several other rooms used to display private collections.

"We entertain our guests with plays and tableaus in here," Willa said, opening a door to show me an auditorium lined with chairs facing a stage.

Their very own private theater, I thought, and larger than some I've worked in.

"I prefer to see real plays in London," Willa remarked as she closed the door.

"I think you just prefer London to Cornwall," I said,

hoping to perhaps gain some insight into her feelings for Hathaway Manor.

She shrugged. "Wouldn't you? Wouldn't anyone?"

She was a surly girl and I doubted I'd have much success making friendly overtures.

I followed her down a long corridor and she stopped before a handsome double door covered in red leather. "This is the large gallery," she said, turning up the gaslit sconces to reveal a room easily seventy feet long. The walls were hung with paintings of all sizes in magnificent gilded frames.

At the far end of the room one very large painting was prominently displayed above a platform. A valance and tied-back drapes in crimson velvet set it apart from the others. Fascinated, I walked the length of the room and stared up at it.

Cherubs and angels stood watch over two children playing near a waterfall. The exquisite beauty of the subjects' faces and the movement suggested in the artist's depiction of the waterfall caught my attention and drew me to the painting. Unschooled though I was in the arts, I instinctively sensed that I was looking at something rare and priceless.

"That is a Botticelli," Willa informed me. "It's been in the family for generations. Nobody knows who acquired it or how." Then she sniffed. "Mama and Papa won't admit it, but it's really stolen goods."

I looked at her in surprise.

"Oh, come on, Katherine. Surely you know that our illustrious family has been involved in smuggling for generations." She pointed to the painting. "That has been the subject of some fascinating rumors."

"Really? I should like to hear them," I said. She seemed as anxious as Stuart to disclose family secrets, and I was certainly willing to grant her the opportunity.

"It's been rumored that Anthony Hathaway, our pirate ancestor, sank an Italian ship, *after* he had removed the cargo and murdered the passengers, of course." She gave me a satisfied smile. "The painting had been aboard, packed and crated for shipment to a private collector."

"And everyone would have assumed it rested at the

bottom of the sea," I added.

"Naturally!" Her pale eyes glowed with unnatural brightness, and she seemed inordinately proud of the ruse. "The other rumor," she said, "credits our beloved grandfather Duncan Hathaway with acquiring the painting through his smuggling operations."

"Was he really involved in smuggling?" I asked.

"Of course." And assuming I had no further interest in the gallery, she led me past the other paintings and back to the corridor again.

"Do you remember Grandfather Hathaway?" she asked suddenly.

"Vaguely," I answered evasively.

"That's not surprising," she said, making me feel relieved. "He was pretty much of a recluse in his later years, spent most of his time searching for treasure." By way of explanation, she added, "Anthony was supposed to have hidden some hereabouts."

"It doesn't sound like I missed anything by not knowing our grandfather."

She gave me a sly smile. "You might get to know him, yet."

"What do you mean?"

Still smiling, she measured me with her pale eyes. "You have his room, you know. After he died, the servants used to say he haunted it."

She was watching me closely, and I met her eyes without flinching.

"They used to hear noises in there, and they refused to go near it, so Mama had it closed off." She chuckled, and added, "Those servants are all long gone, now. Naturally, when they found Lily's body, that bunch of scaredy cats took off like greased lightning."

"Lily!" I cried, suddenly recalling that Maureen had mentioned something about "a Lily."

She looked at me sharply. "Oh, maybe you don't know. They found Lily buried up on the moors." She searched my face. "You do remember Lily Beacham, that no-good servant girl who disappeared."

I nodded, trying desperately to fit this piece into the puzzle of Hathaway Manor.

Willa's eyes widened. "And come to think of it, Katherine, that was the same day you got lost in the cave." She gave me a strange look. "You acted really funny when they found you, like you were in a trance or something." She paused a moment and frowned. "The doctor said you'd had a traumatic experience, but your mind had blocked it out."

I was caught off-guard when she pounced on me with her shrill voice. "What was it, Katherine? Do you remember it, now?"

# Chapter 8

I stared back at Willa with horrified eyes. "I don't remember anything about it." My own voice sounded as shrill as hers had been.

She gave me a searching look, and then shrugged. "The small gallery is just down the hall."

My mind a whirl, I mutely followed her. The shadows are closing in on me, I thought, and suddenly tears of frustration stung my eyes. You can't afford to lose control.

The voice I heard belonged to India Chantelle, Beau's daughter, and my tears suddenly dried up like dewdrops in the sun. Give Willa the satisfaction of seeing a Chantelle reduced to tears? Never!

The small gallery was devoted exclusively to family portraits, and my curiosity about it made me for the moment push Willa's disturbing revelations to the back of my mind.

"We'll start at this end," she said. "Past to present." Before I should ask, she quickly informed me that there was no portrait of Anthony Hathaway. "If there ever was a portrait, it was probably destroyed when the family acquired respectability."

"I wonder what he looked like," I said, hoping to draw her out.

She shrugged; a habit, I had noticed, that she used to convey superiority. "How should I know? Like a pirate, I suppose, dark and dirty and wearing a gold earring."

I was sure then, she didn't know her infamous ancestor

had been an albino. Either that was a secret, or Stuart had been pulling my leg again.

"This is Philip Hathaway," she said, pointing to a portrait of a stern, pale-faced man in a naval uniform. "He was our great-great-grandfather, and the first, 'Lord' Hathaway." She chuckled. "He used his pirate grandfather's money to buy a title, and respectability for the family."

"How could he do that?"

She gave me an impatient look. "I don't know, outfitted one of the king's ships, something like that. You can do anything if you have enough money!"

"Her attitude toward the family is a rather scornful one," I thought and I wondered why.

A plain, grim-faced woman was next. "Philip's wife, I presume?"

Smiling sarcastically, she nodded. "Lady Louise Marchbank. Her family were the bluebloods." She stepped back and recited in a singsong voice, "The Hathaways married the Marchbanks until the Marchbanks were phased out, and the Hathaways were marrying the Hathaways." She laughed. "The Hathaways also acquired the Marchbank money that way. Clever, wasn't it?"

Roland Hathaway, the first, whom Katherine's father was obviously named for, was a rather effeminate looking young man. The small scroll under his portrait read, 1770-1815, and I remarked, "He died young—only forty-five!"

"He was murdered," she said casually, "by one of his brothers, I think."

This certainly is a noble family, I thought, but I made no comment.

The unfortunate Roland's wife resembled him, the portrait showing her to be a thin, washed out young woman with pale eyes, and I thought the kinship to be obvious.

Finally, we had arrived at Duncan Hathaway's portrait. I stared intently at this ancestor, whose ghost, according to Willa, might soon be haunting my room.

He was a harsh looking old man with bushy white hair and a long beard. Willa was watching me, and reading her thoughts, I smiled.

Don't think to frighten me with ghost stories, Willa. I'm too practical for that, I mentally challenged. Then a sobering thought entered my practical mind. "What I have to fear at Hathaway Manor is not a supernatural enemy, but a natural one!"

Early the next morning, we were on our way to London; Beatrice, Willa, Stuart and myself.

I was annoyed when I found out that Stuart would be accompanying us. If he had any common decency, I told myself, he wouldn't force his presence on me after his insulting behavior in the cave. Not that I excused my own behavior! I had acted scandalously, but at least I had the good grace to be ashamed of myself.

Ever the chameleon, Stuart had assumed his shallow guise, and the passionate and intense man I had viewed in the cave was replaced by a handsome dandy who insisted he had had more than enough of the country and could not wait another day to return to London.

Contrary to the norm, Beatrice and Willa seemed overjoyed by his company, and it wasn't until the footman was checking our luggage at the Penzance station that I understood why.

"All the luggage tags must be changed," Beatrice informed the servant. "We will want them sent to Master Stuart's address, not Sir Alex Lighthizer's." Handing him a slip of paper, she pursed her lips and eyed him sternly. "Master Stuart's address is written here. Copy it exactly. If there is any mix-up with the luggage, you will be held accountable."

Taken by surprise, I forgot myself and spoke to Stuart, "We're staying with you?"

"Oh, come on, Katherine. Don't be a prude. I'm not going to ravish you, and besides, it really wasn't my idea."

I gave him a scathing look. "Whose was it, then?"

"Those two," he answered, nodding his head toward Beatrice and Willa who were arguing with the station master about the placement of their luggage. Regarding me with an amused eye, he said, "Don't you know they want you as far

97

away from Sir Alex as possible? Why, they'd stay with me if I lived in a brothel!"

"It wouldn't surprise me where you lived," I said.

He merely smiled. "Just to allay your fears, I'll tell you. I live in a modest house in a perfectly respectable neighborhood."

Beatrice and Willa joined us then, and if I hadn't been so upset at this latest news, I could have laughed at the identical peevish expressions they wore. *Madam and Mistress Scold,* I thought, recalling a hilarious farce one of Beau's sassier lady friends had appeared in.

"That station master is the limit," Beatrice fumed. "He insists on putting our luggage in the same boxcar as the second class passengers."

"Shocking," Stuart said, egging them on. "I do believe they put chickens and goats in there, too."

"Goats!" Willa shrieked. "Mama, if my clothes wind up smelling . . ."

Beatrice gave Stuart an annoyed look. "Don't be ridiculous, Willa. Stuart is being facetious."

We sat down on a hard, wooden bench to await the train, and my thoughts turned to my own problems. I didn't want to stay in Stuart's house. Not that I would be tempted by him; I assured myself that I most certainly would not be. But I didn't relish coming under Stuart's eagle eye every day that we would be in London. For how then could I follow through with my plan to see Beau and Katherine?

The train was late, and we were all growing hungry. Finally Stuart ascertained from the surly station master that there had been a derailment and the train would not arrive for another two hours.

"Two hours!" Aunt Beatrice exclaimed. "I knew I should have had cook pack us a picnic basket."

"I hate that," Willa said. "It looks so provincial."

"There's a nice little inn just over the hill," I said, pointing out the window. "I missed the fly the day I arrived, and spent the night there."

Beatrice gave me a disapproving look. "Alone? Really,

you American girls!"

"Well, she could hardly have slept on one of these benches, could she?" Stuart answered. Standing up, he added. "They're not even comfortable to sit on. So come along, ladies. Let me take you to lunch at Katherine's inn."

Beatrice hung on Stuart's arm, as he propelled her up the steep hill, while Willa and I followed behind them.

"I hope the food will be worth this climb," Willa grumbled, fanning herself with a handkerchief as she walked.

I was almost sorry I had made the suggestion, but anything was better than sitting in the station, trying to make small talk and watching my words lest I make a slip.

At least this gives them something to complain about, and the conversation need not include me. Once on the train, I can look out the window and pretend to be admiring the view, I rationalized.

At last we reached the top.

"This is it?" Beatrice gave the poor little inn a disparaging look, and frowned in my direction.

I'd like to show you some of the other places I've stayed in, I thought, feeling suddenly disgusted with Katherine's pompous, rich relatives who'd never worked a day in their lives. And that includes you, too, Mr. Cousin Stuart Hathaway!

Grace, the same cheerful waitress, greeted us at the door, and seated us at a table. I couldn't help noticing her appraisal of Stuart. When she finally tore her eyes away from him, she met mine. "Oh, aren't you the young American lady who stayed with us once?"

I confessed that I was, and she pointed out the window. "You just missed your friends."

I looked outside and saw the two school teachers who had befriended me. "Why, it's Miss Violet and Miss Clara."

They stood beside their bicycles, looking outlandish and adorable in their bloomers and identical little navy blue, boater hats.

Beatrice looked shocked when I tapped on the window to

99

attract their attention. "Don't bring them in here," she said. "Go outside if you must talk to them."

"I'll do just that," I retorted, pushing my chair back and squeezing past Willa who was sitting on the edge of her seat.

Knocking her hat askew, I forced myself to apologize, and she righted it angrily. "Such a fuss over two old nobodies!"

I hurried outside and the Shaw sisters greeted me warmly. "Why, if it isn't Miss Hathaway. How nice to see you again."

Miss Clara clasped my hand. "We've spoken of you often, dear. We were worried about you crossing the moors in that rickety old fly."

"It wasn't an experience I'd want to repeat, but I made it, safe and sound," I said.

"Are you alone?" Violet asked.

"No. My aunt and two cousins are waiting for me inside. We're taking the train up to London this afternoon."

"But you're coming back," Clara said.

"Oh, of course."

"Good. We'll be staying in Cornwall for the summer." She hesitated a moment and then added awkwardly, "The sudden arrival of a windfall has allowed us to extend our stay."

Violet hitched up her bloomers and gave her sister an impatient look. "The sudden demise of a windbag is what she means. Our cantankerous old uncle died and left us his money."

"Violet!" her sister said. Then turning to me, she added. "Uncle Clarence didn't approve of emancipated women, but he died without a will—"

"And we were his only heirs!" Violet blurted out, hard pressed to contain her mirth. Her expression suddenly turned serious. "Now, we never wished him any harm, you understand, Miss Hathaway."

"Of course not," Clara agreed.

Another twinkle appeared in Violet's eyes. "I do pray every night though that Uncle Clarence is assigned to a celestial choir composed of female angels."

"Violet, you're shocking Miss Hathaway."

100

"Please, call me Katherine," I said. "And don't worry about shocking me. I'm one of those unconventional Americans, remember?"

Violet abruptly changed the subject. "Do you ride a bicycle, Katherine?"

"I most certainly do."

"Good. You must come with us on one of our excursions this summer."

Clara was looking through the window into the inn. "That young man at your table. Who is he, Katherine?"

"He's my cousin, Stuart Hathaway."

"He looks just like the young man we see in the library, doesn't he, sister? The one that's always pouring over those old maps."

Violet gave Stuart a quick glance. "Good-looking devil, pity he's your cousin, Katherine." She shook her head at her sister. "Can't be, Clara. Katherine's cousin's a gentleman. The other one's rougher looking, dirty hands, muddy boots. Remember? We remarked about him tracking up the floor."

We parted then, and I watched them ride away on their bicycles; two unconventional and perfectly charming ladies. Comparing them to the waspish females in Katherine's family, I sighed, and walked slowly back to the inn.

I tried not to think about their remarks concerning Stuart. They had mistaken him for someone else; they were sure of it. But, Stuart did disappear every day after our lesson, and sometimes he didn't come back until late in the evening. Plenty of time to ride into Penzance, I thought. But what would he be doing pouring over old maps in the local library?

"Well, its about time," Beatrice said when I returned to the table.

"I ordered you a meat pie," Stuart said.

"Thank you."

"Who were those outlandish old women, anyway?" Willa asked.

"They're retired schoolteachers," I said. Glancing at Stuart out of the corner of my eye, I added, "They spend a lot

101

of time in the local library."

His expression never changed. But he is a good actor, I recalled.

"How droll," Willa remarked. Grace appeared then with our lunch, and Willa hastily unfolded her napkin. "I hope this food's worth eating," she commented.

Stuart tasted his. "This is delicious," he said, giving Grace a winning smile. "Did you make it?"

She blushed and stumbled over her words. "Oh, no, sir. Me mum's the cook."

"Well, you tell your mum she makes good meat pies."

Neither Beatrice nor Willa made a comment one way or the other, but I noticed they both cleaned their plates.

After lunch, we took a short stroll before returning to the station and its hard, wooden benches.

"There's the local library," Stuart said, pointing to a small, grey stone building.

I stopped in my tracks and gave him a startled look. Good God! The man must be a mind reader! I mused.

He laughed. "Don't look so surprised. I know this town like the back of my hand. After all, I'm a Cornishman. Remember?"


It was late when the train arrived in Paddington Station. Bored with one another's company, we were sick of traveling and anxious to arrive at our destination. Too tired to complain, Beatrice and Willa settled for wearing pained expressions and even the usually loquacious Stuart appeared to have lost his sense of humor.

As for myself, I welcomed the silence. I, too, was exhausted and quick to anger. "The Wheely Woes," Beau calls it, for the affliction seems to follow long rides by carriage or coach.

Consequently, we were in no condition to cope with the pandemonium that awaited us as we stepped down onto the crowded platform.

Frantic lest they miss their trains, men and women

holding food baskets and suitcases in front of them like shields advanced upon us. We had to push our way forward against the tide, and all three of us would probably have been swallowed up in the melee were it not for Stuart's clearing a path for us.

He led us out of the station and in a matter of minutes, we were comfortably seated in a cab. Jogging along through the foggy, damp streets of London, my excitement grew.

I heard, "Katherine and Beau, Katherine and Beau" in every clip-clop of the horses' hooves. They're somewhere in this very city, and soon, very soon, we'll be together! I exulted.

"It's so good to be in London again," Willa crooned, leaning back in the red upholstered seat and closing her eyes. "I do hope our trunks arrive tomorrow."

"They will," Stuart said. "I'll send my man down in the morning to grease some palms. I promise you, the trunks will be delivered in an hour."

Beatrice looked surprised. "You keep servants!"

He laughed. "My dear Aunt, did you think I lived in a tent? I have a house. Naturally, I require servants."

I was surprised myself. From the way Stuart talked, I had visualized him living like a Bohemian, and keeping his father's house merely as a place to sleep and change his clothes.

"How many servants do you retain?" Beatrice asked.

"Only three. Bachelors don't require a large retinue. There's the butler Diggs and Mrs. Diggs, who acts as my housekeeper. They've been with me ever since Father and I moved to London. My valet, of course," he added, and then smiled. "No ladies' maids, though, since I have no ladies, but if you should require such services, perhaps Mrs. Diggs can suggest someone."

Beatrice answered quickly. "Willa and I planned on asking Lady Lighthizer for the loan of a servant, Stuart, if that is acceptable to you."

He said, "Fine."

"Perhaps Mrs. Diggs can find someone for Katherine,"

she suggested.

"That won't be necessary," I said.

Beatrice looked piqued. "Really, Katherine, one servant can hardly be expected to give proper attention to three ladies."

"Of course not," I said. "I meant that I prefer not having a maid at all while we're in London."

Beatrice and Willa exchanged puzzled glances. It was clear they considered me peculiar.

The carriage stopped, and in a matter of minutes, the driver had hopped down and opened the door. "Here we be, Gov'nor, 10 Bleekman Place."

Stuart had referred to his home as a modest house on a respectable street. Modest, perhaps by Hathaway standards, I thought, but certainly not by mine.

The imposing edifice stood three stories high. It occupied a corner lot and reminded me of elegant townhouses in the fashionable neighborhoods of New York's upper fifties.

The door was opened by Diggs, the elderly butler who took our wraps and ushered us into a large, comfortable drawing room. A fire was blazing in the hearth; a welcome sight on such a chilly, damp evening.

Stuart stood in the foyer, talking to Diggs, but presently he joined us and said, "Make yourselves comfortable, ladies. Diggs will be bringing us tea."

I stood with my back to the fireplace, surveying the room which was tastefully furnished, and far more inviting than the cluttered drawing room at Hathaway Manor.

It was definitely a man's room though, with large comfortable looking chairs, rich earth-tone colors, and a noticeable absence of bric-a-brac.

"A suitable house for a bachelor," Beatrice remarked, giving the room a desultory glance.

"On the contrary, it's too large," Stuart said. "Now that I'm spending more time at Hathaway Manor, I don't really require a house in London."

She gave him a disconcerted look. "I thought you were tired of the country."

"Not at all. Oh, I grant you, London's exciting, but Hathaway Manor will always be home for me. I'm sure you feel the same way, Aunt. I dare say I'll be ready to return with you whenever you ladies decide to leave."

What a devil he is, I thought, and almost laughed, as Beatrice struggled to hide her true feelings. "Fine," she said at last, stretching her lips in a vain attempt to smile.

Diggs appeared then with the tea tray, and right behind him came a short, motherly looking woman.

Stuart greeted her warmly. "Mrs. Diggs! Have you missed me?" Before Aunt Beatrice's horrified eyes, he bent down and kissed the woman.

Embarrassed, she shoved him away, "Now, Master Stuart, you behave."

He laughed heartily. "No need for formality, Mrs. Diggs. They're all family," and he nodded his head towards the three of us. "My aunt, Lady Hathaway, my cousins, Miss Katherine and Miss Willa Hathaway." With genuine affection, he put his arm around the little woman and summed up her position with a simple, "Mrs. Diggs keeps me in line."

"Go away with you," she told him, her round, pleasant face all pink with embarrassment. Dropping us an old-fashioned curtsy, she acknowledged the introduction and busied herself beside her husband at the tea table.

I was seeing yet another side of Stuart Hathaway today, I thought. Here, in his own home, he radiated warmth and a sincere affection for these elderly servants.

The tea and little sandwiches Mrs. Diggs provided were delicious, but all of us with the exception of Stuart were too tired to do them justice. I yawned, Willa yawned, and Aunt Beatrice stifled hers and said, "Stuart, we're exhausted. Have that woman show us to our rooms."

He rang and when Mrs. Diggs appeared, we bid him good night and followed her plump little figure upstairs.

The small valises containing our night clothes had been placed in our rooms. Mine faced the front of the house, overlooking the street. It was a plain room, but not unattractive, suitable for either a man or woman with its white crocheted

105

bedspread and blue striped wallpaper.

I went to the window and looked outside. The gas lights cast an eerie glow on the fog laden street, lending an air of mystery to the lone figure who hurried past, tapping his cane on the sidewalk and whistling softly.

"Night of evil, night of sin, wherein a thousand demons lurk. In every dark corner, behind every black tree, they wait, my love, wait for thee!" From a play by Francis Porterfield. Beau performed it in Philadelphia. I can't recall the title, but I never forgot those lines.

I undressed and got into bed. Too tired for sleep, I tossed and turned and worried over getting away to meet Beau and Katherine.

Stuart was the problem. I had a feeling he'd stick to me like glue, especially now that I was under his very roof. But, I would just have to give him the slip.

I'll present myself at Brown's Hotel, I decided, hopefully tomorrow, if possible. Katherine and Beau will most likely be at the theater, but I will leave them a message to meet me later in the day.

The thought suddenly struck me, Suppose they've moved from Browns! I didn't even want to think about that. I certainly couldn't go around checking every theater in London, looking for them.

Don't borrow trouble, I told myself, and concentrated on making a list of the questions I had for little Mary Sunshine.

What a picture of tranquility and beauty she had painted for me at Hathaway Manor! Had she thought I wouldn't ruffle the waters enough to stir up the silt underneath?

I had the doll, safely tucked in the bottom of my valise, and I meant to take it with me and demand an explanation from her about that, and a host of other things as well.

What had happened at Hathaway Manor to make Katherine go to such lengths to avoid going back? What did she know about Lily Beacham's murder? And what did Fenton and Beatrice fear she might remember?

All these questions buzzed around in my head like

106

swarming bees. The tension is too great, I thought. I can't take it much longer, and it is having a devastating effect on me.

I am becoming afraid of my own shadow. Why even fog under a street light conjures up visions of dastardly deeds afoot in the night. I am so morbid, I even reach back in my subconscious and resurrect creepy lines from an old play.

Get hold of yourself, India. You made a bargain and you will see it through.

Even if it kills you! a voice inside me added.

# Chapter 9

"Ssh, be quiet!"

"I tell you, she's asleep."

"Do as I say. Take your shoes off."

The hurried exchange in the hallway drifted up through the transom to assault my ears like the hiss of a stage whisper.

Wide awake, I'd been lying in bed, wondering if it were possible for me to sneak out of the house without being detected, and now it appeared that others had a similar notion. This led me to a rather unflattering conclusion; "Deceivers think alike."

Slipping quietly out of bed, I tiptoed across the room and put my ear to the door. Hearing nothing further, I cautiously turned the knob and peeped outside.

Stifling a laugh, I watched as Beatrice and Willa laboriously made their way downstairs. Desperately, they tried to maintain their balance while holding parasols, reticules, shoes, and skirts. Resisting the urge to shout, "Boo," I closed the door quickly.

Witnessing the two of them tumbling onto their royal backsides was tempting, but it would upset my own plans for the day.

I stationed myself at the window. Looking out through the delicate lace curtains, I had a clear view of the front street.

Sunshine, always a welcome sight in England, had obliterated every trace of fog, and along with it my morbid assessment of Bleekman Place. This was a peaceful, genteel neighborhood, as safe and secure as the social standings of its occupants.

And Stuart Hathaway belongs here, I thought. He may joke about it, but privilege and wealth are intrinsic to him, and as much a part of his background as his name. He is a Hathaway, and as far removed from an insignificant actor's daughter as the separate worlds we inhabit.

Thoughts of Stuart were pushed out of my mind, as Beatrice and Willa emerged from the house, followed by Diggs. He hailed them a hansom cab, one of those picturesque, little two-wheeled carriages that seemed to dominate the streets of London.

I saw them get in and then turned from the window, satisfied that they had made good their escape. Losing no time to make good my own, I washed and dressed and hurried downstairs.

Diggs greeted me with a smile. "Good morning, Miss Katherine. Mrs. Diggs is serving breakfast in the dining room."

My heart fell into my shoes when I entered and found Stuart seated at the table, reading the paper. Looking up, he observed me wryly. "Good morning, sleepy head. You missed going calling with our dear relatives. They just left."

"What a shame!"

Why couldn't I have missed you, as well, I thought, feeling annoyed. I knew he'd stick like glue.

"Take heart. You still have me, old stick-like-glue, Stuart. I won't desert you, Cousin."

Not only do I have to be careful what I say around this man, I even have to be careful what I think! Defeated, I sat down.

He chuckled to himself. "They claim they shouted and pounded on your door, but you just wouldn't wake up."

The lie was so outrageous that I dissolved into laughter. When I recovered myself, I said, "You should have seen them tiptoeing down the steps." Recalling the scene, I started to laugh again. "They were carrying their purses, their parasols, and their shoes, and trying to manipulate the stairs all at the same time."

He sighed. "Ah, to what lengths women will go to capture a man."

I stopped laughing. "Some women," I said. "You need to qualify that statement."

He raised his eyebrow and gave me a bold look. "You didn't stop them. You must have preferred spending the day with me."

"Oh, you are the most insufferable—"

Mrs. Diggs interrupted my tirade when she entered the room, wreathed in smiles. "Now, what can I be fixing her ladyship for breakfast on this beautiful spring morning?"

"Fix her a hearty breakfast, Mrs. Diggs," Stuart said. "She needs to fortify herself." He glanced my way and gave me a rather appealing look. "As Miss Katherine's self-appointed guide, I'm giving her the grand tour. We'll visit Hyde Park and some of the more obvious points of interest today, but I also plan to enliven her stay with some of the lesser known attractions that London has to offer."


I was conscious of Stuart's body pressing against mine as we jogged through Hyde Park in our hansom cab.

"There's nothing like these little cabs for speed, and convenience, too," he remarked. "Private carriages are a bother here. I don't even own one." Glancing out the window, he commented. "This part of Hyde Park is called, Rotten Row."

"Whatever for?" I asked.

He shrugged and smiled. "Probably because it's frequented by the rotten rich."

"Do you include yourself in that category?"

He hesitated, but only for a moment. "Rotten, yes, but not really rich."

I smiled to myself. If Stuart Hathaway is not rich, then surely India Chantelle is a pauper. My eyes took in the fine silk hat that rested on his lap and the heavy gold ring that sparkled on the little finger of his left hand. A hand, I noticed, that was not soft and womanish like those of so many fashionable, and pleasure seeking young men.

He pointed out the window. "Over there is Serpentine Lake. It's an artificial lake, but quite beautiful. I'll take you boating on it sometime."

He talked like my stay in London would be an indefinite one, or perhaps he anticipated another visit. In five months, I'll be gone, and you'll have forgotten you ever knew me, I thought. But will I have forgotten you?

Stuart tapped with his cane on the roof. "When you come out of the park, drive up to Regent Street," he instructed the cabbie. "The Quadrant on Regent Street contains many fine shops," he told me. "I thought you might want to shop and browse a bit."

The shops were indeed very fine, but out of reach of my pocketbook, notwithstanding the generous allowance Katherine had bestowed upon me. I enjoyed window shopping though, and made the mistake of admiring a dainty, lace fan.

My protests to no avail, Stuart insisted on buying it for me. "You can carry it if they let you attend one of the grand balls at Lighthizer House," he said, spreading it in front of his face and peering comically over it. "Use it as a disguise, like this, when you're introduced to Sir Alex."

He can be so much fun, I thought, laughing at his antics despite the disapproving frowns of several dowagers in the shop. If only I could trust him!

"Don't borrow trouble, Indy. Life was meant to be fun!" How many times had Beau given me that little piece of advice? Well, today, I told myself, I will take it. I may never get to London again, probably won't. And even if I do, I certainly won't have Cousin Stuart for a guide. *Katherine's* Cousin Stuart, I corrected myself. But *my* Mr. Cousin, I mused.

"Hungry?" Stuart asked, as we walked down Regent Street toward Piccadilly.

"Not really," I said. "Remember, Mrs. Diggs fortified me with a hearty breakfast."

"So she did, good soul that she is." He took my arm. "You won't mind walking then, and working up an appetite for lunch. I'm going to take you some place very special, and very expensive," he added. "And if you pick at your food like Willa, I'll make you pay for it yourself by washing the dishes."

"I never pick at my food," I said. "I have a healthy appetite and just thinking about this expensive lunch is making it grow. You may have to wash the dishes to pay for my lunch."

"You're a gel after me own 'eart, lovey," he said in a better imitation of a Cockney accent than any I'd ever heard on stage. "I hate women who eat like canaries," he added with a smile.

We crossed the street and in front of us stood an imposing six-columned building.

"Is that a theater?" I asked.

"The Haymarket, no less."

"The Haymarket," I repeated, staring up at the legendary theater with a look bordering on reverence.

"Oscar Wilde's *An Ideal Husband* is playing now," he said. "Would you like to go?"

"Would I!" I answered.

"Great. I enjoy the theater myself. It's in my blood, you know."

Mine, too, I almost said.

"I'll have my valet pick up the tickets," he added casually, tucking my arm in his.

"Are there many theaters in London?" I asked.

"More than we can ever attend. I'll take you to the most important ones, though." He stopped suddenly and gazed intently at me. "By Jove, I think you might enjoy it." Then just as suddenly, he shook his head. "No, probably not. You're too straitlaced."

One look at my face, and he hastened to reassure me. "I'm teasing you, Cousin. I'm talking about a Music Hall. Our's are perfectly respectable, but lots of fun. What do you say?"

"I'd love it. I've never been in one."

"Then we'll go, but don't tell Aunt Beatrice."

He hailed a cab, and told the driver to take us to The Grand Hotel. "I'm anxious to hear how the Grand compares to your New York hotels," Stuart said. "We Londoners consider it one of the best." Like a guide, he rattled off its

112

statistics. "The Grand has several restaurants, a Winter Garden, Palm Court, and I believe, five hundred bedrooms."

"I'm impressed already," I said. "I'm sure I'll love it."

Of course, I'm impressed. I've never seen any of New York's grand hotels, I silently confessed.

My thoughts turned then to The Barclay and the sleazy little desk clerk who'd called us "two-bit actors."

Suddenly, I felt cheap, pretending to be an heiress and moving in circles where I didn't belong. I had criticized the Hathaways, and called them all hyprocrites, but what was I?

"What's wrong, Katherine?"

I forced a smile. "Nothing."

"You look sad," he said, taking my hand. "It doesn't take much to set off an attack of homesickness. Believe me, I know. It's not easy, being uprooted and planted somewhere else."

His sympathy was too much for me to handle. Tears of guilt rolled down my cheeks, and suddenly I was in his arms. His sweet embrace, and the kiss that brushed my lips with tenderness, sought no self-gratification. Overwhelmed, I clung to him, and wondered, Is this how it feels to fall in love?

A week passed, and still no opportunity presented itself for a meeting with Katherine and Beau. Stuart kept me busy sight-seeing, and the time we spent together turned into memories that I pressed like roses between the pages of my heart. Someday, when this masquerade is over, I shall take them out and savor their sweetness. Perhaps, while I sit in some dimly lit theater, repairing a costume, I mused.

And how shall he remember them? Will he slap his thigh, and tell his aristocratic wife, She really had me fooled! That little Chantelle minx was quite an actress.

But, for the most part, I kept such distressing thoughts at bay, and my obsession with Stuart even upstaged my anxiety over Katherine and Beau. You have plenty of time to see them, I told myself.

We drove all over London in little hansom cabs, and I fell in love with the city. Its many bridges, spanning the Thames fascinated me, and I always insisted that we get out of the cab and walk on them.

"London Bridge is falling down, falling down, falling down. Dare we cross it?" I teased.

"Why not," Stuart countered. "A little dunking in the Thames won't hurt us."

Waterloo, Blackfriars, Vauxhall, Victoria, we saw them all, but the most fantastic to my mind was Hammersmith's Bridge, a huge, Gothic structure. Its twin archways were flanked by towers with candlesnuffer roofs. Stuart called it a monstrosity, but I loved the medieval look of it.

We fed the pigeons in Trafalgar Square and I was dutifully impressed by the monument to Lord Nelson which Stuart informed me was called "Nelson's Column." Not being British, I was sketchy about his lordship's accomplishments, and could not offer much in the way of intelligent comment.

Stuart had mentioned that The Strand was noted for its many theaters, so I suggested that we take a leisurely stroll in that direction.

Like a spy, I minutely studied the billboards of every theater we passed, but nowhere did I see the name, Chantelle.

"Are you looking for anyone in particular?"

I jumped, and found Stuart staring at me with a peculiar expression on his face. Realizing how odd my performance must have seemed to him, I smiled and said, "Not really. I was just curious to see if any of our American actors were performing in London, that's all."

I couldn't be sure if he accepted my explanation or not, but he dropped the subject. "If you're ready for lunch, there's Simpson's right here in the Strand. Its by way of being a favorite with Londoners."

I looked forward to these elegant little luncheons I shared with Stuart on our tour of the city. Our evening meals were marred by the presence of Beatrice and Willa who dominated the dinner table conversation with gossip and complaints about everything.

I was also looking forward to our theater nights, and I hoped Stuart hadn't forgotten about them. "Were you able to get tickets for the theaters?" I asked.

We had just been seated in the restaurant, and he eyed me across the small table, a calculating look upon his face. "You seem to be particularly devoted to the theater," he said. "I've never known anyone to read billboards quite so thoroughly."

I laughed, a little nervously. "I like the theater very much, most New Yorkers do." And waving my hand I added, "But, if you didn't get them, it's of no consequence."

He reached into his pocket, and pulled out four tickets. "We have box seats for both performances next week." Then he smiled. "The dates conveniently coincide with two dull *soirées* at Lighthizer House, which I'm afraid you'll have to miss."

I giggled. "What a shame!"

"I know, I'll miss them, too, but I explained the whole thing to dear old Aunt Beatrice. She agreed to let you come with me, since I'd already purchased the tickets. Wasn't that generous of her?"


Beatrice and Willa dutifully took me shopping the next day, and much to my surprise, insisted that I go with them on one of their calls.

We were to visit a distant relative, I was told, an elderly widow who had not left her boudoir for the past five years. I assume Beatrice felt Lady Marchbank eminently qualified to receive me for several reasons; the woman was deaf, demented, and she was obviously no longer a part of London's social set.

Her house, facing Kensington Park, was an imposing mansion four stories high. We were ushered into an opulent drawing room by an elderly butler and presently Lady Marchbank's nurse appeared to escort us upstairs.

"Dear, Cousin Elvira," Beatrice crooned, sweeping into the bedroom, and making a show of embracing the tiny figure who lay propped up on a chaise lounge.

The old lady pushed her away, and reached for her cane.

"Who the devil are you? Smith!" she called, thumping on the floor for her nurse, and narrowing missing Beatrice's foot with the cane.

When the harried woman reappeared, Cousin Elvira demanded to know, "Who are these people, Smith?"

Embarrassed, the nurse leaned down, and spoke into the old lady's ear. "Your cousin, Lady Hathaway has brought her daughter and her niece to see you, Lady Marchbank."

Waving the woman away with a bony hand, Lady Marchbank skewered me with her tiny birdlike eyes and announced, "I know you. You're the actress!"

I paled, and was well on the way to fainting for the first time in my life, when Beatrice said, "No, Cousin Elvira. This is Roland's daughter, Katherine."

"She's Nell," the woman insisted, nodding her head and grinning toothlessly at me. "So, they decided to let Gilbert keep you." Riveting me to the spot with her watery eyes, she said, "Go back on the stage, gel. Run, if you have to, but get away from Hathaway Manor. They'll eat you alive down there!"

Beatrice looked at the nurse, and made a hasty retreat. "She's tired, poor dear. We'll leave and let her rest."

I waited until we were in the cab, and then I asked, "Who's Nell?"

"Nell Bridges."

The name, which meant nothing to me, had barely escaped Beatrice's tight lips, when Willa cried, "Stuart's mother!" Her pale eyes sparkled with malicious glee, and she pounced on Beatrice, "Tell, tell, I'm dying to hear all about the wicked Nell Bridges."

Beatrice's face looked like it had been pickled, but that didn't deter Willa. "Oh, come on, Mama. I'm not a child anymore, and neither is Katherine." She threw me a quick glance, and then doubled back and measured me with jealous eyes. "Does Katherine really look like her?"

"Cousin Elvira is as blind as she is batty," Beatrice retorted. Staring directly at me, she shrugged. "Nell had dark hair and fair skin. She was rather pretty in a common sort of way."

I took that as a backhanded compliment for myself as well, but I hoped she would continue with the story, for I, too, was interested in hearing about Stuart's mother.

Beatrice worked her kid gloves down over her long fingers and appeared to weigh her words. "There's not that much to tell, really. Your Uncle Gilbert had always been a rake."

Folding her hands primly in her lap she continued, "He was quite handsome, blond, of course, but, his coloring was not as pale as most of the Hathaways. I rather think he took after the Marchbanks." She paused a moment and then added, "He had the most incredible violet-blue eyes."

I wondered if she'd been in love with him, but I didn't have time to pursue the thought, for Willa interrupted, "But, Mama we want to hear about *her.*"

Beatrice answered impatiently. "I told you, there is not that much to tell. Gilbert ran around with a bohemian crowd in London, and I suppose that's how he met Nell Bridges. She was already *enceinte* when he eloped with her."

Willa's eyes widened. "She was pregnant with Stuart!"

Beatrice's pale face turned chalk white. "Willa! Kindly refrain from using that vulgar word." She spoke then, almost to herself. "There was no reason for him to marry her. His father would have paid her off."

"Maybe Uncle Gilbert loved Nell," I said.

Two pair of icy grey eyes stared back at me with astonishment, and Beatrice said, "Don't be ridiculous, Katherine. A gentleman of your uncle's background does not *marry* that sort of woman!"

"What sort of woman was she?" I asked.

Beatrice smirked. "She called herself an actress, but she started out as a cheap entertainer in music halls." Wearing a smug expression, she added, "Grandfather Hathaway had her background checked. She was nothing but a Cockney upstart with illusions of grandeur."

I thought of that conversation one week later as I listened to Lottie Collins, the rage of London Music Halls belt out,

"Ta-Ra-Ra-Boom-De-Ay" on the stage of the Tivoli Theater.

I admit, there is snobbery in the theater, and those of the legitimate stage, by virtue of the very name, consider themselves performers rather than entertainers. But talent can never be underwritten, and I found these acts in every way professional performances and worthy of the thunderous applause the audience bestowed upon them.

Vesta Tilley, Queen of the Music Halls, or so Stuart informed me, brought the house down with a catchy little number called, "Jolly Good Luck To The Girl Who Loves a Soldier." Mark Sheridan sang, "Brighton," and "Girly-Girly," two Cockney songs, whose words, because of the accent, sometimes eluded me, but I enjoyed them nevertheless.

My guide also informed me that the theater was nick-named, The Tiv; it's three tiers seated fifteen hundred people and all the Music Hall *Greats* performed there. Looking down, and then up to the balconies from our box, I would have to say that the *Greats* were playing to a packed house this evening.

My mind turned back to some of the empty houses we had played to in the past. Once, out west, our audience had consisted of four drunken cowboys. The play was, *As You Like It,* and I don't suppose they did, for they snored loudly through all the acts.

I wondered what kind of theater Beau was playing to tonight and how his performance was being received, when all too soon, the house lights went up, and the curtain came down.

Now, the performers would hang up their costumes, I mused, take off their greasepaint and turn into perfectly ordinary people.

A few would meet friends and take off for a night on the town, but most would hurry to whatever hotel room they currently called home, to analyze their performances and try to work out a better way of saying it, singing it, or dancing it; never being one hundred percent satisfied, but always striving for perfection. That's the theater, and nobody knows its bright side or its dark side better than I do.

"If you're planning on staying for the next performance, you'll have a long wait."

Stuart's words jarred me out of my reverie, and I looked around to find him standing behind my chair, holding my wrap. "I was daydreaming, but I did enjoy it, ever so much, Stuart."

In a gesture that was intimate and disturbingly sensual, he laid the velvet wrap across my shoulders, brushing my bare skin with his hands. Leaning over me, he hooked the clasp at my throat, and whispered in my ear, "We're not rushing home. You look gorgeous, and I want to show you off."

"Where are we going?"

"To the ballroom of the Claridge Hotel. We're going to waltz the rest of the night away."

His words delighted me. I had dressed up this evening. Not having to worry about outshining Willa, I had worn one of Katherine's more sophisticated gowns, a pale lavender satin with tiny nosegays of violets bordering the daring, off-the-shoulder neckline. The slim skirt clung to my body and ended in a short train.

Stuart looked elegant, and very dashing in top hat and tails. He's so handsome, I thought, wanting to memorize his face: the slate grey eyes that could twinkle with merriment and then turn in a flash to deep, unfathomable pools; his moustache that I loved, and which he kept trimmed to just the right thickness, neither bushy, nor pencil thin; and the sensuous mouth beneath it; the lips that could be hard and bruising and at other times as gentle as the touch of a feather.

He brushed my ear with them now, as he whispered, "Follow me. I know a shortcut."

Grabbing my hand, he led me down a back stairway and through a service door to a side alley that ran alongside the building. We walked around to the front street where cabs were lined up outside the theater, waiting for the crowd to spill out.

An eager cabbie opened his door for us. "Where to Gov'nor?"

119

"Hotel Claridge."

Stuart handed me in, and we were on our way before the others had emerged from the theater.

"My compliments," I said. "That was a very neat little trick."

"I know them all," he answered smugly and we laughed looking out at the crowd of stranded people who stood on the sidewalk waiting for the next available cab.

My laugh turned into a gasp. That face in the crowd. . . . Had I imagined it, or had I really seen Katherine!

# Chapter 10

Like a silly *ingénue* in a bad play, I waltzed around my bedroom, holding a bouquet of flowers and wearing a dreamy smile.

It had been a magic night, and closing my eyes, I transported myself back to the ballroom of the Claridge Hotel. Once again, I heard the strains of a Viennese waltz, and I was in Stuart's arms, dancing as I had never danced before. He was smiling down at me and a thousand stars were in my eyes.

Flinging myself across the bed, I stared up at the ceiling and recalled his outrageous compliments in the carriage on the way home.

*You're a marvelous dancer, Katherine. I mean it. I doubt Vesta Tilley waltzes as well.*

I looked at the scraggly little bunch of flowers I still held in my hand and giggled to myself.

We had arrived home, and after paying the driver, Stuart had suddenly left me standing on the sidewalk and vaulted the fence that separated No. 10 Bleekman Place from No. 8.

I had no idea what he was doing, until a few seconds later when he returned and presented me with this hastily picked bouquet from his neighbor's garden.

*These can't compare with Vesta's, but they're the best I could do on short notice.*

Already withering now, they were still beautiful to me, and I would press them, and keep them, along with the

121

memory of this night.

My thoughts turned reluctantly then to Katherine and Beau. My imagination had been playing tricks on me, for as we had jogged briskly along London's dark streets, I thought I had seen Katherine several times.

This, I interpreted as a premonition. Was Katherine in some kind of trouble, and was she crying out to me for help?

Ever since coming to London, I had been wrapped up in my own affairs, playing my role of fashionable heiress to the hilt with Stuart dancing attendance on me. And loving every minute of it, I must confess.

But, in the meantime, what was going on with Katherine and Beau? Those two lovable, irresponsible people could have gotten themselves into any number of difficulties by this time, and on this very night, they could be desperately in need of my help.

My thoughts were interrupted by tapping sounds coming from the street, and jumping up, I turned out the lamp, and ran to the window. A man, wearing a long, black cloak, stood tapping his cane against the lamp post and whistling tunelessly.

This was the same man who had tapped his cane and whistled in the fog, causing my imagination to run away with me.

"Night of evil, night of sin . . ."

Stop it, I told myself. You're doing it again.

At that very moment, the man suddenly stepped out of the shadows and stood under the street lamp. Pressing my nose to the glass, I tried to see his face, but his black derby concealed it. A match flared, and I caught a fleeting glimpse of nondescript features and a swarthy complexion.

Turning away, I sighed with relief. He only wanted to stop for a smoke.

I undressed, without benefit of a light, for the moon was full, and it shone through the lacy curtains. Wanting one more glimpse of that magnificent orange-colored ball surrounded by stars, I returned to the window.

The man was still there! And more startling yet, Stuart was with him. They spoke in low tones, and then the stranger

122

handed Stuart a slip of paper.

Stuart reached into his pocket and it was obvious to me that money was changing hands. There was something furtive and a little frightening about the encounter and I didn't like it.

A spark of fire glowed in the darkness, as the stranger flipped his cigar into the gutter, and then they both turned on their heels and walked away. Stuart toward the house; the stranger toward Charing Cross. I remained at the window until the tapping and whistling grew fainter and fainter and finally died away.

I felt vaguely troubled, but I did not know why.

The following morning, we were informed by Mrs. Diggs that the master had been called out of town. "He left early this morning, he did, and he asked me to convey his apologies," she said.

The two women facing me across the table looked up in surprise and their expressions immediately showed their chagrin. I knew what was upsetting them. They figured with Stuart gone, they'd be dutybound to include me in their plans.

Beatrice picked at her soft-boiled egg and cast a weak smile in my direction. "Well, Katherine. It looks like your tour of London has been interrupted." Pursing her lips, she added, "I find it strange that Stuart should be called out of town so suddenly."

You'd find it even stranger, I thought, if you'd looked out my window last night.

Willa attacked her sweet roll with a vengeance, but said nothing.

"We feel it's our duty to spend the day with Cousin Elvira," Beatrice lied. "But of course, if you don't want to go, we'll understand, dear."

I would have loved to call their bluff and accept the offer, but this was a golden opportunity to track down Katherine and Beau.

"Thank you, Aunt Beatrice," I replied. "But might I be

123

excused? I have a rather bad headache, and I really think I should rest."

They pounced on me like two cats after cream.

"We'll make your apologies," Willa said, helping herself to another roll. She lavished it with butter and popped it into her mouth. Wearing a satisfied smile, she chewed it slowly.

"Soup and rest, that's what you need, Katherine," Beatrice advised. Then she hastened to add, "Mrs. Diggs will take good care of you, and to make it easy on her, Willa and I will take supper with Cousin Elvira."

A whole day to search for Katherine and Beau. I couldn't have asked for more, but last night's mysterious meeting had put a damper on my spirits.

Beatrice and Willa left on their trumped up mission of mercy, and as soon as they had gone, I jumped out of bed, and dressed for my long postponed appointment.

I wore a lightweight green serge suit with a short jacket that reached just to my waist, and a small straw hat banded with a wide gros-grain ribbon in a darker shade of green.

Checking my appearance in the full-length mirror, I thought of Stuart. He liked me in green and the outfit was becoming. For a brief moment, I wished he were standing waiting for me at the bottom of the stairs, left eyebrow raised, his eyes taking me in from head to toe, grinning that rakish grin that told me he approved.

I took the doll, still wrapped tightly in my old petticoat, and tucked it under my arm. Then gathering up my gloves, and an umbrella, for the sky looked threatening, I hurried downstairs.

Sticking my head in the kitchen, I informed Mrs. Diggs that I was going out. "I had a headache," I said, "But I feel much better now, Mrs. Diggs. I'll be back before my aunt returns, but I'd appreciate it anyway if you didn't mention my little outing to Lady Hathaway."

Placing a plump finger over her lips, she said, "Mum's the word, Miss Katherine." Her wink and my knowing smile branded us conspirators, relieving my mind of at least one small worry as I set out on my quest.

Conscious of the need to take precautions, I had Diggs

124

hail me a cab, telling him I was going to The Strand, but as soon as we had pulled away from the curb, I instructed the driver to take me to Brown's Hotel instead.

My heart was pounding when I reached my destination, and suddenly my list of grievances seemed trivial and downright hysterical. What was I going to say?

Somebody put this doll in bed with me, Katherine, and it frightened me out of my wits.

It did sound hysterical. Why would any normal, sane person be afraid of a doll?

I sensed a presence behind me, Katherine, and I became terrified I might plunge over a cliff. But, when I turned around, no one was there. Oh yes, I did see a tall, lumbering figure disappear in the bushes. It rather resembled a giant possum in the way it moved.

Ridiculous! People have been committed for less.

I paid the driver and walked towards the hotel.

"Miss, you forgot your package."

Wishful thinking, but I thanked him and accepted it. I'll just tell Katherine I found the doll, and thought she might want to keep it.

Entering the lobby, I approached the registration desk.

"Do you have a Mr. Beauregard Chantelle and his daughter, Miss India Chantelle registered?" I asked.

"Yes, indeed, Miss, but they're not here now. They're at the theater rehearsing."

"Can you tell me which theater?"

He thought a moment. "The Avenue, I believe, Miss."

I thanked him and walked outside, feeling suddenly lighthearted. Everything was as it should be. They were staying at Browns and they were working.

A policeman stood on the corner, and I asked him for directions. Perhaps I could walk. I could, he informed me and pointed. "Straight ahead for a block, Miss. Then take a right. You can't miss it."

It was an experimental theater, the sign said, and the play was a new one, *Regrets Only,* by someone named Robert Allen.

I walked around to the back of the theater and entered

through the stage door. The old man who detained me with a curt, "No admittance, they're in rehearsal," might have stepped out of any number of theaters I've worked in. Different accent, but same gruff voice; wrinkled brown trousers, held up by black suspenders; the little cap that covered his bald pate. Every theater in the world had their *Pop*.

"Can I leave a message for Mr. Chantelle?"

"Aye."

I scribbled a short note on the back of an envelope: I'll be at Brown's Hotel waiting for you.

Pausing, I agonized over the signature, wanting to sign my own name, until Pop's curious stare convinced me otherwise. Hastily, I scrawled Katherine Hathaway at the bottom and handed him the note.

Seated in the sumptuous lobby of Brown's Hotel, I had a clear view of the entrance, and I spotted Katherine and Beau before they saw me.

My father cut a dashing figure in his morning coat and fashionable grey trousers with the new, vertical crease down the front and back. With his bowler hat and cane, he could have passed for an English lord, but it was Katherine's appearance that surprised me.

Her brilliant sapphire blue suit and plumed hat gave her a theatrical look that belied her tender years. The impulsive child I had known on shipboard had metamorphosized into a very sophisticated lady who kept her poise, even when I made a spectacle of myself by colliding with several bystanders as I rushed up to greet them.

"You don't know how glad I am to see you," I exclaimed after I had embraced them both.

"Indy, my dear, we have so much to tell you," Beau said, and Katherine gave him a warning glance.

"Let's go upstairs, and then we can talk," she suggested, and I understood her concern. Beau would have to be careful about the names. I would, too, I reminded myself.

We were joined in the lift by a middle-aged lady who greeted Beau and Katherine warmly. "Ah, Mr. Chantelle and India, my dear. I missed you in the dining room this morning."

"We had an early rehearsal," Beau explained.

She gazed up at him with adoring eyes and I recognized the look. Beau had obviously made another conquest.

"Will you be taking the play to New York?" she asked.

To New York! I thought.

Beau never batted an eye. "Not yet, dear lady. There are quite a few changes that need to be made first. I'm still working them out with the author."

She dimpled with delight. "Then we shall keep you in England a little longer."

"I'm afraid so."

She turned to Katherine. "So good of your father to assist these young playwrights. Most established actors would not be so generous."

Katherine merely smiled as the lift halted.

"Your floor, Mrs. Oliphant," Beau said.

"So it is. See you at dinner," she trilled, leaving the elevator.

A man took her place and we rode the rest of the way in silence. Recalling Mrs. Oliphant's conversation with my father, I smiled, Beau's still Beau.

We got off at the fifteenth floor and I followed their lead to a suite of rooms overlooking the Thames. The sitting room was twice as large as Grandma's parlor back in Columbus, Ohio, and not quite as long as the drawing room at Hathaway Manor.

Done in gold and white, the decor was more French than British, and I felt like I had lost two inches in height, as I sank into the plush carpet that stretched from wall to wall like snow over a field.

"What do you think, Indy?" Beau said. "This is a far cry from The Barclay, isn't it?"

"It's just beautiful, but it must be terribly expensive."

Katherine laughed and hugged me. "We knew you'd say that, didn't we, Beau?"

He looked a little uncomfortable. "Don't scold, Indy. Katherine insisted on it. She's being very generous."

Katherine pulled the pins out of her hat and gave me an intense look. "I told Beau, if we want to be successful, we have to look like we already are."

Beau nodded in agreement. "And it works, Indy. We were only in London two days when we got parts in this play."

"It's experimental theater," Katherine said, "But they're doing some wonderful things." Her eyes lit up with excitement. "Last year, they did, *Arms and the Man*, by George Bernard Shaw. It was a huge success and this play will be, too."

Katherine talked like she'd been in the theater all her life, and I marveled at her perception. "Well, tell me about the play," I said.

Beau spoke up. "It's wonderful. Just my cup of tea, a smart, little drawing-room comedy." His face took on a boyish look of anticipation. "I know you think I was talking through my hat down there in the lift, Indy, but I really would like to take this play to New York. It could be the hit of Broadway."

"He's right," Katherine said. "And Beau gives an outstanding performance."

"Now, now, enough of that." Beau waved Katherine's compliment away in a brave show of modesty, and then turned around and said, "The role is just tailor-made for me, Indy. The character has class, he's handsome, debonair. All the ladies adore him." He turned his hands out and shrugged. "Who could play it better than Beauregard Chantelle?"

I was happy for him. "It sounds wonderful, Beau." I turned then to Katherine. "And did you get a part, too, Katherine?"

Beau answered for her. "Did she get a part! Wait until we tell you the news."

Katherine slumped in the chair and pouted. "I still feel bad about it, Beau."

He walked over and gave her a fatherly hug. "These things happen, Katherine. You did beautifully at rehearsal today. Just don't think about it."

Suddenly Katherine jumped up. "He's right, India. I have

# MORE PASSION AND ADVENTURE AWAIT... YOUR TRIP TO A BIG ADVENTUROUS WORLD BEGINS WHEN YOU ACCEPT YOUR FIRST 4 NOVELS ABSOLUTELY *FREE*
## (AN $18.00 VALUE)

Accept your Free gift and start to experience more of the passion and adventure you like in a historical romance novel. Each Zebra novel is filled with proud men, spirited women and tempestuous love that you'll remember long after you turn the last page.

Zebra Historical Romances are the finest novels of their kind. They are written by authors who really know how to weave tales of romance and adventure in the historical settings you love. You'll feel like you've actually gone back in time with the thrilling stories that each Zebra novel offers.

## GET YOUR FREE GIFT WITH THE START OF YOUR HOME SUBSCRIPTION

Our readers tell us that these books sell out very fast in book stores and often they miss the newest titles. So Zebra has made arrangements for you to receive the four newest novels published each month.

You'll be guaranteed that you'll never miss a title, and home delivery is so convenient. And to show you just how easy it is to get Zebra Historical Romances, we'll send you your first 4 books absolutely FREE! Our gift to you just for trying our home subscription service.

## BIG SAVINGS AND FREE HOME DELIVERY

Each month, you'll receive the four newest titles as soon as they are published. You'll probably receive them even before the bookstores do. What's more, you may preview these exciting novels free for 10 days. If you like them as much as we think you will, just pay the low preferred subscriber's price of just $3.75 each. *You'll save $3.00 each month off the publisher's price.* AND, your savings are even greater because there are never any shipping, handling or other hidden charges—FREE Home Delivery. Of course you can return any shipment within 10 days for full credit, no questions asked. There is no minimum number of books you must buy.

# 4 FREE BOOKS

## TO GET YOUR 4 FREE BOOKS WORTH $18.00 — MAIL IN THE FREE BOOK CERTIFICATE T O D A Y

Fill in the Free Book Certificate below, and we'll send your FREE BOOKS to you as soon as we receive it.

If the certificate is missing below, write to: Zebra Home Subscription Service, Inc., P.O. Box 5214, 120 Brighton Road, Clifton, New Jersey 07015-5214.

## FREE BOOK CERTIFICATE

# 4 FREE BOOKS

### ZEBRA HOME SUBSCRIPTION SERVICE, INC.

**YES!** Please start my subscription to Zebra Historical Romances and send me my first 4 books absolutely FREE. I understand that each month I may preview four new Zebra Historical Romances free for 10 days. If I'm not satisfied with them, I may return the four books within 10 days and owe nothing. Otherwise, I will pay the low preferred subscriber's price of just $3.75 each; a total of $15.00, *a savings off the publisher's price of $3.00.* I may return any shipment and I may cancel this subscription at any time. There is no obligation to buy any shipment and there are no shipping, handling or other hidden charges. Regardless of what I decide, the four free books are mine to keep.

NAME

ADDRESS _____ APT _____

CITY _____ STATE _____ ZIP _____

( )
TELEPHONE

SIGNATURE _____ (If under 18, parent or guardian must sign)

Terms, offer and prices subject to change without notice. Subscription subject to acceptance by Zebra Books. Zebra Books reserves the right to reject any order or cancel any subscription.

to put it out of my mind. Beau'll explain." She gave me a quick hug. "I'm going to change, and when I come back, we'll have lunch."

When she had gone, I said, "What happened, Beau?"

He sat down and spoke softly. "Poor kid, she was really upset. One of the girls in the cast committed suicide."

"Oh, how terrible!"

He nodded. "She wasn't much older than Katherine, and they'd gotten rather friendly, you know, giggling backstage together, that sort of thing." He shrugged his shoulders and shook his head. "Veronica's gentleman friend threw her over, so she jumped in the Thames."

"No wonder Katherine was upset," I said.

"It was pretty bad. The police came to the theater and reported it. You can imagine how that was."

Knowing how emotional actors and actresses can be, I could readily understand the trauma such an incident would produce.

"Poor Veronica had no relatives and the director had to identify the body," he added. "Then a couple of days later, they offered her role to Katherine."

Now I understood. Such a decision for a sensitive girl like Katherine to make!

"She didn't want to do it, but I talked her into it, Indy." His eyes glowed with pride. "Katherine's a natural born actress. She has perfect timing, she's fresh and exciting . . ."

I felt a tinge of envy, and then chided myself for it. I never wanted to be onstage. If Katherine can act, more power to her, but it would be nice if Beau could be a little proud of me, too, I thought.

Katherine appeared then, her mood having done a somersault from down to up again.

"So, has he told you about my part?"

"Only that you're wonderful in it."

"Oh, Beau," she said, plainly pleased.

She had changed into a simple blouse and skirt and looked more like the little girl I remembered. Perching herself on the arm of Beau's chair, she bubbled over with enthusiasm, as she described her role, "Vivacious, a little naughty."

Katherine's part sounded like it was tailor-made for her, too.

"And now, tell us what you've been doing," Beau said. But before I could answer, Katherine interrupted, "India must be starving. I know I am. Why don't you order us a nice lunch, Beau?"

"Watch this, Indy," he said, picking up a telephone and speaking to the hotel kitchen right from the room.

"Come, see my new wardrobe while he's ordering," Katherine said, grabbing my hand and leading me into a bedroom that must have been copied from Versaille.

Ruby red was the predominant color, and though it suited Katherine's strong personality, it intimidated me. I preferred my soft green and rose bedroom at Hathaway Manor.

"Oh, India, this is all so exciting," Katherine said. "I just love the theater. Later, I want to read you my lines and I want you to tell me honestly what you think of my interpretation."

"Beau says you're very good, Katherine. His criticism is far superior to mine."

She opened the large armoire and showed me gowns that must have cost a fortune. Like the plumage of exotic birds, the colors were vibrant and lustrous; sapphire blue, heliotrope, reds ranging from ruby to deep garnet, emerald green. Beaded gowns, gowns decorated with ostrich feathers, gowns lavish with lace.

"What's the matter, India? Don't you approve?"

"They're pretty sophisticated for a seventeen year old debutante," I said.

"I'm not the debutante. You are."

I had no answer for that, but I was slightly annoyed with her self-absorption. "Don't you want to hear about Hathaway Manor?" I asked.

Like a child, she showed immediate remorse. "Oh, India, I'm sorry. Here, I've been prattling away about all the good things that are happening to me, and I haven't even asked you how you were enjoying yourself. Are you having a wonderful time communing with nature?"

I ignored her question. "Aren't you interested in hearing about your relatives?"

She avoided looking at me and busied herself rearranging the gowns in the armoire. "They don't suspect anything, do they?"

"I don't think so."

She turned around then and smiled. "I knew you could pull it off, India. You're probably a better actress than you realize. Just don't pay any attention to Aunt Beatrice and Uncle Fenton," she said, making a face. "They're stiff as boards, and besides they never did like me. As for Willa," she added. "She's a mean little chit!"

My sentiments exactly, I thought.

"Is Cousin Jordan still playing with his Bunsen burners?"

I nodded, and Katherine giggled. "I used to hide and watch him, hoping he'd char his nose on them."

"I've met your Cousin Stuart, too."

Katherine's eyes widened in surprise. "You mean, he still keeps in touch with the family!"

"He's been staying at Hathaway Manor ever since I arrived," I said. "And right now, we're all living at his house in London."

She was obviously shocked, and took a moment to collect her thoughts, but I wasn't prepared for her reaction when she finally spoke. "Don't trust Stuart, India. Whatever you do, don't trust him!"

She was staring at me with a strange expression on her face. "You haven't let him seduce you. Have you?"

"Of course not," I said, feeling frightened and vaguely apprehensive. "But why? Why do you say I shouldn't trust him?"

"Because he's a rake, just like his father." She patted my hand like a wiser, older sister, which in itself was absurd and added in a gentle voice. "I'm sure he's charming, India, but be very careful," and then she added emphatically, "And don't believe a word he says!"

We were sitting on the bed, like two schoolgirls exchanging confidences. Yet, we have exchanged nothing, I thought, not even information.

"Katherine," I said. "We need to be honest with each other. I'll admit, I am attracted to Stuart, but I realize the

131

futility of falling in love with him."

I took a deep breath, and continued, "There's something else though. What happened at Hathaway Manor that caused you and your family to leave so suddenly?"

Turning evasive, she resorted to a nervous giggle. "I don't know. I was only ten."

I felt like we were going around in circles. "I overheard your aunt and uncle talking. They don't want me at Hathaway Manor, because they're afraid I might remember something. Stuart keeps badgering me about a cave. He thinks I know something, too." I decided to lay my cards on the table. "Does the name Lily Beacham mean anything to you, Katherine?"

"She was a servant. I think she disappeared."

"She was murdered," I said. "And don't you understand? They think you know who did it."

She shook her head. "If I know, I don't remember."

She thought a moment, and then a chill ran down my spine, when she spoke. "Stay away from Stuart. I have a bad feeling about him, India." Then she added, "Any number of people at Hathaway Manor could have murdered Lily Beacham, but I'd say Stuart or his father would be the prime suspects!"

# Chapter 11

Spurning a cab, I decided to walk back to Bleekman Place. My long awaited reunion with Katherine and Beau had been a disappointment, and depression hung over me like a dark cloud. I couldn't bear the thought of facing Katherine's relatives tonight. I was not up to coping with Beatrice and Willa's snide remarks nor Stuart's false smile.

Katherine had confirmed my suspicions about him, and all the evidence I had tried to overlook came back to haunt me.

I had recognized Stuart Cousin immediately for the scheming charmer he was. Yet, like a fool, I had let my defenses down once I discovered he was really Stuart Hathaway.

And then there were the sudden personality shifts. Besotted, I had thought of a chameleon, a rather bright little creature with a propensity for change, but should I have been thinking instead of a snake that can alter its appearance by shedding skins?

I refused to believe that Stuart would be involved in murder, but the nagging thought persisted. Why would he be so interested in jogging Katherine's memory if not to protect himself in some way?

"No!" I thought, and must have said, for I found myself the object of curious stares from several passersby. Embarrassed, I hurried past them, and when I got the opportunity, crossed the street.

I won't suspect him of murder, I told myself, in spite of Katherine's accusation, but I must accept the fact that she is probably right about the other part. Stuart Hathaway is not to be trusted. He *had* tried to seduce me in the cave, and he has neither apologized nor offered me a decent proposal.

Then there is his mysterious and probably unsavory involvement with the whistler, I thought. Gentlemen do not conduct business in the street, surreptitiously exchanging money for information under cloak of darkness.

My eyes blurred with tears. There was no one to offer me either comfort or advice. My own father was more concerned with Katherine than he was with me.

The doll incident was certainly proof of that, I thought, recalling Beau's awkward hint that it would be better if I took my leave. "Don't feel bad, Indy. You had no way of knowing. Maybe it would be better if you came back another day though. It'll take me awhile to cheer her up again."

After lunch, I had unwrapped the bundle and presented the doll to Katherine, whereupon she had immediately gone into hysterics. Not however, for any reason I might have anticipated.

The doll, she tearfully explained, bore a striking resemblance to Veronica, her tragic friend. Katherine begged me to take it away, for she said she couldn't bear to look at it.

I felt terrible, but she embraced me and said, "Next to you, India, she was my best friend." Then she looked at me with sad eyes, and squeezed my hand. "Please forgive me, but I think I'd like to rest now. You and Beau have a nice chat."

Recalling her sweet young face, I chided myself for being selfish. Right now, Katherine needs Beau, and he's accepting that responsibility. I should be proud of him.

I stopped suddenly. Where was I? Engrossed in my problems, I had wandered aimlessly, and now I found myself in an unfamiliar and rather unsavory part of town. To add insult to injury, fog had drifted in from the sea, and looking around a deserted area of what looked like run-down warehouses, I felt suddenly afraid.

"Lost?"

I heard the voice, but saw no one. Turning around, I began

to walk briskly, retracing my steps. Laughter, low and terrifying, followed behind me. The fog was moving in quickly, and I was becoming confused. If only a hack would appear, I thought, but no carriage, nor person did I see. The laughter had stopped. Was he still behind me? I wondered.

I tried to get my bearings. Crossing the street had been a mistake. To someone like myself, with absolutely no sense of direction, retracing steps could pose a problem if one deviated, even to the slightest degree.

I have gotten lost more times than I care to remember, and for a practical person like myself, this inconsistency in my personality is a source of embarrassment. Beau, on the other hand, is a veritable bird dog, and I've grown used to relying on him to steer me in the right direction.

Well, he's not here now. So, which shall it be? I asked myself. Left, right, or straight ahead?

"Lost?"

The voice, followed again by low laughter, raised the hairs on the back of my neck and without making a conscious decision, I picked up my skirts and ran.

I could feel the doll, still wrapped in my petticoat, slipping from my grasp. I tried to hold onto it, but holding up my skirt was a greater priority. I didn't want to trip and fall down, putting myself at the mercy of my pursuer, so when the unwieldy bundle finally fell to the sidewalk, I kept right on running.

Fog, like the fetid breath of some prehistoric monster, spewed out a heavy, nebulous cloud. It hung like a green curtain over the city, and I ran through it blindly, feeling that at any minute, I could step off the ends of the earth into absolute nothingness.

A stitch in my side forced me to stop running, and panting for breath, I leaned up against something solid. I supposed it to be a wall.

My throat was on fire, and my heart was pounding in my chest. Something brushed against my legs, and I went to pieces. It could be a rat, I thought, and with a sob, I stumbled away, not knowing if I was running *from* danger or *into* it.

The thing, dog, cat, whatever it was, ran between my legs, and sent me sprawling. I felt a sharp sting that reverberated all the way up my arm, as my outstretched hands hit the concrete, and stunned, I lay on the ground, a tangled mass of bruised flesh.

Through my pain, I heard the unmistakable sound of a running footpad, and unable to move, I lay motionless, hoping against hope that the fog would at last work to my own advantage.

Feeling violated, I recoiled from the large, groping hands that found my body and lifted me to my feet. Instinctively, I reacted by trying to beat my attacker off. "Leave me alone," I shouted. "Help! Police."

My cries were effectively muffled as he spun me around and clamped a big hand over my mouth. With his other arm, he grabbed me around the waist and pinioned me tightly against him. My flailing fists beat the air, and frantically I shook my head, too terrified to understand what he was saying.

I was fighting for my life, and hysterical with fear. I could neither punch nor bite, but I could still kick, and I heard his curse, as my high-button shoes met his shins.

Raising me off my feet, he tried to render me helpless, but I continued to kick him in the knees. With a shout of pain, he released me, and I reached up to scratch his face, but he slapped me hard. "For God's sake, Katherine, come out of it. It's Stuart!"

His voice, more than the words, penetrated my crazed brain. "Stuart, Stuart," I repeated with a surge of relief that left me weak.

He gathered me in his arms. "I'm sorry, Katherine. I didn't want to strike you."

I sagged against him, sobbing softly. "I thought you were going to kill me."

"You need a keeper," he said. "What are you doing down here? This is a bad neighborhood."

"I was lost in the fog." And then, wanting to justify myself, I added, "But someone was chasing me. He kept asking me if I was lost, and then he would laugh, and hide."

136

My voice broke, and he spoke matter-of-factly, "Somebody just wanting to scare you. Our London fogs bring out the comedian in people."

His attitude annoyed me. "I've just been scared out of my wits, manhandled and slapped in the face. You'll pardon me if I don't see the humor in it."

Why was he following me in the first place? And why wait until I almost broke my neck to identify himself? I wondered.

"I spotted you from across the street," he said, and then, casually. "Where were you going?"

"Back to Bleekman Place."

He paused, and I thought I detected a challenge in his voice. "And where had you been?"

"Don't trust him," Katherine had said, and I weighed my answer. "Shopping."

"Most of the shops are on The Strand."

I can play cat and mouse as well as you can, Stuart Hathaway, I thought.

"Not all of them. Lots of the hotels have lovely gift shops."

A cab suddenly materialized out of the fog, and Stuart hailed it.

"And in the future," he said, once we were settled comfortably inside, "don't wander around the waterfront alone."

So that's where I had been! No wonder the fog was so thick. I rubbed my sore palms together.

"Did you hurt your hand?"

"Certainly not."

And what were you doing wandering around town when you were supposed to be out-of-town, I thought.

"I had to go to Brighton this morning," he said. "Turned out to be a wild goose chase, so I got back early."

Blast the man for reading my mind again! "It must have been sudden," I said. "You didn't mention it last night."

"So that's it!"

"That's what?"

"The reason you're miffed. You are, I can tell." He touched my lip with his finger. "You have a cute little pout. You didn't always, you know. As a child, your pout

137

stretched for about a mile." He shook his head. "Horrible! Made you look like a fierce little monkey."

I laughed in spite of myself. Oh, why does he have to be so delightful, so disarming, and so disreputable?

We turned into Bleekman Place, and Stuart was suddenly serious. "I have some unfinished business to attend to," he said. "You needn't mention that you saw me, Katherine. I should be back in a few days." He brushed my lips with a cousinly kiss. "Don't forget, we have tickets for the Haymarket on Friday."

The hall clock was just striking four P.M. when I entered the house. Diggs greeted me and said, "Lord Hathaway and Master Jordan are in the drawing room having tea, Miss Katherine."

This took me by surprise. "How long have they been here?"

"They just arrived, Miss."

"Are Lady Hathaway and Miss Willa home?"

"Not yet. Will you be joining the gentlemen, Miss Katherine?"

"In a few minutes," I said, hurrying upstairs to repair the damage incurred by my wrestling match in the fog.

Looking at myself in the mirror, I wondered that Stuart had not laughed at the sight of me. Wisps of hair had escaped my knot, and they hung washerwoman style around my face. My natty little straw boater was squashed, and cocked on my head at a rakish angle, it gave me the appearance of a tipsy tart.

My gloves, of course, were ruined, and would have to be thrown away. Fortunately, my clothes were not torn, and I was able to brush away the mud spots on my skirt.

I ran a comb carefully through my hair and tucked the wispy tendrils back in place. Dusting my nose with a powder puff, I gathered up my courage and hurried to report for tea.

Katherine's uncle and cousin stood as I entered the drawing room. "You're just seven minutes late," Fenton said, pulling out his pocket watch and checking the time.

Jordan frowned. "Father, Katherine has left a sick bed to join us."

"So she has. Good of you to come down, my dear," Fenton mumbled and I mentally thanked Mr. and Mrs. Diggs for covering for me.

"Are you feeling better?" Jordan asked.

"Much better," I lied, for my muscles had suddenly stiffened and I felt about a hundred years old.

"You may pour, Katherine, since your aunt is not here to do her duty," Fenton said, obviously annoyed that Beatrice would not make herself available at teatime.

I wondered why they were in London, but hesitated to ask. "Did you have a pleasant train trip, Uncle?"

"Horrendous!" he said. "Trains are filthy, unsanitary nuisances, belching out smoke, and contaminating the air, assaulting the peace with their infernal clanking and grinding. Confounded nuisances, I say!"

"We'd be isolated in Cornwall without them," Jordan argued.

"Aye, and that could only be a blessing," Fenton retorted. "All those bloody outsiders coming down, scavenging the beaches, digging up the moors. Searching for artifacts, they say. Humpf," he added with a toss of his head. "Tarleton spotted two of them just last week combing the beach right in front of Hathaway Manor. Two old biddies, riding bicycles and wearing bloomers. He tried to run them off, he said, but they threatened him."

I nearly choked on my tea. Violet and Clara! And what I wouldn't give to have heard them telling old Tarleton off.

The tea and Mrs. Diggs's delicious scones put Fenton in a better humor, and he became quite mellow and cordial, asking me how I was enjoying the city, and inquiring about where I had been.

I didn't tell him about the Music Hall, but I made the mistake of mentioning that Stuart was taking me to the Haymarket on Friday, and he said, "Excellent idea. We'll all go. Can't let Stuart monopolize Katherine, can we Jordan?"

In a way, I was relieved. Being alone with Stuart was only asking for heartaches, because in spite of all that I now knew

139

about him, I still could not trust myself to resist his charm.

Fenton finished his tea and setting the cup and saucer down, rose from his chair. Looking peevish, he took out his watch, opened it and then quickly snapped it shut. "It's getting late. They'll barely have time to dress for dinner."

"Oh, they've having dinner with Cousin Elvira," I said.

He gave me an astonished look. "Poppycock! Beatrice can't abide the old troll. They're out gallivanting with that bunch of Sybarites."

Feeling like a mischievous little tattletale, I said, "I only know what Aunt Beatrice told me, Uncle Fenton."

"Humpf."

He left the room, and Jordan said, "Father doesn't think much of London society."

I didn't care where they were or who they were with, and I certainly had no wish to be included, but I felt justified in showing them up for Katherine's sake. It would serve them right, if Fenton packed them off and sent them home. And what a blessing that would be for Sir Alex, I concluded.

"I've missed you, Katherine," Jordan said. "I never thought I'd say that, but it's true." He laughed a little nervously. "You were such a mischievous little girl, and I was so serious. Still am," he added. "I'm sure you thought me quite a bore. I hope you've changed your mind."

Anxious to avoid any chance of Jordan's showing more than a cousinly interest in me, I kept my response impersonal. "I suppose chemistry was beyond my grasp in those days, but I certainly don't find it boring now. In fact, I find your experiments fascinating."

"Thank you, Katherine," he said, plainly pleased. "You see, I've never been able to discuss my work with the family."

He hesitated, and I felt a little sorry for him. "The subject distresses Mother, and Father is only interested in results. He has no appreciation for research. The pace is too slow for him."

Then his eyes took on that strange, otherworldly look, and he stared off into space. "Fitting one tiny piece into the puzzle can make it possible for others to add on, and on, and on."

I found his intensity a little frightening, but there was no doubt in my mind that he was an able and dedicated scientist.

"It might take a hundred years, maybe five hundred," he was saying. "But eventually, we shall find the key to unlocking the mystery of the human mind!"

"A noble goal," I commented. "You should be proud to be a part of it."

He smiled, a little sadly, I thought. "Aye, the goal is a noble one. Therefore, the end must necessarily justify the means."

"Are you still working with morning glory seeds?" I asked.

"You remembered! Ah, Katherine, you are a most unusual woman." He shook his head. "No, unfortunately I've had to curtail my use of both ergot and morning glory seeds." He frowned and studied his hands. "The hallucination they produce is unusually violent and hard to control."

Clenching his hands into fists, he added, "Nevertheless, I'm convinced that these two elements can instigate a major advance for us."

He paused and then continued. "There are some who believe your American town of Salem was plagued by ergot. Hence, all the furor over witchcraft could be attributed to a fungus in the rye."

"How appalling! You mean the whole town could have been hal-hal—"

"Hallucinating. Aye, it's only a theory, but certainly not an impossible one."

"What a pity," I said.

I may have learned my history in the theater, but that only served to impress it on my mind. I can still recall the harrowing scene from *Witch of Salem* when the heroine was burned at the stake. The use of a transparency on stage made the whole thing seem real and utterly terrifying.

"I came up to London to consult with Dr. Cummings," Jordan said. "I'll be working at his sanitarium during the day, but I will be looking forward to the evenings when I can spend my time with you, Katherine."

*       *       *

141

Life became difficult for us all after Fenton's arrival. The former, relaxed atmosphere of No. 10 Bleekman Place was being stifled under rules, regulations, and restrictions. In Stuart's absence, Lord Hathaway and his clock dominated the household and all within it.

Beatrice and Willa, duly chastised, were allowed only short excursions between breakfast and teatime, and then only after asking his lordship's permission; this being the only consequence of Fenton's arrival which gave me pleasure.

As for myself, I was frustrated beyond measure. This would have been a perfect opportunity for me to spend time with Katherine and Beau, but with Fenton in the house monitoring everybody's activities, that was impossible.

Jordan was another source of worry. His budding, romantic interest in me was becoming more obvious and I didn't know what to do about it. Fenton, much to my surprise, seemed pleased.

Just when all of our nerves had reached the breaking point, "The Master," as Mrs. Diggs so charmingly referred to Stuart, returned.

We were in the midst of tea, all of us, I'm afraid, wearing bored, resentful faces, when like a breath of fresh air, Stuart breezed into the drawing room.

"Well, well. What misfortune are we mourning here?" He searched our faces in mock dismay. "Has your watch stopped, Uncle Fenton?"

Fenton gave him a disgusted look and Stuart's eyes riveted on the sullen faces of Beatrice and Willa. Snapping his fingers, he said, "It must be Sir Alex. Has he joined a monastery? Or, did he run away with a lady of the chorus?"

"That will do, Stuart," Fenton grumbled. "Have you no sense of the proprieties, running off and leaving guests to fend for themselves."

"I apologized to the ladies for leaving," Stuart replied. "It was unavoidable, but I'm here now, and we can all be one big, happy family again." Scanning the room, he said, "Did the mad scientist come? Or is my cousin still locked in his laboratory, mixing up some bubbling concoction?"

"Jordan brought a new batch of drugs up to the Sanitarium," Fenton explained. "I merely accompanied him. We shall be leaving in a few days."

Willa brightened, but Fenton fixed her with a stern eye. "All of us," he said emphatically.

She turned purple and I wouldn't have been surprised to see her go into a tantrum, but her mother quickly spoke up. "The Lighthizer Ball is next Thursday, Fenton. The girls have so been looking forward to it." She bestowed a simpering smile on me. "Dear Katherine will be coming out next year, and it wouldn't hurt for her to be seen. Just everybody will be there."

It was the first I'd heard of it, but it might be fun, I thought. At least I'll get to meet the famous Sir Alex Lighthizer.

Fenton reluctantly agreed to staying over for the ball. "But, we shall all return to Hathaway Manor on the following day," he proclaimed, like a general addressing his troops. I knew then I would not get another chance to see Katherine and Beau.

It was obvious that evening that Stuart did not appreciate Jordan's newfound interest in me, and when the tension this engendered began to get on my nerves, I pleaded a headache and retired early.

Fenton's reasons for encouraging a match between his son and myself became clear later that night when I overheard him talking to Beatrice.

Thinking everyone had retired, I was coming downstairs for a book when I heard voices in the library.

"It's the Hathaway way of keeping money in the family," Fenton said.

I would have retraced my steps at that point, but Beatrice's voice was shrill, and it carried.

"But, Katherine, of all people, Fenton. I don't like the girl, and besides, suppose she remembers something."

"All the more reason to have her married to Jordan."

Beatrice apparently made another derogatory remark that I did not catch, and Fenton answered. "Would you prefer that we killed Katherine then, and *inherited* her fortune?"

143

He followed the proposal with a hearty laugh, and I could only hope that he was being facetious!

I'll never get to sleep now. Why did they have to be in the library, I thought, wanting more than ever to forget my own problems by reading someone else's.

Passing through the entry hall, I remembered I had hidden a half-finished romance novel in the credenza several weeks ago. It was a silly story, and I was rather ashamed of being caught reading it. But it'll do for now, I thought.

Stooping down in front of the massive piece of furniture, I opened the large double doors. My novel was just where I had stashed it, but someone else had hidden something in the credenza, too.

The cloth wrapped package was filthy and looked like it had been rolling in a gutter, but I immediately recognized my old petticoat!

# Chapter 12

I touched the bundle gingerly, just to be sure the doll was still wrapped inside it, and when I felt the hard little body, I shrank back, suddenly afraid.

Who had put it there, and why?

Book forgotten, I closed the doors quickly and hurried back upstairs. In the privacy of my room, I paced the floor, my brain whirling with questions that had no answers. "The whole thing is bizarre," I thought.

Someone snuck this doll into my room, and for what purpose, I have yet to figure out. I showed it to Katherine, and she was upset by it, but only to the extent that it reminded her of a *recent* acquaintance. And finally, someone went to enough trouble to retrieve it from the gutter and hide it in the credenza.

And why the credenza, of all places, I mused. Unless that was but a temporary hiding place. Of course, that's it. Whoever brought the doll into the house had to conceal it immediately and the credenza was handy. Later when no one was about, they would retrieve the bundle and find a safer hiding place for it.

Following that line of thinking, I sadly concluded that Stuart again was the logical suspect, for if Fenton or Jordan had placed the doll in the credenza, they would have done so on their arrival three days ago.

That would have allowed them plenty of time to move the doll to a safer place, most likely a locked trunk, but Stuart had only arrived this evening, and knowing us all to be in the drawing room, he stashed the doll in the credenza for safe keeping.

If it's gone in the morning, I'll know for sure, I told myself.

Opening the window, I breathed deeply, and the fragrance of springtime was in the air. A gentle breeze cooled my fevered brow and moonlight cast a soft glow on the budding trees lining the street. How could treachery dwell in such genteel surroundings, I wondered.

Oh, Stuart, I thought. If only you could really be my charming Mr. Cousin, and I could meet you all over again as India Chantelle. With no class distinctions and no secrets between us, we should be free to fall in love.

Looking up at the star-studded sky, I mused, We'd go dancing on a moonbeam, touch a star, and drift happily ever after on a fluffy pink cloud.

A fantasy worthy of a poet, I thought, smiling through my tears. But I'll confess, I'd settle for a wedding ring like my mother did, a one-room flat, and some beautiful, dark haired babies with Stuart's slate grey eyes and mischievous smile.

Every day after that, I checked the credenza, but the bundle remained in place. Perhaps he has decided to leave it here, I thought. After all, as far as Stuart is concerned, it's as good a hiding place as any.

He was noticeably put out when he discovered that Fenton had officiously arranged for the whole family to accompany us to the Haymarket. "Why didn't the old goat stay in Cornwall?" he fumed in one of our now rare moments alone.

"Perhaps it's best this way," I said.

We were lingering over coffee at the breakfast table; the others all having finished and left the room.

He put down his cup and regarded me with eyes dark as thunder. "What do you mean by that?"

Recognizing the signs and wanting to avoid an argument,

146

I rose and mumbled a hurried response. "Nothing, we'll be leaving soon, and—"

"Sit down, Katherine." And something in the tone of his voice made me comply. "You've been avoiding me ever since Jordan arrived. What's going on?"

"Nothing," I said, not wanting to argue with him, but feeling a perverse pleasure at his jealousy.

"Don't tell me that. You let him monopolize you every evening. You sit in a corner, heads together, talking about drugs and planting flower seeds." His eyes flashed, and he shook his head. "It's the dumbest conversation I ever heard!"

*"Overheard,* you mean! Have you nothing better to do than eavesdrop on other people's conversations?" I retorted.

His face turned red. "Eavesdrop! We were all in the same room. For your information, that could hardly be considered eavesdropping!"

"And for your information," I countered like a child arguing with another child, "the seeds were morning glories, and you don't plant them, you ingest them!" His raucous laughter only spurred me on. "Don't put down what you don't understand, Stuart Cousin. Jordan is a scientist!"

I don't know why I called him Stuart Cousin, but for some strange reason, it deflated his anger.

"Ah, Katherine," he said sadly. "If only I could be your Stuart Cousin, and not your Cousin Stuart." Our eyes met, and locked for a moment, and then he said, "Be careful of Jordan, Katherine. And don't under any circumstances go to his laboratory!"

I stood up, and flounced out of the room before he could detain me again.

"Katherine warned me against Stuart. Stuart warned me against Jordan. Oh, why did I have to get mixed up with this insane family!"


After that brief and unresolved discussion, I noticed that Stuart made a conscious effort to intrude whenever Jordan tried to engage me in conversation, and our night at the Haymarket was so marked by tension that I scarcely

147

followed the play.

Fenton, in another show of orchestrating the evening, made reservations for a late night supper at the Claridge Hotel, and the memories that evoked for me were poignant ones. It seemed like a hundred years ago that Stuart and I had danced and fallen in love in this very hotel and I wondered if the memories were as vivid for him as they were for me.

Probably not, I decided. Most likely his memories of the hotel are crowded with many faces, and mine is only one in a long chain of Stuart Hathaway's passing fancies.

I was relieved when the evening finally came to an end. In another week, we would be leaving London and Stuart behind, for he was staying, despite his earlier threat of returning with us; a jest, no doubt made with Beatrice in mind.

The days that followed were devoted exclusively to preparation for the Lighthizer Ball. Beatrice and Willa, with myself in tow, scoured the shops of London in pursuit of any accoutrement that might enhance Willa's chances of enticing the elusive Sir Alex to the altar.

We visited an exclusive wig shop and Willa acquired a false chignon and a generous supply of frisettes to compensate for her own thin crop of hair. To adorn this magnificent illusion, she purchased sprays of tiny satin roses to entwine around it.

Perfume from Paris, skin cream from Sweden; no embellishment escaped their notice, and fool that I am, I looked at Willa, and offered a suggestion. "You're too pale, Willa, but a little makeup could rectify that."

"Makeup!" Beatrice exclaimed in a shocked voice. "Only tarts wear makeup, Katherine."

"That's not so," I answered. "Lots of fashionable women in America wear it, but subtly, so that it appears as nothing more than natural beauty."

"Disgraceful!" Beatrice said, but Willa regarded me slyly. "Do you know how to apply it, Katherine?"

"Yes," I said, taking the plunge, and for the life of me, I don't know why, except that she suddenly seemed rather pathetic. "If you wish, I'll come to your room tonight, and we can try it out."

Beatrice was skeptical, but Willa was game, and if nothing else, I had to admire her persistence.

Using knowledge gained by watching countless actresses tone down bad features and play up good ones, I applied these same techniques to Willa, but with a lighter touch so that she would look natural rather than theatrical.

The result was a marked improvement and Willa was delighted. Even Beatrice had to admit that no one would suspect Willa was wearing cosmetics, but she cautioned us not to let Lord Hathaway find out.

At last the fateful night arrived. Wanting Willa to shine, I wore my own peach silk gown, made over by findings from the Wardrobe Department. Wearing pearls, the only jewelry I owned and carrying the fan Stuart had bought me, I descended the staircase to find both Hathaway cousins waiting for me in the hall.

Diggs had commandeered two hacks which waited at the curb. One was a four-wheeler and the other a hansom which seated only two passengers.

"Katherine and I will take the hansom," Stuart said to Fenton. "You'll be more comfortable in the growler, Uncle."

But Fenton was not fooled. "Nonsense, your aunt and I will take the hansom. You young people go together."

Stuart made sure he sat next to me, and Jordan reluctantly sat beside his sister.

"You look different tonight, Willa," Stuart commented, and I prayed he would not say anything flippant. "More sophisticated somehow. Don't you agree, Jordan?"

Jordan gave his sister a disinterested look. "Very nice," he said.

Willa looked pleased, and I found myself hoping that tonight Sir Alex would finally make her an offer.

Overdressed as usual, she wore a pink chiffon creation embellished with flounces and bows and her flat bosom looked weighted down by the long antique necklace that hung around her neck, but the blush on her cheeks was becoming and her thin lips were enhanced by the touch of rouge I had applied with a delicate stroke.

The Lighthizer estate was situated just on the outskirts of the city, and my excitement mounted as we approached a stately mansion, blazing with lights, its driveway sprinkled with handsome carriages.

Beautiful music drifted out across the lawn to us, and I forgot for the moment all my troubles and looked forward with pleasure to attending my first, and probably my only, ball.

The house was the most magnificent I had ever seen, making Hathaway Manor appear seedy in comparison. We entered a hall lavish with frescoed plaster work picked out in gold. Two butlers, one on either side, collected our wraps and cards, and we were escorted to the ballroom by a liveried footman who announced us by name to the more than one hundred elegantly attired guests.

We descended a short marble staircase to the huge ballroom lit by sparkling cystal chandeliers where we waited to greet our hostess Lady Lighthizer in the receiving line.

She was a formidable-looking woman, as tall as Beatrice with a florid complexion and a mass of mahogany colored hair that had probably once been red.

She greeted Beatrice and Willa with enthusiasm, and it was obvious that she, too, was anxious to promote a match between the two families. "How charming you look tonight, Willa, dear. Alex won't be able to take his eyes off you." No doubt she had already heard about me, for she eyed me suspiciously and said, "So this is the American cousin! So nice to meet you, Katherine."

"Thank you for inviting me, Lady Lighthizer," I said, feeling suddenly awkward and outclassed. I had managed to scrape by thus far, but this was a formal ball and I had absolutely no conception of the protocol involved.

A portly man with flaming red hair suddenly appeared beside Lady Lighthizer. "Ah, Alex here you are," his mother said. "Doesn't Willa look charming?"

He peered myopically at me through thick, horn-rimmed spectacles. "This is Katherine!"

His astonishment was so obvious I was certain he'd been

led to expect a hag with no teeth and a wart on her nose.

Willa instantly stepped between us. "My cousin, Katherine," she said, and giving me a murderous look, mumbled, "Sir Alex Lighthizer, our host."

That said, she reached for his hand and pulled him onto the dance floor.

I heard Stuart chuckle behind me, and then I felt his arm encircle my waist. "An excellent idea. Shall we dance, Katherine?"

The gesture and his casual manner smacked of ownership and it riled me. "I don't feel like dancing now," I said.

Jordan, standing on the other side of me, indicated a secluded alcove with comfortable chairs banked by palms.

"Let's sit over there. We can watch the dancers, and I'll get you a glass of punch, Katherine."

I could sense Stuart's anger. "In that case, you'll excuse me. When I come to a ball, I like to dance."

He drifted away and the next time I saw him, he was dancing with a small blonde who was gazing up at him with adoring eyes.

I fanned myself rapidly, and the most outrageous notion popped into my head. I want to flirt with every man in the room, have them all one by one whirl me about the floor while Stuart, consumed with jealousy, watches from the sidelines.

"Miss Katherine, may I have the honor of this dance?"

The words jolted me out of my reverie, and I turned to find Sir Alex Lighthizer standing in front of me.

With his thick glasses, he rather resembled a giant toad dressed in evening clothes. I started to refuse, and then thought better of it. After all, he is our host. It would probably be considered rude to refuse him, and I certainly don't want to show myself up by committing a social blunder.

Imitating the simpering smiles I saw all around me, I thanked him and let him escort me to the dance floor.

Holding me stiffly, he stared down into my face. "Upon my word, Miss Katherine, you are quite the loveliest gel I've ever seen." And blushing to the roots of his fiery red hair, he added awkwardly, "Please don't take offense. I'm not usually so bold, but I've been carried away by your beauty."

Oh, no, I thought. Sir Alex is the last man I need to impress!

"You are most kind, sir, but have you noticed how charming our Willa looks this evening? I declare every gentleman in the room is fascinated by her."

Over his shoulder, I caught a glimpse of Willa and Beatrice standing on the sidelines. If looks could kill, I'd be dead on the spot, I thought.

"Willa? Aye, charming gel. My mother's most fond of her," he said, squeezing my hand and holding me a little closer.

Much to my relief, the dance finally ended and I was overjoyed to see Jordan waiting in the alcove for me.

"Thank you, Sir Alex." Glancing up, I feigned surprise. "There's my cousin with our punch."

He released my hand and murmured, "It was my pleasure, Miss Katherine. I'll be back to claim another dance after you have refreshed yourself."

Not if I can avoid it, I thought, reaching out to Jordan like a lifeline. "How nice, you have our punch. Let's sit down and just be spectators."

My eyes scanned the floor, looking for Stuart, and when I found him, he was surrounded by a bevy of debutantes. Like a sultan with his harem, I thought, quickly turning away and concentrating my full attention on Jordan.

We finished our punch, and Jordan said, "I'm a poor excuse for a dancer, but I'd love to have this waltz with you, Katherine."

"I thought you'd never ask," I said, wanting to put him at ease for I sensed a tenseness in him tonight, and I thought he looked even paler than usual.

He didn't have Stuart's natural rhythm or smooth self-confidence, but he wasn't a bad dancer, and I rather imagined he had learned the steps and then memorized them like a scientific formula.

We were halfway to circling the floor when I felt him miss a step, and sag against me. Looking up, I found him deathly pale, and beads of perspiration glistened on his brow. "I'm sorry, Katherine. Would you mind . . ."

I took him by the hand and led him from the floor. "Let's sit down," I said, and conscious of the fragile male ego, added, "I was feeling a little faint out there."

His glassy eyes held a vacant stare and his pupils had all but disappeared, giving him that strange, alien look. He gripped my hand and spoke hurriedly with a panic that bordered on hysteria. "Katherine, I must leave. It's nothing to concern yourself about."

"But, Jordan, you look ill."

He shook his head vigorously. "No, I'm all right. Please, I apologize, but it can't be helped. You must say nothing to the others. I want your word on that. Do you understand?"

I nodded, feeling helpless to do otherwise and he hurried off, pursued as it were by his own invisible demons.

Feeling vaguely disturbed, and wondering if I should have insisted on alerting Fenton, or even Stuart, I looked up just in time to see Sir Alex heading my way.

Counting on the man's poor eyesight to effect my escape, I quickly ducked behind a massive display of palms and held my breath. The whole thing was so utterly ridiculous, like a scene from some bawdy French farce, that I almost laughed.

He looked around in complete amazement, took his glasses off, wiped them with his handkerchief and then put them back on again. Finally convinced that I had indeed disappeared in thin air, he placed his hands in his pockets, and rocked back and forth on his heels.

Caught in my own trap, I stood a prisoner behind the palms waiting for him to leave when in typical farce fashion, Lady Lighthizer arrived.

"There you are, Alex. I'm simply appalled at your behavior—dancing with that hussy, Katherine Hathaway and leaving poor Willa alone."

"And I shall dance again with Katherine Hathaway, Mother. In fact, if I have my way, I shall marry Katherine Hathaway!"

"You have lost your mind," Lady Lighthizer exclaimed. "Have you no sense of honor, no sense of duty?"

"You want me to marry a Hathaway, Mother? I pick Katherine."

Afraid to bat an eye, lest I betray my hiding place, I listened to this exchange with horror. Oh, Lord, I thought, on top of everything else, why do I have to be plagued with Sir Alex?

"Well, you can just unpick her," Lady Lighthizer commanded. "Katherine's to wed Jordan, and heaven help him!" She leaned slightly forward and lowered her voice. "Leopards don't change their spots, Alex. Katherine was a hellion and still is in spite of that angelic face!"

I shrank back in horror as I saw Stuart approach and bow. "A charming ball, Lady Lighthizer. I'm honored to be invited."

She smiled coyly and wafted her fan over her ample bosom. "Always a pleasure to entertain a personable young man." Then she giggled like a simpleton and asked, "How many hearts have you broken tonight, you naughty boy?"

"You flatter me, Lady Lighthizer. All your lady guests are safe with me, I assure you. But, have you seen my young cousin, Katherine?"

"No, but we were just speaking of her," Alex said eagerly.

"The naughty child is probably hiding somewhere," Stuart said. "I've been trying to keep an eye on her. She's rather skittish, you see." He laughed indulgently. "A pretty little thing, but quite a handful, she is."

Lady Lighthizer gave her son a smug look that said, "You see? Mother always knows best."

"I'll walk around and have a look for her," Alex said.

"That's good of you, old man. I'd appreciate it."

Mortified beyond words, I couldn't wait for them all to leave so I could escape. I was beginning to feel claustrophobic and the palms were making my nose itch. Oh, God, don't let me sneeze, I prayed.

Alex and his mother walked off, both in different directions, and Stuart's grinning face appeared through the potted palms.

"Ah, there you are, Katherine. Everybody's been looking for you." He raised an eyebrow in his exasperating way. "I've

154

heard of wallflowers, but isn't this a little extreme?"

I stepped out and confronted him. "You're impossible, Stuart, telling the Lighthizers all those outrageous lies about me."

"Oh," he said. "Were they lies? Perhaps then, you should tell me the truth, Katherine."

"I'll tell you nothing," I said, and started to leave, but he caught me by the arm.

"Here comes your latest admirer to claim a dance. What'll it be, Katherine? Alex or me?"

"Get me out of here, Stuart," I said. "Willa will be furious."

"Come on, then."

They were playing a polka, and grabbing me around the waist, he whisked me off my feet, twirling me around and around until we had advanced to the other side of the room.

French doors opened out to a flagstone terrace that overlooked the garden, and as the music slowed and drifted into a waltz, he danced me outside onto our own private dance floor under the stars.

Holding me close, and with his lips brushing my ear, he whispered, "This feels right, having you in my arms again."

"And didn't all your other ladies feel right?" I asked.

"No. Some were too skinny. Some were too fat." He rubbed his hand over my waist, and his touch ignited a spark within me. "You fit my arms just right."

He smiled down at me, and I felt my foolish heart begin to melt.

"Some were too tall. Some were too short." Pressing my head down on his chest, he said, "See, your head just fits under my chin." I looked up and met his eyes. "Your lips fit mine just perfectly, too. Let me show you, Katherine."

Time stood still under the magic of his kiss. I forgot that this love could never be, forgot who I was and who he was.

Let us have these precious moments, I prayed. All too soon, they'll be gone, and then I shall have only the memories to last me for the rest of my life.

Arm in arm, we walked down the garden path on a night made for love. A new moon beamed down on us and stars flickered in a black velvet sky. A gentle breeze brought us a fragrance of lilacs, and we sat on a stone bench and kissed. Hypnotized by a force I could no longer control, I let his hands caress me, for we would be leaving for Cornwall on the morrow and I didn't know if I would ever see Stuart Hathaway again.

# Chapter 13

With stars still in my eyes, I awakened to relive every precious moment in that beautiful, moonlight drenched garden. My lips still burned with Stuart's kisses, and my body tingled with the magic of his touch; those strong, gentle hands that could leave me weak with desire and aching to surrender.

Dancing on a pink cloud, I hummed and waltzed around the room; tossing gowns, slippers, and stockings haphazardly into my trunk. Shoving it closed, I took a deep breath and then laughed aloud at my own stupidity. I was still wearing my nightgown, and my traveling suit was packed inside!

Too happy to be annoyed, I patiently unpacked, repacked, and calmly dressed myself. Then checking my watch, I hurried out of the room. Stuart rose early, and I wanted to see him alone before the others came downstairs.

Shoes in hand, I smiled to myself, recalling Beatrice and Willa sneaking down these same steps, just as quietly to avoid arousing me.

Glancing cautiously over the balcony, I was overjoyed to see Stuart come out of the dining room and enter the hall. On the verge of attracting his attention, I paused when I saw him stoop down and open the credenza.

Taking a step back, I held my breath. Let it not be there, I prayed. Or if it is, let him pull it out and by his actions prove himself innocent to me. Let him give it a puzzled look, perhaps unwrap it, and then let me hear him say something typical like "What the hell is this doing here?"

But, he did none of those things. With tears stinging my eyes, I watched him as he matter-of-factly removed the doll, still wrapped in the petticoat, and closed the credenza. He made no move to look inside the bundle. Why should he? I asked myself. He knows exactly what is inside that petticoat.

I saw him put on his hat, and then I quickly returned to my room. Looking out the window, I watched him walk down Bleekman Street with the bundle tucked securely under his arm, and suddenly, like sand castles under a violent wave, my fantasy world crumbled and was washed away.

Stuart's deception reduced all my beautiful memories to cheap thrills, and my cheeks burned as I recalled the liberties I had allowed him to take, justifying them to myself in the name of love.

I stayed in my room until I heard the others going downstairs and then I joined them in the dining room for breakfast.

Jordan sat hunched over his tea, looking miserable, and Beatrice said, "You must be coming down with *la grippe.*" Then she sighed and placed her hand over her heart, a gesture that vividly bespoke her inner thoughts. It wasn't enough that she had to contend with Willa's disappointment, now Jordan had to be sick!

He got up then and left the table, and my thoughts turned to another puzzling aspect of Jordan's affliction. He had left the Lighthizer Ball because he had felt unwell, and yet he had not come home and gone to bed as one would naturally assume.

Unable to sleep myself, I had watched the sunrise, and alerted by the click of the gate, I had looked down to see Jordan, still attired in evening clothes, quietly enter the house.

Where had he gone? I wondered. And why?

I drank my tea, but my throat was too tight to swallow anything solid, and looking at the sideboard with its untouched buffet, I saw that I was not the only one to be leaving London with shattered dreams.

Willa shoved her cup and saucer aside and stared gloomily into space. Her failure to wangle a proposal out of Sir Alex was a stich in her side, and somehow I knew the blame for it all would be leveled at me.

Beatrice suddenly threw down her napkin and stood up. Her voice dripping with sarcasm, she said, "Come along, Willa. We've wasted enough time dawdling over breakfast. Your father can't wait to get us out of London, you know."

I felt sorry for them. Fenton's arrival had certainly put a damber on their fun, and now they were being forced to return home before reeling in the catch of the season.

I heard Stuart's voice then, and not wanting him to find me alone, I quickly followed Beatrice and Willa outside.

Diggs and the cabbie, hindered by Fenton's supervision, were nevertheless managing to pile our considerable luggage into one carriage, while another stood curbside, waiting to transport the five of us to Paddington Station.

Stuart, wearing a puzzled expression, tried repeatedly to engage me in conversation, but I barely answered him, and then only in brief, staccato-voiced sentences.

All the affection I had felt, and so foolishly demonstrated last night in the Lighthizer Gardens, had evaporated upon my discovery of his treachery.

Jordan had already taken his place inside the carriage and Stuart dutifully embraced his aunt and cousin. "Have a safe trip, ladies." And then with a devilish smile at Beatrice he added, "Don't fret, Aunt. I'll be down soon for another long visit."

Infuriated by his guile, I wanted to slap him when he turned to me and said, "Don't you fret, either, Katherine. We shan't he parted long. I'll get down to Cornwall as soon as possible."

"Don't come on my account," I said. "I'll be busy helping Jordan in his laboratory." I don't know what possessed me to say that. Jordan had not even hinted at such an arrangement, and I certainly had no intentions of suggesting it.

I was not prepared though for Stuart's violent reaction. With a curt, "Wait for Katherine a minute," to Uncle

Fenton, he grabbed my arm in a bruising grip and propelled me back inside the house.

In the foyer, he turned on me with a vengeance. "I don't know what's gotten into you, except perhaps you've reverted to form. Last night you were one person; today, you're another. But I'm telling you right now. Stay away from Jordan's laboratory!"

His eyes glared at me like smoldering ashes, and grabbing me by the shoulders, he shook me. "Do you understand me, Katherine. That's an order!"

"An order!" I shrieked. "What right do you have to give me orders? I'll do as I please."

He released me suddenly, and searching my face, he shook his head. "I don't know you, Katherine, but maybe Anabelle does. Shall I ask her what she knows?"


Traveling through the beautiful English countryside, I saw whitewashed cottages with their charming little gardens speed by. Sadly I recalled that the last time I had traveled in this direction, Stuart had shared the compartment with me.

My thoughts turned then to that strange conversation in the foyer. Who was Anabelle? I wondered. The name was not familiar to me. Certainly Katherine had never mentioned it. I didn't know of anybody at Hathaway Manor by that name either. But then, I only knew some of the people by their last names. Mrs. Janney, for instance!

"Anabelle Janney," I rolled the name over on my tongue. But, I found it hard to reconcile old stone-faced Mrs. Janney with a name like Anabelle.

Who could she be? And more importantly, what could she know that Stuart would threaten me with her? I can't ask anyone at Hathaway Manor, I thought, for to do so would brand me an imposter. Of course, I could always ask Katherine, but there is no way for me to get in touch with her.

And would she tell me the truth even if I asked? After all, Katherine had been more evasive than truthful about a lot of things. Sweet, but self-centered child that she was, she was not going to tell me anything that might jeopardize her chance to play actress.

I sighed. *Oh, what a tangled web we weave, when first we practice to deceive!*

I turned from the window and my eyes rested on Jordan. He was sleeping, and his dreams must have been tormented ones, for every now and then his body would twitch convulsively, as if he were trying to throw off the demons that haunted him.

I did not understand Jordan, and sometimes when the pupils of his eyes disappeared and he took on that alien look, he frightened me. I had the strange feeling that he was not really of this world, but he had never shown me anything but kindness, which was more than I could say for all the other Hathaways.

Beatrice and Willa sat beside him. Too angry to make conversation, they also dozed. I know they blamed me for last night's fiasco, and were it not for Fenton's presence, I'm sure they would have given me the tongue lashing they thought I deserved.

Too depressed to care, I made no attempt to justify myself in their eyes. I was sick of the Hathaways, all of them. I was fed up with their mysteries and tired of their secrets.

I just wanted to go home, see my sisters and spend some time with real people for a change. Maybe I'd stay in Ohio, forget the theater, and find work as a dressmaker.

I could be a doting aunt to my nieces and nephews, I mused. Just because I'd never marry and have children of my own didn't mean I couldn't enjoy other people's. Beau can go back to the theater alone; he doesn't need me anymore. He's gotten along just fine without me in London.

Stealing a glance sideways at Fenton, I saw that he was still engrossed in his book. It was a thick, heavy volume and the print was so small I couldn't even decipher the title, but I imagined it to be about economics, since that was the only subject of interest to him.

The book also served to isolate Fenton from the rest of us, and I'm sure that was its purpose. He was still out of sorts with Beatrice and Willa for what he considered their frivolous behavior in London, and I gathered he was disgusted with Jordan for being ill.

The Lord and Master of Hathaway Manor was not a tolerant man, and I suddenly wondered what would happen should Fenton discover he was harboring an imposter in his home.

He slammed the heavy volume shut, and I nearly jumped out of my skin.

Fixing me with a steely eye, he said in a cold voice, "Nervous, Katherine?"

Was he mocking me? I wondered. Perhaps he already knows, and is just playing a cat and mouse game.

"No, I'm not nervous," I answered. "Just tired, Uncle."

He said nothing more, and in a short time, we were pulling into Penzance. I was relieved to see that Fenton had wired ahead, for two carriages from the manor were waiting to transport us, luggage and all, home in comfort.

Jordan looked terrible, and as we were ready to step into the carriage, Beatrice turned to her husband with a worried frown. "The doctor's right here in Penzance. Shouldn't we . . . ?"

Jordan held up his hand in protest, and Fenton answered curtly. "Get into the carriage, Beatrice. He can rest when we get home."

The ride across the moors proved to be smoother, but no less harrowing than my first trip in the fly. This time because of my concern for Jordan.

Wedged between his mother and sister, he appeared to be in a coma, eyes closed, and lips parted with a thin trickle of saliva oozing from the corners of his mouth and running down his neck.

I was reminded of a scene I had witnessed once in a hot, little Texas town. A crowd of people had stood in the square, watching a large dog in his death throes, panting pitifully as he lay in the road.

"Stand back," a man shouted. "He's foaming at the mouth!"

162

A woman grabbed me by the arm. "Don't get no closer, little girl. That poor, dumb animal's plumb mad!"

The carriage lurched as it climbed the steep hill to Hathaway Manor, and Jordan suddenly opened his eyes and stared vacantly at us. Not wanting to embarrass him, I turned to look out the window and caught the look of disgust on his father's face.

The carriage jolted to a stop, and servants poured out of the house. Fenton stepped outside and bellowed out orders; the first, to all of our reliefs being, "Assist Master Jordan into the house, and get him into bed immediately!"

I felt like going to bed myself. My head ached and I was exhausted physically and mentally.

Just as I was wondering how I should cope with that rigid Hathaway ritual known as four o'clock tea, Beatrice surprised me by announcing it would be cancelled because of Jordan's illness and our late arrival. Tarleton's puckered-up old face told us in no uncertain terms how he felt about that.

I imagined him pouting, as he refolded the cloths and returned the silverware to its drawer. This was his big act, and Beatrice had just given him the hook. Small wonder the old fuss-budget was upset!

Dinner was served at eight o'clock, and I was shocked to find Jordan present and looking completely recovered.

He smiled and scoffed at Beatrice's comment that he should have stayed in bed another day. "I'm fine, Mother, really I am."

Fenton said, "Humpf," and Jordan returned his father's grunt with a defiant scowl. I thought his reaction was a little out of proportion to the offense, and it surprised me.

As if to punish us for skipping tea, Tarleton took an eternity to serve dinner. His every movement seemed calculated to consume time, and given the state of our collective dispositions, I think we all could have applauded the arrival of the finger bowls.

I saw the summer stretch ahead like the long run of a bad play. Without Stuart to liven up my days with his sparkling wit and engaging personality, Hathaway Manor would be devoid of excitement, I thought. But I was wrong, as I would later discover!

Weeks passed, and I found that I missed Stuart terribly. But, I reminded myself, the man I had fallen in love with had never even existed. All along, he was wearing a mask, a charming one, to be sure, but his intentions had never been honorable. And like a fool, I had come close to letting him seduce me.

The pain will lessen as time goes by, I told myself, but it didn't. I pictured myself an old maid in my sixties, still stargazing and daydreaming about the handsome cad who had broken my foolish heart.

Every day I promised not to think about him, but every night I did, and I would cry and finally fall into a deep, exhausted sleep that would last until morning.

But one night something woke me, and I sat up suddenly.

Fear, irrational but strong, wrapped itself around me like the coil of a snake, and not to be fooled twice, I ran my hand cautiously over the opposite side of the bed. There was nothing there, and with a sigh of relief, I lay down again.

It started out as a moan so low that at first I thought I had imagined it. As it grew in intensity, I sat up and looked around me.

Moonlight cast an eerie glow on the room, but I saw nothing amiss, and thinking it to be an animal outside, I lay back down and tried to go back to sleep.

A loud shriek split the air and jarred my nerves like chalk screeching across a blackboard. I jumped, reached blindly for the lamp and sent it crashing to the floor. It broke, and the glass shattered like an explosion in my ear.

I sat up and listened, trying to pinpoint the direction of the moans. They were not in the room, of that I was certain, and I finally determined them to be coming from a position several feet below, and directly under my bed.

I recalled Willa's warning that Duncan Hathaway's ghost might be paying me a visit. I wondered if she, Beatrice, or both of them together were trying to frighten me into leaving

Hathaway Manor. I can't leave this house fast enough, I mused, but nobody's going to scare me away with ghost stories!

The sounds grew fainter and softer until they ceased altogether, but I did not court sleep. I waited patiently, my eyes peeled on the window. When daylight came, I got to work.

First, I cleaned up the broken glass from the floor; then, I got down on my hands and knees and crawled under the high poster bed.

Running my hands over the wooden floor, I traced the square that had been cut so perfectly that it would have escaped notice even if the bed had not been placed over it.

The trapdoor was just wide enough for a man to squeeze through, but in order to examine it, the heavy, solid mahogany bed would have to be moved. This required time, and an absolute assurance of privacy, for what could I say if someone came in and caught me?

I decided to wait until after breakfast when I should have more time. Fenton and Jordan would be gone by then, Fenton to badger his poor tenants and Jordan to work in his laboratory. The female Hathaways never bothered about me anyway. They would simply assume I was engaged in one of my more peculiar habits, like beachcombing or bird watching, and be grateful for my absence.

My real problem, I suspected, was going to be Maureen. We had resumed our friendly relationship after my return from London, and I was no longer suspicious of the girl, but I really couldn't trust her to keep this a secret.

Being Irish, Maureen would embrace the ghost theory with open arms, and there would be no way she could keep from regaling the other servants with such a delicious yarn.

But luck was with me, or so I thought at the time, for everything fell very neatly into place. Fenton and Jordan were already gone, and Beatrice and Willa informed me they would be attending a gathering in Newquay.

"It's a sewing bee," Beatrice explained. "I don't imagine you'd like to come along, Katherine, since you don't sew."

The irony of her backhanded invitation struck me rather funny. I'll be back to sewing soon enough, I thought, and not for my own amusement.

"You're right, Aunt Beatrice. I'm afraid I wouldn't feel comfortable at a sewing bee." I returned her false smile. "Thank you for asking me, and do give the ladies my apologies, but I plan to do some exploring today."

As soon as their carriage had pulled away, I rang for Maureen, and sent her into Penzance on an errand. "Danny can drive you," I said, making her blush with pleasure. The young groom was a handsome lad, and I doubted if Maureen would rush home.

I hurried upstairs to my room, my heart beating with wild excitement. I had no earthly idea what I would find when I opened that door, but I wasn't afraid.

I should have been, but at the time, I was more curious than concerned.

The old-fashioned bed must have weighed a ton, and I pushed and shoved with all my might before moving it so much as an inch. Grunting and groaning like a thing alive, it gradually gave way to my efforts, and the trapdoor was exposed.

Soaked with a most unladylike sweat, I pushed the hair out of my eyes and knelt down on the floor. I saw no handle or latch, and I suddenly wondered if this was one of those insidious devices that the unsuspecting stood upon and thus were dispatched forthwith to their doom.

I shrank back a little and shook my head. I refused to stand on that square! The thought that others, in another time, might have done so, and plunged to their doom haunted me, and my courage began to waver.

But this is 1895, I told myself. Relics of more violent times abound in a house as old as this, but such things are obsolete in an advanced society.

I laid my hand on the square and pushed, at first gingerly, and then when I heard a squeak, a little harder. The door swung inward and I found myself staring down at a flight of steep, stone steps.

I don't know why, but I felt a compulsion to find out where they led. Stuffing the pockets of my skirt with matches and a candle, I lowered myself into the hole in the floor.

There was a slight drop to the first step, but I never hesitated. I had a phobia about heights, but this didn't bother me.

The light from above did not carry far, and I lit the candle and held it out before me. Nothing but endless steps, leading down, I was sure, to a dungeon underneath the house.

The Hathaways had been smugglers, I recalled. I supposed this concealed stairway had been used in their clandestine operations.

Suddenly I regretted coming. What did I expect to find?

The air was growing dank and a musty odor rose up from below me. Looking down, I saw that the steps did indeed end in a dungeon, as I had deduced, but I was not prepared for what I found there.

Iron chains were attached to the wall directly in front of me. No doubt, they had been used to restrain prisoners in an earlier time, but I froze in horror. I realized they had been used again, and as recently as last night, for the floor where I stood was spattered with blood and the stains were still fresh!

I backed away, feeling a nameless panic rise up like bile in my throat. This was no prank perpetrated by jealous women to scare me away. There was something diabolically evil here.

I held the candle high, and my eyes traveled around the room. It was a small cell, an *oubliette,* the French would call it. An open door led out to a wider section of the dungeon, but it, too, appeared to be empty.

I looked up at the steep steps. I decided they must have been put in at a later time, when smuggling had become more important to the Hathaways than taking their enemies prisoner.

But who was chained here last night? I wondered, and where is he now?

A noise, coming from the top of the stairs, sent chills down my spine. Someone's up there, I thought, and right now, concealed in those shadows, he's watching me like a tiger stalking his prey. And you, like a fool, are helping him, I told myself.

Taking a deep breath, I blew out my candle, and immediately plunged myself into a deep, black void.

> "Night of evil,
> Night of sin,
> Wherein, a thousand demons lurk.
> In every dark corner,
> Behind every black tree,
> They wait my love, wait for thee!"

Oh, God, I thought. I can't get back. He's hiding on those steps, and he'll keep right on waiting. *Waiting for me!*

# Chapter 14

There must be another exit, I thought, recalling that before extinguishing the light, I had noticed an open door leading from the cell to another part of the dungeon. If I could just get to that other area, I might have a chance to escape while my stalker waited, expecting me to take the steps, I calculated.

Like a blind person, I groped my way slowly, feeling my other senses heighten to compensate for my loss of sight.

I sniffed, picking up sea smells in the musty, stagnant air that surrounded me, and my ears caught the faint, but unmistakable, sound of water dripping somewhere. Reaching out with my hand, I touched something solid and felt the rough texture of a warped wooden door.

Sliding my hand alongside it, I passed outside the cell and into the dungeon. When I was sure that my faint light could not be seen from the stairway, I struck a match and relit the candle.

The cellar was large, but I only gave it a cursory glance. I was looking for a way out, and later, I could recall only its many doors and my own desperate feelings about them. Where did they lead? To other cells, a torture chamber, maybe? Perhaps there was even a snake pit!

Never lifting my eyes from the ground, I moved cautiously toward the closest door, and setting my candle on the ground, I grasped the handle with both hands and pulled.

The rusty old hinges shrieked with outrage, and I found

myself looking into a long, tunnellike passage. Not knowing where it led, I entered it without hesitation, conscious only of the fact that I was distancing myself from whomever or whatever lay in wait for me on the stairs.

I hadn't gone far though when I realized with mounting panic that I was no longer in the dungeon; no longer even in the house. I was in a cave!

Water dripped from the ceiling and slithered down the walls in between the rocks. It splashed on my head and ran down my face. Brushing it away, I shivered.

Should I try to find another exit, or take my chances in the cave? Perhaps he is no longer waiting on the steps. He could be in the dungeon right now, searching for me. Do I dare confront him?

*Or her,* a voice inside me added. *It could be Mrs. Janney, you know.*

I didn't want to think that, and I had deliberately avoided all speculation about the identity of my stalker for that very reason. Somehow, confronting Mrs. Janney on those steps or anywhere in that dungeon would be so terrifying that I had refused to consider it a possibility.

I faced that fear now, and forced myself to make a decision. Which way to go?

I held the candle high, and in its flickering light, I saw something back there, something I had missed that encouraged me to go forward.

A lantern hung above the door I had just closed!

Hurrying back, I lifted it down. It was a large lantern, and when I lit the wick, it threw out a bright, steady beam of light. Blowing out my feeble candle, I held the lantern high, and headed into the cave.

There may be dangers ahead, I thought, but at least now, I shall be able to see them, and though I was still afraid to go forward, I was more afraid to go back.

I hadn't gone far when the passage took a sharp turn and I found myself in a chamber about the size of my bedroom.

Water, oozing from the cave's walls, had collected in drops to form pools, some no bigger than puddles, but others had grown to pond size, and setting the lantern down,

I knelt beside the largest one and gazed into it.

An abundance of tiny, white fish were swimming around in the pool, and drawing closer, I suddenly realized that they had no eyes.

There was something grotesque and frightening about them, and I was reminded of Jordan, the whiteness of his skin, and those crystal eyes that could blend into his overall paleness and seem almost to disappear.

Glancing over at the other side of the pool, I noticed an opening in the rock wall. Not much more than a space to crawl in, but I wondered if it could lead to another series of tunnels.

I assumed this was the main one, for it was cleared and had obviously once been used, but no doubt there were others, perhaps leading to chambers that had been undisturbed for centuries.

The thought intrigued me, but I was not about to go exploring on my own. Under other circumstances though, this may have been a wonderful adventure, I mused. There was something fascinating about this underground maze with passageways and chambers hidden in the bowels of the earth.

I was reluctant to leave the spacious chamber and enter another long tunnel, but picking up my lantern, I trudged purposefully on.

The passageway took another sharp turn and suddenly narrowed, causing me to cringe and suck in my breath. The walls seemed to be closing in on me and I wanted to run back to the chamber, but I forced myself to move forward, one step at a time.

Let it widen, I prayed, feeling the cold and clammy walls scrape my arms as I passed through the narrow opening. Then a horrible thought struck me, and I stopped dead in my tracks. Maybe this exit was closed! Didn't rock slides sometimes occur in caves?

The ground was slippery and I inched my way along cautiously. I couldn't risk falling and injuring myself. What a horrible way to die, I thought, alone and lost in a dark cave.

171

The passageway was not widening. If anything, it was becoming narrower, and I was forced at times to move through it sideways. Despair was nipping at my heels, and I was almost ready to go back to the chamber when suddenly I heard an eerie whistle. A cold draught hit me in the face and I knew then that wind was blowing through the tunnel.

Bracing the lantern against a large rock, I crawled on my hands and knees, as the ground rose under my feet. Sharp rocks tore my hands, but I continued to dig like a frantic mole reaching for the surface. I shoved a large boulder with strength born out of sheer desperation, and was rewarded with a patch of light.

Like a snake I wiggled through the opening and found myself looking into another chamber. But, this time it was at the mouth of the cave, for I could see sand and the glittering sea.

Tears of relief suddenly stung my eyes, blurring my vision and making me wonder if the sea and sand were nothing more than a mirage and I would step out into yet another chamber strung between endless tunnels that reached to infinity under the ground.

Tossing rocks aside with wild abandon, I widened the opening enough to scramble through it, and landed in a heap on the floor of the grotto.

Looking out through the gaping hole, I saw blue skies above me, and I heard the familiar sound of waves rolling into shore.

Overcome with relief, I jumped up and ran outside into brilliant sunlight. Never had it seemed so welcome, and I wanted to kick off my shoes and frolic for joy in the warm sand, but I dare not waste a single minute.

I had to sneak inside the house and set my room and myself to rights before the others returned. I must look like a chimney sweep, I thought, glancing down at my dress which was torn and caked with dirt.

Running down to the water, I scooped up foam from an incoming wave, and splashed it on my face and arms. With the hem of my skirt, I patted myself dry and then headed up the beach to the manor house.

The only satisfaction I gained from the whole horrible episode in the cave was the expression on Tarleton's face when he opened the door to me.

"My word," he exclaimed, pursing his lips like a prissy old woman and stepping sideways to avoid contamination as I passed.

I took the stairs with the elegance of a queen, knowing his disapproving old eyes were riveted on me, but once I had reached the balcony, I hurried down the corridor to my room.

I had no qualms about entering it. My stalker, if indeed there had been one, would never confront me here, I told myself.

Thank God, I did not encounter any of the more loquacious servants in the hallway. Tarleton, for all his faults, was not a gossip and although my bedraggled appearance must have certainly aroused his curiosity, his butler's code of ethics would never allow him to comment on it.

I opened the door, and stood back in surprise. The bed had already been pushed back into place and the room was in perfect order.

I knelt down and peered under the bed. The trapdoor was closed and a large rock had been placed over it. My blood turned to ice. Someone had deliberately sealed it, knowing I'd be trapped down there.

As with the doll incident, the more I thought about the trick that had been played on me, the angrier I became. I blamed Mrs. Janney for both pranks, but I no longer felt she was working alone. Not after I had seen Stuart remove the doll from its hiding place and walk down Bleekman Street with it under his arm.

But why? I asked myself. Why were they so anxious to frighten Katherine away from Hathaway Manor? For I must remember that it is Katherine they are trying to frighten away, not I.

The ghost of an idea suddenly popped into my head. What if I led them to believe that Katherine's disturbing presence might become permanent? What if they thought there was a possibility that she might have a lifetime at Hathaway

Manor to recall whatever it is they want her to forget? What would Stuart do then, or Mrs. Janney? Or anyone else for that matter, who is concerned about Katherine's lost memory?

I took a long time to dress that evening, and to Maureen's delight, I chose a gown that I had never worn before. One of Katherine's, it was a frothy debutante creation in pale green chiffon. The demure neckline and huge puffed sleeves gave it a little girl look, and though it was far too fussy for Stuart's more urbane taste, I was sure Jordan would find it irresistible.

"Aye, but you look like one of them Botta-Botta. . . . One of them angels in that painting upstairs," Maureen said.

"The Botticelli painting?"

"Aye, that's the one." She eyed me from head to toe. "Lady Hathaway's emeralds would set it off." Then she shrugged, and wrinkled up her nose. "Maybe not. You don't need them. You've got emeralds in your eyes, Miss Katherine."

My eyes did appear more green than ever with the gown, and I hoped nobody would remember that Katherine's eyes were hazel.

Maureen opened the dresser, and taking out the fan Stuart had bought me in London, she said, "Would you be wanting your fan?" Gazing lovingly at it, she sighed. "How dainty and old-fashioned it is, Miss Katherine."

Looking at it, I saw him again, clowning in the shop, and remembering made my heart ache. I had been so happy that day. "You're right, Maureen," I said. "It is old-fashioned. Fold it neatly, pack it in moth balls and put it away."

Like my memories, I thought. What good are they now?

She gave me a peculiar look and I left her gazing at the fan with admiring eyes.

The family was gathered in the drawing room when I floated in, trailing wisps of chiffon behind me.

Willa looked me up and down and made a sarcastic comment. "Katherine must be expecting the Prince of Wales."

"I hope not," Jordan said, giving me an intimate smile.

174

Then, taking my arm, he whispered, "I don't want to share you with anyone tonight, Katherine."

Beatrice looked at me, and then at her son. It was obvious she was not pleased. "You should have come with us," she said, eyeing me coldly. "Emily Wilson's brother dropped in for tea. He had hoped to meet you, Katherine."

Fenton snorted. "That popinjay? Did he bring his sewing, too?"

Beatrice gave her husband a murderous look. It was plain she did not want me for a daughter-in-law, and just as plain that Fenton favored such an arrangement as a means to gain control of Katherine's money.

I felt like a lamb surrounded by wolves. Certain people at Hathaway Manor had something to gain by keeping me here, and others had everything to lose. Either way, one set of wolves might devour me.

Tarleton tiptoed in to announce that dinner was served, and Jordan gallantly offered one arm to his sullen sister, and one arm to me.

As Fenton came forward to join his wife, I was shocked to see that his hand was bandaged. "Uncle Fenton," I asked. "What happened to your hand?"

"He was bitten by a dog," Beatrice said. "We were discussing it before you came down."

"Nothing serious," Fenton added. "One of the tenant's dogs suddenly took a dislike to me."

"You should have shot the beast," Willa said.

"Was it O'Hare's?" Jordan asked.

Fenton turned around with a scowl. "What?"

"The dog." Jordan said. "Was it that mongrel that belongs to Will O'Hare?"

Fenton looked annoyed. "No, some other dog. Now let's go in to dinner."


Later, as I lay in bed, going over the events of this long and confusing day, I wondered about the dog bite. I found it hard to imagine that any dog would have the nerve to bite Lord Fenton Hathaway, the Master of the Manor. But I found it even harder to imagine the alternative, that it was Fenton's blood on the floor of the cell.

The thought was just too preposterous, and I refused to entertain it. Fenton *was* the Master of the Manor and there was just no way that he could have been confined and injured in his own dungeon.

But who had been down there, then? I had seen the blood and heard the screams. But, surely, in this day and age, dungeons were no longer used to confine and torture people.

Could it have been an animal? I wondered. It seemed the only logical explanation, but still my muscles tensed as I recalled that horrible dark place, and I wondered if I should hear those chilling screams again tonight.

Turning over, I wrapped my arms about my pillow like a child clutching a plump, stuffed animal. I tried to concentrate on other matters and my thoughts centered on Jordan. Why was I encouraging him? Did I really want to smoke Katherine's enemies out, or was I using Jordan to soothe my wounded pride?

*Hell hath no fury like a woman scorned!* Stuart warned you to stay away from Jordan and his laboratory. Is that why you consented to go?

I overrode my nagging inner voice. What I once might have felt for Stuart had nothing to do with it. This masquerade had inadvertently involved me in Hathaway Manor's secrets, and I meant to ferret them out. Furthermore, I'll not be scared off by Stuart or anyone else who has something to hide, I told myself.

I sat up and fluffed the pillow. I must get some sleep. Tomorrow, Jordan would be showing me his laboratory.


The small, thatch roofed cottage on a barren stretch of the moors looked unpretentious, and I rather expected to find a tenant working in its neat little garden.

We reined in our horses, and Jordan pointed to it with pride. "There's my laboratory!"

"I thought it was a tenant cottage," I said.

"It used to be, but the old fellow who lived here died, and

176

Father never bothered to rent it again. I took it over when I was about fourteen." He smiled. "That was before you came to Hathaway Manor, Katherine. I was interested in explosives then, and Father wasn't exactly pleased when I blew the window out of my bedroom."

"I can imagine."

Urging our mounts forward, we rode around to the back of the cottage and tethered the horses. There was a small garden, and I said, "Are you also a farmer?"

"Of sorts," he answered. "I use these plants in my experiments."

Mushrooms grew in profusion under a large, shady tree, and I said, "I never saw mushrooms like that." They were of a reddish color with white flecks, and I thought perhaps they were peculiar to England. "Are they good?" I asked.

He looked at me strangely. "Have you never heard of fly agaric?"

"No. What is it?"

"That's what they are called," he said. "They were originally used to poison flys; hence the name, fly agaric. But, they have a side effect on human beings," he added. "They produce hallucinations and delirium."

Suddenly, I felt a shadow fall across the pretty little yard, and the garden took on a sinister quality. "All these plants are poisonous, aren't they?" I said.

"Aye, to a degree, but more importantly, they all produce hallucinations." He pointed to a beautiful bush overflowing with bell-shaped flowers in a lovely bluish-purple color. "That's belladonna," he said. "It belongs to the nightshade family—henbane, belladonna, and mandrake. They were all used by the ancients in witchcraft."

I began to regret coming. There was something a little scary about this garden and its deadly crops that appeared so innocent.

"In the Middle Ages, they thought mandrake was satanic," Jordan was saying. "It resembles a human form, you know." He reached down and grasped a small plant with his hand. "They say it shrieks when it's pulled up. Listen." With a quick movement, he wrenched it from the ground, and I did hear something, or thought I did.

I shuddered when he showed it to me, for it did indeed resemble a human form and I could readily understand how it would strike terror into superstitious minds.

Jordan laid it carefully on the ground to dry in the sun, and reaching into his pocket, he brought out a large key. "Let's go inside, and I'll show you the laboratory."

The door opened into a small room. An old-fashioned wood stove stood in the corner and a cot neatly covered with a blanket occupied the other wall.

"Sometimes, I need to spend the night," he explained, looking a little embarrassed, as if he thought I might misconstrue his intentions. "The laboratory is in the front," he added.

Hurriedly, he began to unbolt another door. The sliding locks were made of heavy metal and there were three of them; a precautionary measure that seemed a little ludicrous to me, considering that it was an inside door. Finally, he got it opened, and we entered the laboratory.

A long table dominated the room. It was filled with glassware; funnels, beakers and test tubes of all shapes and sizes, and funny looking little metal candles that Jordan informed me were called Bunsen burners. "They produce a smokeless flame that gives off intense heat," he explained.

"And those are my latest samples," he added, pointing to a rack which held several test tubes. Selecting one, he held the liquid up to the light. "This was extracted from one of those plants you saw in the garden."

"It looks like wine," I said.

"You wouldn't want to drink it."

"Would it kill me?"

"Worse," he answered, returning it to the rack without further explanation. A look of disgust suddenly crossed his face, and he ran his fingers through his hair in a gesture of futility. "It gets so discouraging at times. I take one step forward and two back, but that's the nature of research. My father doesn't understand that. He wants me to quit."

"It's for a noble purpose," I said. "Surely, if you can be instrumental in wiping out mental illness your efforts will not have been in vain."

He gave me a weak smile. "That's why I wanted to show you the laboratory, Katherine. You're the only one who understands." His eyes took on that far-off, alien look again, and my uneasiness returned.

Anxious to bring him back to reality, I asked the first question that popped into my head. "How do you extract drugs from plants?"

Immediately, he turned teacher, grabbing mortar and pestle and showing me how he ground the seeds to a fine powder. "Then a solvent is added," he enthused, "alcohol or benzene. The solution is then heated in a water bath, using the Bunsen burner. The end product is tested and results are duly recorded."

"I see," I said.

I didn't, really. "How did he test them?" I wondered, but I was afraid to ask.

My suspicions were soon confirmed when he pulled the cover from a cage and said, "The rats are used for testing purposes."

Huge, grey rats fixed me with fierce, beady eyes and I shrank back, overcome with revulsion. My hand hit the test tube rack, splashing the liquid onto the table. "Oh, I'm sorry," I said, reaching out to steady the shaking tubes.

"Don't touch them!"

His panic was contagious, and I jumped back.

Grabbing my hands, he ran his fingers over them. "Did any of it get on you?"

"No." I said.

"Are you sure?"

I was almost in tears. "I don't think so, Jordan. Why?"

His hands were holding mine in a vice-like grip, and his face was contorted with pain. For an instant, we just stood there, staring into each other's eyes, and then gradually, I felt him relax. Dropping my hands, he reached up and very gently touched my cheek. "I shouldn't have brought you here," he said. "Come along, I'll make you a cup of tea."

He hastily covered the cage, but not before I'd had a second look at the ugly rats inside. Feeling queasy, but not wanting to admit it, I followed Jordan to the back room.

I sat on the cot, and while he busied himself making the tea, my thoughts kept returning to the rats in the next room. I was terrified of them, obsessively so, ever since the night I'd almost been attacked by one.

I'd been about two years old, and still taking a bottle to bed with me. The rat had wanted the milk, and I can still recall the terror of waking up to see that hideous rodent poised on my crib rail, ready to pounce.

I had screamed, waking the whole hotel, and my fastidious father had beaten the rat to death with his cane. Outraged, Beau had threatened the concierge with a similar fate, but suffice it to say, I no longer took a bottle to bed with me.

Jordan handed me a cup of tea, and pulling out a battered chair, sat down. "I'm sorry, Katherine. I should have told you about the rats."

I gave him a weak smile. "It's all right, Jordan. I have an excessive aversion to them. I hope I didn't disturb your samples though."

He frowned. "No, just so none of it spilled on you. You're sure it didn't?" he added, looking at me anxiously.

"Quite sure, but I'm too clumsy to be around a laboratory," I said. "I'm going to ride back to the manor and let you get some work done."

I hoped I wasn't insulting him, but I'd seen quite enough of the laboratory, and knowing those creatures were in the next room was making me nervous.

"As you wish," he said, reaching over and patting my hand. "You're a jolly good sport, Katherine. Most women would have fainted. Please forgive me for startling you like that."

"Of course," I said.

"Drink your tea. It'll calm your nerves."

"I'm all right now," I said, dutifully sipping the tea, which was hot, but not particularly good. I finished it quickly though, for I was anxious to be off. Jordan's hideaway with its deadly garden and scurvy rats had a depressing effect on me. I set the cup and saucer down and stood up. "Thank you for showing me the laboratory, Jordan. I found everything fascinating, with the exception of the rats," I added with a smile.

"Thank you for coming," he said, grabbing my hand, and continuing to hold it as we walked outside to where the horses were tethered.

He helped me mount, and looking up at me with concern, he said, "Now, you're sure you know how to get back."

"Of course," I answered with more confidence than I actually felt. My sense of direction was notoriously poor, but I didn't want to force Jordan to leave on my account, and yet I simply could not bear to remain another minute in such close proximity to rats, caged or not!

"I'll be fine," I said, as I waved him goodbye, little knowing that I was about to embark on the most terrifying experience of my life!

# Chapter 15

I looked around in confusion and berated myself for lacking a sense of direction. I could hardly believe I'd done it again—gotten myself lost!

Looking skyward, I feared the unpredictable Cornish weather was about to add to my problems. The sun had disappeared behind grey clouds and the wind that whistled across the barren moors told me we were in for a thunder storm.

I recalled Stuart's warnings about bogs that the unwary could step into and be swallowed up in. "There's a wild sort of beauty about the moors," he had said, and I had to agree.

Nature at her most desolate carried herself in awesome splendor, I thought, looking out over a windswept wasteland, untouched by the passage of time. Patches of purple heather softened its starkness, but this was a hard land where few living things survived.

Two large tors loomed ahead of me and I thought perhaps I should make for them. I didn't want to be caught out in the open in a violent thunderstorm.

Digging my heels into the mare's flanks, I urged her ahead, but she reared up, as if reluctant to follow my lead.

"Come on, girl," I crooned, but she would not budge. Can anything else go wrong? I wondered. I knew horses were afraid of fire. Perhaps this one is afraid of storms as well, I thought. Grumbling to myself, I dismounted, and wrapping my shawl around the mare's eyes like a blindfold, I led her toward the twin peaks.

The wind whipped my hair about my face and looking up, I saw that the sky was now black. A loud clap of thunder suddenly split the air, making the horse whinney and toss her head nervously.

"Easy, girl," I said, holding tightly to the reins, as the mare balked, moving backwards. The makeshift blindfold dropped to the ground just as a shriek of lightning lit up the sky. I dropped the reins and staggered back, narrowly escaping the mare's deadly hooves, as she reared up on her hind legs, eyes wild with fright.

I sprawled backwards over a large rock, and looked up with horror to see the huge animal soar over me as she jumped the boulder and raced like a wild thing over the storm tossed moor.

I called to no avail. Her primal instincts had taken over, and my voice could not penetrate her fear. Standing up on legs that were weak from fright, I counted myself fortunate. I could have been trampled to death!

Big, pelting drops of rain hit me then, and picking up the shawl, I raised it over my head, and ran. The tors were farther away than they had seemed; an illusion peculiar to the moors I would later discover.

Panting for breath, I stopped several times, placing my hand on my brow and peering through sheets of rain to find the peaks no closer than before. I was soaked to the skin and terrified of the lightning that seemed to play about me like a fierce dog nipping at my heels.

My only hope lay in trusting that the mare would find her way home. Then a search party could be sent out to rescue me.

No longer able to run, I dragged myself over the coarse ground, stumbling over moorland scrubs until I reached the tors. They were not as close together as they had appeared from a distance, but they did offer more protection from the storm than the open plain.

Taking refuge behind a large boulder, I waited out the storm, which gradually subsided until nothing was left, but a fine, misty rain.

I began to assess my situation. I can't just stay here, waiting to be rescued, I decided. That could take hours, days, even. I shuddered at the thought of spending even one night alone on the moors.

Stepping out from behind the boulder, I resumed my hike; this time in the opposite direction. Perhaps I can find my way back to Jordan's laboratory, I thought. The terrain was more rugged on this side of the tor, and at one point, I found myself looking down into a deep gorge. I was about to turn back when something in the distance caught my eye. It was a small cottage.

I made my way down the rain slick path. It was steeper and more treacherous than I had imagined, and I soon regretted the impulse that had forced me to take such a foolhardy risk.

I should have looked for another, more accessible path to the lowlands. I shall break my neck on this one, I predicted. A moment later, I lost my footing and was sliding down the pass.

In desperation, I reached out for something to grab hold of, but the rain had turned the path into a mud slide and I skidded all the way down, scraping my arms and legs every inch of the way.

It was a miracle I was not seriously hurt, but I was too sore to be grateful. My hands stung from brush burns and every muscle in my body ached. I was covered in mud, and I don't think I have ever felt more miserable.

Looking around me, my heart sank. I was in marshland, and remembering Stuart's warning, I stood up and tentatively patted the ground with my foot. It was soft, and overwhelmed by this new danger, I shouted at the top of my lungs. "Help, somebody. Help!"

Turning suddenly, I looked up from where I had come. There was no way I could climb back. I was lucky to be alive, and I dare not tempt fate a second time.

I sat back down, and hugging my knees to my chest, I cried until there were no tears left. I either fainted or dozed at this point, for it seemed much later when I sat up suddenly conscious of some movement nearby.

I knew there were wolves on the moors, and I was instantly

alert. Looking around frantically for some protection, I picked up a large rock and held it in my hand.

The mist had formed a vapor on the air and I could not see clearly. I might have imagined it, I thought, or it could have been some harmless, small animal.

My eyes were riveted on the tall grass, and very slowly, I saw it move. I'll only get one chance, I thought, and raising my arm, I hurled the rock with every last ounce of my strength. The tall grass parted and what I saw froze me to the spot.

Larger than life, he lumbered toward me out of the mist. His ghostly face wore a weird smile, but it was his eyes that terrified me. They were the color of blood!

I must have fainted, and when I came to, I felt disoriented and sensed that I was in a different place. Thoughts began to gather in my head. The last thing I remembered was the ghost of Anthony Hathaway coming toward me out of the bog. As hideous as the apparition was, there was something vaguely familiar about that face.

Afraid to open my eyes, I moved my hand and felt, not the dampness of earth, but the coarseness of straw. Very cautiously, I peered through hooded lids, and saw that I was in a room. The cottage! I thought with relief.

A woman came toward me, tall, somber-faced. I opened my eyes a slit wider and recognized her. "Mrs. Janney," I cried, shrinking back on the straw mattress.

"I be Mrs. Cull; Mrs. Janney's sister." She spoke in that strange, Cornish accent, and like her sister, her voice had a soft, spooky quality about it.

"Where am I?" I asked weakly.

"You be in Cull cottage on Bismooth Pass."

"I lost my way," I said, and then because she had the same uncomfortable effect on me as her sister, I added regally, "I'm Katherine Hathaway from the Manor House."

Her cold eyes stared into mine. "I be knowing who 'ee are, Miss."

I glanced nervously around. "I saw a man. He came after me. He . . ."

She averted her eyes, but not quickly enough to hide the

lie. "There be no man. You had a bad fall. The dog found 'ee." She jerked her head toward a large, brown animal, dozing beside the hearth. It appeared to be more wolf than dog. My face must have betrayed my fear, for her thin lips curled, and I was reminded of Mrs. Janney's secret little smile.

Pride made me meet her eyes without flinching. "And how did I get here?" I challenged her, for even a big, raw-boned woman like herself would have been hard pressed to carry me such a great distance.

"In the wagon," she said sharply. "It be still hitched, so if 'ee feel up to it, I be taking 'ee home."

I liked her no better than her sister, and I would be relieved when I was no longer in her presence, but she had saved my life. "Mrs. Cull," I said, "I'm very grateful to you, and I know Lord Hathaway will be, too."

That smile again, and I cursed myself for sounding supercilious. "Come, Drake," she shouted, and roused from sleep, the animal jumped to attention. Suddenly aware of my presence, it growled, a low and menacing growl.

I'd always heard that animals can sense a person's fear, and I did my best to hide mine, but my blood turned to ice ⁿ the dog bared its teeth and still growling, approached

ake!" she shouted, and it stopped dead in its tracks. a satisfied smirk, she added, "'Ee won't hurt you, Miss. only attacks on command."

Reaching up, she pulled a thick chain off a peg in the wall, and my heart sank. The beast was going with us!

Once outside, Mrs. Cull took the driver's seat in the wagon and I climbed up beside her. The dog jumped in the back where he positioned himself directly behind me. I could feel his hot breath on my neck and I held myself erect, afraid almost to breathe lest I attract his attention.

The ride across the moors in the ancient wagon made my first journey in the fly seem tame by comparison. Not only were the roads rough, they were slippery from the rain. Nevertheless, Mrs. Cull drove with a recklessness bordering on frenzy. Like a charioteer in the Roman arena, she charged up the steep hill leading to Hathaway Manor, rising from her seat as she flicked the whip, urging the horse to go faster and faster. It'll be a miracle if this rattletrap of a wagon doesn't overturn, I thought, hanging on to the sides for dear life.

By the grace of God, we made it to the top of the hill, and rumbled noisily into the driveway. Taking a deep breath, I turned my head slowly, hoping that the wild ride might have done me one favor. Unfortunately the dog was still there. As if reading my mind, he snarled, black lips curling back to show me his sharp white teeth.

I sat motionless until Mrs. Cull spoke. "Stay, Drake," she commanded the dog, and then turning to me, she issued another command. "Stay away from Bismooth Pass, Miss. The dog'll attack 'ee next time."

Although certain that sarcasm would be lost on the old witch, I nevertheless looked her in the eye and said, "You needn't worry, Mrs. Cull. I wouldn't dream of imposing on your hospitality a second time."

At that point, Fenton and one of the grooms approached, walking briskly from the direction of the stables. Lord Hathaway wore a deep scowl, and if he was relieved to see me, he certainly didn't show it.

"We were about to send out a search party," he said, giving me a perfunctory glance and then turning anxiously to Mrs. Cull. "Where did you find her?"

"In Bismooth Path, Master." She spoke in a properly deferential manner, but I detected an undercurrent of triumph in her words.

Fenton's eyes locked with Mrs. Cull's for a moment before he turned to me. "My God, Katherine. You're covered with cuts and scratches. We must get you into bed, and call the doctor."

"I look worse than I am, Uncle. I'll be fine," I assured him. "I don't need a doctor."

He turned to the young groom standing beside him. "Carry Miss Katherine into the house, Danny, and have Tarleton summon Lady Hathaway."

I knew it would be useless to protest, so I submitted when the groom reached into the wagon and effortlessly lifted me out in his strong arms.

I was weaker than I had suspected, and my tired body sagged against the powerful young man, finding security in his strength. Fenton remained behind and I thought that rather peculiar under the circumstances. What would he have to discuss with Mrs. Cull now, I wondered.

Danny carried me into the house under Tarleton's disapproving eye. Neither my mud spattered clothes nor Danny's dusty riding boots had gone unnoticed by the meticulous little butler, and I'm sure he would have preferred that we use the back entrance.

"Where's Lady Hathaway?" Danny inquired in clipped tones.

"Her ladyship is resting and cannot be disturbed," Tarleton replied with ludicrous formality.

Danny countered, "Can't you see Miss Katherine's been hurt? Go get Lady Hathaway right now. And them's orders from Lord Hathaway!"

I was beginning to feel light-headed, but I managed to suppress a giggle. What a hilarious play, I thought, teetering on the edge of delirium.

At that moment, Fenton swept into the house like a commanding general. "Where is Lady Hathaway?" he bellowed.

Tarleton who had been regally ascending the staircase suddenly moved faster than I would have thought possible, and disappeared from sight in a matter of seconds.

"The butler's after summoning her ladyship," Danny replied with a smile.

"Aye. Well, in the meantime, we must be getting the young lady to her room," Fenton said.

Danny, following his master's lead, carried me up the steps and down the long, winding corridor to my room. "I must be getting heavy," I murmured drowsily, but he laughed and said, "You're light as a feather, Miss Katherine."

I was deposited on the bed and would have drifted off to sleep, but Beatrice appeared, accompanied by Maureen and another maid. Lady Hathaway took one look at my bloody scratches and mud encrusted clothes and hastily retreated, leaving the servants to help me undress and to cluck over my bruised flesh and the blisters that had started to appear on my brush burned hands.

With tender concern, they assisted me into a tub of soothing, hot water and Maureen gently washed away the mud from my face and hair.

"There now, 'tis lucky you are to be alive, Miss Katherine. You'll be sore for a day or two, but then you'll be good as new." She looked at me with fear in her eyes. "When I heard you were lost on the moors, I thought about Lily Beacham. Thank God, Miss Katherine, the bad thing didn't get you."

"What bad thing?" I asked.

She shook her head. "I wouldn't be knowing, but there's something out there on the moors. All the servants say so."

Wearing a fresh, lavender scented nightgown, I gratefully crawled into my soft, clean bed, determined to put my harrowing experiences behind me until I could sort them out and think about them with a clear head.

Dreams were beyond my power to control though, and I relived the day with bizarre distortions that kept me tossing and turning fitfully.

I kept seeing those eyes and that white face staring back at me through the mist. In my dream the ghost, or whatever it was, kept advancing. Closer and closer it came while I lay, unable to scream, unable to move, and just when my terror had reached unbearable heights, the scene shifted and I was being carried in strong arms. Feeling protected and secure, I looked up with gratitude, thinking to see the handsome young groom, but instead I found myself staring into the face of a monster with red eyes!

It took several days for my sore muscles to heal and during that time, I avoided thinking about what I had seen on the moor. I have never believed in spirits, but the alternative to the ghost theory was too bizarre to contemplate. I preferred settling for the obvious—I'd had a fall and my mind had played a trick on me.

The family couldn't have been more solicitous, wanting me to remain in bed, but bowing to my wishes when I insisted I was well enough to come downstairs.

Jordan was full of remorse and blamed himself for allowing me to roam the moors on my own. "I should never have forgiven myself if you had been seriously hurt," he said.

His father gave him a caustic look and added. "All's well that ends well, Jordan." Turning to me with a benign smile, he used the incident to make a point, as one would do with a recalcitrant child. "Katherine has learned a valuable lesson. I doubt she'll visit the moors again."

I doubted it, too, but my proud nature would not let me admit it. "Oh, I don't know," I said. "I'm still fascinated by the place, but next time, I'll be more careful."

Fenton exchanged hurried glances with Beatrice and Jordan. His pale face colored slightly and he fixed me with eyes that were no longer benign. "I forbid it, Katherine. You are not to go up on the moors again. Is that understood?"

I nodded, angry with myself for promoting the confrontation, and he suddenly switched from stern disciplinarian to affable host. His eyes traveled from Willa to me and then rested on his wife. "I'm thinking that our young ladies could do with a bit of fun, and you, too, my dear. How would the three of you like to run up to London for a few days?"

His suggestion caught us all off guard. Was this the same man who only a month ago had equated London with Sodom and Gomorrah? And hadn't he dragged his women-folk home to spare not only their virtue, but his pocket-book?

"Do some shopping and visit your friends," he was saying, as the three of us stared at him with open mouths. "You can stay with Cousin Elvira this time. I'm sure she could use some company."

We arrived in London and summarily descended on Cousin Elvira's household. Our unannounced visit was presumptuous and an imposition, but Cousin Elvira was oblivious to it. The poor old lady had no conception of who we were or even that we had barged, uninvited, into her home.

Her senility worked in our favor though, and I am ashamed to say that all of us, myself included, were eager to take advantage of the opportunities it presented.

With no hostess to answer to, we would be free to come and go as we please. The Hathaway ladies could continue the chase, hopefully this time to ensnare the elusive Sir Alex Lighthizer. As for myself, I could check up on Beau and perhaps wheedle some necessary information out of Katherine.

*And what else, India?* my inner voice insisted.

I shrugged and silently answered, Perhaps, I'll pay a call on Stuart.

*Why, India?*

I argued, "Why not? There's nothing forward about making a courtesy call on the man. And besides, there's always the possibility that he might have a logical explanation for—"

I put my hands over my ears. I didn't want to listen to what my inner voice was saying.

"What's the matter with you, Katherine?"

Willa's shrill words brought me immediately back to Cousin Elvira's old-fashioned drawing room, and reminded me sharply that I had been daydreaming.

"Nothing," I said.

"Well, pardon me," she answered haughtily. "I'm not used to people making nasty faces and then clamping their hands over their ears when I'm talking!"

Oh, God, I thought. "I'm sorry. It had nothing to do with you, Willa." And thinking quickly, I added, "I get a buzzing in my ears sometimes."

She withered me with a glance. "There's already enough crazy people in this family. If I were you, I'd see a doctor." Suddenly she laughed. "Maybe Jordan can prescribe one of his drugs. He takes them himself, you know." She studied me a moment and then added, "He used to be sane, but now he has crazy spells. Maybe they'll work the other way on you."

"What do you mean he has crazy spells?" I asked.

She never answered me, for at that moment, Beatrice walked into the room.

Lady Hathaway gave her daughter a warning look and then said, "We thought we'd shop tomorrow. Would you like to accompany us, Katherine?"

Wanting to avoid a repetition of all the sneaking around the three of us had engaged in the last time, I'd come up with a possible solution, and now was the time to try it out.

"Thank you, Aunt Beatrice, but if you don't mind, I'd like to visit a friend. She's a young woman I met on the crossing," I added hastily. "She's traveling with her father, and right now they're in London."

Out of the corner of my eye, I saw Willa sit up straight in her chair, but I could only imagine the smile that suffused her face.

Beatrice hesitated, but only for a minute lest I change my mind. "Of course you may visit your friends, Katherine. Are they staying close by?"

"They have a suite at Brown's Hotel."

This was an endorsement as far as Lady Hathaway was concerned, and she asked me no more questions. They could have been anything, even actors, I thought, smiling at the irony, and Beatrice would have given them her unconditional stamp of approval. The important thing as far as Katherine's aunt was concerned was getting Katherine out of her hair!

My conversation with Willa in the drawing room came back to me later, as I tried to sleep in a room reeking of stale, bottled-up air. I had tried to open a window, but the sashes had been painted shut. This house is like poor Cousin Elvira, I thought, suspended between life and death!

My thoughts picked up on several strange incidents concerning Jordan Hathaway. "He used to be sane, but now he has crazy spells." Aside from the vagueness and that alien look that would sometimes appear in Jordan's unique eyes, there had been other things. The time he had left the Lighthizer Ball, claiming to be sick, and yet I had seen him coming home at daybreak; his sudden recovery after we had arrived home from London; and those cries in the night! Could it have been Jordan down in the dungeon, making those half-human, half-animal sounds?

Suddenly the face I had seen in the mist flashed across my mind. There had been something vaguely familiar about that face. Did it resemble Jordan? I rather thought it did, and my vivid imagination conjured up bizarre implications around that resemblance.

Was Jordan a Doctor Jekyll and Mr. Hyde? And if he was, could it have been Jordan's Mr. Hyde who had murdered Lily Beacham?

# Chapter 16

We had just finished breakfast, a meal which must have strained the help's patience to the breaking point.

Beatrice's eggs were too soft, Willa's were too hard, the cream was not thick enough, the tea was not strong enough. Their complaints went on and on in an endless litany.

I felt embarrassed to be considered one of them, and I would have been happy to see the harrassed little maid dump Beatrice's and Willa's eggs in their laps, take off her apron, and tender her resignation!

But, alas, the poor girl was British and to her way of thinking, it was her lot in life to put up with the demands of the aristocracy.

I almost laughed out loud when Beatrice said, "We shouldn't be a burden to Cousin Elvira's staff, Katherine. So, why don't you just dine with your friends this evening?"

I couldn't resist saying, "How considerate of you, Aunt Beatrice, but where shall you and Willa dine?"

"Lady Lighthizer is going shopping with us," Beatrice replied stiffly. "I'm sure she'll insist that we dine with her."

And Sir Alex, I mentally added. Not that I cared. I certainly had no wish to see Sir Alex again, but their elaborate machinations never failed to amaze and amuse me.

"In that case," I replied, "I shall dine with the Chantelles."

Beatrice frowned slightly. "Chantelles? I thought you said they were Americans."

"They are."

"Of course. I keep forgetting that America is a hodge-podge of nationalities."

"How droll," Willa said. "I should hate to live there among all those foreigners."

I smiled. "But, they're not foreigners, you see. They're *all* Americans!"

My words went over her head. "That is my complaint about Italy," she said. "It's a beautiful country, but I can't stand all those Italians being there."

Beatrice shoved her cup and sauger aside. "We must hurry, Willa. It's after nine." Turning to me, she smiled sweetly. "Have a lovely day, Katherine. And don't wait up for us. The Lighthizers dine late."

After they had gone, I poured myself another cup of tea and began to plan my day. The theaters back home were closed on Mondays, and I imagined it would be the same over here. Nevertheless, I reminded myself, Katherine and Beau are late sleepers. I shouldn't barge in on them too early.

Looking out the window, I saw that it was a lovely day for a stroll. Stuart is an early riser, I recalled. Since Bleekman Place was only a few blocks away, it seemed logical that I should walk in that direction.

Before leaving, I made it a point to seek out Nurse Smith. She appeared to act as Cousin Elvira's housekeeper, companion and all-around *chargé d'affaires*. It seemed rude in my opinion to use the house as a hotel and not even accord the woman common courtesy.

I found her in Cousin Elvira's room. The little old lady was propped up in bed and Nurse Smith was serving her breakfast.

I tapped lightly on the open door and they both looked up in my direction. Evidently Cousin Elvira could not see well, and she grabbed the nurse's arm and said in a stage whisper, "Which one is it, Smith? If it's Beatrice, or that sassy gel of hers, throw them out."

Nurse Smith looked embarrassed. "Lady Marchbank, please don't be naughty." She paused. Evidently in her nervousness, she had forgotten my name. "It's the other

195

young lady," she said.

"Nell Bridges?" Cousin Elvira crooked a bony finger at me. "Come in, come in, gel."

I stood at the foot of her bed. "I'm not Nell, Cousin Elvira. I'm Katherine," I said. "Roland's daughter."

Her watery eyes studied me and recognition slowly dawned. "Roland's gel, you say? Aye, I remember you. A hellion, you were, but you seem different."

"I've grown up, Cousin Elvira," I said.

"Aye, but leopards seldom change their spots." She cackled to herself and then turned to Nurse Smith. "Gave them all a merry chase, this one did."

Nurse Smith looked at me and shook her head. "Pay no attention. She gets confused sometimes."

"The hell you say!"

I thought Nurse Smith was going to faint. "Lady Marchbank. You're being very naughty!"

Lady Marchbank waved her away. "Out, get out, Smith. Let me talk to this gel without your damn interruptions."

I was hard put to contain a giggle, but I nodded solemnly to Nurse Smith. "I won't stay long."

When the nurse had gone, Cousin Elvira turned to me like a fellow conspirator. "She's an old maid. I like to shock the pants off her. I can curse better than that though. Lord Marchbank was in the navy, and he taught me everything I know."

I thought that Cousin Elvira must be the bane of the Hathaway family, and I gathered she was far more rational than she appeared. "I'm sorry to impose on your hospitality this way, Cousin Elvira," I said.

She locked eyes with me. "No, you're not, gel. This is a golden opportunity for you."

I gasped. "What do you mean?"

Her shrewd little eyes gleamed wickedly. "Fenton's in Cornwall, and all Beatrice cares about is landing that pompous ass, Lighthizer for a son-in-law. That leaves you unchaperoned and what young gel would object to that?"

"But, I . . ."

She bobbed her head up and down. "You can't fool me, gel."

"About what?" I asked warily.

"That scamp, Stuart Hathaway! I heard he'd been squiring you around." She cackled again. "A handsome devil that Stuart is, just like his father." She shook her long, bony finger in my face. "But he won't marry you, gel, just like his father wouldn't marry Beatrice!"

I recalled Lady Hathaway's bitterness about Gilbert's marriage. "Beatrice and Gilbert were in love?" I probed.

She laughed derisively. "Beatrice was, Gilbert wasn't." Shaking her head, she continued. "A plain gel with a nasty disposition couldn't interest a man like Gilbert Hathaway." She looked me in the eye then and spoke in a gentler tone. "Even if she'd been a beauty like you, Katherine, it wouldn't have mattered."

"Why not?"

"Because Gilbert would never have married his cousin." She shrugged. "He felt strongly about it, and he was probably right. Too much intermarriage weakens the strain, either physically *or* mentally," she added.

"But, weren't you a Hathaway?" I asked.

"Of course, and I loved Charles Marchbank, but we could never have children. Perhaps that was a blessing rather than a curse," she added caustically. "Anyway, Stuart feels the same way as his father. I've heard him say so."

"Well, I certainly don't care," I said. "I don't want to marry him either." Wanting to change the subject, and hoping for some insight into family secrets, I said casually, "Beatrice settled for Fenton, then."

"Aye, that she did, and her love for Gilbert turned to hate. She poisoned Fenton and Duncan's minds both against him. Cut Gilbert and young Stuart off without a penny, Duncan did." She shook her head and mused. "People wondered why your grandfather did that, but the Hathaways would never tell."

She gave me a sharp look. "And you, Missy. Why did your father run off to America? What happened down there at

Hathaway Manor?"

"I don't know," I said. "I was only ten years old."

"Ten years going on a hundred." She eyed me critically. "The family in London heard you'd had a fit of some kind, but I must say you seem normal enough now. Even likeable," she added, patting my hand. "Unless you're good at pretending."

She looked suddenly very tired, and I smiled and said, "You get some sleep now, Cousin Elvira. We'll talk again."

She waved me away. "Run along, gel. I know you're up to no good, but at least be careful," she added with a bawdy laugh. "What the hell! You're only young once."

My face burned, but I made no attempt to defend myself. Good heavens, I thought, what did the outrageous old lady think I was going to do?

Nurse Smith met me in the hall. "I hope she didn't shock you, Miss Hathaway."

"We had a nice little chat," I said with tongue in cheek.

"I'm glad. She can be very naughty sometimes, but we have to make allowances for her condition, don't we?"

I nodded and thought that Cousin Elvira had probably been naughty long before her condition warranted excuses from Nurse Smith.

"You won't have to bother about us for tea or dinner," I informed the woman. "We won't be back until late this evening."

She looked relieved, and again I felt guilty about the extra work we were causing the household. I bid her good day, and opening my parasol, I stepped outside.

The entrance to Kensington Park was directly across the street and the shady trees that lined the walks looked inviting on this warm August day. Crossing over, I opened the wrought iron gate and entered the park. I could do with a quiet stroll after Cousin Elvira's confusing conversation, I thought.

Two gentlemen, sporting canes and wearing identical bowler hats, passed me, going in the opposite direction. They smiled and tipped their hats, and I wondered if I was committing a social error, walking unescorted into the park.

What the hell! Cousin Elvira's favorite expression suddenly popped uninvited into my head. I giggled, thankful that the gentlemen had passed, or they might have thought I was trying to attract their attention.

Cousin Elvira was a character straight out of a play, and I couldn't wait to regale Beau and Katherine with an account of her antics.

She certainly knew a lot about the Hathaways, and she wasn't reluctant to let skeletons out of closets either. I wished I had asked her more questions, and I suddenly wondered if Cousin Elvira knew the identity of Anabelle! I must find another opportunity to chat with her again, I thought.

Several nannies approached pushing perambulators and holding tightly to the hands of their more rambunctious charges. They were young women, about my own age, and the thought struck me that had we not met Katherine, I might have wound up being one of them.

Without connections or money, theater work is difficult to come by, and Beau and I would probably have been forced to seek other employment in England.

The thought only served to emphasize the difference between Stuart's class and mine. He was a British aristocrat and there was no getting around that fact. He might not consider marriage to his cousin, but neither would he consider marriage to anyone who was his social inferior.

"What the hell!" I could hear Cousin Elvira say. "You're only young once, gel!"

She had thought I was going to see Stuart, and she was sure I was up to no good. Was she a senile old lady with a naughty mind, or had she astutely read mine?

Looking up, I realized that I had wended my way out of the park. If I turned left, I'd be walking in the direction of Brown's Hotel, but if I turned right, Bleekman Place was only a short distance away. My feet automatically turned right and I justified my decision by reminding myself that it was now late August and I would be leaving England behind in a few short weeks.

My heart was pounding when I opened the gate to No. 10 Bleekman Place. He may not even be home, I reminded myself. But surely Diggs will tell him that I called. Will he get in touch with me, or is it over as far as he's concerned? Should I tell him why I was angry? Ask him to give me explanations about the doll and ultimately about Lily Beacham?

My hands turned clammy at the thought. In that case, I should also have some confessions of my own to make.

*You made a bargain with Katherine,* my inner voice reminded me. *The masquerade is not over yet.*

And I wondered, Once I have removed my mask, will Stuart smile? Or laugh?

My hand hesitated, and then reached for the door knocker. I knocked once, and then almost fell off the step when the door was opened by Stuart!

"Katherine!" he exclaimed with genuine surprise.

Expecting to see Diggs, I was as taken back as he. "Stuart!" I exclaimed stupidly.

He had already recovered his composure, and was regarding me with a self-assured smile. "Now that we know who we are, won't you please come inside?"

His easy banter unnerved me and I shrugged in a vain attempt to match his poise. "Oh, I don't know. I was just passing by."

He laughed and grabbed my arm. "What are you talking about, Katherine?" Pulling me inside, he shook his head. "You were just passing by. From Cornwall? Come, have some tea, and tell me what's going on. What are you doing in London, anyway?"

He took my parasol and led me back into the dining room. "Where's Diggs?" I asked.

"It's Monday. Servants' day off," he said, pulling out a chair. "Sit down. I was just eating breakfast. Will you join me?"

I said, "I've already had breakfast, but I will take some tea."

He reached into the buffet for a cup and saucer, and I suddenly realized that Mrs. Diggs was absent, too. That meant that we were alone in the house, and the thought made me suddenly nervous. "I can't stay long," I said.

200

"Relax. You just got here, Katherine." He poured my tea and handed it to me. "Now, take off your gloves and drink your tea."

His patronizing attitude made me angry, and I jerked on the finger tips of my kid gloves to pull them off.

"Why are you angry with me?" he said.

"If only I could tell him," I thought. "Lay my cards on the table and just ask him, but I couldn't without giving myself away."

I replied, "I'm not angry."

He shrugged in a good-natured way. "You could have fooled me. Why don't you take your hat off? I can hardly see your face."

"I can't stay," I offered, but I did remove the hat, laying it on the empty chair next to me.

"So you said. And where are you going in such a hurry, or is it a secret?"

"No secret," I said. "I'm going to spend the day and have supper with friends."

"Might as well let him know that I will not be available to him," I thought.

He looked at me sharply. "Friends? You never told me you had friends in London."

"Might as well stick to the same story," I thought.

"I met them on the crossing, a young American woman and her father. They're in London now," I added, giving him the impression that they had only recently arrived.

"So, is that why you came up to London?" he asked.

"Hardly," I said. "Fenton suggested we go on a shopping spree."

Too late, I realized I'd said, *Fenton,* and not *Uncle Fenton!*

He raised an eyebrow, and I didn't know if he'd caught my slip of the tongue, or if he was merely surprised that Fenton would suggest we shop.

"We're staying with Cousin Elvira," I explained.

He smiled. "Another of Uncle Fenton's suggestions I would imagine. No doubt he doesn't trust me to keep the three of you in line."

I avoided commenting by sipping my tea, but I could feel his eyes on me.

"Did something happen at Hathaway Manor to make our uncle suggest a trip to London?" he asked.

Not knowing how far I dare go, I hesitated before answering. "I became lost on the moors. Perhaps he thought we could all do with a diversion."

He looked at me sharply. "What were you doing up on the moors alone?"

"Jordan took me to see his laboratory," I said.

He slammed his fist on the table, making me jump. "Didn't I tell you not to go there!"

My temper flared. "You are neither my husband nor my father, Stuart!"

"Fortunately for you, I'm not!" We glared across the table at each other and then he said, "All right, finish the story. How could you get lost if the great scientist was with you?"

"I left," I said. "He had rats in cages, and I was afraid they might get out. It wasn't Jordan's fault. I told him I knew the way home."

He sniffed. "Just like you knew your way through the streets of London, no doubt."

"Something like that," I said. "Anyway, I got back safe and sound. Uncle Fenton just wanted to be nice about London, I suppose."

"Uncle is not nice about anything," he said caustically. Then under his breath, he added, "You can bet there was some purpose behind it."

Wanting his help, and wanting to trust him, I spoke without thinking. "Stuart, I think I saw the ghost of Anthony Hathaway on Bismooth Pass."

His eyes were wary. "Oh? What did it look like?"

I told him then about stumbling onto Bismooth Pass, and what I had seen, or thought I had seen, and about Mrs. Cull.

He listened intently, and when I had finished, I saw the mask drop down over his face. "You probably imagined it," he said. "As for Mrs. Cull, she and her sister are typical old Cornish. Peculiar, but harmless!"

I reserved my opinion, recalling that he and Mrs. Janney

were coconspirators.

We lapsed into silence. After a moment, he reached across the table and covered my hand with his. "I've missed you, Katherine," he said simply.

In spite of all the lies between us, I wanted to believe him. "It's been a long time," I said. "You could have written, or come down to Hathaway Manor."

"I didn't think you wanted to see me. As I recall, you were not exactly friendly the day you left for Cornwall."

"No, I wasn't," I thought, "and all because of a stupid doll. Who am I to demand honesty? If Stuart has deceived me, so have I deceived him." I confessed, "I'm sorry. I've missed you, too, Stuart."

He got up and came around to my side of the table, and taking my hand, he raised me to my feet. "God, I've been going crazy, thinking about you." His voice was husky with passion and he crushed me to him in an embrace that took my breath away. His lips met mine, and I forgot about the doll, and that Katherine had said I shouldn't trust him.

Reveling in his touch, I let his hands roam over my body while I tasted the sweetness of his kisses. His lips moved from mine and I felt his hot breath in my ear as he whispered. "Let me make love to you, Katherine."

The only word I heard was "love," and wrapping my arms around his neck, I pressed my hungry lips to his. Swooping me up in his arms, he carried me out of the dining room, into the hall, and up the staircase.

The realization of what he expected suddenly hit me when he carried me into his bedroom and deposited me very gently on the bed. A sudden panic brought tears to my eyes, and my voice broke as I said, "I can't, Stuart. I'm sorry, but I just can't."

"But, surely you're not. . . . I thought all. . . . You're a virgin?"

I nodded my head, too ashamed to look at him. I had led him on and now I was backing down. I might be innocent, but with my theatrical background, I was by no means ignorant. I knew Stuart had every reason to be angry with me.

His hand was under my chin. "Look at me, Katherine," he said. Afraid to face him, I bit my lip, and then reluctantly met his eyes. They were gentle eyes, and bending his head, he kissed away my tears. "It's all right, sweetheart. Please don't cry."

He took me in his arms and held me close, and pressing my head to his shoulder, he lightly stroked my hair. I felt safe and secure like a wanderer who has finally found her home.

Placing his hands on my shoulders, he gently pushed me away, and raising an eyebrow, he said, "Now, get out of my bedroom, lady, before this soft-headed little gentleman shows his true nature and turns into a cad!"

I brought his hand up to my lips and said, "You could never be a cad, Stuart."

He gave me a wicked smile, and stood up. "Don't be too sure about that, me proud beauty."

I stood up, too. "I'll go wash my face," I said.

"Good idea. I'll meet you downstairs."

Checking the mirror above the sink, I splashed cold water on my face until the puffiness around my eyes had all but disappeared. Then I pulled the pins out of my hair, recombed it, and swept it up on top of my head.

Staring back at my reflection, I saw kiss swollen lips and starry eyes, telltale signs of a woman in love. My breasts ached with longing for the touch of his hands, and a vague sensation of wanting made my body throb for a fulfillment that was mysterious and so powerful, it frightened me.

With nervous hands, I smoothed the wrinkles from my skirt and hurried downstairs. He stood, waiting for me in the hall, and our eyes met. Both of us a little shy now, we reacted by being overly polite.

"I think I left my hat in the dining room."

"Aye, I'll get it for you."

"Don't bother. I can get it."

"No, please, let me."

"All right. Thank you."

"Here you are. You can use the mirror over there to put it on."

"Yes. Thank you."

"It's a very attractive hat."

"Thank you, again. Well, goodbye, Stuart. Thank you for the tea."

"Dammit, Katherine. Stop thanking me." He pulled me to him and kissed the top of my head. "Don't make any plans for tomorrow night. I'm picking you up at Cousin Elvira's at seven P.M. We'll have dinner at home." Holding up his hand, he smiled and said, "Don't worry. You'll be well chaperoned. Mrs. Diggs will be here and someone else that I'd like you to meet."

# Chapter 17

"Here ye be, Miss. Brown's Hotel."

The cab halted, and before the driver could jump down, the doorman had the door open and was handing me out of the carriage.

My thoughts still on Stuart, I automatically entered the hotel and walked up to the front desk. Like a sleepwalker, I stood there until the clerk politely cleared his throat.

"Mr. Beauregard Chantelle," I said quickly. "Would he or Miss Chantelle be in?"

"Aye, they're both in," the man said. "Which one shall I ring up?"

"Mr. Chantelle, please. I'm his daughter . . . 's friend." He didn't catch the slip, but I chided myself for being careless. "Just tell him Miss Hathaway is downstairs," I added.

He spoke first to the switchboard operator. "610, please." And then, "Mr. Chantelle, there's a young lady at the desk, a Miss Hathaway." He paused, listening. "Quite. I'll tell her, Mr. Chantelle." Then he turned to me. "Mr. Chantelle will be down directly, Miss."

I took a chair discreetly behind a giant palm and sat, facing the lift. Feeling the clerk's eyes on me, I suddenly realized that I had probably given the man the wrong impression by asking for Beau instead of Katherine, but I wanted a little time to speak to my father alone.

The gilded lift which resembled a giant bird cage descended, and Beau along with several other gentlemen emerged from the cage.

He wore a black frock coat with silk-faced lapels and grey striped trousers. With his handsome face and trim figure, Beau stood out from the other men like a peacock among barnyard roosters.

Shielded by the tall palm, I studied my father. He glanced almost frantically around the lobby, and when he didn't see me, began tapping his cane with impatience on the floor, a habit Beau uses to relieve frustration."

I stood up quickly then and walked towards him. Poor Beau, I thought. Katherine's mercurial moods are probably getting the best of him.

I announced, "Here I am," and he looked up and smiled.

Careful to appear properly formal, I extended my hand. "The desk clerk is watching," I warned in an undertone.

"My dear, Miss Hathaway," he said, slipping naturally into the act. Executing a courtly bow, he kissed my hand. "India is resting, but let us have lunch together. Not here," he added quickly, dismissing the hotel. "Some place else where we can talk."

Always the actor, I think Beau enjoyed the cloak and dagger aspect of our little masquerade, and I smiled indulgently. "I should be happy to have lunch with you, Mr. Chantelle. Lead on."

Out on the street and safely past the desk clerk's eagle eye, I entwined my arm in Beau's and squeezed his hand. "I've missed you, Beau. How have you been?"

"Fine, fine," he said absently. "But, I'm concerned about Katherine."

Always Katherine, I thought, and then chided myself for being jealous.

Beau doesn't know anything about your problems. He's assuming as always that you can take care of yourself! Not this time, I answered. I could use some fatherly advice, or maybe just a shoulder to cry on.

"There's a little restaurant around the corner," Beau said. "Nothing fancy about it, but at least we won't run into anybody we know."

It was a carbon copy of all the restaurants we had dined in

back home. Plain and inexpensive, its working class patrons looked more like small town Americans than Londoners. A far cry from our present lifestyle, I mused, wondering if we would find it hard to adjust once the masquerade was over.

I turned my attention then to Beau. He seemed preoccupied and uncharacteristically oblivious to his surroundings. "You said you were worried about Katherine," I prompted.

He sighed and shook his head. "She's terribly upset, Indy. I don't know if I can get her to go on tomorrow night." He paused and then looked at me with tormented eyes. "She acts strange sometimes, like she's in a trance or something."

"Beau," I said, "there's something about Katherine that you don't know."

He waved the approaching waitress impatiently away. "Later," he told her, giving me his undivided attention. "Go on. What do you mean?"

"As a child, Katherine had a traumatic experience," I said. "She can't remember what it was, but the Hathaways all seem to think she witnessed a murder!"

All the color drained from Beau's face. "Oh, my God," he said.

"That's why her family took her to America. And that would account for her reluctance to come back to Hathaway Manor. Subconsciously, of course. Poor Katherine was afraid of something, but she really didn't know what it was."

He appeared deeply disturbed by what I had told him. Finally, he spoke. "The police came to the theater yesterday and questioned the cast. It seems Katherine's friend Veronica did not commit suicide. She was murdered by her boyfriend!

"How horrible!" I said. "And this is what caused . . ."

He nodded. "Katherine's been in a trance ever since." Grabbing my hand, he said. "I don't know what to do. Oh, Indy would you talk to her? She looks up to you. If anybody can help her, it'll be you."

"Of course, Beau. Let's have lunch and then we'll go back to the hotel. I don't have to get back until late tonight."

"Oh, good," he said. "I knew I could count on you, Indy."

I patted his hand and sighed. True, but who can I count on, Beau?

Beau seemed nervous and anxious to get back, so we ordered lightly and both of us picked at the ill-prepared food.

"Ready?" he asked, and I nodded. The place depressed me for I could foresee countless meals in identically dismal surroundings stretching ahead of me. Katherine's check, as agreed upon, would be made out in my name, and I had no intentions of letting Beau squander the money when we got home.

Very soon now, I mused, the carriage will turn into a pumpkin, and Cinderella will run away, leaving her handsome prince behind.

"How are things with you, Indy?" Beau asked as an afterthought on the way back to the hotel.

"Fine," I said.

We entered the lobby, and I noticed that the nosy desk clerk was not at his post. Probably gone to lunch, I thought with relief.

We were silent in the lift, both of us wrapped in our own thoughts. Mine were on Stuart, and already I was regretting what I had not done.

Who are you saving yourself for? There will never be another Stuart in your life.

"This is our floor," Beau's voice brought me sharply back.

Katherine, I remembered. Beau expects me to have a magic wand and turn her into a sparkling, fun-loving girl again. Hastily tucking my own problems back into a corner of my mind, I gave Beau an encouraging smile and stepped out of the lift.

Beau unlocked the door and we entered the suite's magnificent drawing room. Both of us eyed the closed door to Katherine's room. "She's probably asleep," Beau said, and putting his ear to the door, he knocked softly. "Katherine, wake up. India is here."

I saw the knob turn, and braced myself for an emotional scene, but I wasn't prepared for the shock I received.

Wearing a gay smile and a pink, feather-trimmed dressing gown, Katherine glided into the room like an exotic bird. "India, what a pleasant surprise!"

My eyes met Beau's and he shrugged in amazement. "You're feeling better?" he asked her.

She gave him a brilliant smile. "I feel fine, Beau." Her cheeks were flushed, and her eyes danced with merriment. "How long can you stay, India? I hope you don't have to hurry off like the last time."

"I don't have to get back until late," I said. "We can all have dinner and spend the evening together."

"Did you hear that, Beau? Isn't it wonderful?" Bubbling over with enthusiasm, she grabbed my hand. "We don't have a performance tonight, so we can do the town." And giggling, she added, "I don't suppose my straitlaced relatives showed you any of London's nightlife."

Not wanting to mention Stuart, I said nothing, but she took my silence for affirmation and turned to Beau. "Let's see, the Claridge has a wonderful orchestra."

I stiffened. I wanted to help Katherine, but I would not subject myself to all the beautiful, but painful, memories I associated with the Claridge. "Some other place," I said. "Fenton took us all to the Claridge after the theater one night."

Katherine made a face. "What a shame! But there's lots of other exciting places. What do you suggest, Beau?"

He had sat down in a chair by the window, and for the first time in my life, I thought Beau looked his age. "Why don't you check that list the hotel provided?"

"Of course. There's a printed list of places to go and things to see," she explained, looking at me. "I'll see if I can find it."

She swept out of the room, leaving several pink feathers floating behind her, and Beau and I exchanged glances. "I don't understand," he said.

"She's blocked it out," I answered. "Just like the other time."

"That's good," he said. "If we don't mention anything of a disturbing nature, she'll probably be fine."

I didn't agree. Katherine was sticking her head in the sand.

How were we helping her if we did the same thing? And what about all the questions I had planned to ask Katherine? Like, who was Anabelle, and what did she know? *What,* or more importantly, *who* did Katherine see the night Lily Beacham was killed? Would all these questions have to be swept under a rug now? I asked myself.

Probably so, but I couldn't help wondering, "Was Katherine's peace of mind more important than exposing a murderer?"

After much indecision, Katherine and Beau finally settled on the Savoy for dinner. They were anxious to show me a good time, and Katherine offered me the pick of her wardrobe. "You can't go to the Savoy in an afternoon dress," she insisted.

At that point, I didn't care if I went in my petticoat. Katherine's ability to suppress unpleasant facts made me both worried and angry, and I alternated between wanting to shake her and comfort her. Was she a spoiled brat or a deeply disturbed girl? I pondered.

My thoughts kept returning to Stuart, and I ached to be in his arms. Dare I beg off, give Katherine and Beau some excuse about having to get back to Cousin Elvira's right after dinner? And dare I instead go to Stuart, and give myself to him?

"Which one?" Katherine's voice shattered my daydream, and I stared stupidly back at her.

She shook her head. "Which dress, India? I told you to take your pick."

We were standing in front of the open armoire which was bulging with gowns in every color of the rainbow. "You choose," I said.

Pulling out an exquisite Venetian lace gown in white, she held it up to me. "Gorgeous. It makes you look like a bride, India."

Something I'll never be, I thought rather sadly, as I put it on.

Katherine wore peacock blue, her favorite color. The soft silk gown clung to her body, adding years to her age, and I jokingly told her so.

"That's a nice compliment," she said. "I hate being young. You might think it shocking, India, but I'd like to be forty with a husband and two lovers," she added impishly.

I shook my head. Shades of Cousin Elvira! I thought.

Beau was waiting for us in the drawing room. He looked anxiously at Katherine, and when she smiled, he seemed relieved. With forced heartiness, he extended his arms, and said, "An arm for each fair lady, and a fair lady for each arm. What man could ask for more!"

We feasted on lobster and drank French champagne in the elegant dining room of the Savoy Hotel. Katherine's eyes sparkled like the diamond cut prisms twinkling down on us from crystal chandeliers. "A toast," she said, raising her glass. "To my forthcoming birthday, and the end of the masquerade."

We clinked our glasses together and drank. Tasting the bitterness of regret like vinegar on my tongue, I thought that once the masquerade had ended Stuart would be lost to me forever!

"Don't look so sad, India. You only have two more weeks to go," Katherine said.

"That's right," Beau added. "And before you know it, we'll all be on the other side of the ocean again."

Katherine smiled. "I'll be free," she said.

Beau laughed, "I'll be safe."

And I'll be miserable, I thought, fighting back angry tears. Suddenly I reached a decision. "It's getting late," I said. "I have to leave, but you two stay and enjoy the evening."

"But why?" they both protested.

"The night is young," Katherine said.

I smiled. "Not for me. Time is running out like sand in an hourglass, and I must hurry or it'll be too late." I stood up, puting my hands on my father's shoulders before he could rise. "Don't get up, please. The doorman will get me a cab." Standing behind him, I kissed his cheek and looking over his head to Katherine, I said, "If you don't mind, I'll just keep the bridal gown on. I'll return it later."

While they were still in shock, I hurried out of the room,

feeling like Cinderella leaving the ball. But I was not hurrying away from my prince, I thought. I was hurrying to him!

I felt daring and a little nervous as the doorman handed me into the cab and asked, "Where to, Miss?"

"No. 10 Bleekman Place," I said, trying to keep my voice steady.

"No. 10 Bleekman Place," he shouted up to the driver, and we were off, the horses prancing noisily over the cobblestoned streets of London.

What shall I say? *I've changed my mind, Stuart.*

The very thought of it made me blush. It won't be necessary to say anything, I decided. Stuart will open the door and take me in his arms, and then everything will be all right.

I had no illusions about our love. Nothing would change. We'd be back in America in two weeks as planned. Katherine would have her freedom, Beau his security, and I would have my memories. They would last me the rest of my life, and that would be enough for me.

We turned the corner into Bleekman Place and I tapped on the roof of the cab. "You may stop here, driver," I said. We were a few doors away from No. 10, but I preferred not to stop directly in front of the house.

I thought the driver's dour face registered disapproval as he handed me out of the cab. Fool, I chided myself. How could the man possibly know? I paid him and was relieved when the carriage clattered past me and disappeared quickly down the street.

Walking slowly, I savored the night. Summer was coming to an end, and its beauty was fading like an aging courtesan. Hot August days melted into nights that held a hint of autumn in the late summer air. Soon it would be fall and our little masquerade would come to an end.

I, too, wanted to fade away like these lush summer days, never letting Stuart know that I was not Katherine. Perhaps then, he would keep a place in his heart always for the cousin he could never marry. Better that, than to have him hate me for deceiving him, I mused.

213

Opening the gate very quietly, I entered No. 10. A soft light shone through the bay window in the front of the house. Picturing Stuart reading in the drawing room, I tiptoed up onto the step and peeped inside.

He was pouring himself a drink from the decanter on the wine table, and my heart turned over when I saw him. There was something so vital and exciting about Stuart that seeing him after even a brief absence took my breath away.

I felt like a stagestruck female ogling an actor, as I stood at the window, feasting my eyes on the man I loved. Deeply tanned, he radiated robust health and a virile masculinity that was refreshing in this age of pasty-faced dandies.

His lips moved in speech, and I sucked in my breath as the drawing room's blue velvet portieres parted and a woman entered the room.

She was exquisitely beautiful, small and dark-haired, with the finely chiseled features of a dainty Dresden doll. Her flawless figure was enhanced by a stunning black gown that hugged her hips and bared her creamy bosom.

I watched, stupefied as she took the glass from Stuart's hand and smiled up at him with adoring eyes. His lips moved in a toast, and they touched glasses and drank.

I should have left then, but I could not tear myself away until Stuart bent down and swallowed her petite figure up in an embrace. I could not bear to see him kiss her, so I turned quickly, losing my balance and almost giving myself away.

The last thing I wanted to do was to attract their attention, so I practically crawled down the steps, my eyes brimming over with tears.

At last I reached the gate, pushed it open, and ran outside. I never stopped running until Bleekman Street and my faithless lover were far behind me.


"Suit yourself," Beatrice said.

We were seated at the breakfast table, and I had just proposed my early return to Cornwall, chaperoned by the Chantelles who were supposedly traveling there themselves.

"But just make sure you tell your uncle this was your

idea, Katherine," she added, wagging a finger in my face. She stared pointedly at my swollen eyes. "Are you catching cold? You look terrible."

I forced myself to smile, though I had a violent headache, brought on no doubt by all the crying I had done the night before. "I'm fine," I lied. "I just want to spend a little more time with my friends."

She nodded, and dismissed me from her thoughts, for which I was supremely grateful.

Early this morning, still wide awake and with no tears left to cry, I had decided that I could not remain in London. To see Stuart again would be just too painful.

There was no excuse he could give me for what I had seen with my own eyes. The truth was plain. Stuart had wanted a woman last night, and when I had not made myself available, he had simply replaced me with someone else.

A predictable end to a romantic illusion, but one I simply could not face, so I had come up with what I hoped would be an acceptable excuse to escape London. It had worked and I thanked God for small favors.

We got up from the table and Beatrice said, "We must run. Willa has a fitting with the dressmaker." She brushed my cheek with cold lips. "Have a safe trip."

Willa missed my cheek altogether and kissed the air between us. "Goodbye, Katherine."

I waited until they had gone and then I went upstairs and packed. I had no idea what time the train left, but I'd be waiting at Paddington Station to board it.

Before leaving, I looked in on Cousin Elvira. "I've come to say goodbye and to thank you for your hospitality," I said.

"Threw you out, didn't they? I'm not surprised," she said. "What will you do now? Go back on the stage?"

Her words shocked me until I recalled that she habitually mistook me for Nell, Stuart's mother. "I'm Katherine, Roland's daughter," I said gently.

She spanned the generations in a blink of the eye. "So you are." Then she gave me an impish smile. "Did you let that rogue Stuart seduce you?"

"Cousin Elvira!" I said.

"Oh, don't have the vapors, gel. Stuart's probably good in bed. Like Lord Marchbank," she added, rolling her eyes. "Oh, the things that devil would do!"

I said, "Cousin Elvira," but she ignored me.

"My father wanted me to marry your grandfather, Duncan Hathaway, but I wouldn't do it." A look of disgust suddenly crossed her face. "Duncan was a mean cuss, and ugly as sin, crooked as a ram's horn, too. He turned Hathaway Manor into a smuggler's haven. It was a scandal, but the family kept his secret."

I said, "The family has many secrets, doesn't it, Cousin Elvira?"

"Aye, we're a scurvy lot," she said with a cackle.

Her eyes gleamed with sudden clarity. "You've kept your share of secrets, too, haven't you, Katherine?"

"I don't know what you mean."

She frowned impatiently. "Oh, come on now, gel. That business about Lily Beacham. You know what I mean."

"I don't remember," I said.

She nodded her head vigorously. "Aye, that was your tune, gel and you played it for all it was worth. I don't remember. I don't remember," she mimicked in a childish voice.

"I really don't," I insisted. "But perhaps if you filled me in on some of the details, it might come back."

She gave me a skeptical look, but I could see she was enjoying being taken seriously for a change. "Well now, let me see. We'll begin with Lily—" She stopped abruptly and glared at her nurse who was standing in the doorway.

Nurse Smith winked her eye at me, a universal sign to politely dismiss either the very young or the very old when they had become a nuisance. "It's time for our nap," she said loudly.

"Fine. You take yours then," Cousin Elvira shouted back. "And close that damn door. This is a private conversation."

Despite my distraught state, I smothered a smile. Cousin Elvira was the only one of Katherine's relatives that I would miss.

"Now, where was I?" she asked when the door had been gently closed.

"Lily," I said.

"Aye, Lily Beacham. She was a servant girl and a tart if ever I saw one. Lily was a looker though, and she had enough brass to start a band." Cousin Elvira shook her head and I visualized the cobwebs disappearing inside. "She hadn't been at Hathaway Manor long when she was carrying on with anything in trousers. And that's not excluding the aristocratic trousers inside the mansion," she emphasized.

"Go on," I urged, hoping against hope that she would not lose the slim thread of thought that was giving me a glimpse into the past.

"You, of course, were always running around, sticking your nose into things that were none of your concern."

As I feared, she went off on a tangent.

"My Willie, Lord Marchbank," she explained, "used to say, 'Katherine Hathaway ought to convince anybody that cousins shouldn't beget children!'" She laughed. "Where was I?"

"Lily Beacham," I insisted.

"Aye. In the meantime, you had disappeared. Your mother had the whole household in an uproar over it. Emily was a typical hen with one chick, I always said. She was a nervous wreck about you—"

I interrupted quickly before she got off on another tangent. "I disappeared, you say."

"Aye, that's what I said. For pity sakes, pay attention, gel!" I apologized, and mollified, she continued. "Servants, the whole family—they were all out searching, combing the grounds like a pack of dogs, but it was your grandfather who finally found you."

"Where?" I said without thinking.

She looked at me sharply. "You really don't remember!" She shook her head and continued. "He found you in the cave near Pirate's Cove. You were hiding behind a boulder, and not ten feet away was Lily Beacham's dead body!"

"How awful!" I said, feeling a surge of sympathy for Katherine.

"Aye, so awful you'd gone into shock, couldn't talk, just stared straight ahead like a dummy. A trauma, the doctor called it, course he was never told about Lily. Nobody was. The Hathaways keep their family secrets!"

"But all the servants at Hathaway Manor know about the murder," I insisted.

"Of course," she answered impatiently. "That's now, but nobody knew then because old Duncan Hathaway swore his family to secrecy. They buried Lily up on the moors that very night. Duncan, Fenton, Gilbert, and your father."

"But why?" I asked.

She smiled. "Why indeed? Because Duncan Hathaway suspected it was one of his own who'd murdered Lily, that's why."

I swallowed a lump in my throat. "Who did he suspect?"

"Gilbert," she answered. "And it was Beatrice who pointed the finger at him."

"How do you know all this?" I asked.

"Gilbert and I were kindred spirits," she said, and then added a little sadly, "He was the son I never had."

"And you don't believe he did it?"

"I know he didn't, but somebody did."

She was staring intently at me, and I felt compelled to add, "I wish I could remember."

"What difference would it make now? Gilbert went to his grave being blamed for it."

Her sudden show of outrage quickly evaporated, and then she said something so profound, I was to recall it later.

"The answer to a riddle is usually as plain as the noses on our faces." Looking at me with sad old eyes, she patted my hand. "It wasn't your fault, gel. One of us adults should have figured it out right then and there instead of depending on a child."

I could see she still felt deeply about Gilbert, but there were other things I wanted to know as well. "How was Lily's body finally discovered?" I asked.

"Some of those diggers were scratching around up on the

moors, looking for artifacts. They'd carry away the bloody tors if they could manage it," she added. "Anyway, they uncovered the chit's body, but the authorities didn't do much investigating." She shrugged a bony shoulder. "After all, she was only a poor gel with no family and with her reputation, half the men in Cornwall might have had reason to bash in her skull."

She leaned back and closed her eyes for a moment, and I suddenly felt guilty about pumping her. "I'm sorry if I've tired you, Cousin Elvira," I said. "Just one thing more," I insisted, for I had to know. "Do you remember Anabelle?"

She opened her eyes. "Of course, I remember. She was your doll, your funny little alter ego. Whenever they asked you something that you didn't want to remember, you'd say, 'Ask Anabelle. She knows.' And, when you got yourself into trouble, you'd blame it on the doll. 'Anabelle did it,'" she mimicked in a childish voice. "That's what you told me once when you scribbled on my best tablecloth." She gave me a smug smile. "Spoiled rotten, you were, but I pinched your behind good when nobody was looking."

"Do you know what happened to the doll?" I asked.

"You left it at Hathaway Manor, didn't want anything to do with it after you lost your memory," she said. "It's probably still there."

Oh, no, it's not, I thought, but knowing that Anabelle was a doll made Stuart's comment even more cryptic.

*I don't know you,* he had said. *But maybe Anabelle does. Shall I ask her what she knows?*

# Chapter 18

"Earl's son charged with murder!"

Holding the lurid tabloid out in front of him, the newsboy wended his way through the crowd at Paddington Station. "Read all about it," he shouted shrilly. "Scotland Yard says actress was murdered!"

His words gradually penetrated my brain. Could he be talking about Katherine's friend? I stood up and raised my hand. "Over here! I'll take a paper," I said.

"Here ye are, miss." He eyed me boldly and grinned. "Like to read *The Tattler,* eh? Plenty in 'ere to keep you awake."

I paid him and took the paper without comment. It was one of those trashy editions that thrived on sensationalism, but I was only interested in the feature story.

Folding it up, I tucked it in the wicker basket that contained my lunch. Nurse Smith had the cook pack enough food for an army, but I was grateful for her thoughtfulness.

Once on the train in the privacy of my compartment, I took the paper out and read with interest the account of Miss Veronica Mayfield's tragic involvement with The Honorable Roger Cranston, youngest son of the Earl of Havenwood.

According to *The Tattler,* the young *ingénue* was swept off her feet by the wealthy young man who attended nightly performances and filled her dressing room with flowers.

"The poor girl fell madly in love," the article stated, and then posed a question, "But would she be accepted by such an aristocratic family?"

Perhaps as a mistress, *The Tattler* insinuated, but never as a wife!

The article went on to suggest that Veronica Mayfield's insistence on a wedding ring caused her lover to resort to murder rather than risk a breach of promise suit.

Poor girl, I thought. She should have known better. Even in America, lines are drawn to separate society into classes, but there the gap can sometimes be bridged. Not so here, I mused, thinking of my own situation. The English aristocracy is sacrosanct, and this tragic affair had brought that fact home to me in no uncertain terms.

I didn't care if Veronica Mayfield had threatened Roger Cranston with a scandal. He had no right to kill her, and I gathered from the tone of *The Tattler* that most of the common people in England agreed with me.

How much better not to take the risk of rejection, I thought, for to see Stuart look at me with contempt would be more than I could bear. Never, would I give him that satisfaction. Let him think that "his cousin" rejected him first!

Leaning back in the seat, I closed my eyes, hoping the motion of the train would lull me to sleep, but my restless mind would not be stilled. I couldn't stay in London, but I wasn't anxious to return to Hathaway Manor either.

Why not stay in Penzance? I thought. Beatrice's letter announcing my return won't arrive at Hathaway Manor for several days. I'll be back before I'm missed. Of course, Fenton will be outraged and accuse me of heaven knows what when he finds out I didn't come straight home, but why should I care? Everybody expects Katherine to be daring.

That decision made, I relaxed and drifted off into a deep and dreamless sleep.

When I awoke, we were crossing the Tamar, and I could hardly believe that I had slept so soundly and so long. Raising my arms above my head, and holding my legs taut, I stretched, savoring that moment of utter peace that suffuses us when first we wake.

Almost immediately my mind began to tally up the score of unsolved problems that sleep had laid to rest, but I pushed them aside. Right now, I was ravenously hungry, and reaching for the picnic basket, I opened it eagerly.

The contents looked delicious—biscuits, cold chicken, eggs and fruit, with a generous slice of gooseberry pie for dessert. Quickly pulling off my gloves, I started to eat. Thank God Tarleton can't see me now, I thought as I devoured a biscuit with unladylike haste and daintily licked the butter off my finger.

Munching on a chicken leg, a ridiculous riddle made popular by old minstrel shows suddenly popped unbidden into my head: *Why does a chicken cross the road? To get to the other side.*

"The answer to a riddle is usually as plain as the noses on our faces," Cousin Elvira had said.

An astute observation, I thought, turning it over in my mind. We wrack our brains to answer a riddle and invariably overlook the obvious. But, what is obvious about Lily Beacham's murder?

I never expected to learn the answer, for time was running out. I pictured sand trickling relentlessly through an hourglass, the top almost empty now, the bottom almost full. But as Cervantes said in *Don Quixote, Murder will out,* and so it did when least we all expected it.

When the train arrived in Penzance, I checked my bags at the station, and carrying only a small valise, walked the short distance to the inn.

Grace recognized me at once and gave me a welcoming smile. "Miss Hathaway, it's ever so nice to see you again."

"Thank you, Grace," I replied. "I'd like to stay for a few days if you can accommodate me."

"Aye, I'll give you the same room you had last time." She reached into her pocket for keys. "The Shaw sisters are still here," she informed me. "I suppose they'll stay until the weather changes."

I followed her upstairs and she continued talking. "They like to go exploring," she confided and smiled. "Waste of time if you ask me, but then they were school teachers," she added indulgently. "Here we be, Miss. Same nice view."

As soon as she had gone, I opened the window and took a deep breath. Like a runaway, I felt the exhilaration of complete freedom. It was a rather heady feeling and one completely new for me.

For the first time in my life, I had no one to answer *for* and no one to answer *to*. I can eat when I want, sleep when I want. I have no responsibilities beyond those I impose on myself, and for the next three days, I did not intend to impose anything on myself!

Glancing at my watch, I saw that it was four o'clock. A vague sense of something forgotten tugged at my conscience, and then I laughed out loud.

Feeling as outrageous as Cousin Elvira, I said, "To hell with your bloody teatime, Tarleton!"

The Shaw sisters sought me out before dinner. "Here she is, Violet," Clara exclaimed, coming out on the inn's front porch where I had seated myself to watch the sun go down.

"Grace told us you were here," she said, taking a chair beside me.

"And that you were staying for a few days," Violet added as she joined us.

"Yes, my aunt and my cousin are still in London, so I thought I'd sightsee in Penzance before going home."

Violet looked at me sharply. "Home? Do you mean home to Hathaway Manor or home to America?"

I was a little surprised that she had stumbled on the truth, but I saw no reason not to tell them. "Home to America," I confessed. "In two weeks time, I shall reach my majority. Then I shall no longer require a guardian."

Violet's shrewd eyes took me in, and then with her customary candor, she said matter-of-factly, "I'm sorry things didn't work out here, but Clara and I are not surprised. You may technically be a Hathaway, Katherine, but you're nothing like this branch of the family."

Curiosity aroused, I said, "Please tell me what you mean." And quickly I added, "I promise, I shan't take offense."

"No reason that you should," Violet said emphatically. "We're none of us responsible for our relatives."

"Certainly not," Clara acknowledged. "We'd hate to be held responsible for Cousin Clarence."

"That old fool! Don't mention his name," Violet retorted. Turning back to me, her expression softened, and she said, "I'm glad you're leaving, Katherine. Don't let your uncle persuade you to stay. There's something evil about Hathaway Manor."

Clara joined in. "That's right, Katherine. We've heard things, and. . . ." She looked at her sister. "You tell her, Violet."

Violet then proceeded to tell me an involved story which began with the two sisters being confronted by Tarleton on the beach near Hathaway Manor. "We didn't give that prissy little man a second thought," she explained, "but the next day Lord Hathaway himself came after us with a gun!"

I was shocked. "He threatened you with a gun just for walking on the beach!"

Clara nodded, and Violet said. "We did a little investigating and we think we know why."

I listened intently as she told me how they had come back to the Penzance Library and delved into old accounts of buried treasure, piracy, and smuggling along the coast of Cornwall.

Confirming Stuart's story, she related the tale of Anthony Hathaway, the infamous, albino pirate who had been Katherine's ancestor.

"He had a falling out with his cohorts," Violet said. "It ended in murder. Their's by Anthony, of course, and he hid the spoils, reputed to be treasures from a Spanish galleon somewhere along the coast. The Hathaways have been searching for it for generations," she added.

I didn't interrupt and she continued.

"Duncan Hathaway became obsessed with finding it, they say, but no one knows if he ever did. He was a strange man and it's rumored he was deeply involved in smuggling back in the old days. Not many people in Cornwall are willing to

224

talk about that even now. I guess they're a little ashamed," she added. "They were more than smugglers, you see. They were wreckers and the poor souls who survived the shipwrecks didn't survive the wreckers, if you know what I mean!"

Clara spoke up. "But, we're just telling you this so you'll understand the rest of it."

"There's more," I said.

Violet stood up and placed her hands on her hips. "Well, you didn't think we were going to let your uncle scare us off, did you?"

I smiled. "I should have known better."

"Of course you should," Violet quipped.

Clara said, "This is the exciting part."

Violet glared at her sister. "Do you want to tell this story, Clara?"

Clara looked at me with mock dismay, and turning to her sister, she said, "No indeed. You go right ahead."

Violet cleared her throat. "There's a cove a little way down from Hathaway Manor."

"Pirate's Cove?" I asked.

She nodded. "You're familiar with it then."

Not wanting to disclose information yet, I shrugged. "I've heard of it."

"There's a cave there, and someone has recently been exploring it because we found a lantern at the mouth of the opening."

The one I left after my harrowing escape, I thought. Perhaps I should tell them, but the words stuck in my throat as Violet said, "We lit the lantern and crawled inside."

Taking note of their ample figures, and recalling the narrow passageway, I spoke without thinking. "But wasn't it an awfully tight squeeze?"

Violet shrugged. "You couldn't get a hack through it, but it wasn't all that narrow for pedestrians. The fallen rocks made walking a little difficult though."

I smiled to myself and mentally concluded that the pounding surf had evidently widened the passageway since I had

225

opened it up.

"Anyway, we followed the tunnel until we came to a large chamber."

"There were ponds in there, and little fish with no eyes," Clara exclaimed, unable to curb her enthusiasm.

I was dying to find out if they had discovered it led directly to Hathaway Manor, and I said, "Did you go through the chamber to the other side?"

Clara thought I hadn't heard. "They had no eyes, Katherine. I mean that literally. These little creatures simply had no eyes, and they were white," she added. "Totally without color. I've never seen anything like it!"

Neither have I, I thought, but right now, I'm more interested in what else you saw.

Violet picked up the story. "We were about to leave the chamber and explore the rest of the cave when we heard a tapping noise. It was coming from another passageway on the far side of the large pond."

I recalled seeing that other opening and wondering where it led.

"Well, considering that your uncle had threatened us with a gun," Violet continued, "we decided discretion was the better part of valor, and we'd best leave the cave."

"But we were too late," Clara added, her eyes wide with excitement. "Rocks started to slide out of the opening and we could hear a man's footsteps coming out of the other passageway."

"We hid behind a big boulder," Violet said, quickly regaining the floor. "The man came out, and you'll never guess who it was." She paused dramatically, daring her sister to give away the surprise ending. "It was your cousin, the good-looking one who was with you at the inn."

"Stuart!" I said.

They nodded their heads. "The same," Clara said. "You know Katherine we didn't recognize him that day at the inn, but we figured it out later. He's the same young man we used to see in the library."

"When did all of this happen?" I asked.

Violet frowned in concentration. "I can't recall exactly.

Can you, Clara?"

Clara shook her head.

I thought back to when Fenton and Jordan had come to London. Stuart had been off on a business trip then. Had the business been in Cornwall?

"We never did get to explore the cave," Clara said.

"No," Violet added. "And it's probably just as well. I've been reading about them and sometimes there are cave-ins. We could have been trapped down there."

A chill went up my spine. I could have been buried alive and never been found. Had the watcher on the stairway lured me there hoping that might happen?


I returned to Hathaway Manor, feeling refreshed and competent to cope with Fenton's anger. I needn't have worried though, for Beatrice's letter did not arrive until the day I did. Tarleton handed it to his master in the drawing room just before tea, and after reading it, Fenton wore a look of disgust and tossed it aside.

"Your aunt is getting as skittish as a Londoner," he remarked. "Giving a young woman permission to travel alone and unchaperoned."

I glanced at the open letter. In her haste, Beatrice had forgotten to date it, and he must have assumed she'd written it several days before I left.

"But Uncle," I said, "I traveled across an entire ocean alone and unchaperoned."

"Aye and it's a miracle you didn't get waylaid and wind up in London!"

Oh, but I did, or the real Katherine did, I mused. Only Katherine wasn't the one who was waylaid. I was!

Watching Fenton sip his tea, I wondered what he would say if I told him his niece was on the stage and he was entertaining a wardrobe mistress from Columbus, Ohio.

But he'll never know. He'll reluctantly kiss his assumed niece goodbye. And he'll do it reluctantly only because he'll be saying goodbye to Katherine's money.

At least I hope he'll be saying goodbye to Katherine's

227

money, I thought. The only way Fenton stands to get it is by marrying Katherine off, or killing her off, and since I'm still masquerading as Katherine.... I let the thought dangle. Fenton's face held a menacing look as the shadows of twilight crept into the room.

"How is Jordan?" I asked with genuine interest for Jordan's strange illness concerned me, particularly after Willa's alarming remarks.

My question seemed to pique Fenton's interest and he regarded me with speculation. "I'm surprised you're interested, Katherine."

"Of course I'm interested," I said. "Jordan is my cousin. He was feeling better when I left and I hope that hasn't changed."

He leaned closer to me and spoke in a confidential manner. "He's been spending his days and nights in that confounded laboratory up on the moors. Perhaps you can persuade him to give up his experiments, my dear."

"I wouldn't presume to do that, uncle," I said. "Jordan is a dedicated scientist. I have no right to interfere in his work."

His pale eyes turned to granite and he regarded me with sudden anger. "His work will be the ruin of us, and as for Jordan being a 'dedicated scientist,' as you so dramatically put it, that's all poppycock. There's some things better left alone."

"But Uncle," I said. "No new discoveries would ever be made if every man thought as you do—"

"Don't contradict me, Miss," he stormed. "This is England, not America, or even London, for that matter." He shook his head and muttered, "Which is almost as bad. This is Cornwall," he proclaimed. "Women are chattel and they defer to their husbands and guardians." Draining his teacup, he looked me in the eye. "You've been in America too long, Katherine!"

My own anger rose up and spilled over, and I heard myself say, "And I can't wait to get back!"

Deathly silence followed, as we stared into each other's eyes, both of us shocked by my outburst.

Fenton spoke first. "Your mind's made up. That's wha'

228

you plan to do?"

"Yes," I said.

His expression turned shrewd. "Perhaps you'll change your mind. Jordan is the heir to Hathaway Manor. He's taken with you, Katherine, and think about it. Your combined fortunes would be almost limitless. You'd acquire a title, something most American heiresses would die for."

His closing statement rang in my ears and a cold fear crept up my spine. I didn't want to give Jordan any false hopes, and I thought the time had come to lay our cards on the table.

"I'm sorry, Uncle. I'm fond of Jordan, but I'm not in love with him. I'm grateful to you and Aunt Beatrice for taking me in, but America is my home, and I plan to return right after my birthday."

The strangest expression crossed his face, and his words turned my blood to ice. "So be it. I shall honor your decision, Katherine, but I wipe my hands of it. What you have decided may have alarming repercussions. You have always been willful, and I shudder to think now how you shall end!"

Needless to say, my conversation with Fenton did nothing to raise my spirits. Like the fog that continuously shrouded Cornwall in a swirling mist, distorting it, revealing it, and then suddenly concealing it again, my mind struggled to see through the masks so artfully worn by all the players in the masquerade at Hathaway Manor.

It was customary for the family to gather in the drawing room before dinner, and knowing Fenton's obsession with punctuality, I wanted to be on time.

"Hurry, Maureen," I said, as the girl dawdled over arranging my hair. "Lord Hathaway does not like to be kept waiting."

I felt edgy tonight, probably as a consequence of my argument with Fenton, but more than that, autumn had arrived early up here and it added a spooky atmosphere to the place.

I had noticed it even before I had alighted from the fly. A penetrating chill was in the air, and clouds obscured the sun, whereas in Penzance it had still been summer.

Stabbing pins hurriedly into the French braid she had fashioned in my hair, Maureen chattered away. "There, Miss Katherine. If you didn't have such thick hair, I could have finished quicker, but then it's lucky you are to have it. Some ladies have to depend on false plaits. They say a lady in London lost hers at Covent Gardens. A gentleman in the seat behind her picked it up and handed it to her."

"Yes, thank you, Maureen," I muttered, hastily dabbing cologne behind my ears.

"You'll be needing a shawl," she reminded me. "Summer's gone and these old houses get drafty in the fall."

I took the shawl and hurried downstairs, anxious to arrive in the drawing room before the clock struck eight o'clock.

I saw Fenton as I entered. His back was to me and he was alone. I had hoped Jordan would be present, but I assumed he was still holed up in his laboratory, working.

"Good evening, Uncle," I said.

I hoped we could get through this awkward evening without further unpleasantness. It was unfortunate that Jordan would not be here, I thought, but I intended to act as if nothing had happened.

My smile froze on my face as he turned and looked at me with a contemptuous expression. His lips curved into a sneer, and he said, "You're right on time, Katherine. Most unusual for such an independent young woman, but then you won't be subject to the rules of Hathaway Manor much longer now, will you?"

Refusing to be goaded into another argument, I sought to change the subject and walking over to the fireplace, I said, "It's a good night for a fire. It's chilly here, but it was rather warm in Penzance."

He said, "Humpf," reached for the decanter, and poured himself another glass of wine.

I remained standing, staring into the fire and wondering how I should manage to get through these last days at Hathaway Manor when my thoughts were interrupted by Tarleton's somber announcement.

"Dinner is served, your lordship."

We ate in the small salon, each of us at opposite ends of the table, with Tarleton in rigid attendance. I tried several times to initiate a conversation, but Fenton was preoccupied and uncooperative.

At last the meal ended, and I hoped he would remain in the dining room for his brandy and cigar, but he turned to me and said, "We shall retire to the drawing room now, Katherine."

I fully expected to be questioned about my plans, and perhaps pressured again to change them, which I had to admit seemed the logical thing for a guardian to do. Fenton, however, did none of those things. He spoke not one word to me and immediately buried his nose in the newspaper.

Beatrice's needlepoint easel stood in a corner of the room, and for wont of anything better to do, I sat down and began to work on it. The silence was so acute, I could hear the pin-prick of my needle going in and out of the canvas.

"Master Jordan is home, your lordship." Tarleton's words startled me, and I stuck my finger with the needle.

Fenton jumped up. "Where is he?"

"He's gone upstairs to his room, your lordship."

Fenton was very white, and he seemed extremely nervous as he paced the floor.

"If I may be excused, Uncle," I said. "I should like to retire, too."

He waved me away impatiently. "Aye, that's best. Go to bed, Katherine."

"Goodnight, Uncle," I said and left the room.

I was halfway up the staircase when Fenton called my name. Gripping the bannister, I turned and saw him looking up at me from the bottom of the stairs. "Katherine," he said, and I had to strain my ears to hear him. "Don't come out of your room tonight. Do you understand me?"

My blood turned cold. "Aye, Uncle, but—"

"Bolt your door," he ordered. "And don't leave your room, no matter what you hear. Is that understood?"

"Yes, Uncle."

Picking up my skirt, I ran upstairs and down the long, dark corridor to my room. I flung open the door, and leaning against it, I gasped for breath. Then remembering

Fenton's warning, I slammed the flimsy bolt into place.

The room was icy cold and I was trembling all over. I could hear the roar of an angry sea, but the night was heavy with fog, and as I looked out the window strange shapes seemed to materialize out of the mist, and move like phantoms over the ground.

My heart was beating wildly. But, I'm safe in here, I told myself. Then I remembered the trapdoor under the bed!

# Chapter 19

Consumed by an anxiety that bordered on hysteria, I knelt down and peeked underneath the bed. The rock was still in place!

Overcome with relief, I slumped to the floor and leaned my head against the bedpost. I consoled myself with the thought that even without the rock, the trapdoor could not be opened with the bed in place. But, my peace of mind was short-lived.

There may be other secret entrances to this room, I thought, and my eyes darted frantically around, pausing at the large, walk-in closet whose door was slightly ajar.

*What are you afraid of?* my inner voice asked, and it forced me to face the ugly suspicion that Fenton meant to do away with me.

The possibility that I might never leave Hathaway Manor alive had occurred to me in the past, but I had pushed the ugly thought to the back of my mind, not wanting to admit it, even to myself.

Now, I reluctantly examined the evidence. Hadn't I signed a paper in Katherine's name stating that should she die before reaching her majority, all of her assets would revert to Lord Hathaway? And hadn't I overheard Fenton tell Beatrice that a match between Jordan and Katherine would be a good way to keep her money in the family?

*Or, would you rather we killed Katherine and inherited her money?* Fenton's own words came back to haunt me.

He had raised the question in jest, but what will he do now after I have taken away his first option by refusing to marry Jordan? I cannot stay in this room, I told myself. If he means to do me harm, he'll do it while Beatrice and Willa are away. I must hide, but where?

Suddenly I remembered the secret staircase that I had stumbled upon that very first day when I had become lost in the maze of Hathaway Manor's corridors. Nobody would think of looking for me there.

My decision made, I pulled a blanket and pillow off the bed. Folding the blanket as small as possible, I used it as a pouch, stuffing a candle and matches inside of it. Then I cautiously slid the bolt back and opened the door. The dimly lit corridor looked so spooky that I hesitated, vacillating between taking my chances in the room or daring to leave it.

I turned around. Suppose I have misjudged Fenton? He told me to stay in my room. If I leave it, will I be putting myself in even greater jeopardy?

My ears picked up a faint, scraping sound. It could have been the wind rattling the window or a mouse scurrying for a hole, but it made my decision for me. I closed the door and ran down the corridor so fast my feet scarcely touched the thickly carpeted floor.

My heart was pounding in my chest and every time I turned a corner, I held my breath, but I encountered no one. At last, I reached the hidden staircase. Terrified lest I trip on the treacherous stairs, I sat down and slowly inched my way down on my bottom.

It was pitch black down there and I was cramped for space, but I felt safe in this small area. I unfolded my blanket and wrapped it around me, spilling out the candle and matches which I had rolled inside. I would not use them now for they would be a fire hazard down here, and the fact that I had even brought them testified to my irrational state of mind.

I stuffed the pillow behind my head and tried to relax. Consoling myself with the thought that Beatrice and Willa could return at any minute, I rationalized that I should not have to spend many more nights down here.

"You sent for me, Father?"

I jumped, hearing Jordan's voice on the other side of the wall. So Fenton had remained in the drawing room, I thought. I felt a little silly recalling the scraping noise and my conviction that Fenton had been hiding in my room.

"Aye, I sent for you. You haven't been home for a week, and then you sneak upstairs without one word to me."

"I'm very tired, Father. I thought to save the inquisition for morning."

"Don't push me too far, Jordan. I'm your father and still the Master of Hathaway Manor." Fenton's voice rose, as he added, "And at the rate you're going, you might not live to inherit the title."

Jordan answered him in a weary voice. "I don't care about the title, Father."

"You're a fool, Jordan." The brief pause was shattered when Fenton exclaimed in a tortured voice. "Oh, God, why have I been cursed with idiots? Would you have Stuart declared heir-presumptive?"

Jordan's voice was low. "It doesn't matter."

"It matters to me," Fenton shouted. "Never, I say! Do you understand?"

Jordan gave him no answer, and Fenton continued to rail. "The title, the house, the land, and aye, even that accursed treasure, wherever it is, belong to my heirs, not Gilbert's. Stuart shall have none of it. Is that clear?"

I had to strain my ears to hear Jordan say, "Aye, now if I may be excused, I would like to go to bed."

"I'm not finished yet," Fenton said. He had calmed down, and not wanting to miss any of the conversation, I leaned closer to the wall. "Your mother and Willa are still lolly-gagging around London, and if they don't come home soon, I shall go up there and bring them back." He paused a moment and then added, "But your cousin Katherine came home today."

Jordan's voice picked up in tempo. "Katherine is here?"

"That is what I said. She plans to return to America, but it would be advantageous if you could persuade her to stay. As your wife."

I held my breath, waiting for Jordan's answer. "Katherine is everything I could ask for in a wife, but I shall never marry, and I think you know why, Father."

"I told you to stop the experiments, but you're pig-headed."

Jordan interrupted. "I have explained this to you innumerable times, Father. I am no longer experimenting with that substance. All of the attacks that I have since had are classified as residual effects. Neither Dr. Cummings nor I understand it, but that's evidently the nature of this particular drug. I no longer work with it. In fact, I've stopped using ergot in my experiments entirely, but the attacks keep recurring."

My blood ran cold as Fenton screamed, "Liar! I don't believe you. You've been fooling around with the devil's brew longer than you'll admit, and you're still using it."

"Think what you like."

"Think what I like? Ah, no, it's not what I like. Do you think I like to recall that I saw my own son, the heir to Hathaway Manor, foaming at the mouth and writhing in chains? Do you think I like to remember that right before my eyes you turned into a monster and bit your own father?"

"What are you talking about?"

Fenton's voice took on a tormented tone. "Just what I said. It wasn't a tenant's dog who bit me. It was my own flesh and blood!"

"You came to the dungeon, didn't you?" Jordan's voice broke. "Oh, God! Why did you think I had myself chained to the wall? I never wanted to hurt anyone. I'd go to any lengths. . . ." He paused and then added softly. "When it's over, I remember nothing."

"Aye, and what happened when you had attacks and weren't chained to the wall."

"I don't know. I can't remember." Then his voice sounded stronger, and he said, "But, I get a warning before they strike. I always try to restrain myself—to make sure I don't do violence to anyone else."

"God only knows what you've done in the past," Fenton said. "But I beg you to stop. Your crimes can't always be

236

covered up, Jordan."

I stuffed my fist into my mouth to keep from crying out. What did Fenton mean? Could Jordan have murdered Lily Beacham?

In a voice devoid of guile, he answered. "I have stopped, Father. I know you don't believe me, but it's true. My attacks are left over. Hopefully in time, they will disappear completely. I ask your forgiveness for whatever pain I might have caused you. Good night!"

No further conversation ensued, and I gathered they had both left the room. Shivering under my blanket, I turned this new information over in my mind. Jordan's was the voice I had heard, crying out in anguish from the cell under my bedroom, and in his altered state, he had been violent enough to bite his own father's hand and then remembered nothing about it.

He could have murdered Lily Beacham and forgotten that, too. He would have only been sixteen, but hadn't Jordan told me once that he'd been conducting chemical experiments up on the moors since his boyhood?

Poor Jordan, I thought. Such a gentle, dedicated man.

It was hard to believe that he could turn into a monster! Suddenly I remembered the thing I had seen on Bismooth Pass. There had been something shockingly familiar about that weird, distorted face. . . . Was that strange, lumbering creature the ghost of Anthony Hathaway? Or could it have been Jordan in his altered state? I hated to think the latter, but then I have never really believed in ghosts!


I was only forced to spend that one night in the secret staircase, for the following afternoon, the fly stopped at Hathaway Manor to discharge three passengers—Beatrice, Willa, and Stuart!

Observing their arrival from the window, I looked down on my unfaithful lover with mixed emotions. A small part of me was glad to see him, and I chided myself for being a fool.

He probably expected me to run outside and greet him

237

with open arms, but I hurried upstairs to my room. Oh, why did he have to come back! But, he doesn't know you saw him through the window. He's probably wondering why you rushed back to Cornwall.

That's right, I answered, he doesn't know, and I shall never tell him. Let him think that I didn't care to see *him*. Let him think I forgot! Yes, that's it. I *forgot* he had invited me to dinner.

That ought to deflate his swollen head to the size of a walnut shell, I decided.

Looking at myself in the mirror, I frowned. With my stiff-necked white shirtwaist and plain black skirt, I looked like a wardrobe mistress.

*All you need is a pincushion at your waist,* my inner voice said. *And you've aged, too. You could pass for twenty-five!*

Frantically, I pulled off my clothes, and throwing open the armoire, I brought out one of Katherine's favorites, an apricot taffeta gown with a Paris label. Then I opened the makeup kit and applied some of the techniques I had used on Willa, to myself.

He'll see me at my best, or he won't see me at all, I decided.

I waited until the stroke of four, and then I walked regally downstairs. I could hear the murmur of voices and the distinctive sound of Stuart's laughter.

Holding my head high, I entered the drawing room, and to my surprise, Willa rushed up to greet me. "Katherine, I'm so glad to see you." She was bubbling over with excitement and stooping down, she whispered in my ear. "I'm engaged!"

Caught off guard, I said, "Sir Alex has proposed!"

"Ssh." Taking my arm, she led me over to a corner of the room. "It's not official, yet. Alex has to speak to Papa, but of course, he'll give his consent." A startled look crossed her face. "If he doesn't, I shall simply die! Mama and I have already invited the cream of London society here for an engagement ball!"

I tried to match her enthusiasm, and I really did wish her well. "Nonsense," I said, "Of course, your father will give his consent. That's wonderful news, Willa."

Stuart sauntered over and joined us. Regarding me with a puzzled expression, he said, "I hear you're going back to America."

News travels fast, I thought and hoping he'd believe I'd been toying with him all along, I answered, "It's not a hasty decision. I always intended going back."

"I guess you forgot to mention it," he said. "Like you forgot our dinner engagement."

I feigned surprise. "Oh, dear! Did we have a dinner engagement?"

Willa giggled, and tapped Stuart coyly with her fan. "What a blow to your ego, cousin!"

He put his hands on either side of his head and grinned at me. "I think I'm down two hat sizes already."

Rogue, I thought. Doesn't he take anything seriously?

Ignoring him, I turned back to Willa. "When is Sir Alex coming down?"

"In a few days. We're planning the ball for the four-teenth."

Katherine's birthday is the day after, I thought.

"I know it's close to your birthday," Willa said. "We can make it a double celebration, though, especially since you'll be leaving."

I smiled to myself. She probably hadn't *meant* to imply they would be celebrating my departure, but I was sure that would be the case. Willa usually wound up saying exactly what she was thinking.

"It's going to be a Masquerade Ball," she confided eagerly. "I haven't decided what I'll be," she said, and then looking me over sharply, she added, "Naturally, Katherine, I have first choice on costumes."

"Of course." I knew she feared competition and I had no desire to give her any. I just wanted it all to be over. Let me take off my mask and quietly slip away, I thought, no post-mortems, no goodbyes. Just like the song: "Many the hopes that have vanished, After the ball."

"What are you thinking about?" Stuart asked, measuring me with eyes that seemed to see right through me. "Just a song. You wouldn't know it," I added.

"I know lots of American songs. What is it?"

I answered him impatiently. "'After The Ball'!"

"I know it," he said.

Willa's thoughts were still on costumes. "Maybe I'll go as Juliet and Sir Alex could be Romeo."

The thought of Sir Alex dressed as Romeo was just too ludicrous to contemplate and neither Stuart nor I dared comment. Willa was already thinking about something else though, and she turned eagerly to Stuart. "You haven't told Katherine the secret." Catching my eye, she smiled. "It's a surprise for you, Katherine."

"Let's make her wait," he said jokingly, but his expression had turned serious.

Jordan came into the room then, and Willa dashed off to tell him her news. Watching her from across the room, I couldn't help noticing the change in Katherine's sullen cousin.

There was a sparkle in Willa's pale eyes, and a rosy glow colored her face, making her look downright vivacious and almost pretty.

"So, we're to have a wedding in the family, after all," Stuart remarked.

"That should please you," I said. "You told me once you liked weddings as long as they were held for *other* people!"

"Ouch," he said. "Those are the sentiments of a true cad."

I don't know what possessed me to say, "We all play the roles we choose."

"Very profound, Katherine. And what role are you playing, if I might ask?"

I looked him squarely in the eye. "I never play the fool," I answered.

"Aren't those lines from a play?"

Are they? I wondered. Oh, blast him! I thought.

My face must have registered my confusion, for he regarded me smugly. "You don't have to confess, Katherine. I know you're a . . ." He paused as if searching for a word.

The cat toying with the mouse again, I thought, but I

met his eyes without flinching.

"Connoisseur!" he said triumphantly. "Aye, that's what you are, a connoisseur of the theater. I remember how you studied the billboards all along The Strand."

My relief turned to anger, and I could have slapped his smiling face. Moving slightly away, I regarded him coldly. "Aunt Beatrice is pouring the tea. I think we should join the others."

His smile vanished, and grabbing my arm, he held it in a vice-like grip. "You're staying here. I want to talk to you."

His words pushed me out onto thin ice, for I did not want to be alone with him, and I particularly did not want to discuss my sudden decision to leave London. Stuart asked too many leading questions, and he had an uncanny ability to read my mind.

I would rather die than have Stuart find out that I had come back that night. Recalling how I had stood outside his window like a lovesick fool, I was overcome with shame.

Feeling desperate, I caught Jordan's eye and waved him over. Stuart groaned and made a motion to leave. "I'm going over and stir our old uncle up a bit."

"Please don't stir him up about Willa and Sir Alex," I pleaded.

"What? And spoil my chances to attend a wedding *and* a Masquerade Ball! Give this cad credit for more sense than that, Katherine!"

Passing Jordan, he poked him gently in the ribs. "You're losing weight, Jord. Eat something besides those damn seeds!"

Jordan joined me, wearing a puzzled expression. "What's Stuart talking about?"

I couldn't help laughing. "Pay no attention to him. Our erudite cousin thinks your experiments with seeds involves eating them!"

"What ever gave him that idea?"

"Stuart has big ears to go along with his big head," I explained. "He was eavesdropping on one of our conversations, and muddled things up a bit."

241

He turned suddenly serious. "How I shall miss you, Katherine! You don't know what it has meant to me to have you here."

Reaching for my hand, he pressed it to his lips, and now that I knew his secret, I found the gesture a poignant reminder of his tender feelings toward me. Dear, sensitive, Jordan, I thought. Why couldn't I have fallen in love with you?

Looking up, I saw that Stuart was watching us from the far corner of the room. Ignoring him, I turned back to Jordan. Stuart's obvious jealousy gave me pleasure until I remembered how shallow it was. He can't stand it if he's not the object of every woman's attention, I thought.

Suddenly recalling that I had as yet spoken to Beatrice, nor had my tea, I said to Jordan, "Let's join the others. Your mother will be angry with us for hiding in a corner."

"Do you care?" he asked. "I don't. These last few days are precious, Katherine. I want to crowd them with memories, so that after you're gone, I can console myself with them."

"Oh, Jordan," I said. "We'll keep in touch. I'll write you long letters, and I hope you'll answer them."

He smiled. "Aye. I shall answer them, but I shall miss your sweet face . . ." He paused, and his eyes, which had once frightened and repelled me, glistened with tears.

Touched beyond measure, I turned my head away, as guilt overwhelmed me: *Oh, what a tangled web we weave, when first we practice to deceive!*

I dutifully paid my respects to Beatrice before teatime was over, and she accepted my polite small talk with no degree of increasing warmth. I supposed the fact that my imminent departure had removed me as a threat to both her daughter and her son was not sufficient reason to overcome her dislike for me.

Fenton had buttonholed Stuart and was expounding his views on the tenant issue. I was grateful that Stuart was thus occupied, but out of the corner of my eye, I saw Tarleton approach Fenton with a message, and I hastily took my leave.

Disappearing into the morning room, I opened the French

doors and slipped quietly outside. It was chilly and I could have used a shawl, but I had escaped, and no one would presume to look for me here.

I was just about to walk down to the beach when I heard the front door close. That eagle eyed Stuart, I thought, and ducking behind a tall boxwood, concealed myself.

But it wasn't Stuart who walked down the steps and hurried around to the side of the house. It was Fenton!

Curious, I followed him at a discreet distance, taking advantage of the large shrubs that banked the house. To my surprise, I saw Mrs. Cull's rickety old carriage parked in the driveway.

The old woman was seated in front with the dog beside her. And Fenton, after an animated conversation with the woman, climbed up into the buggy and the three of them took off and roared out of the driveway!

Dinner that evening was a lively affair. Lord Hathaway's absence allowed the family to openly discuss the two issues that were foremost in their minds—the masquerade ball, and Willa's upcoming wedding.

Willa did not trust Tarleton to keep secrets from his master, so Beatrice had cleverly banished the old butler by having him set up an informal buffet. She thought to soften the blow by giving him the night off and blaming the whole idea on "the young people." Naturally he was in a snit about it and to everyone's relief retired to his room, no doubt to sulk.

Beatrice was as excited as a general after a successful campaign, but she nervously reminded everyone that all plans were subject to Lord Hathaway's approval of the match. "Lord Hathaway will surely give his permission," she explained, "but he would not appreciate our making plans in advance."

That said, she launched into an account of the upcoming ball, concentrating on the guest list. With more animation than I have ever seen her muster, Beatrice began ticking off the names of prominent members of the ton. "Anybody who is anybody in London has been invited," she gloated.

"Now, tell Katherine the surprise," Willa said.

Beatrice fixed me with a cold eye. "Oh, that. Aye, those friends of yours, the Chantelles have been invited, Katherine. We thought it would be nice for you, since you don't know the other guests, and since you'll be going back to America anyway . . ."

I was stunned. Katherine and Beau were coming here!

"Well, for heaven's sake. We thought you'd be pleased," Willa said.

My head was spinning, but I tried to gain control of myself. "I'm pleased, of course," I lied. "Just surprised. How did it come about?"

"Actually, it was Stuart's idea," Willa said. Tittering behind her hand, she looked across the table at him. "He was upset, naturally, when you stood him up, Katherine, and he thought perhaps you might be spending the night with your friend."

"But, you and Aunt Beatrice knew I was going back to Hathaway Manor," I said.

Stuart suddenly joined the conversation. "They told me you'd left that morning for Paddington Station, but no one had seen you off, so I decided to check up on you."

The nerve of him, I thought, feeling my face burn with anger.

"Mr. Chantelle was charming," he said. "We had quite a long chat, in fact."

Good Lord, I thought, getting more nervous by the minute. "Did you meet India?" I asked and held my breath, waiting for his answer.

"Unfortunately no. India was resting. It seems she's been upset by something to do with a friend of hers. Her father's concerned about her, so I suggested they get away, come to Cornwall for a visit with you, Katherine. Chantelle thought it was a capital idea, and I invited them to the ball." He gave Beatrice a charming smile. "I knew our good aunt wouldn't mind. The more, the merrier, right, Aunt Beatrice!"

She returned his smile with a look of resignation, and went on to supply the names of those important personages she might have missed the first time.

I felt physically ill. What was Beau thinking about? I couldn't believe even he would be so irresponsible as to accept an invitation to Hathaway Manor.

Frantically I searched for a way out of the mess my father had gotten us into, and then I remembered Katherine! She'll veto it, I thought. Katherine will never agree to come here!

But I was wrong and never in a million years could I have foreseen the consequences of that visit!

# Chapter 20

Sir Alex Lighthizer and his mother arrived at Hathaway Manor several days later. To everyone's relief, Fenton and Willa's reluctant suitor emerged from their meeting with satisfied smiles.

The terms of the agreement were naturally not discussed, but Stuart was convinced that Fenton had sweetened Willa's dowry to include lands promised to his father by old Duncan Hathaway.

"That has to be it," he confided on one of the rare occasions when we accidentally found ourselves alone. "I recall it now. Lighthizer's father owned property that adjoined ours in Sussex. No wonder the little toad was smiling." His eyes turned dark with anger. "That land should have been mine," he said.

Fenton was not an indulgent father, but he placed a high priority on peace and quiet, so I didn't doubt he considered the land a small price to pay for placating a nagging wife and disposing of a difficult daughter.

Forthwith invitations to the gala Masquerade Ball were hastily written and dispatched to London and Cornwall. Although some had already verbally accepted, etiquette decreed that they do so formally, and Beatrice and Willa constantly bemoaned the fact that mail arrived sporadically from Penzance by way of the fly.

I anticipated an early reply from Katherine declining the invitation, so I was not surprised when Willa retrieved the mail and commented. "This is from your friends, Katherine. They're probably anxious to come."

She ripped open the envelope and I prepared to act disappointed.

"I won't be surprised if they decline," I said, and for some reason, I felt a sudden compulsion to dignify Beau. "Mr. Chantelle is a rather important American actor. It's hard for him to get away."

Willa tossed her head with impatience. "Don't be ridiculous, Katherine. No actor would refuse an invitation to mix with artistocrats. Of course they've accepted!"

I was dumbfounded, and could only assume that Katherine must be in a comatose state due to developments in her friend's murder, and that Beau was making the decisions.

From past experience it was easy to see that Beau's first decision would involve seeking me out. How could he extricate himself from this hopelessly tangled web if I wasn't around to unravel it?

His irresponsibility and dependence on me was a burden I was tired of assuming. Didn't I have enough problems of my own without having Beau dump more on me? I wouldn't put it past Fenton to have me arrested if he should discover the truth. Hadn't I forged Katherine's name to a legal document?

And suppose Katherine winds up having a nervous breakdown. Who is to speak for us then? My blood ran cold as I suddenly saw this whole little game through accusing eyes. *The Tattler* would eat it up, I thought, visualizing the headlines: *Two-bit actor and his slick daughter persuade an innocent heiress to change places.*

My God, I mused, to what lengths could this scenario be carried? We could be convicted of fraud, perjury, attempted larceny, and Lord knows what else!

Willa was eyeing me strangely. "What's wrong with you, Katherine? I swear sometimes you act as spooky as Jordan."

"I'm fine," I said.

"Well, you certainly don't look it. You're white as a sheet, and I thought for a minute there you were going to have a fit.

Do you still get them?"

"No, of course not. I just need some air. It's stuffy in here," I said.

I excused myself and hurried outside. A punishing wind whipped the shawl from my shoulders and carried it off the porch where it skittered playfully along the ground like a living thing.

Running down the steps, I tried to retrieve it, but it tumbled over the cliff, and looking down, I watched as a wave swallowed it up and carried it out to sea.

I was reminded of the day I had stood on deck and watched the ocean claim my scarf. I had found a romantic significance in the incident then, but not this time. The sight of my shawl disappearing under angry waves depressed me and I shuddered.

Looking down the beach from my high vantage point, I spotted a man in the distance. As he approached, I saw that it was Stuart.

He walked slowly, dragging his feet through the sand like someone exhausted from doing manual labor. He's probably still trying to break through that passageway, I thought recalling Violet and Clara's eyewitness account.

Now that I knew Lily had been murdered in the cave, Stuart's obsession with it bothered me. I didn't know why until a saying, tucked away in the grab bag of my mind, suddenly emerged: "A murderer always returns to the scene of the crime."

I refused to entertain such a thought. Stuart was fickle, of that I was painfully aware. But, I like to think that for a little while, and in his way, he had loved me. I could accept that he was a rogue, but if he had a darker side, I didn't want to know about it.

The week passed quickly, as Beatrice crammed every day with activities designed to entertain and impress the Lighthizers. All of us were expected to take part in these events, but Stuart, ever the maverick, took off on his own pursuits. It was left to the rest of us to present a false, but picturesque, view of life in the country.

The overnight guests from London were expected to

arrive on Friday and Fenton had commandeered the fly plus his own two private carriages to transport them from Penzance to Hathaway Manor.

I had been apprehensive all week just thinking about Katherine and Beau's arrival, and now that the day had finally come, I was in an acute state of anxiety.

I rushed to the window every time I heard carriage wheels clatter up the hill, but the faces I sought were never among those that emerged laughing and chattering to converge on the manor house.

The last train from London was due in Penzance at six o'clock in the evening and when the carriage returned to Hathaway Manor empty, I breathed a sigh of relief. Katherine and Beau were not coming.

Either Beau had had second thoughts or Katherine had recovered in time to thwart his plans. At any rate, Beau's blunder had turned into a blessing in disguise, for when the London guests departed, I would accompany them.

I would voice concern for my absent friends, pointing out that India had been ill. Fenton could hardly refuse, especially since I would be accompanied by his own departing guests. Once in London, I would wire Fenton that I would be leaving for America. Katherine would be legally of age then, so there would be nothing her uncle could do about it.

Now that my anxiety over Katherine's appearance at Hathaway Manor had been laid to rest, I welcomed the coming festivities. I began to look forward to the ball. No longer my first, it will surely be the last one I shall ever attend, I told myself.

Maureen gasped as she buttoned me into my costume. "Miss Katherine, you'll be the most gorgeous lady at the ball."

I sincerely hoped not. This was Willa's night and I did so want her to shine. I had designed and made both of our costumes, swearing Willa to secrecy and threatening to cut up the gown if she told her mother I sewed.

The little dressmaker in Penzance had done a sorry job of transforming Willa's conception of Marie Antoinette into reality, and moved by Willa's tears, I had offered to help.

I ripped the whole thing apart and redesigned the ruby red gown, copying it in my head from one we had used in the *The Rein of Terror*. I lowered the neckline two inches, added a panel widening the skirt eight inches and then used bands of black bugle beads for trimming. Willa had been ecstatic and in a fit of generosity, I had offered to give her a full theatrical makeup the night of the ball.

I had just left her room and the transformation I had effected was nothing short of miraculous. Powdered hair, rouged cheeks, eyes outlined with kohl, and a black beauty patch had turned Willa into a vivid and engaging courtesan.

My own gown, desiged to represent a medieval lady-in-waiting, was not as elaborate as Willa's, but the very simplicity of it apparently appealed to Maureen who had a flair for fashion and more taste than many of her so-called "betters."

It was made of shimmering, emerald green satin and the neckline and wide sleeves were trimmed with bands of black fur. My hair hung loose, and Maureen brushed it out, letting it fall like a dark curtain over my shoulders. Then she placed on my head the tall, cone-shaped headpiece whose pointed crown exploded in a waterfall of wispy chiffon.

I had painstakingly sewn hundreds of tiny beads on the veil, and Maureen said, "Lord, Miss Katherine, but it sparkles like diamonds against your black hair."

She handed me my mask and I put it on. "You haven't told anyone what I'll be wearing, have you, Maureen?" I asked.

She turned bright red and lowered her eyes to the floor. I had only meant to tease her, knowing that Maureen could never keep a secret. My costume had probably been described in minute detail to all of the servants in the kitchen, but I really didn't mind.

Her confession, however, astounded me!

"I didn't want to tell him, Miss Katherine, but he wormed it right out of me. Master Stuart has a way of doing that, he does."

I could not believe he would resort to pumping a servant over something so silly and trivial. "Master Stuart *asked* you what I would be wearing?"

Still looking guilty, she nodded. "Aye, down to the last detail, he did. You're not angry with me, are you, Miss Katherine?"

"No, of course not," I answered, more piqued with Stuart than Maureen. He always has to show off, I thought, picturing the satisfaction he would derive from such childishness.

Since this was a masked ball, there was to be no receiving line and naturally no announcements so guests would merely be escorted upstairs by Tarleton to the massive theater which doubled as a ballroom.

After leaving the main wing of the house, I let the sound of music direct my way to the bizarre sight of masked figures in odd assortments of disguises whirling across the dance floor to a lively polka.

A portly, knobby-kneed man wearing a false beard and kilts was bouncing across the floor with a tall, Spanish lady whose mantilla had slipped to the side of her head.

Good Lord, I thought, suddenly realizing that it was Sir Alex and his mother.

A well-padded Henry VIII was dancing with none other than Beatrice, easily recognizable in a handsome Regency gown that looked like it might have been authentic.

Someone tapped me on the shoulder, and I turned around to confront a court jester who pantomimed his request for a dance. Most of the guests were unknown to me, so I was spared speculation as to his identity. He was too short to be either Stuart or Jordan, and too young to be Fenton, and they were the only male guests I might possibly recognize.

At least, that's what I thought at the time.

I recognized Stuart right away, and he made no attempt to conceal his identity, as he strode purposefully toward me from across the room. He made a swashbuckling pirate and I thought the costume appropriate to his character. "Have you a dance for your old friend, Mr. Cousin?" he asked with a grin.

Without waiting for an answer, he gathered me into his arms, and I let him hold me close, as the orchestra drifted into a plaintive refrain. "Here's our song," he whispered.

I didn't recognize it until they played the chorus, and then the words tugged at my heartstrings as he sang them softly in my ear.

> "After the ball is over,
> After the break of morn;
> After the dancers leaving
> After the stars are gone.
> Many a heart is aching
> If you could see them all,
> Many the hopes that have vanished,
> After the ball."

"Now, that song will always remind you of me," he said. His arm tightened on my neck, as he drew me closer. "Will you think about me just a little bit when you're back in America spending all that money?"

I stiffened. "Spending all what money?"

"Your inheritance, of course. What money did you think I was talking about?"

"Oh, I don't know," I said. I couldn't read his expression because of the mask, but I got the feeling that he was deliberately goading me, and again I wondered if Stuart had guessed my secret from the very beginning.

Had he known all along that I was just a nobody? And had he gone along with the game just for the fun of it? That would be something that Stuart would do, I thought, and then gasped, as I caught a glimpse of someone in the doorway wearing a costume identical to mine!

Stuart suddenly spun me around and I lost sight of the woman. It can't be, I thought. I must be mistaken. Similar, perhaps, but the costumes couldn't be identical.

"I like your costume," he said, and Maureen's words rang ominously in my ear. *He wormed it right out of me, he did, down to the last detail . . .*

But why would he? Oh, no, I thought. My imagination

252

is running away with me. Feeling an urgent need to sa
my own curiosity and regain my sanity, I murmured
excuse and broke away from him. Making my way to the on
place he could not follow me, I glanced hurriedly around,
but the woman had disappeared.

When I returned, I accepted a dance from Jordan whom I
recognized right away in a monk's brown habit. He said,
"Katherine?" I smiled, but didn't answer him, and he added,
"I know you this time, but I was confused by your double. I
had quite a one-sided conversation with the woman, whoever she was."

I said, "Someone else is dressed the same as I?"

"Well, she had me fooled," he said. "I'll confess, I knew
what you'd be wearing. Willa took pity on me," he confided.
"She said you'd be wearing a green gown and a tall hat with a
lot of chiffon on it."

"Where is this woman?" I asked. "I'd like to see her
myself."

He glanced around without interest. "She could be anywhere. You'll run into her sooner or later."

I had just about convinced myself that the costumes would
wind up being close, but hardly the same, when I spotted the
woman, standing beside a tall man in a black cape.

Her costume was an exact replica of the one I was wearing,
and I felt a creepy feeling pass over me as my eyes traveled
from her gown with its identical bands of black fox to the tall
headpiece whose trailing chiffon veil glittered in the candlelight.

There was something familiar about the man standing
next to her, too, and I wracked my brain for a connection. At
that very moment, he turned and as his hand emerged from
the cape, I saw that he was holding a heavy, black cane. A
picture flashed immediately across my mind. I saw a man
standing in the street. Similar height, similar build, he wore a
black cape, and he carried a heavy cane that he tapped as he
whistled.

I am losing my mind, I thought. This cannot be!

Feeling like I had stepped through The Looking Glass, I
murmured an apology to Jordan and threaded my way

through the crowd towards the couple. I had a desperate need to confront them directly and convince myself that they were strangers and not the people I feared them to be.

"Pardon me. May I get through, please?"

A tall man, wearing a suit of armor blocked my view and slowed my progress across the dance floor, and when I finally reached the other side, they were gone!

Jordan caught up with me, and I apologized for running off. "I wanted to see my double," I said.

He looked a little surprised, and I'm sure he thought it a poor excuse for leaving a partner stranded on the dance floor, but his mind was on other matters. "Be careful tonight, Katherine."

"What do you mean?"

He hesitated. "I don't quite know how to say this." A pained expression crossed his face and then he continued. "You see, Hathaway Manor holds some dark secrets. Murder has been done here, and more than once," he added.

I stopped looking at the dance floor and faced him. What was he trying to tell me?

He continued in a rush. "One of the Hathaways murdered his own brother so he would be next in line to inherit, and several years ago a servant girl from the manor was murdered."

"What are you saying, Jordan?"

His eyes took on that pupil-less guise, and a chill ran down my spine, as he said, "Don't trust any of the Hathaways, Katherine, not even me. Tomorrow you'll be of age and free to leave. Take my advice, and go, but be careful tonight!"

His face had turned chalk white, and he was breathing rapidly. "Jordan, are you all right?" I asked.

"Aye, but for God's sake, heed my warning, Katherine." Standing up quickly, he seized my hand and pressed it to lips that were as cold as death. "Good night, my dear," he said, and in the next instant, he was gone.

The ball suddenly lost its gaiety and took on the aura of a nightmare. The heavily masked figures that surrounded me now appeared grotesque and threatening. Jordan's warning rang in my ears, and panic overwhelmed me, making me gasp. My throat constricted as invisible hands wrapped themselves around my neck like snakes squeezing tighter and tighter until I could scarcely breathe at all.

Using every ounce of strength I possessed, I stood up. I must get out of here, I thought. I must hide. The secret stairway immediately entered my mind. It had been my sanctuary once before and it beckoned me into its dark abyss.

Moving at a normal pace, I skirted the dance floor, and was heading towards the door when a voice I could not place spoke in a commanding tone. "I believe this is my dance."

Before I could refuse, I found myself in the arms of the armor-clad man I had noticed earlier in the evening. His authentic looking costume had been ingeniously cut from heavy cloth and painted over in silver. He was the tallest man in the room, and I was certain I had never seen him before.

He looked down at me from his great height. "Do I know you, my lady?" he asked.

"I don't think so," I answered.

"Ah, this one's not afraid to talk," he said, grinning with amusement. "I danced with your twin sister, but couldn't get a word out of her."

His eyes glittered through the black slits in his mask, giving him a diabolical look and I plunged through The Looking Glass again.

All the grinning, masked faces seemed to be staring maliciously at me, and with a strength born of panic, I broke away and ran from the ballroom.

Ducking into the first room I came to, I found myself in the gallery. It was hardly the room I would have chosen for a haven. Portraits of the Hathaway ancestors lined the walls and in the flickering candlelight their ghostly faces seemed to taunt me.

I tore the mask from my face and brushed tears of frustration from my eyes. Take hold, India, I cautioned myself. You'll need all of your wits about you to get through this night!

Brave words. Had I known the terror I was about to face, I think I would have spent the night in the gallery, in the company of the dead Hathaways rather than the living ones.

I waited until I was sure I had not been followed and then I removed my tall hat, which would surely give me away, and left it behind. Slipping cautiously out of the gallery, I ran quickly past the open ballroom door and down the corridor to the main wing of the house.

As I rounded the balcony, I saw Tarleton coming up the staircase. Spying me, he called out, "Miss Katherine, wait. I have a message for you."

I leaned over the balcony and looked down at him. "Ssh," I hissed, putting my finger to my lips. Retreating back into the shadows, I waited while he climbed the stairs at a snail's pace.

When he finally reached the top, I impatiently grabbed hold of his skinny arm and pulled him into the corner with me.

"See here," he protested, but I was too frustrated to care.

"I don't want to be seen, Tarleton. Now what is it?"

He adjusted his coat sleeve with maddening deliberation, and gave me a petulant look. "You should curb your boisterous behavior, Miss Katherine. You're a grown-up lady now."

I was in no mood to receive a lecture from Tarleton, and I said, "Yes, yes, I'm sorry. Now, please, what is the message, Tarleton?"

I suppose I expected him to deliver some silly request from Beatrice, as to where I should sit at supper or with whom, so I was surprised when he reached into his pocket and handed me a sealed envelope.

Perplexed, I stared at it blankly for a second before my head cleared. "Wait," I said, "there might be an answer." Ripping it open, I unfolded the single sheet of paper, and holding it out into the light, I read,

Indy,
Come at once to the cave at Pirate's Cove. Tell no one about this. I need you. Beau.

I recognized my father's handwriting immediately. "Who

256

gave this to you, Tarleton?" I demanded in a voice shrill with terror. When he didn't answer quick enough, I seized the old man's arms again and shook him. "Who gave this to you?" I repeated.

He scowled back at me. "How should I know? They're all wearing masks, aren't they?"

We stared mutely into each other's angry eyes, and I knew it would be useless to question him further. He had done his duty and delivered the message, and that was as far as Tarleton would go. With a contemptuous smirk, he turned on his heel and left me standing there.

I have no choice, I thought. Beau is counting on me, and I cannot turn my back on him. Without a moment's hesitation, I ran down the steps and out the door.

The night was black and the roaring surf pounded out a warning as I ran down the beach.

> "Night of evil,
> Night of sin,
> Wherein a thousand demons lurk,
> In every dark corner,
> Behind every black tree,
> They wait, my love,
> Wait for Thee!"

# Chapter 21

Those lines from the old play had never seemed more apt, and looking back toward the brilliantly lit house, I paused. Had I been hoodwinked into leaving it?

Shutting out my inner voice which cautioned me to beware, I rationalized that the note *had* been written in my father's handwriting.

Beau is irresponsible. Yes, and sometimes selfish, I admitted. But he would never let himself be used to entrap me. I'd stake my life on that. Placing my hands over my ears, I turned and ran toward the beach.

Foamcapped waves exploded on the sand and then quickly receded into the dark unknown from whence they came. There was something terrifying about that vast expanse of black sea, and I pulled off my slippers and ran where the sand was deepest and driest.

Overhead, a bright, full moon hung in the sky like a lantern. It cast shadows on the beach, turning rocks into menacing faces and a gnarled piece of driftwood into a sea monster. I had slowed down, but now adrenaline shot through my arteries, and I ran like a fox with hounds nipping at its tail.

As I rounded the bend into the cove, I spied a torch moving toward me. The dark figure of a man was moving with it, and I had a sudden urge to turn and run the other way, but in the next instant, he was upon me.

It was Stuart, and in the eerie glow of the torch, his pirate's disguise gave him a menacing look.

"What is this all about?" I cried. "My father sent me a note . . ."

Oh, God, I thought and stopped, clamping my hand over my mouth.

"I know he's your father, India. I've been on to your little scheme for some time," he said.

"Where is Beau? What have you done with him?"

"Be quiet, and listen to me. Beau and the real Katherine Hathaway are both in the cave."

I uttered a strangled cry, and he grabbed my arm. "Take hold of yourself. You'll need all your strength for what you may be about to hear."

"What are you talking about?" I said, struggling to release myself from his grasp. "Take me to Katherine and Beau. I want to hear what they have to say about this."

"Katherine won't even know you. She's been in a trance for a week. Now, listen to me carefully, India. This is a psychological experiment. It just might remove the mental block in Katherine's brain and bring her memory back. Don't spoil it. Say nothing to either Katherine or Beau when you see them in the cave. Is that clear?"

My head was whirling. What was he up to?

"Is that clear?" he repeated, giving me a shake.

There was no trace of affability in him now, and I slowly nodded my head. The identity of Lily Beacham's murderer was locked in Katherine's subconscious and Stuart wanted her to point an accusing finger at the killer.

Suppose she pointed to Stuart, himself? Was that what he feared? And if so, what did he plan to do about it? *None, save one, might ever leave that cave alive,* my inner voice warned, as Stuart pushed me ahead of him into the mouth of the cavern.

The opening through the grotto had been cleared, but the passageway leading to the chamber was still extremely narrow, and we had to move through it single file. Stuart followed behind me, holding the torch high. It cast eerie shadows on the walls and the spooky atmosphere combined with a feeling of sudden claustrophobia scraped my nerves raw.

At last we emerged into the large chamber where I had seen the eyeless fish. The room was lit by several torches that had been secured to the walls and in their eerie glow, I saw Beau and Katherine seated on the cavern's floor.

I gave an involuntary gasp, and Beau, more serious than I had ever seen him, shot me a warning glance. Katherine sat staring vacantly into space, and she did not so much as turn her head or blink an eye when we entered the chamber.

I followed Stuart's lead and sat down on the floor. The situation was strange; all of us sitting there in silence like we were waiting for a performance to begin.

Suddenly a torch flared on the opposite wall, and the faces of two women materialized. I was sure the pictures had been painted on a transparency, a stage prop commonly used in the theater to produce dramatic effects.

The cloth, usually made of loosely woven gauze, is painted with transparent dyes. When lit from the front, it appears as a normal painting, but when lights are placed at the back, the picture fades.

I had no earthly idea what this was leading up to, but my attention was caught, and stealing a glimpse at Katherine, I saw that her vacant stare had been replaced by a wide-eyed interest in the strange exhibit.

I was waiting for the light to be thrown to the back, and after several moments, it was. The women's faces disappeared and the torch threw its illumination on Anabelle, the doll!

A macabre feeling overwhelmed me and my skin crawled. At that very instant, a deep, masculine voice spoke from the shadows. My body jerked, and Stuart placed a firm hand on my shoulder, warning me not to break the spell.

"Who are you?" the disembodied voice demanded.

I was certain I had lost my mind when another voice answered. "Anabelle Hathaway."

"Who are the two ladies in the picture?"

"Veronica Mayfield and Lily Beacham."

The voice was well-modulated and self-assured, and it definitely seemed to emanate from the doll. Is it a gramophone? I wondered. But the tones were almost too natural to have been mechanically reproduced.

"They're both dead. Aren't they?"

"Yes."

"Do you know who killed them?"

"Yes."

"Who?"

"I did!"

My eyes had been racing around the cave, looking for the gramophone, but in that instant they had settled on Katherine. I saw her lips move.

She's throwing her voice, I thought, like a ventriloquist!

"Why did you kill Veronica Mayfield, Anabelle?"

I stared at Katherine in horror, and watched her lips move as she answered simply, "Because I wanted her part in the play."

"How did you lure Veronica to the embankment?"

"I wrote her a note and signed Roger Cranston's name to it. I asked her to meet me there, and she did; then I pushed her in the water."

Dear God, she's sick. This can't be true, I thought.

"Did you kill Lily Beacham, too?"

"Of course. My papa was going to run away with her. He was going to leave Mama and me at Hathaway Manor." Her voice was out of control now and she shouted. "I hated Hathaway Manor. Grandfather Hathaway would have been in charge of me, and I hated him, too."

"How did you know this, Anabelle?"

"Katherine and I were hiding in the cave when they met in the chamber. We listened."

"I don't believe you killed her, Katherine. You were only a little girl."

"Katherine didn't kill her. I did!" she shouted. My blood curdled as she added, "Papa left first and then while she was

261

leaning over, looking at the blind fish, I bashed her head in with a big rock." She smiled with satisfaction. "She deserved it. She was going to get all Papa's money, and we'd have to live on charity at Hathaway Manor!"

At that point, an ominous rumble reverberated through the cave and I thought, That's a drum roll. This has all been an act! I had been confused enough at the Mad Hatter's ball, but this was even more bizarre.

The drum roll rose to an earsplitting crescendo and I watched in horrified fascination as the transparency crumbled before my eyes in a hail of tumbling rocks.

"Cave-in," Stuart shouted above the din, and grabbing my arm, he dragged me behind a huge boulder.

Things were happening so fast that my confused brain refused to function. For an instant, I thought crazily that this must be the grand finale to the whole bizarre performance.

Beau and Katherine took refuge behind another boulder and I watched as Stuart dashed across the chamber, dodging the still falling rocks to lead a black-cloaked man to safety.

It was the Whistler, and I screamed as I saw blood pouring from a wound in the man's head. Sanity returned to me in that instant and I rushed forward to help.

"Get back behind that boulder," Stuart yelled. "This isn't over yet!"

I ignored him, taking the man's other arm, and together we led him out of danger.

When we were all three crouched behind the huge rock, Stuart tried to stanch the flow of blood with the man's black cape. "No, the dye might get in it," I said, and without a moment's hesitation, I pulled up my skirt and ripped my petticoat in half, pressing the cloth to the man's head.

Stuart shouted to the others, repeating his warning, "This isn't over, yet. Stay right where you are."

Katherine let out a strangled cry. "Anabelle's in there," she shrieked.

Beau shouted, "No, come back." But before he could stop her, she had raced across the rock strewn floor to the other side of the chamber.

Another deafening rumble shook the cavern and before our horrified eyes, the wall collapsed. I saw Katherine fall, and then the whole horrible scene ended in blackness as the curtain fell on the final act.


I must be bleeding, I thought, as something wet trickled down my neck and in between my breasts.

I heard Beau's voice, weak with fear. "Please, Indy, open your eyes."

Stuart said, "She's coming around now. Wet the cloth again."

I opened my eyes. "I'm not bleeding?"

Stuart answered. "No, you fainted."

"Katherine!" I cried, trying to sit up.

I was lying in Stuart's lap, and very gently he pushed me back down. "Just take it easy a minute."

Beau suddenly materialized. "Oh, thank God, you're awake." He placed a wet cloth on my head and I pushed it away. "Where's Katherine?" I insisted.

Both Beau and Stuart hesitated, and another voice answered. "We couldn't save her, Miss India. We all tried."

I looked up into the face of the man I knew only as the Whistler. "Katherine and Anabelle Hathaway are in better hands now, Miss," he said simply.

Katherine dead! It was hard for me to believe, and sudden tears streamed down my face.

Beau patted my hand. "I'll miss her, too, Indy, but she was a very sick girl. Mr. Donovan is right. It's better this way."

"Are you sure she's dead?" I asked.

Stuart merely nodded, and I turned my head and saw a massive pile of rubble. With a gasp, I realized that this was all that was left of the opposite wall.

Stuart placed my head on his shoulder, and spoke softly. "There's much you don't know, India. You see, Beau and I planned this together that day at Brown's Hotel. Your father suspected that Katherine had murdered Veronica Mayfield."

263

Beau cut in. "She was completely unstable, Indy. I began to realize it months ago, but I didn't want to burden you with my suspicions."

Stuart continued with a nod toward the man I had called the Whistler. "I asked Floyd Donovan to help us. Floyd is a private investigator, recently retired from Scotland Yard," he explained.

I was surprised. But why had the man come to Bleekman Place those other times, I wondered.

Stuart gave Mr. Donovan a knowing smile. "Floyd had just concluded another investigation for me, so I decided to seek his assistance on this one as well." Looking at Beau, he said, "The three of us got together and set up this test to force Katherine to remember the past."

"We didn't like doing it, Indy," Beau added. "But we couldn't let an innocent man go to the gallows."

"Katherine Hathaway would never have been convicted," Mr. Donovan said. "The poor girl would have been judged insane. She was literally two people. A rare and strange affliction," he added. "I've only come across one other such case in all my years at the Yard."

The full impact of our precarious situation did not dawn on me until Stuart looked anxiously around and said, "We can discuss this later. Are you up to exploring a new passage, India?"

Fear made my voice tremble. "We're trapped in here, aren't we?"

Beau and Floyd Donovan exchanged hurried glances, and Stuart looked to them, and finally to me. "There is a hidden passage out of here. I know I can find it, but all of you will have to follow my instructions to the letter." He stared intently at the two men. "There can only be one leader. Are you willing to place your lives in my hands?"

Beau nodded. "You haven't been wrong yet, Stuart."

Floyd Donovan said, "You saved my life once. I guess I can trust it to you a second time."

"Do I have your trust, too?" Stuart asked, looking at me with eyes that were very gentle. I blushed, recalling the many times I'd doubted him. "I trust you, Stuart," I said.

"Then, if India is up to it, I think we should move on."

Beau looked at me with fatherly concern. "What do you say, Indy? Do you feel well enough to go?"

Stuart made my decision for me by glancing around and making a calculated observation. "This whole section could go up in another cave-in, so it would be expedient to—"

"I'm ready," I said quickly and without hesitation.

The three men nodded. We were all of a singular mind, and that knowledge brought us together as comrades in this incredible adventure that we were about to embark on.

We didn't know it then, but our quest was to take us on a journey that would pit us against the forces of nature in a setting so spectacular, we would wonder for the rest of our lives if we had only imagined it.

Stuart confided that he was an experienced underground ranger. "The Hathaways have been searching for old Anthony's treasure for generations. I'm no exception," he added with a shrug. "After my grandfather died, I became obsessed with finding it."

A bitter expression crossed his face, and he paused, making me recall that neither Stuart nor his father had been mentioned in Duncan Hathaway's will.

Shrugging, he continued in a matter-of-fact tone. "I studied old maps, dug up the moors, even tried diving!" Then he smiled. "Had a brilliant idea the old devil might have sunk it in the shallow waters off this cove. Nothing!" he said, throwing up his hands. "Then I decided to concentrate my efforts on exploring this cave, and that's what I've been doing, off and on for over a year now."

"Are you saying that you've already explored other passageways in this cave?" Donovan asked, and when Stuart nodded, he said, "But where did they lead?"

"Nowhere," Stuart answered. "They were all dead ends, but this time, I think I have something." He pointed to the opening I had noticed the first time I'd entered this chamber. "I've been working in there recently. I think it connects to another cave."

Beau looked wary. "But what if it doesn't?"

"Do we have another choice?" Stuart asked.

"What about equipment?" Floyd asked, giving the two torches on the undamaged wall a skeptical look. "How long will they last?"

"About an hour," Stuart said. "But, I have two good lanterns and plenty of cane to make more torches. We'll have enough light to last us for days."

The thought of spending days in this underground world was sobering and Stuart hastened to reassure all of us. "I have food and water already in the passage, some tools. I'm not saying it's going to be easy, but I'm confident we'll survive and see the sun again."

"Let's stop talking then, and go," Floyd said.

We had to crawl, one by one through the entrance. Stuart led, I followed, then Beau, and Floyd Donovan brought up the rear. We were to keep these positions while traveling, Stuart informed us.

Sharp rocks ripped through my flimsy gown and when we emerged from the tight space I was embarrassed to see a slit in my skirt that reached all the way up to my thigh.

The men in their sturdier clothes looked none the worse for wear. If we have to do any more crawling, and if we do indeed escape from this cave, I shall be naked! I thought.

We were now in another chamber. This room was smaller than the one we had just left. But, at least all its walls are intact, I mused.

The thought took me back to Katherine, and the knowledge that she was buried back there in the ruins brought tears to my eyes again.

Stuart noticed, and put his arm around me. "Don't think about it, India. We have to look ahead." Then typically, he appealed to my sense of humor. "How do you like my parlor, Miss Chantelle? I think Mother Nature has decorated it rather nicely, don't you?"

He led me over to a huge boulder. "Here's a comfortable chair. Rest yourself while I check our supplies."

The giant rock did resemble a chair, and I smiled in spite of myself.

Stuart had stocked the passage with varied supplies: blanket, hammer and pliers, several hundred feet of rope, stalks of cane for making torches, some wire, lots of matches, and several tins of food.

"We'll eat here, and carry the rest of the supplies with us," he said, so we sat in a circle on the floor and feasted on tins of salmon and dry, preserved fruit.

"It's not up to Tarleton's standards, but it's not bad," Stuart quipped.

"It's delicious," I said, and giggled. "Wouldn't he be horrified if he could see us now."

Stuart puckered up his face in a hilarious imitation of the old butler and we both burst into laughter. The joke of course meant nothing to Beau and Floyd, but it lightened their spirits nevertheless.

Stuart then set Beau and Floyd to work assembling torches by binding three pieces of cane together with a length of wire.

I offered to help, too, but Stuart shook his head, and took me aside. "I hate to have you hide those gorgeous legs, but I think a change of costume is called for."

I blushed and tried to cover myself with the shreds of my gown.

Reaching into his supply box, he brought out a heavy shirt and trousers. "Put these on, India. They'll keep you from getting scratched. The dressing room is over there," he said, pointing to a large column that looked like white marble and grew from the ceiling to the floor.

I discarded my medieval lady's costume and put on the shirt and trousers. The sleeves of the shirt covered my hands and I rolled them up, along with the pants legs. Stuart had handed me a length of rope along with the clothes and I tied it around my waist to hold up the trousers.

With my hair streaming down my back, I must have made a strange looking boy, but the clothes were warm and comfortable and I was glad to have them.

Draping the remains of my gown over the boulder, I smiled to myself. Some unsuspecting explorer will discover it and think the passage was used as a trysting place for knights and their ladies long ago.

Stuart was waiting for me, and he said, "You make a cute

little boy, but I'm glad you're a girl."

I wondered how he viewed me, now that he knew who
was. Of course, I was completely out of his class and it wa
ridiculous for me to entertain the fantasy that he might be
love with me.

Hadn't he tried to seduce me, knowing I was India, ar
not Katherine? He'd thought I would be easy because I wa
connected with the theater, and when I'd refused him, he ha
merely found a replacement. I'll not encourage him,
thought. Having him turn away from me after this is all ov
would just be too hard to bear.

"Thank you for the clothes," I said and quickly joined th
others.

The new torches cast a soft glow on the chamber and I wa
reluctant to leave it, but Stuart wanted to move as far a
possible from the fault on the other side of the cave.

We entered another tunnellike corridor that twisted ar
curved in an endless maze. After an hour of this, I was read
to turn back. "Why couldn't we just sit in the supply roo
and wait to be rescued?" I asked.

"Because nobody knows we're here," Stuart patient
explained. "Sit down and rest awhile," he suggested, and a
of us slumped down on the narrow floor.

The walls began to close in on me and I felt myself teete
on the brink of hysteria.

> "T'aint nothin can hurt me
> I say,
> T'aint nothin can hurt me
> No way,
> An Irishman's stuck
> With his own good luck,
> There's no doubt about it,
> I say."

Beau's voice rang through the cave and I joined him in
song that had calmed our childish fears and lulled us to slee
in so many strange hotels when my sisters and I had bee
little.

It was from, *The Rainbow,* a short-lived play that had marked my father's first and only singing role on stage. We children had loved the song, though, and whenever things went wrong, and so often they did, Beau would sing it. It had gotten us through tough times before, and my spirits soared as Stuart and Floyd caught on to it and sang along with us.

We called it our "Marching Song" and all through that narrow tunnel, we improvised and harmonized, concentrating all our thoughts on the song, and in so doing left our individual fears and doubts behind.

Dear Beau, he'd always been there for us. Maybe he had chased after rainbows, and maybe sometimes he'd used poor judgment, but he'd never given up. And he's not giving up now, I thought, glancing back at my father, smiling and singing like he was marching in a parade and not through an eerie tunnel that nobody had walked through before.

Stuart's a lot like Beau, I thought, handsome, witty, impractical. No wonder I fell in love with him. Oh, God, why did he have to be British and an aristocrat?

We must have gone on for another half hour and then suddenly Stuart stopped. The rest of us crowded behind him and to our amazement saw that we were standing on the brink of a valley in a passage easily forty feet wide and equally as high. We could see a river below us, and a skiff lay on the bank, anchored with rocks.

We gazed in awe at this underground landscape. Beautiful beyond description, it sparkled with crystal vines that hung from a ceiling more magnificent than any ornamental plaster work ever devised. Delicate sprays of multicolored flowers decorated the dome and glittered in the glow of our torches.

Stuart was beside himself. "Those flowers are formed from gypsum," he said. "And look, over there, that's flowstone."

He pointed to a large formation that hung in folds like a piece of drapery.

"It's most unusual for flowstone and gypsum to be found in the same area," he explained.

269

I felt like I was in a crystal palace, a wonderland of suc[h] incredible beauty that it took my breath away, yet there wa[s] something macabre about it, too, for everything here wa[s] but an illusion. The flowers, vines, and trees—even th[e] drapes that hung so gracefully in folds—were imitation[,] lifeless and hard.

"I think we're on to something," Stuart was saying. "Th[at] skiff isn't made out of gypsum."

"Could we get to it, and follow the river?" Floyd aske[d]

"It'll be quite a climb. You brought the rope, didn't you[?]"

"Aye," he answered.

I walked to the edge and looked down. Climb down th[at] cliff, I thought. Not me! Never in a thousand years!

# Chapter 22

Stuart was uncoiling a hundred feet of heavy rope, and while my body protested, my conscience reminded me that I had promised along with Beau and Floyd to follow Stuart's instructions without question. Neither Beau nor Floyd seemed unduly alarmed about the climb and they were both men in their fifties, I reminded myself.

Stuart tied the rope several times around one of the large columns. Then he secured it with an intricate knot. "That'll hold us," he said, pulling it taut.

Beau and Floyd nodded their agreement, and their acceptance of the inevitable bolstered my own courage.

Of course, I'd go. The last thing this expedition needs is an hysterical female!

"I'll go first," Stuart was saying. "Then the rest of you follow one at a time, using the same order."

He grabbed the rope with two hands and began to lower himself down, all the while shouting encouragement to the rest of us. "It's not bad. There are several good footholds in the rocks."

I couldn't look. Dear God, I prayed. Don't let him fall!

I held my breath until I heard Beau shout, "He made it!"

Then I opened my eyes and looked down. Stuart was waving his arms and grinning rakishly up at me. Tears of gratitude filled my eyes and unconditional love filled me with joy. He was fickle, he had deceived me, and hurt me beyond measure, but no other man could ever take Stuart Cousin's place in my heart.

Inching his way down a rocky slope, he stood on the river bank and shouted up to us, "It's a beautiful river, clearer than the Thames."

Then we watched as he inspected the skiff. "Looks sea-worthy," he shouted. "Even has oars!" He held them up for us to see, and then scampered back up the embankment. "Your turn, India," he called out gaily.

Something fluttered in my chest, traveled up my throat and right out my mouth. I think it was my heart!

Beau put an arm around me. "You'll make it with no trouble, Indy. Remember when you were little, and you and your sisters used to play hide and seek in the stage rafters? You always climbed the highest, and you could skitter down like a little monkey."

I had forgotten. We had played that game until our mother had caught us and forbidden it. When had my fear of heights begun? I wondered.

"Pretend you're nine years old and in the old Memphis Opera House," Beau said.

He was looking at me with so much love and trust that I couldn't back down. I grabbed hold of the rope. "I'm ready."

Hugging me close, he whispered, "Good girl!"

I lowered myself down, following Stuart's instructions from below and my father's encouragement from above. Wrapping myself in the illusion that I was a pigtailed tomboy again, I slowly descended, giving no more thought to danger than a nine year old should.

Suddenly hands encircled my waist. My father and Floyd shouted for joy, and I was safe at last, locked in Stuart's strong arms.

"You made it, India. Thank God, thank God," he cried, locking me in an embrace that took my breath away.

Looking over Stuart's shoulder, I gasped as I saw something slither down the cliff and land with a thud below. "The rope!" I screamed. "The rope!"

Stuart released me so suddenly that I almost fell.

272

Stumbling across the rocks, he picked up one end of the rope. "It's been cut! How? Why?"

We both looked up to find Beau and Floyd staring down at us. "What happened?" we shouted up in unison.

Beau answered. "Don't be mad, Indy. I'm staying here with Floyd. You young people go on without us."

Floyd shouted down. "He could have made it. I know he could. It's all my fault. I never dreamed he'd cut the rope." His voice shook with regret. "I told Beau I was staying behind. I'm dizzy. I knew I couldn't make it."

"Why didn't you tell me?" Stuart shouted. "We would have waited."

"No, no," Beau answered. "We're two old men. I couldn't have made it either."

"That's not true," I said in an undertone to Stuart. "Beau's in great physical shape. He knows he could have made it."

My father was calm and completely in command. "This was my decision, Indy. Respect it, and go with Stuart. When you find your way out, send a rescue team for us."

Ah, Beau, I thought. How could I ever have thought you weak?

Stuart collected his wits, and shouted up. "We'll find our way out, and I'll be back in no time with help. We'll bring a rope ladder," he added in a cheerful voice.

"That ought to do the trick," Beau said. "Now, get moving. I tied half the supplies on your rope. We have our half up here, so Floyd and I will be fine."

Stuart searched the ground and picked up a blanket that had been tied to the other end of the rope. "What a man your father is," he said, for wrapped inside were matches, reserve torches, a hammer and two tins of food. Waving his arms, he shouted, "Good show. Thank you, sir. And don't worry, I'll take good care of India."

"I know that," Beau answered.

"God speed," Floyd shouted, as Stuart lit the torches and handed me into the little boat.

As we pushed off into the winding river, I shouted back, "I love you, Papa!" My words echoed through the canyon. "I love you, Papa, I love you, Papa, I love you Papaaaa!" And then as we rounded the bend, Beau's voice echoed back, "Me, too, Me, too, Me, toooooo."

Stuart reached over and squeezed my hand. "We'll get them out, India. I swear it!"

I brushed away tears. Beau had made a noble gesture. There had been nothing maudlin or egocentric about it, and I owed it to my father to dignify his sacrifice and not turn it into a cheap melodrama. "I know that, Stuart," I said. "Beau has complete faith in you and so do I."

As we traveled down the river, the coastline dropped, allowing us to view more magnificent underground formations along the way. Stuart was very knowledgeable, and he explained that the icicle-like shapes that hung from the ceiling were called stalactites, and those that grew up from the cave floor were called stalagmites.

At one point the waterway narrowed and we found ourselves in a canal. Dripping down from the ceiling were strange formations that resembled twisted fingers and claws. I shrank back, but Stuart assured me they were harmless deposits of calcium carbonate. "They're called helictites," he informed me, and then made me laugh when he said, "Pay attention, because I'm going to give you a test on all of this."

How shall I live without him, I thought. Stuart has shown me a whole new world of beauty and laughter. How can I expect to go back and pick up where I had left off six months ago? He's taught me too much. I'm not the same, self-righteous prude I used to be.

My inner voice reminded me, *And Beau won't need you. He has more courage than you ever gave him credit for.*

I thought, Maybe he never did need me. Maybe it was I who needed him. Could it be possible that I have been using Beau as an excuse for not living my own life? No, he did need me, I insisted. He still does!

"I'll settle the argument for you, if you'll tell me what it's about," Stuart said.

I jumped. "What do you mean?"

"Come on. You're at war with yourself over something. It's written all over your face. I can always tell when you're having one of your little inner discussions. You scowl, you

274

bite your lip, sometimes you even smile. It's very enlightening," he added.

"Oh, you make a joke about everything," I said.

He pulled the oars inside, and let the boat drift. "I'm sorry, India. I guess I learned to do that a long time ago. Disappointments don't hurt so much if you joke about them."

I gathered he was referring to his unhappy childhood, and I melted a little. "I was thinking about Beau," I said. "And how all my life I misjudged him. I guess I tried to keep him weak so I could be strong."

"You're too hard on yourself, India." His lips curved in a gentle smile. "Have I told you I like your name? India," he said softly. "It's beautiful and mysterious, like you are."

"There's nothing mysterious about me anymore," I said. "I'm just a wardrobe mistress from Columbus, Ohio."

"I know your occupation and where you're from. I want to know what you think, and what you feel," he said. "When we were in the garden that night at the Lighthizer ball . . ."

He paused and I thought, How can he bring that up?

"I thought you were in love with me then, but the very next morning, you gave me the cold shoulder. Why?" he demanded.

"Because I saw you leave with the doll, and I didn't trust you. You terrified me once before with it."

"So, that was it!" he said. "Putting the doll in your bed was Mrs. Janney's idea, India. I had nothing to do with that and I'm sorry if it frightened you. I thought you were Katherine then, and I knew that damn doll was the key to unlocking her memory." He paused and then added. "Everybody thought my father had murdered Lily, and I was determined to clear his name."

"But where were you taking it that morning?"

"To be repaired," he answered. "I had to have the doll, as you now know, but when I retrieved it from the street, the head had been broken."

A simple explanation, I thought, recalling Cousin Elvira's saying: *The answer to a riddle is as plain as the noses on our faces.*

And so it had been with Katherine. The signs were all

there, but none of us had seen them.

"And what about this last time when you blew hot and cold?" he was saying, his voice rising in anger. "You came to my house, acted like you were crazy about me."

"I did not," I said outraged.

"Well, you gave a good imitation of it, so much so that I misunderstood and was ready to seduce you. Be honest, India! You acted like a woman in love, and then you ran back to Cornwall and gave me the cold shoulder again. What's wrong with you?" he demanded.

"Hypocrite!" I shouted without thinking, but I was sick of his games. "I saw you through the window that night. You lost no time replacing me!"

He stared back at me with dawning realization, and without a word, picked up the oars.

We had come out of the canal and the passage had sloped down and widened out. Steering the boat to shore, he said, "We'll get some sleep and then continue."

Now, he knew, and I hated myself for telling him. He held out his hand to help me out of the boat, but I ignored it and got out by myself.

Our lights were growing dim, and I supposed we should have to light new torches. That meant we'd been on the river for almost an hour, I calculated.

We walked up a much lower embankment and were on the cave floor again. Stuart took my torch and his, and stuck them both in crevices in between the rocks, making them look like sconces on the walls of a room.

"India," he said, suddenly pulling me into his arms.

"It's over, Stuart," I protested. "Let me go!"

Triumph was in his voice. "You came back that night. You were going to let me make love to you, weren't you?"

I struggled in his arms. Oh, was there no end to his conceit! "It's no use, Stuart. It's over," I shouted, kicking him. Our legs became entangled and we both fell to the ground. He leaned over me and pinned my arms above my head. "Wild cat! She was my mother!"

I stopped struggling. "Who?"

"The woman you saw through the window. If we ever get

out of this bloody cave, I'll prove it to you."

"That beautiful, *young* woman was your mother!"

"She's forty-four," he said. "But I'll grant you, she looks much younger." He pressed his lips to mine in a chaste kiss. "If I let you up, will you promise not to kick me?"

I nodded, still confused, but a faint glimmer of hope flickered in my heart.

We sat up, and he said, "My father confided many things to me before he died, India. He was a weak man, but he hadn't killed Lily Beacham, and he begged me to clear his name." Stuart paused, and ran his fingers through his unruly hair. "As for my mother, my father admitted that he had treated her shabbily. He hadn't stood up to my grandfather. Instead, he'd taken the easy way out, by allowing her to be banished from both our lives."

I saw the hurt on his face, and I could have cried for the child inside him.

"After he died, I searched for my mother. I couldn't locate her, so I hired Floyd Donovan." The ghost of a smile lit up his face when he said, "Floyd found her in Italy three months ago. She had remarried after the divorce but her second husband had since died. I asked her to come to England, and she agreed. She had only just arrived when you saw her. I wanted to surprise you the next night. Don't you remember I said there was someone I wanted you to meet?"

Oh God, he had said that, I recalled.

"I couldn't understand why you'd raced back to Cornwall. Of course, I knew you weren't Katherine. I'd followed you to Brown's Hotel that first time. The desk clerk told me what I needed to know, and one night I went to the theater. As soon as I saw Katherine on the stage, I knew."

Reaching for my hand, he said, "She had a twisted personality, even as a child." And when I shook my head in disbelief, he added, "She probably learned to cover it up as she grew older, but it was there, India. Beau discovered it, too."

He pulled me into the circle of his arm, and this time, I did not protest. "Beau told you his suspicions then, when you went to the hotel to look for me?" I asked.

"Yes. We had a long talk. He's quite a man, your father.

We liked each other right away." Then his eyes danced with mischief again, and he raised an eyebrow. "Incidentally, I want him for a father-in-law, so I guess I'll have to marry you."

I opened my mouth, but he smothered my outrage with a kiss that deepened and set my pulses to racing with the sure knowledge that Stuart loved me, passionately, honorably, and completely.

When his lips finally left mine, he whispered in my ear. "I love you, India. Say you'll marry me."

"But, Stuart," I said. "I'm—"

He finished my sentence. "A Wardrobe mistress from Columbus, Ohio. It sounds like a song, but I'm sick of hearing you sing it, India. I don't care what you think you are. You're going to be, India Chantelle Hathaway, not a wardrobe mistress or any other kind of mistress. You're going to be the wife of Stuart Hamlet Hathaway."

"Hamlet?" I said. "Your middle name is Hamlet?"

"Don't you dare laugh. My mother was only nineteen and stagestruck when she named me."

We spent the night, or was it day, curled up in each other's arms, and I don't think I have ever been so happy. Stuart's optimism was contagious and I was convinced that we would find our way out, rescue Beau and Floyd, and all live happily ever after.

Basking in my own contentment, I slept, convinced that all the questions had been answered, all the riddles had been solved. But I was wrong. One more startling revelation would present itself before the masquerade would finally come to an end!

It was cold, and I pulled the blanket up to my chin, and snuggled closer to Stuart. He was sleeping soundly, but something had awakened me, and I sat up.

The torches had burned down, so that only a very faint glow illuminated the cave, but I thought I saw something move on the opposite side of the chamber, and my blood turned to ice. It had been large and lumbering in its movement.

A bear! I thought. Frantic, I nudged Stuart.

"There's a bear in the cave," I hissed in his ear.

He was instantly awake and alert. "You were dreaming, India. There are no bears in these parts, believe me."

"But I saw something," I said. "Over there in the corner."

He stood up. "I'll have a look."

"No, Stuart. Don't go back there. Please!"

He leaned down and grasped me by the shoulders. "I'll be fine. I just want to convince you that there's nothing there."

Picking up a torch, he walked over to the other side of the chamber, disappearing almost instantly from my sight. I sat, frozen in fear, and then I heard Stuart say, "What the hell!"

There was a scuffling noise, and I screamed, "Stuart, Stuart!"

Jumping up, I grabbed the other torch and the only weapon I could find, the hammer, and ran to his aid.

Raw terror rooted me to the spot, as I confronted not a bear, but the red-eyed ghost of Anthony Hathaway!

"Don't throw that hammer!" Stuart commanded, coming up behind me, but my body had turned to stone, and I could not have thrown the hammer if both our lives had depended on it.

Stuart grabbed me and pried the hammer out of my hand. "He's not a ghost, India, and he won't hurt you."

The creature stared back at me. His skin was stark white, as was his hair, but he was not old.

He's Anthony Hathaway, my confused brain insisted. But how can this be?

"Don't be afraid," Stuart was saying. "I know who he is, and he's harmless. Trust me, India."

"But, he looks like . . ."

"He looks like his albino ancestor," Stuart said. "And I'll wager his name is Anthony."

At this, the creature nodded his head vigorously. Then he held up two fingers, and pointed to Stuart.

When he repeated the gesture, Stuart turned to me, and

279

said, "He can't speak, but I think I know what he's trying to tell us."

Staring directly into the other's face Stuart spoke in a loud voice. "You say there are two more men in the cave. Where are they?"

The strange creature called Anthony nodded and pointed, and gestured for us to follow him.

"Wait, I'll get our supplies," Stuart said.

I followed closely at his heels. "Are you sure we can trust him? Maybe we shouldn't go."

Stuart was rolling the blanket out and placing the supplies inside. "India, he's going to lead us to Beau and Floyd. We must follow him."

"But we left them back on the upper level. How could they have gotten down here?"

"I don't know, but we're going to take the chance and follow him for awhile at least. We'll leave a rope trail, so we can find our way back."

I was still wary, and I tugged at his sleeve. "Stuart, you've never seen him before, have you?"

"No."

"Then how do you know who he is?"

"My father told me. We can't discuss it now, India. I'll explain later."

We lit new torches and joined Anthony who carried a lantern. Perhaps Stuart has never seen him, I thought, but I have, three times. Twice at Hathaway Manor, and once on the moors at Bismooth Pass.

We followed him into a narrow passage, and I held tightly to Stuart's hand. This mute, wild-looking creature must surely be deranged, I thought. How can Stuart trust him? He could be leading us into a trap!

We followed the passage for what seemed an interminably long time, though it was probably only fifteen minutes or so. My head was still reeling from shock. Three times, I had seen this strange creature, yet I had been led to doubt his very existence by everyone!

I recalled how Fenton, Jordan, and even Stuart had dissolved into hoots of laughter over the "giant possum" I had seen in the garden. My description had been absurd, but they had embraced it, and used it to silence me.

Then there had been the old crone, Mrs. Cull. She denied I had seen a man on Bismooth Pass, but she couldn't get me out of there fast enough. Fenton, too, I mused, recalling how he had packed us off to London the very next day. And, when I had related the incident to Stuart, he had sloughed it off again, preferring to let me think I had imagined my red-eyed ghost.

What does it all mean? Is there no end to Hathaway Manor's secrets? I wondered, feeling resentful. All my dreams for a lifetime of happiness with Stuart were now dependent on the whim of a madman. Would he lead us to safety or everlasting doom?

Surely, Stuart must have read my thoughts, for he stopped and spoke impatiently. "We're turning back, Anthony. You've lost the way."

Thank God, I thought. We should never have trusted the fool in the first place.

Anthony's face contorted, and the savage, animal sounds he uttered chilled me to the bone.

Stuart seemed more annoyed than terrified. "Dammit! You said it wasn't far."

I dug my nails into Stuart's hand, and whispered, "Don't argue with him, Stuart. We can outrun him. Let's just go!"

But, it was Anthony who took off, running with his lumbering gait down the passage. I was still pulling on Stuart's hand, but he said, "Wait!"

Anthony turned a sharp corner and we lost sight of his lantern. "Hurry, before he comes back," I pleaded.

"Be quiet," Stuart shouted. "Listen."

I strained my ears, and then I heard it. Voices, and not Anthony's, were calling from the other end of the passage.

Who can describe the joys of reunion? My father and I laughed, then we cried. We embraced, and Beau, always the consummate actor, resurrected lines from some half-remembered, and I suspect, appropriately fractured sonnet.

"The lost has been found, and joy abounds. Ring ye bells throughout the realm. Unfurl the flag, let flow the wine, the lost has been found, and joy is mine!"

"Bravo," Stuart shouted, and Floyed joined in. Our rescuer looked bewildered and Beau spoke to him like he was a perfectly ordinary man, and not a figment of my wildest dreams. "Don't mind us, Anthony. We're all a little daft!"

"He led you here?" I asked, finding it all hard to accept.

"Oh, quite," Floyd answered. "The chap obviously knows this cave well."

"How did you know his name?" Stuart asked.

"He wrote it down on a piece of paper," Floyd said.

I was flabbergasted. "He can write!"

"He's dumb, Indy, not stupid," Beau answered.

"He drew us a map, too," Floyd informed us, pulling it out of his pocket and handing it to Stuart.

I leaned over Stuart's shoulder and was amazed to see a detailed blueprint, obviously drawn by a person of above average intelligence.

"You made the boat, too, didn't you?" Stuart asked, looking at Anthony.

He nodded his head. I thought, Of course, the boat. I, like a fool, had merely taken it for granted, but someone had built it and placed it in the cave.

"I knew it couldn't have been used by the pirates," Stuart was saying. "It would have rotted out to nothing, ages ago."

"Well, that mystery's solved," Floyd said. "Now, didn't I hear you say something about wine, Beau?"

They both looked at Anthony. "Now's the time, Cull," Floyd said, and Anthony took off.

"Did you say, Cull?" I asked.

"Aye, Anthony Cull. That's the chap's name," Floyd answered.

I looked at Stuart, and he shook his head. "Poor fellow, he only thinks that's his name."

At that moment Anthony returned, holding a flask which he handed to Floyd. He drank, sighed, and said, "Ah, excellent. This is vintage wine, try some, Miss Chantelle."

I thought of refusing, but somehow it didn't seem very polite, with Anthony standing there, looking on expectantly.

Never have I tasted such wine. "It's delicious," I said,

passing the flask to Stuart who drank and then handed it down to Beau.

I looked at Anthony for the first time as a human being and not a freak. "Thank you, Anthony. That was delicious," I said.

He smiled at me, and I was reminded once again of Jordan, but this time the resemblance was a deeper one. I saw kindness and great suffering in those eyes that were not so much red as pink.

They looked at me with the same admiration I had seen in Jordan's pale eyes, and I felt ashamed of my own prejudice and that of those who had banished this poor soul from their sight because he was different from other men.

He motioned for us to follow him, and Stuart said, "There's probably casks of the stuff hidden away down here."

There were four, we soon discovered, huge, old wine barrels with spigots attached. Anthony turned the handle on one, and the wine flowed.

"Don't waste it," Floyd said, closing the handle.

Anthony pointed to two of the barrels and indicated by gesture that they were empty. He opened first one spigot, then the other, but nothing came out.

Floyd was looking at the map. "I say another hour should bring us out of here."

"What are we waiting for then?" Beau said, but Stuart seemed more intent on examining the barrels. "Get the hammer," he said, looking at me.

"Stuart, we can be out of here in an hour," I protested.

He raised an eyebrow. "Love, honor, and obey, woman! Fetch the hammer, and I think you'll be surprised."

"Just this one time," I said. "And don't let it give you any grandiose ideas."

I ran back, unwrapped the blanket, and grabbed the hammer. Stuart proceeded to pound on the barrel with it, and when the wood had started to splinter, he used the claw end to tear it apart.

I sat down on a boulder, and the men all stood around Stuart. The barrel at last split open, and all of us stared in spellbound wonder as a cache of gold coins and glittering jewelry spilled out of the barrel and sparkled all over the cave floor.

"Anthony Hathaway's treasure!" I shouted.

Stuart grinned. "We found it! It belongs to us, all of us," he proclaimed.

Forty minutes later, we emerged from the cave and found ourselves on Bismooth Pass.

The sunshine had never looked so bright or so welcome. We had been in the cave for twelve hours, but to us, it had seemed like an eternity.

The cave had opened up another world to all of us. But for me, it had marked a turning point in my life. The masquerade had ended. And in that dark, underground world, I had seen clearly for the very first time. In the dim labyrinth of those winding passages, I had faced the truth about myself and those I loved.

Katherine had deceived, and used me, but she was more to be pitied than blamed, and her death would take time for me to accept.

My father had proven himself to be a man of noble spirit and rare courage, and in those twelve hours my respect for Beau had grown to match the love I'd always held for him.

Anthony Hathaway, who had haunted my nightmares, had turned out to be a friend, and worthy of compassion.

And Stuart, my beloved rascal, had shown himself to be the man of my dreams, a prince who could love a wardrobe mistress from Columbus, Ohio and make her his queen!

# Epilogue

A year has passed since Hathaway Manor's Masquerade Ball, and drastic changes have taken place in the lives of all of us who figured so prominently in the cast.

Stuart and I have married and are deliriously happy. Our share of old Anthony's treasure has allowed my husband to buy back land his father had been promised in Sussex. We have built a gracious and beautiful home on the estate, and I have a morning room like the one I so admired at Hathaway Manor. It overflows with cabbage roses and I write my letters at a beautiful, hand-carved desk.

My husband is busy running the estate, and under Stuart's fair and able guidance the satisfied tenants are reaping us a bountiful harvest.

Ours was not the only wedding to take place this year. Willa and Sir Alex were married and are living happily in the glittering world of London society.

The third wedding of which I speak is the most recent and the most surprising of all. My father and Stuart's mother were wed last week. It was love at first sight from the day they were introduced and we are overjoyed about it. I love Nell, and Stuart and Beau have always been bosom buddies. Of course, my husband had to pretend to be shocked.

"E'gad! I was afraid to marry my cousin, and I end up married to my sister!"

My thoughts turn more poignant when I speak of Anthony Hathaway. I did not learn his identity until after we were out of the cave. "Now, tell me who he is," I had demanded. And Stuart had answered, "He's the heir of Hathaway Manor!"

He was Fenton and Beatrice's oldest son. To her credit, I must say, Beatrice did not know the child lived, but Fenton did. The midwife had branded Anthony a monster, and Fenton's vanity had made him reject the infant and give him to Mrs. Cull to raise. Beatrice was told she had lost a son in childbirth.

Because he was dumb, Anthony was treated as an idiot by Mrs. Cull, although in her way, she loved the boy and did her best for him.

He is twenty-five years old now, but the years spent in isolation out on Bismooth Pass make him appear younger. He is completely without guile and harbors no resentment toward his parents.

Jordan has been more than a brother to Anthony, and the bond is close between them. They are now in London sharing Stuart's old house at No. 10 Bleekman Place.

Anthony is being tutored, and will someday take his rightful place as Lord and Master of Hathaway Manor.

Jordan is happy to release the title and all it entails to his older brother. Jordan is doing what he loves—working in the hospital laboratory with Dr. Cummings. His seizures, brought on by experiments too radical to be safe, are still with him. They don't come as often, and someday we hope they will completely disappear.

Beatrice confessed that she feared Jordan had killed Lil during a seizure, and Fenton confided that he feared either Jordan or Anthony had committed the crime.

Secrets—they abounded at Hathaway Manor, and almost destroyed all within it, but the masks have been lifted. And all, save one of the masqueraders, have escaped the net.

> "Oh, what a tangled web we weave,
> When first we practice to deceive!"

# Author's Note

In 1943 the German chemist, Albert Hoffman accidentally stumbled upon a powerful hallucinogen when a trace of lysergic acid, diethylamide (LSD) was absorbed through his skin. Suddenly he was plunged into the strange and terrifying world of the insane. His scientific curiosity compelled him to repeat the experiment a few days later. This time he drank a very small amount of the drug and the visions that followed convinced him that this drug could make normal people psychotic.

Jordan's introduction to LSD in *The Lost Lady of Hathaway Manor* was based on this incident which actually occurred almost fifty years later. Dr. Hoffman believed LSD could turn normal minds into psychotic ones. Drawing on that conclusion, the character in my novel applied that same theory to the abnormal mind.

Other hallucinogens mentioned here were commonly known. Henbane, belladonna, and mandrake were used in witchcraft during the Middle Ages, and belladonna was often added to the wine at ancient orgies. Fly agaric, the exotic red mushroom, was once regarded as an actual god and a mystic cult developed around its use in a substance called *Soma* in India.

Ergot, a fungus that attacks grain, contains lysergic acid, one of the basic compounds of LSD.

Katherine Hathaway was a split personality. This mental condition was recognized by a few pioneering physicians at the turn of the century, but did not receive widespread notice until much later in the twentieth century.

# MORE THRILLING GOTHICS FROM ZEBRA BOOKS

**THE MISTRESS OF MOONTIDE MANOR** (3100, $3.95)
by Lee Karr

Penniless and alone, Joellen was grateful for the opportunity to live in the infant resort of Atlantic City and work as a "printer's devil" in her uncle's shop. *But her uncle was dead when she arrived!*

Alone once more, she encountered the handsome entreprenuer Taylor Lorillard. Danger was everywhere, and ignoring the warning signs — veiled threats, glances, innuendos — she yearned to visit Moontide Manor and dance in Taylor's arms. But someone was following as she approached the moon-drenched mansion . . .

**THE LOST HEIRESS OF HAWKSCLIFFE** (2896, $3.95)
by Joyce C. Ware

When Katherine McKenzie received an invitation to catalogue the Fabulous Ramsay oriental rug collection, she was thrilled she was respected as an expert in her chosen field.

It had been seven years since Charles Ramsay's mistress and heiress had mysteriously disappeared — and now it was time to declare her legally dead, and divide the spoils. But Katherine wasn't concerned; she was there to do a job. *Until* she saw a portrait of the infamous Roxlena, and saw on the heiress' finger the very ring that she herself had inherited from her own mysterious past.

**THE WHISPERING WINDS OF**
**BLACKBRIAR BAY** (3319, $3.95)
by Lee Karr

Anna McKenzie fulfilled her father's last request by taking her little brother away from the rough gold mining town near City. Now an orphan, Anna travelled to meet her father's sister, whom he mentioned only when he was on his deathbed.

Anna's fears grew as the schooner *Tahoe* reached the remote cove at the foot of the dark, huge house high above the cliffs. The aunt was strange, threatening. And who was the midnight visitor who was whispering in the dark hallways? Even the attentions of the handsome Lyle Delany couldn't keep her safe. For he too was being watched . . . and stalked.

*Available wherever paperbacks are sold, or order direct from the Publisher. Send cover price plus 50¢ per copy for mailing and handling to Zebra Books, Dept. 3634, 475 Park Avenue South, New York, N.Y. 10016. Residents of New York and Tennessee must include sales tax. DO NOT SEND CASH. For a free Zebra. Pinnacle catalog please write to the above address.*